# SILLY AMERICANS

## CHRISTIAN SONNIER

## ACKNOWLEDGMENTS

Thank you Alecia Stoesz for doing such a fine job as editor.

Thank you Matthew Hansen for your creative cover design.

Also—you, reader—thanks for taking a chance!

Introducing...

## The McCreeley's

Once again it was time for an escape into the netherworld for Johnston McCreeley. Pushing off a brown cloud through his bloodstream was the locomotive to his destination; a heaven not arrived through faithful belief and contemplation—something to be earned—but rather a heaven arrived at instantly.

For Johnston, the conscious world was a hell he no longer wished to bare. In that world he was simply a speaking animal sequestered to live out his days dreadfully busting up rocks to procure three essentials for human life: food, water, and shelter. Each day he arrived at the yard, a proverbial town of Bedrock, to endure only one outcome—to lift pieces of earth without pause. His tools were a hammer and pick ax. Down an industrial conveyor belt rolled a block weighing a ton, passing underneath a chomping rock cutter. The biting machine chipped off the block at measured increments as they sloppily tumbled down onto a lower conveyor where Johnston stood to stack the pieces on a wooden pallet twelve levels high. Once that was done, a fork lift would come and take the pallet away. Johnston could then start a new pallet. The one personal power he possessed was a cable running alongside the conveyor, which he could tug on to halt the flow. That was it. Forty hours a week of bitter monotony for food, water, and shelter—at the very least. None of this was endured in the netherworld which came to be as he sat on his recliner, in the shelter of his trailer, sweating profusely, and drooling slightly.

Johnston was raised in rural Texas where it was fully understood and wholly accepted that the state itself was superior to all others. He was not a city boy raised where the sun reflected off massive amounts of concrete, creating an island of scorching heat where everyone scurried about in a semi-organized frenzy. He was a country boy preferring isolation, though deep down in his heart of hearts he despised both. In both places he was subordinate. Both had betrayed him. Both had gravitating systems crushing down upon him.

He wore cowboy boots, a brush popper and blue jeans, and a revolver wedged between his belt buckle and belly button. He drove an old truck, rolled his own cigarettes, and drank to excess. He spoke with a pronounced drawl and was ready to fight at the drop of a hat if his honor was taken for granted. And, like most of his kind, he hated the government. He was an old soul born into the era of American exceptional-ism framed with a frontier mentality. Of course, he found out that was a bunch of bullshit. As it was, he was just another sucker, scraping and clawing for printed money that was just as worthless as his existence seemed to be. Despite all that, Johnston was exceptional. He was just unaware of it at the time.

The heroin habit was a fairly recent phenomenon. It marked the only time he went to the concrete city; it's only use for him. Never had he seriously considered suicide as a viable solution to arriving at perpetual bliss. He wasn't grief-stricken over a failed romance. He hadn't lost the love of his life suddenly. He hadn't lost a child which could never be replaced. The horrors of war hadn't capsized his ability and desire to function in society. He wasn't afflicted with an impenetrable mental disorder, nor was he suffering a terminal malady counting down his days to a dismal zero. The only plausible explanation for his wish to die was that he would have to endure carrying pieces of earth from a conveyor belt to a pallet for the unforeseeable future, putting his body through the fire of severe manual labor until he eventually dropped dead. Even strippers and hookers had it better. At least they got off from time to time. Above all, he just wanted to be out from underneath the crushing system. That was why he began pushing off into the netherworld.

And what a world it was! He couldn't keep his eyes open as he floated down a warm stream through a kaleidoscope of color without the slightest effort; without the slightest concern. The water held him in a comforting motherly embrace. There were others contently floating along with him, none of which he knew; and all the creatures of the earth were standing on the banks of the stream, reveling and cheering him on as he moved past. Even the stones poking out of the water celebrated, sliding out of his path so as not to impede his progress. As he drifted along his excitement grew to the greatest of heights. He could see the drop-off ahead where the waterfall awaited his arrival. Rays of golden sunshine tattooed with sparkling rainbows spewed high from the base of the waterfall he was about to slip over. Down below, a blissful plunge.

His speed accelerated as he approached the drop off, but not to a frightful pace. It felt like an amusement park ride where safety was assured. He smiled and laughed, knowing he was almost there. His escape was at hand. His great release was to be forever secured. At the bottom churned perfect oblivion. He felt the warmth of the rays on his face that would fully consume him at any moment. There it was! So close! At the crest, finally liberated! Yippey!

It was a gasp. The sacks she was holding hit the floor. Covering her mouth in horror, she cried out, "Oh my God, Johnstie!"

He was suddenly yanked away from the stream where precious peace had just been in his grip. She had called him back from his wonderful ending. His plans were ruined again and she was to blame. He came back to with the needle still dangling from his vein and the belt strap loosely clinging to his pronounced bicep. As his motives became clear, tears began to well in her eyes. Johnston wiped the drool from his mouth and sat forward in disappointment, chuckling that death by his own hand was simply another addition to a long list of failures in life. He should have used his gun. It would have been messier, but instant and certain. He was thinking of the mess she would have to clean up, which turned out to be his downfall. Peg was always getting in the way.

"You knew." He grumbled, still somewhat detached. His vision began to steady, but he was looking at everything except Peg.

"Knew what, Johnstie?" She delicately inquired with a certain tenderness, invoking her pet name for him, which incensed him all the more. Death was what he wanted. Not love! Not sympathy!

He sloppily removed the needle from his arm and the strap from his bicep. His initial comment back from the dead was not so well thought out. He was going to place the blame elsewhere. "You knew what you were marryin' into…you knew!"

Peg remained silent. She was yet to close the front door, and did so to contain the madness. How to react was foreign to her. She knew she married a heavy drinker prone to frequent bouts of depression; a man with secrets he would never tell, and a sharp edge never to be blunted. He had never lain a finger on her, though he had been chauvinistic and condescending. She could handle those things. He made her feel safe with him. Still, this was the most fearful sight.

Johnston scanned their modest home with glazed and foggy eyes. He tired of looking at everything placed around him. The furniture, the lamp, the tacky prints hanging on the walls, the soiled brown carpet, the cluttered kitchen, and the dust-crusted box fan. Most of all, he was tired of all the cheap little figurines his wife collected and displayed as her prized possessions. It was as if it were their home, these inanimate objects of Johnston's disdain.

There was the one with the seal balancing a red ball on the tip of its nose. There was the clown wearing a big smile holding a bouquet of balloons. There was the cowboy riding the storm that was a bucking bronco. And of course, the ballerina appearing to be in a twirl of perfect symmetry. There were so many more, but Johnston had not picked a single one of them. Peg had collected them at a steady and deliberate pace as if Johnston was never going to notice. One by one these miniature stills invaded their home. Each one unflinchingly stared at Johnston, which he viewed as impolite. Moreover, they were special to Peg. She adored them, and now he saw a way to get back at her for foiling his attempt.

"It's your damned fault!" He loudly accused.

She knew what he meant, but would act otherwise. "About what, Johnstie?"

He laboriously came to his feet with a detached sense of balance, leaving him wobbly. He was still going to make his statement. He grabbed the clown and threw it to the floor, stomping on it with his boot heel until it broke into pieces. "Clown ain't so funny now, huh?"

He moved on to the seal; the second victim of his boot heel. "Cute little trick with your red ball!"

Peg deteriorated into a full bout of hysterical bawling as the cowboy atop his bucking bronco was no exception, certainly the most masculine of the figurines. No mercy. Under his boot heel it went. "I did him a favor!"

Johnston was loving every second of Peg's desperate sobbing. His sights fixated on the twirling ballerina as did hers in frightful anticipation. They locked eyes in the hesitation; his glowing with contempt, hers pleading for him to relent. It was her most treasured figurine handed down by her beloved Ga-ma who understood and spoiled her affectionately like no other in the family. It was given with the best of wishes when she was a child dabbling in ballet. It was a symbol of encouragement she had always cherished.

But it had ruined his cherished moment!

The apathy on his face was evident as the deviousness clearly showed through. She cringed as he snatched up the ballerina, raised it above his head, and sent it crashing to the floor, extinguishing the light of its perceived innocence. "Not so perfect now, sweetheart!"

After the stomping came to an end the most profound sadness swept over Peg. Johnston wasn't done, either. In sweeping motions with both arms he sent the rest of the figurines crashing to the ground. Up and down he jumped, losing his balance and grunting like an animal. His temper tantrum through the living room resembled the effects of an earthquake, shaking the foundations of everything, real or imagined. He didn't stop until they were all broken into little pieces at his feet. Then, exhausted and delirious he plopped back down on the recliner, wishing for a speedy return to the netherworld he had been yanked from. Peg, lost in dismay, could only conclude that she was going to stay—for better or worse.

Luckily, the sacks she dropped upon her entrance had a brand new figurine. It was a ranch hand leaning on a fence pole, his cowboy hat drawn low over his eyes, toothpick fixed to his mouth, arms folded across his chest, looking measured and tough. It was exactly the way she saw Johnston. Really, she had brought him a present. He had seemed so down as of late.

The numbing effects of his post-tantrum were setting in, rendering him motionless, staring at nothing as sniffles sputtered from Peg leaning against the tobacco-stained wall. She had some news; the best she had heard in a long time. Perhaps the last time she swam in such excitement with rippling anticipation was the time Johnston unceremoniously confessed to her, stumbling drunk; "You've put up with my shit for so long, Peg. We might as well get hitched." The next day Johnston had completely forgotten what he proposed. One thing Peg knew about the drunk she loved was that he only told the truth when fully intoxicated. It was the only thing she liked about his drinking. After Johnston took her word for it, they drove to the Justice of the Peace and made it official. The rush from that snap decision had subsided, but now the rush was set for a comeback. She knew everything was going to be just fine now.

"Johnstie, I'm pregnant."

He was like a statue sitting in the recliner who had looked into the eyes of Medusa. His thinking brain had powered down at the revelation. Immediately following a failed attempt at suicide he was blasted with the news that another life was headed into the world; his own little speaking animal to raise as he saw fit. When he finally snapped out of his conscious coma as Peg submissively waited for his reaction, he slowly nodded his head in approval, and stated, "Well…he's gonna be a big boy."

## The Golden's

Ralston Golden's eyes menacingly scanned the scene; one in which he loathed. The return on his investment was not exactly minimal. The costly spot of air time was essential to remaining on top. He was dominating the Oklahoma auto market in the capital, as well as in Tulsa. He considered the state itself a launching pad for his grand plans of national expansion, busting out at the seams, spilling to the edges until he faced each continental shoreline, leaving all his competitors choking from the smoke kicked up by his screeching tires.

That would mean a lot more of these stupid commercials. His goal—even if it made him old and gray— was to realize Golden Motors as the standard bearer for the American automobile industry. Once that was secure, he would turn to the rest of the globe. His brand would be recognized as the first stop in the buyer's journey for the right vehicle. Never was he to let up on the gas; never was he to downshift, and always would he keep his eyes headed for a horizon he never intended to meet. Word of mouth and strong advertising would one day see him with a thirty-second spot mixed in with the big dogs of alcohol, soda, insurance, and sports-related products during the most viewed annual sporting event in America—the Super Bowl.

Until that ambition was realized there would be Ralston Golden with his menacing eyes overseeing a commercial production fitted with an inflatable bounce house for the kids, face painters doodling on their canvasses—and just to go all the way overboard—a miniature petting zoo. It was a fun-family-friendly environment; a place any potential buyer would call home after their fair and delightful experience. All those affiliated with the production at hand knew better than that.

"Damn it! This is the final take!" Ralston Golden yelled as the director stoked the urgency of everyone to get in their proper positions, knowing fully well his utterly frayed patience was at an end, which would then precipitate a sudden termination of services rendered. It was the ninth film crew in a span of three years. Ultimately, Ralston Golden was the director.

Like he was counting down to the punishment of a petulant child, he loudly belted out, "FIVE!...FOUR!...THREE!...TWO!..." Everyone had hastily shuffled into position and took up their frozen stances. Even the carefree kids in the bounce house knew it was time to get serious, even though their only part to play was to look like they were having fun. He took one last look around with his hand raised above his head, and when he saw all the pieces were set in place, he swung down his hand in a chopping motion to initiate the action.

"Hey! Ralston Golden here wanting to tell you about the shiny deals we're doing for you folks this summer. We have a deal for everyone!"

The kids bounced behind him, but were told to be quiet about it. His navy suit and perfectly layered hair gleamed in the afternoon sun as he stepped to the first deal of the summer. "Here we have this tough full-size crew cab with $13,000 off MSRP, and that's just the beginning, folks!"

His gesticulations were overly enthusiastic as he moved on to the next deal. Just as the shiny black four-door SUV came into the shot a clown ran in front of him, made some silly gesticulations of his own, and left as quickly as he came. "He's clowning around, but I'm not! Here we got something sleek and great on gas. Perfect for the family. We got this gem for $299 a month. Wow!"

On he went to the next one; a white two-door coupe with a sunroof. He gestured to it like it was a prized to be won on a game show. "And here we have this sporty, fully-loaded coupe, with a sunroof, so that Oklahoma sun can shine down on ya'. $19,999! It's like I'm just givin' it to ya'!"

The camera panned out so all three deals were in the shot, along with the bounce house and the impressive edifice of the main showroom. "Folks, come down and see us for a stress-free, no hassle, vehicle-buying experience that's fun and family friendly. Every weekend we have a bounce house, and we've just added..." the camera shifted to encompass the miniature petting zoo with a pony and a goat, along with face painters brushing on a few children wearing big smiles "...a petting zoo and face painting for the kiddos! Come on down and enjoy yourself, but remember, these deals won't last forever because they're just too good!"

Thirty seconds were coming to a close as the director sent up her own countdown. Finally, into the shot came Ralston Golden's personal whipping boy, technically referred to as his assistant. The costume he begrudgingly donned was a huge shiny bar of gold. A circular cut-out in the middle of the bar fitted a smiling face also painted gold. He shook the bar of gold's hand with a hearty smile, and concluded, "I personally promise the deal we make will be good as GOLD-en!"

"Annnd…cut!" the director shouted just as Ralston Golden shouted the same. The crew began to disperse in haste as the director clapped her hands together in praise. "That's a wrap! Great job everyone! Especially you, Mr. Golden!"

Her flattery was taken with less than a grain of salt as he rolled his eyes, responding, "Oh, good for you, stating the obvious. Just remember, I made this commercial happen. You just set up the equipment. You can leave now."

The director did an about-face wearing a smile that harbored a killer's intention behind it, and facing her grip, said through her teeth, "I really hate that man."

Ralston Golden veered over to his costumed assistant who wore an unabashed frown of humility. After a few snickers of enjoyment at his assistant's expense, he said, "Gee, you look ridiculous. Go get changed and pull up the car. Hurry, we'll be out of here sooner than later."

"Yes sir." He humbly replied.

Doused in a sweat of nerves behind Ralston Golden was Stuart, the general manager of the Tulsa dealership. His back also received the whip on occasion. "Welcome back, Mr. Golden!"

Ralston Golden slowly turned around. "Ah, Stuart. I would say it's a pleasure, but it's not. How are you today? Or, should I say, how are we?"

Stuart knew he meant the operations of the dealership as a whole. Finding an urge once again to resist pummeling his boss to death, he answered in a positive tone. "Very well sir, and I hope you are very well too. Are you ready for a walk through, Mr. Golden?"

"Lead the way Stuart, but stay behind me at the same time. I'm ready to get out of here, so make this snappy." He said to Stuart's delight, though he knew the end game of walking through each department was to pick the candidate for termination, which the veterans of the dealership knew fully well.

"How do you think the commercial went, Mr. Golden?" The much shorter Stuart inquired, making an attempt at small talk, risking the inadvertent ignition of a bomb. He cringed inwardly at the foolish attempt. Say less. Rush him along. Get him out of here!

"Hogwash and monkey business, Stuart. A waste of time and resources, but unfortunately necessary. The public likes it. It's all that matters. One day I'll only have to use my brand…a symbol…while my tanned ass is sitting on a beach in Fiji, reaping the whirlwind. Until then, bullshit like this."

"Well, I'll still be here, sir." Stuart said; one of those statements of personal commitment meant to impress, but instead making him look all the more pathetic as if Golden Motors in Tulsa was his total sum of life ambition. Another cringe in the bowels. Shut up, Stuart!

Ralston Golden smirked, noticing the same, and simply admired the groveling. Not in himself, of course, but always in others. He knew the answer to the question he was about to ask. It was only said to hand Stuart some purpose for the moment. "So where are we headed first?"

"The collision center, sir. After that, the service center, then finance, and then the showroom sales floor. A nice little round-a-bout." Stuart answered with a cheesy smile, viewing his summation of the tour as rather humorous, aiming at levity with the auto industry tyrant.

Ralston Golden did find humor in it, only for the reason that Stuart's reddened chubby cheeks resembled that of a chipmunk, jiggling slightly when he got a little frisky.

Stuart opened the door to the lobby of the collision center as the estimators, receptionist, dispatcher, and collision manager all continued their tasks diligently, even if they were pretending to do so. Everyone knew the standard. It was like a celebrity walking into an exclusive fine dining restaurant, expecting the staff and patrons to let them be, since the hassle of fame was so overwhelming and inconvenient to a private, yet grossly public figure. The only difference was that none of these people wanted his autograph—only his demise.

In the customer seating area of the lobby a homely woman with her little daughter recognized him from the local commercials. His celebrity aura had arrived. She pointed her finger, and proclaimed, "Hey, you're in the commercials! Y'all just had one, right?"

Ralston gave her his golden smile as Stuart shuffled behind him like a grotesque beast that could possibly startle the child. "Why, yes ma'am, another tour de force of film. What might your name be?"

He extended his hand as she shook it gladly. "I'm Shelley and this is my daughter, Taffy."

He gently offered his hand to little Taffy with a toy smartphone stuck in her hand instead of a doll. "Well, hello Miss Taffy. That's a very unique and pretty name."

By unique he meant ridiculous, and by pretty he meant unbecoming, but nonetheless; "Is everything going well with your experience, Shelley?"

"Oh yeah, this has been a great experience compared to that jackass plowing into me! Justin has been there every step of the way and…"

Ralston Golden escaped with a nod and a smile behind the wall leading to the body shop where the paint sprayed, the putty dust circulated, the sparks flew, and the racket echoed; leaving Shelley to finish her thought on her own. "People are funny, Stuart. What do the numbers look like for the body shop?"

"Better than ever! Each quarter we see at least a two percent gain from the previous quarter, and that's been going on for two solid years now. Thanks to a yearly round of tough hailstorms, we're growing. To be honest, sir, extending the body shop may be a good…"

Stuart had become background noise with ease. Ralston Golden was always fascinated by the grime. These were the supposed salt of the earth. He watched the Mexican sprayer dousing his hands in paint thinner with cracked bloodshot eyes that said only one thing as they walked by; Pinchè gringo. Ralston knew they hated him, but he wasn't the one intentionally poisoning his nervous system and literally painting the inner lining of his lungs, picking out the most colorful boogers each night. Besides, painters were some of the most well paid in the body shop just beneath the body men. Business was booming. Jose—or so he guessed his name—would be fine just so long as something was in his wallet. There would be no victims in the body shop. He paid them to be that already.

They walked on through the parts department where a white-headed elderly man sat behind the desk with an old word processor reflecting a dull green off his flushed cheeks spurred on by high blood pressure. A lit cigarette hung from his mouth, looking like it had been there his entire life. In reality, it nearly had been. Stuart nearly collapsed in shock, and even though the old man had been there long before Ralston Golden purchased the dealership, he still had to glance at his nametag. "Ernie! Have you lost your mind? Put that out!"

"It's fine, Stuart. I'm sure they smoke in hell, and since he's already there, smoke on." Ralston Golden said with a look of assurance as Ernie shrugged his shoulders, fully accepting the crude assessment as his squinted eyes returned to the screen. "Keep up the good work, Ernie!"

They moved on as Stuart nervously pondered the consequences behind his lapse in oversight. The parts department of the body shop was like a basement operation; out of the way and altogether forgotten. "Sir, about Ernie, I…"

"No need for an explanation. That's all he has left. Let him have it." Ralston Golden quickly interrupted, ending the topic.

They snaked their way into the service area where hoods were propped open, men were operating on lifted vehicles, power tools zoomed, and expressions instantly hardened. "What's it been looking like here, Stuart?"

Still shaky from the Ernie debacle, he queerly answered, "The service department maintains equilibrium and really the only time we see a positive swing in numbers is in the summer months when it's too hot, and things start breaking on cars. Other than that, it's fairly consistent."

Into the finance department they strolled where the looks drastically changed from hardened grime to cheery cleanliness. Here the employees appeared to bask in their roles. They were overjoyed to be a part of Golden Motors, and kept the caffeine levels high to remain as such. Now it was blazers, ties, and dress pants; handsome young faces delighted to be in the presence of the big boss. Of course, that was all just part of the act. The financiers and the salespeople were the front-stage personas, always putting on a show for the enjoyment of the audience. The grime in the back showed how everyone felt deep down inside.

"And here we are, Mr. Golden, the cream of the crop. Sales have never been better. We've added some really bright players, concentrating on recruiting recent and attractive college graduates. You know, keeping it fresh…"

Once again, Ralston Golden trailed off, ignoring Stuart's assessment as he admired what he alone had built. Yes, in his mind of minds, he had built it alone and everything on the property he owned. He owned the Mexican paint sprayer and Ernie in the body shop, the mechanics and estimators in service, the financers and sales force, and most of all, Stuart. Everything revolved accordingly because of his illustrious efforts, and that would always be the case. To the breadth of the national stage! To the total domination of the industry! To the—

"Mr. Golden?" It was a female's voice of squeaky-soft purity that abruptly ended his self-proclaiming deluge of greatness. He looked to her as if he was about to harm the pretty young receptionist who wore a cute thin headset. She cheerfully added, "Your wife is on line five."

He went through his pockets and realized he must have left his phone in the car. This was surely his assistant's fault. No telling who had been trying to reach him since his separation from the hand computer. Cynthia, his wife, was especially a rarity in this instance. An emergency concerning her well-being was the last thing he wanted to hear. His only hope was that she had not been eclipsed by her day-drinking habit, wrapping her car around a pole—or even worse—hit someone else. That would be so inconvenient. He went into the conference room, closing the door behind him, and picking up the receiver. He only assumed it was a matter of life and death. "Yes, Cynthia."

"Hmmm…a surprise awaits you, Mr. Golden."

In the sarcastic tone with which she spoke he could only suspect one thing. After all, she did not appear to be hurt. "You must be drunk, or have taken too many of your happy pills to be calling me at the dealership."

"Not the case, my humble heart of hearts. We will soon have an addition to our family."

"I told you, Cynthia! I don't want any slobbering dogs, or shitting cats, or any other…"

He was in mid-sentence when it struck him like a lightning bolt as the hairs on his body stood upright. A snicker still laced in sarcasm followed from Cynthia, finalizing his innate suspicion. It was a matter of life after all. Never did he think her toxin-soaked womb could house a human life. "Oh Cynthia, is it true? My heir is growing inside you?"

"That's right, Mr. Golden."

Silence fell between the lines as it felt like a brick had splashed into his stomach. There was only one thing he could think to say. "Well…no more vodka presses for a while. I want it to be a boy."

"Me too."

He hung up the phone without a word of salutation as he did with everyone. Everything had changed so suddenly. He began conjuring the development of the child. He was to be raised a fierce competitor with all the calculated cunning of an indomitable force that would undoubtedly end up the victor in all of life's plentiful challenges. He would be molded in the Golden likeness, and unmercifully at that. He would love every second of being the heir of Golden Motors! It did not happen often, but quite unexpectedly Ralston Golden found himself in a good mood, and that was not just brought on by who he was. He was given a golden opportunity to set the boy on the right path to secure a legacy.

He exited the conference room with Stuart waiting like an obedient pet. "Mr. Golden, is everything okay?"

"Just fine, Stuart. I'm going to head out now."

Stuart instantly became ecstatic in a bottled and tightly sealed fashion. Not only he, but the entire dealership would uncork with relief at his departure. As Ralston Golden walked through the glossy showroom with depreciated assets being bought and sold on friendly terms, he admitted being enthralled by the eager anticipation of what was to come nine months down the road. Only one thing could add to his cheery disposition—a vulgar display of power.

Stuart courteously opened the glass door as Ralston Golden exited the dealership. He offered a friendly farewell-for-now wave, and said, "Good to see you, Mr. Golden! Have a good one!"

"Oh, I will." He responded, walking to his black luxury sedan with his assistant at the wheel awaiting his dreadful company. He opened the passenger door and upon turning around for one last thing, said, "Oh, and Stuart…you're fired!"

As Stuart's jaw dropped to the pavement in agonizing disbelief, Ralston Golden plopped down on the cool leather seat and closed the door without a second thought. He grabbed his phone wedged between the emergency brake and seat, held it up, and said, "Thanks for reminding me to grab my phone, ace."

## The Fellowship of the Enlightened

He had always been a meticulously groomed and tailored gentleman. Nothing was going to change in the rapid approach of his golden years. He wore fine tasseled leather loafers, which were essentially mirrors with the color of a well-traveled penny. His silk knee socks were as red as Old Saint Nick's breast coat on Christmas Eve. His grey slacks were imported from Italia, cinched up by an ostrich-skinned belt with the gold bust of an owl's head as the buckle. And yes, every gram of it was pure bullion. His starched crisp white dress shirt had a powder-blue collar and French cuffs; buttons made of ivory he bought in Calcutta. His cuff links resembled a minted coin with his profile raised upon them with Est. 1940 etched just below the profile—the year of his birth. And yes, they were also pure bullion. He wore a grey vest to match the dress pants, and attached was a diamond-crusted pocket watch secured by a thin silver chain. He procured the timepiece at a card game in Amsterdam from a member of the Saudi royal family in 1976. His blazer was made of crushed velvet from Budapest; a shade of the deepest violet with a red handkerchief square poking out of the breast pocket so as not to leave his red silk knee socks alone in the fashion scheme. Just for flair, a yellow and black tiger-striped silk scarf rested around his neck and was strategically fluffed out of the top of his dress shirt; purchased in Morocco. Sitting above his thin lips was a bushy gentlemen's moustache, colored silver, with oiled twirls at each end. His snow white mane was fused with pomade; styled with the deep part of a Hapsburg aristocrat. Though he lacked the necessity of it, he accessorized with a cane made of mahogany finished to a fine gloss holding a silver globe atop the staff, manufactured in his birthplace, London. The agent of his musk came from the enchanted city of Paris, brought in from the flowery fields of the French countryside. And yes, he was quite prepared to face another day with effortless class.

On this day he was strolling the sunny streets of San Francisco on a breezy Sunday morning. He had fallen in love with the city quickly, particularly for its eclectic character and boundless tolerance for the inherent peculiarities evident in nearly every human being on the planet. The Bay City had been founded by the stuff of his belt buckle and cuff links. The drive and ambition had led to a diversified population that built a charming sprawl on the immaculate hills of coastal northern California. It was not a cheap place to live by any means, but this socioeconomic reality was not a concern he harbored. It certainly didn't seem to be a concern for the high concentration of homeless people throughout the city as well. He was rarely pandered to, and when he was, he did not mind handing over whatever he had. That segment of society was also eclectic. Some were resigned mainstays on the streets, some were well-traveled gypsies, and even some had filled their minds with minimalist works of literature that viewed traditional nesting as one of the most suffocating lifestyles. They were on the road just like Kerouac. But then again, some could not get off the needle or the bottle, and their existences were far from a transcendental separation from the grinding routine of societal survival. They were the ones actually in the grinder; not just simply waiting their turn. He felt just fine retiring where his old bones could find fair weather year-round for the remainder of his days. Yes, it was a beautiful city!

He walked past the coffee shop he frequented almost daily, peering inside to see the usual suspects. A hippie gay couple owned the pocket café that looked more like a bizarre depot for modern and post-modern art. What made his attendance so regular was the scenery. It was typically frequented by young people with all of their identities in full-blown crisis. The skin art was exceptional and vibrant; some of them he considered walking murals, art in living motion. They must have hated going to the airport with jewelry hanging from ear lobes, eyebrows, nostrils, lips, intercostal spaces, and genitalia. He enjoyed conversing with all of them, as he found them inquisitive and thirsty for progressive modes of thinking, and even considered some of them friends. A few inside began pleading for him to join them as he walked past, but he just showed those bulging yellow teeth of his, and quipped with a civilized British accent, "We will play again soon, you poor wretched souls of depravity and wonder! And I mean that as the highest of compliments."

He was off to other business, and so they wished him well. This other business had flared his interest as a new hobby; a way to pass the days remarkably, just as he always had in life. He followed the numbers on the street curb that dialed him into his destination. A few blocks from the coffee shop sat a massive two-story burgundy mansion of Victorian inspiration. A tall black cast-iron gate encircled the property, nestled in the thick of a hilltop neighborhood. The front gate had an arched banner that read, The Buckey's. As he walked through the gate and under the arch, he stepped upon a cobblestoned walkway leading up to the front steps of the home. On each side of the walkway was a section of finely clipped St. Augustine blades, which were a glowing green. Resting in the center of each section was a concrete fountain, each hosting the sculpture of a nude woman bathing on her knees, arms stretched over her head, holding a sea shell for her fount. He thought their breasts were sculpted perfectly, certainly by a humanist who knew a thing or two about the finer things in life. A meticulous squared bush line ran along the front of the house, also separated by the walkway, and sprinkled on top were assorted light-colored flower petals that made a most inviting entranceway. As he walked up the stained wooden steps to an open front door, he said aloud to himself, "This will do."

The portico entrance had a darkened hardwood floor with a thin Persian rug stretching to an open foyer where he saw a few people mingling in conversation. He noticed next to him a candlelit table tucked to the vinyl wall that held a framed printed message that read, "Please fill out a name tag. Welcome to the Fellowship of the Enlightened!"

He detested name tags his entire life and mostly traveled under aliases, but here he felt compelled to cooperate. After all, if one should be humiliated, then so should all the rest in kind. Perhaps it was a team effort in making an effort to bring all the participants on the same level. At least the insignia was emblazoned in the center of the name tag—FE—and matching the shine of his belt buckle and cuff links. He pressed it to his crushed velvet breast pocket and moved forward with his usual air of confidence.

His polished and aristocratic appearance eclipsed the attire of all else present. Their eyes darting to his person confirmed the obvious. From the side, out of the shadows of another room emerged a petite woman with black and gray-streaked hair, pulled back tightly into a pony tail. Her attire was modest and neutral, along with her approach. Everyone else gradually began to murmur amongst themselves as she squinted her eyes at his name tag, offering her delicate hand in greeting. "Mister…?"

"Sir Monty Lincoln madam. Pleased to make your acquaintance. Might I add that you have an impeccable taste in dwellings? Truly a gem of yester-year never to be forgotten. Is it Misses or Miss Margaret Buckey?" He said, introducing himself, handing over a compliment, and posing a question at the same time.

She didn't like him already, but indulging people was her new lot in life. That was the consequence of building a congregation. "It is Miss Buckey, Sir Lincoln. My husband, Edward Buckey, died some years ago. By your British accent and the designation of Sir I am sure you've been in finer residences than this one."

He kept his eyes rolling around with a fixed smirk. "Oh, it was quite a boring ceremonial affair, but nevertheless a title one must never turn down. I do have a distinct accent, but it is rather English—not British. It is a shame our island has such linguistic contrast, but it is typically an incorrect observation, which is not in the least bit offensive."

Margaret kept her own ingenuous smile fixed, yet it was slowly losing definition due to his backhanded remark, whether true or not. She would attempt to switch gears with a description of what she was establishing. "Well, Sir Lincoln—

"Please, Monty will suffice, Miss Buckey." He interrupted.

"As will Margaret." She nearly snapped back. The tension was laid out, and then brushed aside momentarily for comfort's sake. "This is the Fellowship of the Enlightened where all belief systems are accepted and tolerated equally. It is our motto that each spark is furnished with the current to illuminate the darkness where religious intolerance flourishes. We believe this is one of the main causes of discord and tragedy throughout the world; not religion itself. We do not think that any belief system should be fueled by a duality; an eternal clash of good and evil. Nor should this conflict exist between the spirit and the flesh, or the material and ascetic planes. The inherent worth of each individual will be extracted, and the end result is harmonious coexistence."

Monty nodded along with a curious expression, attentive to the detail of her description, but willing to call it what it was. "So this is Unitarian Universalism?"

"Essentially, it is. We intend to make it our own. Let me introduce you to some of our congregation." She offered, turning to the few gathered in the foyer. "Here we have our Islamic friend, Tarid."

Tarid was of usual Arab complexion. He maintained a tightly trimmed black beard, donned a multi-colored hijab, and hanging around his neck was a beaded wooden necklace with a pendant of the crescent moon and star of the Islamic faith. In his hand was the Qur'an and his expression was not the least bit inviting, but he did manage to offer a rigid single downward nod, which was entirely more than Monty Lincoln expected. He rarely came across a cheery Arab Muslim, but Monty Lincoln knew he was a pompous British imperialist in the eyes of a Palestinian refugee as Tarid was; so he bowed before him as he would of all with aged faith.

"This is Billy: a southern Baptist from Mississippi. He's our soulful songbird."

Billy was an older black man with a thick moustache and a healthy afro. He carried a working man's build; stout and weathered to a formidable muscle tone. He wore jeans, work boots, and a t-shirt. He came up to Monty Lincoln in a near stride, grabbing his hand and shaking it vigorously. Monty Lincoln feared his shoulder would dislocate from the socket, but forgave him the violence of his introduction when Billy said, "Good ta' meet ya'! God bless ya', suh!"

"This is Josiah. He is of the Jewish faith."

Monty Lincoln extended his own hand as none was forthcoming from Josiah whom with a slight apprehension completed the handshake. Both Billy and Tarid shot conspicuous looks towards Josiah that only Monty Lincoln seemed to notice. Josiah donned a Yarmulke that fortunately covered the bald spot on the back his head and wore the wiry beard of dark and gray as if he were a scribe who had just crawled out of his cavernous study. He solemnly said, "Shalom."

"Here we have Cindy, our lovely Buddhist addition."

She was indeed lovely, Monty Lincoln thought. She wore cropped blonde hair with bright vibrant blue eyes, which appeared as if you could swim in them. She had the build of a Yoga practitioner, wearing a sleek lavender jumpsuit with white ninja-style slip-ons of which ten percent of the retail price went to charity. She pressed forward unabashedly and lightly shook his hand as he ever-so lightly placed a kiss atop her own, generating an immediate frustration within Margaret. For Monty Lincoln, her smile had been birthed in the heights of Nirvana. She blushed, and said, "Nice to meet you, Monty."

"Enchanted." He softly said, pulling back to his own space.

"And finally, we have Baltasar. He is of the Wiccan belief."

Baltasar was a slight man of Armenian descent in his late twenties who maintained a posture like he hated every waking moment of his life, perpetually curled into himself, hiding behind a bulging shoulder bigger than the other. He wore black from head to toe, along with black eyeliner and black lipstick. His thin dyed black hair was pasted down to his starkly pale scalp, and just as he was repulsed by the world, so were the others repulsed by him. He simply and awkwardly grunted forth, "Hey."

Following the norm of classifications and introductions they all gazed at Monty Lincoln, awaiting the revelation of his personal belief system. According to the meticulous and gaudy way in which he dressed and the manner of his speech, they all churned different conceptions of what he might have been. Tarid thought he was probably a Catholic, but not just a Catholic—a Holy Roman Catholic. Josiah thought that whatever he may have been he must not be practicing, and certainly not as diligently as himself. Cindy merely thought he was strangely debonair, but if she had to take a stab at it she would have to pick Episcopalian. Baltasar merely thought that if the Devil had a wardrobe, he would have the outfit hanging in his closet. Billy simply didn't care either way. And yet, Monty Lincoln beat them all to the punch. "And what might you be, Margaret?"

"I am agnostic." Her answer was just as he expected. She exemplified the moderate stance of Unitarian Universalism. "And what are you, Monty?"

"I am a proud and devout worshipper of Realism." He answered, as all present were effectively taken aback.

"That's not a form of faith. It's an ideology associated with the world of politics." Josiah quipped, as if undeniably correct.

"Rightly so, Josiah. But it is also a belief system happening to end with an –ism just as your heralded and ancient Judaism." Monty Lincoln replied with a confident smile. Tarid thought that finally he and Josiah were on common ground, though their religious texts supposedly mirrored each other in so many respects.

Margaret thought Monty Lincoln's admission was rather odd as well, but she was willing to move antithetical to the core principle of the Fellowship of the Enlightened. "Well, I'm sure we could all live with and learn about your interesting belief system as we are all here to do. Welcome to the Fellowship of the Enlightened, Monty. We are all happy to have you."

Monty Lincoln saw some faces of happiness. Cindy nodded in approval with a genuine smile. Baltasar, though naturally looking repulsed by everything, gave an awkward nod and the faintest shade of a smile. Tarid and Josiah nodded, but refrained from smiling. Of course, Monty Lincoln bowed in reverence to them all, fully exposing his bulging yellow teeth. The wheels of his mind were already turning and building steam for a creative explosion. He had plans. Grand plans!

"This will be a very enlightening adventure, indeed!"

**The Power Couple**

The studio was at a dull glow in the perfect blend of light and dark, where shadows drawn upon the walls was his inspiration. Seated in a sound booth, absorbed in the atmosphere with his elbows on his knees, was Jeremy Boland. He wore black polished jump boots, black denim jeans, and a white t-shirt that read—*Hot*—with a color spectrum that ran through the letters resembling the ensemble of a rainbow. A platinum chain hung from his neck with an oversized pendent of the letters, *GJ*, in the style of Old English. The Rolex watch wrapped around his wrist complimented his chain, and a black ball cap with the bill straight as a board was tucked low to his brow. He was preparing to do what he loved once again, and his producer standing against the wall in the sound booth was ready to fluff his ego for another outpouring of flows, to some raunchy beats manufactured to the specifics of his personality in general. That life was Jeremy Boland, but more importantly the moniker for the extension of his identity—Gay J.

"And again, you got dis. It's the last track. You started out hard. Now you gonna end hard. Ain't nobody doin' it like you. Nobody could these days. Dey too soft. Worry too much of what the media gonna say. What dey mommy and daddy gonna say. You above all dat shit. You da trailblazer. You da frontrunna. You da avant-garde, nigga. Take this moment and blow dey minds away. Leave em thinkin, 'Damn, Gay J real! Can't wait for that next EP!' Let's give em what dey want. Let em have it, nigga."

At that, his producer, who had worked with him on his two previous albums, exited the sound booth to take his seat behind the soundboard where he would await the signal from Gay J. He had done it again. This was the final track of the album, and a pep-talk of sorts was always in order. Gay J stood to his feet in the sealed sound booth and drew in a deep breath. As he released the breath he had taken in, it was time. He went through his ritual warming motions, motioning as if already flowing like a fighter throws shadow punches before each bout. He bobbed his head, anticipating the rhythm of the beat; its temporal tone, and the preciseness of his delivery. It was complete. He fastened the headphones about his ears. The countdown was on: 5…4…3…2…1!

*Talk about Brokeback Mountain, nigga, I'll break yo back wit my dick in yo ass NIGGA!*

The beat, in fact, did drop hard as if a cosmic orb of the most evolved energy hovered overhead just for a moment, and then whizzed away. It was immediately followed by a loud clap as if done in unison by a village of bamboo-wielding Japanese percussionists. The clap dribbled forward to accentuate its presence, and then the energy returned to hover overhead again. That was the arrangement for the time being. A precedence had been set: hard and pounding.

*This goes out to all you hatas*
*May you end up face down in the swamps with the gatas*
*Preferably sooner than motha fuckin lata*
*Told you I'd be around like a flu you can't kick*
*And I'm here to make sure that conscience stay sick*
*And as always, you can slobba on my dick*
*Don't do it quick*
*Slow and sloppy so you know I get my fix*
*No teeth*
*No breath for you beasts*
*Bottom line, gonna put some asses in da seats*

*Worldwide*
*As I glide in the high*
*My shit some fucked up equation times Phi*
*When dey put me in da ground*
*I'm never gonna die*
*So come get some*
*Grab yo mic or yo strap*
*Whateva, cuz you know I'm gonna snap*
*No peace*
*Boy, don't expect an invitation*
*All props to the rainbow nation*

The beat pressed on as Gay Jay stepped back from the microphone momentarily to shore up his energy. As he bobbed his head he looked at his producer who was doing the same; both thinking a cut then would be completely out of the question if the track kept flowing as flawless as this. He stepped back to the microphone.

*Now that I got that off my chest, let's follow the yella brick road all the way to that man behind the curtain with da levers, and da lights, and da smoke. He's gonna tell ya a lil somethin.*

The original cadence of the beat was brought to an abrupt close as the time doubled into a fluctuating baseline vibrating on a running string, pulsing ferociously. It was the heartbeat during a marathon and the thumping engine of a race car on its final lap. It was exertion at its highest level of performance—out of control—yet in perfect balance.

*Just so ya know*
*There's no equal*
*There's only people*
*Proddin and plottin*

*For da next evil*
*Swim in da depths*
*Keep it all cerebral*
*Climb for da best*
*Build your own steeple*
*Get it off your chest*
*Always in da end*
*You're your own keepa*

A company of flutes joined the streaming baseline; subtle yet pronounced with a hint of mysterious tragedy that ironically drove the mood towards a sweet-natured sensibility. It was all melding together into a fine shine.

*All I know*
*We all wanna live*
*Get wit da flow*
*It's all I can give*
*Shine a light in da cave*
*The dark got rights too*
*Learn to behave*
*And see it all through*
*Gotta understand*
*Gone is the hero*
*Don't stand wit da man*
*Cuz the sum is the zero*

Joining the baseline and the flutes came a chorus of further harmony, emanating from a choir of unknown dimension. The body of the voice stated nothing in decipherable lyric, but held a hymning air of rejoice like the sun's rays had just penetrated through the dark clouds to once again bring hope upon pale faces.

*Can't stress enough*

*The tough gonna make it*
*Get ready for da rough*
*Cuz you know you can't fake it*
*Shake it up a bit*
*Make it all spicy*
*If ya never quit*
*It fits real nicely*
*Run and I gun*
*Till I fall flat on my face*
*Rock your ear till it bleeds*
*Then I'm gone without a trace*

Suddenly—the baseline, and the flutes, and the choir was replaced by the hovering energy followed by the bamboo-clapping Japanese percussionists from the beginning of the track. It was a full circle as Gay Jay removed the headset clamped around his ears as his producer began fading the beats away. Not one flaw could either of them detect. The album was complete and the message was sent. Gay Jay was here to stay!

Just because, Gay J threw in one last thing. "Bitch ass niggas!"

*

The spotlight was not so gracious for Tommy Bloom. Regardless, he would remain caught in its flash. In his sport and chosen profession he was certainly a rare breed. It began when he was a child, marveling at the circus performers twirling effortlessly through the air where they relied on one another, toying with death at each gasp of the crowd. He liked the tight suits with sparkling and glossy bright colors wrapped around firm bodies. Prior to one Christmas as a child he dropped hints that he wanted one of those suits. It quickly evolved to persistent pleading, and finally shameless begging as only a child can expertly pursue. He eventually got his suit for Christmas, parading around in it as much as he could, which eventually led to foolish attempts at stunts from the roof, the tree, and the unsecured rope hanging from an outstretched branch. What followed was a broken wrist, a sprained ankle, and a slight concussion. None of this served as a deterrent to future daring acts. He was a growing boy who healed fast and only grew bolder. With his fascination in the lives of the circus performers he realized they primarily came from the same sporting background— gymnastics. He then discovered only a select few from the gymnasiums achieved the glory confined within the time-honored tradition of the Olympic Games. The circus performer was a novelty, but the Olympian was entirely something else; a weighted brand that lasted one's entire life. It became Tommy Bloom's personal dream and driving ambition. One day he would be awarded the gold medal under the flag of the United States of America. All would be proud of him, and instead of anguish, he would cry tears of joy as he waved his hand to an adoring world that would forever remember him.

As it goes, not everything follows as one meticulously dreams. He did become a gymnast, and a damn fine one at that. He had only one significant shortcoming; his feelings got hurt if he failed. This hypersensitivity diminished what a champion needed the most—unshakable resolve. This discouraging state of affairs was exasperated by a fierce identity crisis. The world of gymnastics was not exactly a cesspool of machismo, but the young men were still beginning their journey of lust for the opposite sex, even if misplaced. Tommy Bloom had not come along on that particular leg of the journey. He was rather fixated on the clear lines of his teammates' muscles, the roundness of their butts, and the bulge of their crotches, pronounced by the squeezing effects of their tights. This was Tommy Bloom's dirty little secret at the time, although entirely natural. Internal and external forces forbade him to think clearly at such a frenetic stage of development. He began seeking a cure to this inner desire which seemed to be on a different path to the prevailing herd. As with secrets, they distort reality until life becomes disorganized and costly. To combat these persistent and innate desires he joined the high school wrestling team to—quite literally—submit those desires by force, and ultimately conquer them. He became a damn fine wrestler, but a far cry from the grade of an Olympian. To supplement his highly physical existence he studied and practiced theatre. This effectively fed his ethereal sensibilities that were being constantly battered in the wrestling circle. The division of his personality was forged, thus setting the stage for his walk through adulthood.

This all led him to the present spotlight of the EAW (Elite American Wrestling) Association. The backdrop he stood in front of had a clipper ship painted on it, sailing on blue waters with cumulus clouds above as the sun penetrated through with an effervescent presence. The sails attached to the masts were emblazoned with rainbows, and just above the painted scene was The Buccaneer in a flashy neon glow readily scene on the Las Vegas strip. Tommy Bloom, The Buccaneer, wore black pirate boots that stretched around his bulging calves. He wore cream-colored tights accentuating his broad and muscular physique. He donned beautiful brown locks of hair down to his shoulders; wore a black patch around one eye, and a pink bandana around his forehead. His front tooth was deliberately blacked out. He wore red lipstick, rosacea on his cheeks, black eye-liner around his exposed eye, and large gold hoops from his lobes. In short, he was not the most menacing of action figures, but that wasn't his role. He stood in the front of the camera waiting for the cue to begin his vitriolic diatribe intended to shock and offend. Like sex; it all sold well. The cameraman counted down to zero, and Tommy Bloom—The Buccaneer—better known on the streets as The Butt Pirate, was ready to spew forth.

"The Buccaneer is here to get in your face once again, and now I'm setting sail for the Engine Man! Yeh, that's right, it's going to be a fun little date! And lucky for him, The Buccaneer's in love…again! But I'm not gonna whisk you away by candlelight, Engine Man! We're gonna get dirty, and the bill's on you, chump! First, I'm gonna get you all hot and bothered with a few slaps to the face! Ya know, get those juicing flowing! Then after you're all lubed up I'm gonna lay you down flat on your stomach to teach you what it's like to be a real man! To cap off a perfect evening I'm gonna check that oil, Engine Man…so I suggest you have your levels right! Oh, this gonna be such a delightful evening! Here I come, Engine Man! Marvin Gaye put it best…let's get it on!"

At that rundown, he charged the camera as the operator stepped to the side. He toppled it onto a padded surface so as not to damage the equipment. Down the corridor he strutted with purpose as the sold-out arena awaited his entrance, having watched his smack-talking on the jumbo-tron. Only a few thoughts were slung through his head before he smashed through the wall separating the persons of Tommy Bloom and The Buccaneer.

*Am I really still doing this? The pay's not bad. But gosh, I hate these people. Do the routine, Tommy. They're going to hate you either way. You win.*

Out he stepped through the curtains to see what never became dull in his routine—the sight of a fully packed crowd swaying in colorful beams of light. They erupted at the sight of The Buccaneer just as they did in every city, and Atlanta carried a special charge. The pathway leading to the ring was lined with burly security guards preserving a buffer zone between the crowd and The Buccaneer. He was the only wrestling personality requiring it to the degree presented. His personal safety was in question in each and every city, but the southern states seemed to carry out the most graphic responses. He was guaranteed to be showcased where the reaction would be the most palpable. That's what sold tickets.

He began to walk forward in usual fashion; a fine line between masculinity and femininity. His bulging frame significantly contributed to the perception of toughness, but the runway strut complimented his feminine side. The boos from the crowd beat on his eardrums as he showed them how much he loved it. The faces through the crowd were mixed and divided. Some spewed horrible obscenities and threw gestures of contempt. They were the ones attempting to claw at The Buccaneer through the line of security guards, and would have thrown cabbage at him if at hand. Some just stood still in reverence to what they saw as the perfect balance of toughness and sensitivity enshrined in The Buccaneer. Yet still others wore expressions of indifference, not knowing quite what to think and feel. However, all the faces were clearly aroused to amusement.

Halfway down the aisle The Buccaneer shifted his attention from the fans to his opponent standing in the middle of the ring. Engine Man wore a black beard riding the line between kept and chaotic. He wore a navy mechanics coverall that was artificially stained like he rolled around in the greasy muck all day. He wore work boots that were actually wrestling shoes made to look like the former. His shaved head gleaned off the arena lighting. He looked the part of the blue-collar worker, and the color commentators quickly leapt to draw the contrast between the styles of the two about to square off in the ring.

"I tell ya, Donny, Engine Man hasn't looked more revved up than tonight. He's just disgusted by The Buccaneer!"

"Bobby, The Buccaneer isn't too fond of Engine Man, either. This ain't gonna be smooth sailing for The Buccaneer, but he's strutting with confidence up to the ring. This'll be a doosy!"

"Sure will, Donny…and the crowd is electric!"

The Buccaneer went into a full sprint, diving into the ring beneath the bottom rope, sliding in on his washboard abs. Engine Man took the opportunity to stomp the heel of his boot on The Buccaneer's upper back, causing him to dramatically collapse back onto the springy mat. The crowd met the assault with a roar of satisfaction. Engine Man followed the stomp with a close-fisted hammer-strike to the upper back which made getting to his feet impossible. Engine Man began with a confidence which rode on the edge of cockiness, grabbing The Buccaneer's long locks. Clutching them lightly was the cue for them to move on to the next move.

The Buccaneer willingly came to his feet, displaying the pain on his face from the initial blows. Now it was time for a little ride in the routine. Engine Man grabbed him by the arm and flung him to the opposing side of the ring, bouncing him off the ropes so he could run back directly into the vicinity of Engine Man's beefy outstretched arm for a clothesline. The Buccaneer landed violently on his back, clutching his head like his brain had been rattled away from the stem. The crowd reacted boisterously, but Engine Man was to keep the pace high with the next move in mind.

It was time to compound all the pain being dished out with the advanced move of a suplex. He brought The Buccaneer to his feet again, flung him against the ropes, but this time it was up to The Buccaneer to garner the momentum necessary for a turn in mid-air; and Engine Man would play as the vault. It all had to be done convincingly, and as The Buccaneer's back landed squarely on the mat once again, clutching it as if it were broken it two, the crowd went wild as he grimaced in false agony, although it always hurt a little.

Engine Man paused the onslaught to deliberately walk around the ring in folly, nodding his head as the cockiness fully consumed his demeanor. Visceral praise was reserved for Engine Man, and curses were such for the downed Buccaneer. Only a few rainbow flags flew in the crowd as Engine Man went back to work, bringing him back to his feet for another measure of pain.

First, an ear clap. Then a gut shot, followed by a foot stomp, and finished off with a close-fisted punch to the forehead. They were all to be gently placed, and they were, except for a minor miscalculation as the last strike landed just below The Buccaneer's brow. Blood was now drawn and the roar from the crowd was salaciously surprising. Engine Man flung him to the corner where the scantily padded tensioner awaited his violent arrival. The Buccaneer executed a back flip swung from his own momentum that was stopped in its tracks by the immovable corner pad. Upside-down and appearing caught in the ropes as if tangled in barbed wire, his accidental cut began to spill on the mat.

Engine Man untangled him, bringing him back to a standing position, and just before he was about to fling him again to the opposing corner, he whispered in his ear, "Sorry, Tommy."

"No worries, Kev." he responded underneath his breath as he ran to the opposing corner for another self-imposed entanglement with the tensioners.

The fight wore on with dominance on Engine Man's side as he stretched The Buccaneer all over the ring, throwing him from the ring, throwing him back in the ring, and all of it feeding an utter humiliation. Blood was in their hair, on their tights, smeared to their skin, serving as proof of reality for any skeptics out there. It became apparent The Buccaneer could not take anymore. The crowd chanted for him to be finished. An equally exhausted Engine Man dragged him by the arm to the center of the ring like he was moving a fresh corpse. Engine Man flipped him over on his back; The Buccaneer's long and blood-soaked locks draped over his face as Engine Man stomped around the ring, foretelling that his signature move was coming up next. Vroom! Vroom! The crowd insisted as Engine Man climbed up to the top tensioner and gave the signal for the Piston-Hitter. He would jump at a near straight line like a piston firing through a cylinder block. With the crowd counting down along with him, he leaped from the tensioner to make an explosion with The Buccaneer's unconscious being.

At just the right moment The Buccaneer rolled out of the way, and instead of the broad forehead of Engine Man finishing the job—a symbolic attack, not in the least bit scientific—he knocked himself out cold. Engine Man laid lifeless on his stomach as the crowd had been fooled once again, voicing their displeasure as The Buccaneer came to his knees in heaving breaths, but wearing a look some would have considered naughty. The game was up now. Unless an ally surprisingly ran out to the aid of Engine Man, he was about to be degraded and violated.

"Donny, it looks like the Engine Man cracked the head of his piston! Oh no! I think The Buccaneer is about to do a little diagnostic check, and I doubt Engine Man's gonna like it one bit!"

"Bobby, this is a real shocker, but Engine Man's about to get the shock of his life in just a minute! You can feel it all over this arena!"

The Buccaneer had laboriously come to his feet in a puddle of blood and sweat. He hoisted his right thumb in the air to signal it was time for his signature move—The Oil Check, aka The State Inspection, aka The Butt Plug. And yes; its name and function had nothing to do with physical mechanics just as the Piston-Hitter. Regardless of its farcical enterprise The Buccaneer was about to put his own finishing touches on Engine Man with the crowd and viewership at home hypnotically tuned in.

The Buccaneer made a few circles around the play-dead body of Engine Man. He then proceeded to come down on one knee at the Engine Man's rear and kept his thumb lifted high as the majority bristled at yet another shocking turn of fortune on behalf of the reviled Buccaneer. With a chopping single downward thrust he theoretically plunged his thumb into the anal orifice of his working friend, Kev— or so the crowd thought, but didn't, but somehow did, in some strange way.

Engine Man instantly came to consciousness like adrenaline had been mainlined to his heart. The Buccaneer's thumb was the current of electricity as Engine Man contorted himself into an upward parabola, eyes rolling into the back of his head for effect. Tommy removed his thumb and back into unconsciousness Engine Man fell with a pronounced deflation as there was only one thing left to do. The Buccaneer turned him over, pinned down his shoulders, and then waited as the referee slapped the mat with the palm of his hand three times. The bell rang out, ending the fiasco to the relief of the wrestlers and to the dismay of the fanatical base.

As the bloodied Buccaneer slid under the bottom rope down to floor level it was clear their work had been masterfully served. Walking back up the aisle to seventies dance music, The Buccaneer looked at all the faces in the crowd. It was always the same: disgust, shock, indifference, and lightly sprinkled smiles of approval. A spitball from a child's arsenal lodged into his hair with a few minor scuffles breaking out in the crowd. He looked back at them for his final farewell of the night. He pointed his butt out towards the crowd, licked his extended index finger, and touched his bum like it was too hot to handle. He, and some of those in the crowd, audibled, *"Tssss!"* His work was done for the night as he retreated behind the curtains where he became Tommy Bloom again in an instant.

When he got back to his dressing room he plopped down in front of the mirror; first carefully removing the heat-conducting wig and then seeing how bad the cut actually was, but it failed to draw any concern. Now reflection was all he had left to do. There was nothing won in the match. That was something he had learned in theatre. The only prize was the enraptured reaction of the audience. He was to be the profitable, rate-generating pariah to bring out the divisions encased in a sensitive societal matter. His body ached, but he was used to that. The mirror would be his comfort as he began removing the make-up from his face.

He could only think about the one he loved and where exactly he could be at that moment. They were both men on the run, chasing fame and fortune; both unable to realize that fame and fortune only existed in the times they shared alone together. Tommy thought he may be in town, and if so, he had to find him as soon as humanly possible. Comfort was desired, and not by hugs and kisses and rolling in the bed—though pleasant as well—but by the company they mutually enjoyed. That was the best. The simultaneous laughter drawn from complete understanding. The falling asleep at the same moment, and waking up to a gentler reality away from the devouring monster which was inevitably the way of their world. He missed him so much that it began to tear into his psyche as he realized the futility of his walk without—

"Wuz up, baby boy?"

Tommy whipped around in his chair to a mix of fear and delight. In the darkest part of his dressing room sat the man he had been longing for, and would always long for. "J! You came!"

Gay J stood up with confidence as he always did, stepping into the light. He drew close to Tommy, brushing his fingertips across Tommy's elated face. There was only one thing he could say. "Let's go home, baby."

## Malcolm Grace

Make-up was putting the final touches to the face of Bill Doody, the neo-conservative pundit whose nightly news commentary, *The Clear Line*, enthralled the hawks of the political landscape. He was a man of hot temper who brought half-truths to full proof with a certain charisma and knack for persuasion. Responding to everything rhetorically, and especially theoretically, was his method. He even discredited and stomped on ideological allies just so he could keep his preeminent aura of innate rightness alive. Of his enemies, one stood next to him with a clipboard in hand, though he had very little use for it. The program director had four basic bullet points: news of the day, conversation, fielding inbound calls, and the guest of the show. The first three had been crossed off and he was eagerly awaiting the opportunity to cross out the fourth. He knew that in reality, Bill Doody only needed a dash of make-up and a camera pointed in his direction to hammer down his views on mammoth issues of complexity. It all came down to how people felt at the moment, stuck on what's *popular*. That was Bill Doody's operation. He called all the shots like a schoolyard bully no one really respected at the end of the day. The program director's job was to be agreeable with Bill Doody, but most importantly—to encourage him.

"Who the hell is this?" Bill Doody growled, looking through the curtains at his inconspicuous guest calmly taking in his surroundings. In no way was this man a somebody of any sort. It only made Bill Doody minutely contemplate his own decline. "Can we get anybody to come on this show anymore?"

"Bill, we had the Speaker of the House on last night." pointed out the program director without seeming condescending. It was in Bill Doody's nature to exaggerate. Also, it was the main ingredient of his business model.

"Yeah, that guy's a weirdo. Some people like him, some people hate him, but at least he's got those two things working for him. Who hates or loves this guy?" Bill Doody frustratingly posed.

"Make him interesting, Bill. Introduce him to the world. Bust him up a little. Let him know he just stepped up a level. Do what you do best." He half-heartedly encouraged.

"Well, let's get this over with." Bill Doody stated, waving away make-up and pressing through the curtains. A spontaneous burst of clapping erupted from the live audience, but he quickly motioned for them to cease as they were to remain silent for the most part. After all, it wasn't a game show with prizes to be won and games to be played. Well, maybe some games were involved.

He approached the table separating the two of them without even taking a glance in the direction of his guest. He was too busy adjusting his tie, checking the time, making sure the papers on the table were evenly stacked, and that his fancy pen was in hand to add some sophistication and refinement to an exterior resembling a porcupine. His guest had been watching him and without revealing it, laughed inside. The commercial break was over and it was time to roll.

"Welcome back to *The Clear Line*, where tonight we have a special guest. His name is Malcolm Grace. He received his law degree from Tulane specializing in civil liberties legislation. He has been a keynote speaker for influential independent and moderate leaders across the country. He's penned, *How's That Working Out For You?*—

a study and commentary into recent government policy. So let's to get to know a little more about Malcolm Grace."

Bill Doody finally turned his attention towards the faintly smiling Malcolm Grace, dressed down for the occasion. Sure, he wore a white dress shirt with a dark blazer, but no tie to keep him restricted with an appearance of containment. His complexion was clear and his body fit. His hair flowed a fitting blend of gray and black housing a clear and sharp mind for the outing at hand. It was truly nice to be there; his first shot at national exposure with the American masses, especially with an extreme pundit like Bill Doody. There was a plan, which was also a bit extreme. All he had to do was put it in action.

"So what are you doing? What's your purpose? You're obviously shooting for some kind of political points." Bill Doody tersely began, immediately placing Malcolm Grace in a corner to defend a barrage. As usual, Bill Doody just didn't like the looks of him.

"Well, it's not points. I'm not running for election, so I'd rather refer to it as attention. And there are certain matters that need to be brought to attention." Malcolm Grace confidently asserted, maintaining his faint smile to match Bill Doody's condescending one.

"Is that what your book is about? Is it another map to all the answers? Personally, I haven't opened it up." Bill Doody pressed, as a few chuckles came from the audience.

"Yeah Bill, just like your book." Malcolm Grace strategically reversed, keeping his answers short and precise. Bill Doody's most recent work was titled, *Liberal Loonies*. The real difference was that his was a best seller.

"Okay, we'll see if you can get on the best seller stand—three times!" Bill Doody mocked, smiling like a hyena, yet already showing the signs of cracking. His vanity was taking the controls. Now with his ego fully inflated Malcolm Grace would pursue a full-frontal attack. "So where along the fence do you ride, Malcolm?"

"I ride where it makes the most sense. Remaining in one spot would not make much sense. Then you're not going anywhere. I think knowing the entire breadth of the fence is the most important thing."

"Oh, so you don't believe in taking stands? Having some resolve? Let me put it this way..." Bill Doody said, swaying his fancy pen in the fashion of a laser pointer. "You're telling me you don't lean either way on the political spectrum? That you're far too intelligent for that? That you're far more intelligent than the voters of this country— conservative or liberal? You're just somehow above it all? Is that fair?"

This was the tone of the show each and every day as it gorged on the adversarial. Malcolm Grace was fully prepared for the challenge, especially on such foreign ground where he hadn't a friend in sight. "Certainly not above it. Submersed within it, yes. I know we all sink or swim together."

Dismissing his answer as vague, it could have been construed as patriotic, and also collective at the same time. "So what are you?"

"I'm a citizen of these United States of America. I believe in utility, in constructive dialog, in choice and variety, and the power of numbers to bring about the greater good. The only things absolute in my mind is that I live, breathe, and will eventually pass as a citizen of this great nation. Everything else is open for thoughtful refinement and fervent debate. I believe in the betterment of those things that are undeniably absolute." Malcolm Grace answered with a calm delivery; the faint smile remaining fixed.

"Okay, this fluffy existentialism sounds pretty and nice, but if you have political aspirations, then where exactly do you stand? Are you a wacky libertarian that believes people should do whatever they want and not pay taxes; a progressive that only looks towards the future; or a liberal looking to control the mind, body, and finances of everyone, while simultaneously telling people they're being liberated? I know damn well you're not a conservative!" Bill Doody shot forth as his audience rolled out their judgmental chuckles of approval. His expertise for humiliation and verbal combat were grown with care over the years. The ratings had him on an eight year run at, or very near the top of the political commentary business. He was nowhere close to a passing fad.

"No Bill, I'm not a conservative by your standards nor a liberal by anyone else's. I do hasten to progress, but not at any fixed rate, and I don't think a free-for-all is the answer either. There is a large gap on the political spectrum occupied by those who have fallen out of love with the proto-typical configuration of Democrats and Republicans, blue and red, donkeys and elephants, liberals and conservatives. This configuration places restrictions on the democratic process within our Republic—

"Let me stop you there!" Bill Doody hastily interjected as he found his own mind drawn to the oratory of Malcolm Grace. He had to kill that ability to listen to a well-drawn argument on his own show. Things were to be black and white. He continued his attack. "So the time-honored political divisions of this country; that in effect built this country, are no longer viable and make our democratic process a sham?"

"First off, this a Republican form of government and democracy is only the institution that brings it to form. Look at national elections versus local elections. The most voter turnout indisputably is that of the Presidency, which is not decided by the popular vote. During that same election cycle members of Congress are elected as well, though typically very few people know their Senators or Representatives by name, much less what district they're in. Yet, their vote counts more in their local constituencies. If you get down to municipal elections for city council or the mayor the turnout is laughable. The American voter has proven more interested in the majesty of high office, but my original contention is that there are only two primary choices—Democrat or Republican—through which the voter can exercise their freedoms. Unfortunately, the bulk of those who vote do so through the lens of family tradition, populism, or uninformed engagement…like voting down a straight Democratic ticket or Republican ticket. This is what the two parties want the most."

"So all Democrats and Republicans are stupid?! You have all the answers and none that you're presenting, by the way! How's that working for you, Malcolm?" Bill Doody stabbed, as he shook out some more chuckles from the audience. He felt the time was ripe to slam rejection down Malcolm Grace's throat as he had done to countless other guests attempting to use his show as a launch pad for their whimsical musing of a theoretically better United States of America.

Malcolm Grace paused to allow the audience time to recover from Bill Doody's reactionary rebuttal to irritate, and not at all to tantalize. Malcolm Grace's faint and peaceful smile was entirely more condescending than Bill Doody's snap violations of courtesy and reason. In Malcolm Grace's capable eyes it could be seen that he was the one holding session. He slowly sat back in his chair as the smile disintegrated into a look of sincere severity, indicating a shift in the flow. He couldn't hold it too long, or it would lose effect. It had to be brought out and put back in with precise timing. Malcolm Grace's following words had already been chosen and he would not be looking for a rebuttal. The perfect time of delivery was between the longing for words, and the ultimate frustration of not receiving them. He would begin with what could be unanimously understood. "With only two choices, if you take one away, you are just a single step away from full-blown tyranny."

It was an observation; a simple problem of subtraction, but the implication of that sum was what they all received. He figured it was the most dangerous implication he could have put forward with so much confidence; so much inevitability that the implication would soon become a reality that affected the lives of all. He took into consideration that things were to get nasty from this point on, but it had to be done. He was no different from the public. He also blindly followed his feelings.

Just as Bill Doody's lips began to curl and his tongue to wag at another stab of humiliation, Malcolm Grace suddenly stood to his feet and made a swift left-face, making his way in front of the camera stationed at the foot of the audience. Bill Doody was unable to respond to such unconventional behavior. Too much was happening at once, along with the shock that he was doing it without the slightest permission or fear of immediate consequence. "There is another way! I, Malcolm Grace, am here to announce the creation of a new political party!"

"What in God's name are you doing? Security! Security!" Bill Doody frantically cried out. His mouth ran a good game, but his physical prowess lagged.

"We will be called many names. We will be the Balance. We will be the Ground. We will be the wildest notion. But most of all, we will LEAD." He announced to a frozen live audience and a viewership of millions witnessing something that hadn't gone to plan. It was actually a welcomed delight to most, except for Bill Doody who stood aside in absolute horror. Malcolm Grace circumventing the status-quo political system was not his beef, but that he had lost all control of his baby—his show—to a *nobody* at that.

In the panic induced by this, whoever the hell he was, Bill Doody shrieked out loudly, "Where's the fucking security?!"

With Bill Doody on the ropes there was only a small window of time before security arrived, and a likely uncontrollable scene would ensue, definitely leading to Malcolm Grace's incarceration, even if for a short amount of time. The audience looked amongst each other in bewilderment, silently asking, *"What are we supposed to think about this? We guess it doesn't matter. We're being entertained!"*

Bill Doody was running his thumb across his neck, indicating a stop to the filming of the show entirely. The wide-eyed cameraman looked to the seemingly useless program director for confirmation. He was indicating differently, using his one and only veto against Bill Doody, motioning with a smile to keep on rolling. Bill Doody's consternation and inner rage turned him into a tea kettle. *No one was going to take over his fucking show!*

"We will not have all the answers, but we will find those we can, without appeasing to a mass of people carrying the same signs with all the wrong answers."

Security had arrived, but was stopped from intervening by the seemingly useless program director, to the unbearably drawn out horror of Bill Doody. The program director knew there was a chance it could go viral, skyrocketing the viewership to new heights. Sure, Bill Doody's implacable tough guy reputation would be tarnished, perhaps beyond buffing out, but he was enjoying this progression. It was almost as if a dream never dreamt had come true. He never thought this asshole would ever be put in his place. Not even in his wildest dreams.

"Our way is not the highway, but rather the one-way and two-way streets; sometimes leading into the back alleys, and sometimes into a stretch without highways, streets or alleys, where there is no defined path. Regardless, we will get there."

The audience was stupefied. He was not a stark-raving maniac—at least not yet. He was in the prime of his own times, fit and sharp with a staunch confidence. He spoke fluidly without the ums…the awes…and all the stalling tactics before the next round of bullshit could escape his mouth. His seemed to belong in these states naturally. Despite all of these unique and rare qualities, Bill Doody had seen quite enough. "Cut! Cut! Cut!"

"The power is in all. Not just a few. Join us! We will have a good time making it all right. It will be filled with danger, action, and love for the faceless. It's time the sovereign took it back!" Malcolm Grace stated just before they were officially off-air; not because Bill Doody had demanded it, but because commercials trumped a continuation of coverage. Corporations and others paid for that airtime. The only things that could interrupt them was a state of emergency or an address from the President directly. Bill Doody, the program director, and Malcolm Grace had very little control—just a controlled moment.

Malcolm Grace quickly realized they were off-air as he looked at the stunned audience with a furrowed brow. It seemed to him that his initial breech was successful. He knew most people feared public speaking more than their own deaths. It was the catalyst to achieve a consolidated admiration, or a fomented hatred. He wanted to establish both, and there was still much more work to be done. He had birthed the charisma needed to be taken seriously, which was the sole motive for sitting opposite a scoundrel like Bill Doody.

He turned his back to the audience to face Bill Doody who did not know whether to speak, move forward, run away, or just stand still. Malcolm Grace cared less either way. Bill Doody had built his career on intolerance, vehemently dismissing views contrary to his own, and he was just handed a bitter taste of his own medicine. As Malcolm Grace walked past him without apologies, Bill Doody thought about something that he rarely considered—murder. Not physically, but rather the murder of Malcolm Grace's public standing and reputation.

Malcolm Grace then walked past the very useful program director and the line of security guards who were still suspended in disbelief, yet underlined by a strong sense of intrigue and respect. He had penetrated the most stubborn consciousness without the undesired consequences of violence, jail, or even worse—never being heard at all. He was a commander among them. Seeing it in the flesh was different from seeing it on the tube.

"Thank you for your time." He said, making his unfettered way to the exit door.

If Bill Doody had one last viable recourse, it was to yell at the top of his lungs to the much bigger man leaving the scene untouched, and now fully noticed. "You're not going to win, Grace! You're going to lose! Better listen up, Grace! We're going to eat you alive!"

He certainly hoped they would eat him alive. It was exactly what he needed. Ignoring him was the worst thing that could happen. He needed enemies just as much as he needed supporters. He looked forward to having a quiet dinner that evening before the flood of inquiries he anticipated the following day. His movement had begun, or so he hoped.

## Wink Broadcasting

He never thought looking out on New York City from the top floor a skyscraper housing the command center of his media empire, Wink Broadcasting Company, could ever become dull. But, as it was, the romance had fallen away. There was a distinct lull; a pause in progress that bored him to the point of reassessing an already luxurious and accomplished life. Wink Broadcasting had stake in many facets of the television entertainment industry. The media conglomerate was at the top of 24-hour news coverage, movie channels, cartoon networks, sporting events, music venues, and seasonal genres that catered to holiday programming year-round. His competitors were on the fringes, only existing to serve as a kind of mom-n-pop store, strictly out of mercy.

The time had come to outdo what had already been done. There was one market grown from amateur roots that was more volatile than the stock market. People the world over were obsessed with reality television, but were eating up the themes like a pregnant woman with a craving. Nothing seemed to quench the public's appetite, and quite true, ideas were running thin. Reality programming was quite different from the watchable forms of sitcom, original series, or movies. The life of the reality show only lasted one viewing, since there would be nothing left to meaning. Everything was floating on the surface like oil, or plastic on an abandoned beachhead. Mass consumption without the slightest flutter of the intellect was the objective. The only creative aspect of reality television was coming up with another idea that would further butcher the sanctity of reality itself. No, the skyline was not helping Frank Winkelshten on his quest for a new concept. *Where could this new reality be?*

Sitting behind him at the round boardroom table were those who had braved the winds of Wink Broadcasting. They had been there the longest, never defied Wink, and were unconcerned about garnering any personal spotlight. They served as the idea farm Wink could harvest as his own. He had just turned into his seventies and discovered as the years wore on that he was becoming ever more detached from what the public wanted to watch. Everything was moving entirely too fast, and the attention span of the masses fell right into a positive diagnosis of robust ADHD. Adderall was not the answer. It would have to be an idea that could keep their asses seated without wanting to use the remote for at least thirty minutes. Those sitting around the table knew full well they were to speak only when spoken to, and as Frank Winkelshten turned away from the skyline to face them, it was their time to listen.

"So what the hell are we doing?" Wink asked in his raspy voice, always beginning there like his entire empire was perpetually crumbling beneath his feet. The question did not require an answer. It was purely rhetorical and marked the beginning of his many diatribes. Staring off as if peering into some foresight he alone possessed, he continued, "We have a stalemate out there. For a whole year, a stalemate! Granted, we're not losing ground, but we're not gaining any either. Can we keep up? I ask myself that question each and every day I get out of bed."

A few laughs gushed forth as he did use levity from time to time, but those that blundered forward wildly misinterpreted him. "Not a joke, people! I can't keep up with these ingrates! None of it makes sense anymore. Television is all people have nowadays, and there's nothing to watch. You know why there's nothing to watch? Because everything is virtually the same. And it's all this staged reality. It's even spilt into documentaries about real people that are still alive. Those are fake, too. The only thing real is the news, but it's all one-sided. By that, I mean pretty much all bad news. And then it has to be this 'us against them' thing. It's good fuel for the fire. Pit something against something, and people will watch it every time. Look how it stands now: humans against zombies, humans against aliens, humans against ghosts, superhuman against superhuman, and humans against the law. I guess it could all come to a head with a good old fashioned apocalypse. What does anybody have to look forward to?"

It always took Wink a moment to realize when he was mounted on his soap box, and needed to step down as not to appear a manic old man. It was unproductive after all. The real reason for their assemblage was to encourage and feed the evolving debacle. No profit was to be had in reversing the order of things. But every once in a while, it was quite refreshing to dip one's thoughts into the true state of affairs and then quickly return to the muddy banks for another search through the dense brush of nonsense. He was now ready to roam in the pasture of new ideas, which had to carry some kind of new edge. "So what the hell are we doing?"

The bravest of the boardroom bunch spoke up first. "What about a show involving all the unsung heroes—so to speak—from around the world? I'm talking about the people behind the scenes who really advance the lives of normal people. Like engineers, computer programmers, neurosurgeons, astronauts, and the special innovators of high technology. We steer away from the military, civil servants, law enforcement, activists, and any other kind of social discipline. This will be all about those most important people who don't require fame or honorable recognition. They make the world better by keeping their heads down, absorbed in fantastic ideas that we can put to practical use; who are unconcerned about a blatant show of force. We could simply call it, *Thinkers*. What do you think, Mr. Winkelshten?"

He was not only the bravest, but the youngest of the executive think-tank, always willing to break the ice among them. Wink appreciated him for that, but he was an idealist that oftentimes made too much sense, which was not what Wink looked for in an idea. Completely rebuking his idea was the best thing for the meeting, as it only encouraged the others to top it. "I like that, but unless we're moving into public broadcasting, thinking is the last thing I want our viewers to consider. Then they might think to become engineers, computer people, doctors, space junkies, and hi-tech gadget geeks. People like that don't watch too much television, and the people that do watch television would be bored to tears. Sounds like watching a Senate confirmation hearing. Not much juice in that lemon."

A uniformed laugh tumbled forth, even from the young and brave idealist. Wink smiled along as he traipsed around the outer edges of those seated. He wanted the wheels of his own imagination to spin as well. "Come on people, who and what is popular right now? Nobody gave a damn who designed the pyramids. It was all about the Pharaohs and the dirty laundry they carried around. Who can we exploit? How can we shed light into the darkest parts of the lives of the famous? That's what people watch—human frailty!"

The idea had been brewing a while inside the mind of Wink's finest idea-maker, Joshua Bannister. He was a youthful fifty-something executive with a vulgar taste for populism, and he studiously consumed it from all over the world each day. His most recent creation had done very well. *Last Ditch Effort* was a series about celebrities attempting to remain in the limelight by whatever means necessary. One was faking a drug addiction to keep the paparazzi around him. Another was an aged painter working vigorously to put together a gallery showcasing her life's work, and another who was a burnt-out football star who was re-directing his energies to become a professional poker player.

As it all went, the celebrity, yearning to be under the glare again, subsequently lost the minimal gain of fame. The sympathy aroused from suffering drug addiction, and it being uncovered he was addicted to nothing—except for relevance—had brought him to his end. By the end of the series he was bawling about how he would be forever shunned by the public to die alone like most people. The painter did finish her compilation, proudly putting it on display to the most discerning and harshest critics who proceeded to strip her work down to amateur status at best, pointing to everything from form to finish. In her devastation she burned all the things associated with her craft in the flames of a backyard bonfire, while dousing her wounded heart in cheap wine. The football star plagued by a career of scandals—from steroids to sex—did play his hand at poker, making it to a private game with some big time names, putting everything he had left on the line in his final sit-down. He held the chip lead by far, but only one hand was going to change that. He had the high-end straight on the flop, unsuited. Three spades were showing with the turn dishing out a club; one that gave him both ends of the straight. The river flooded forth another spade, which his lone opponent had patiently waited for, betting in big just for the possibility of a flush. It was just a slow, embarrassing death after their hands were shown. His final comment as he left the table at the end of the night said it all; "I could kill myself."

Joshua Bannister knew failure exceeded success in entertainment value. He had hit a home run with *Last Ditch Effort*, and he intended to do it again. "I have an idea."

Wink was instantly interested, along with the other stiffs at the table. Joshua Bannister was a running faucet of ideas. Not all were put in motion, but none of them were boring. "Whatcha got, JB?"

His smirk defined what was to come next. "You know what's popular right now, and has been since society began?"

It was a big question, and oddly enough, nothing obvious popped into any of their minds.

"Minorities. People who are not of the majority."

"*Fair enough,*" Wink thought while he nodded along.

"Do we know who is popular right now?"

Again, they all drew blanks.

"Gay people."

The sparkle in Wink's eye said it all, "*Ah-hah!*"

"They're making it cool these days, and we need to board that ship because it's-a-steamin. Not since the seventies have they been so popular and their causes taken so seriously. I'm pretty impressed.

"But as for me, I'm definitely straight. I know that for a fact. I find the female form to be universally attractive, but in no way, shape, or form—the male body. I think it may be safe to say that both sexes can agree the female form is much more appealing. With a woman it's easier to lose sight of which team you're batting for.

"My point is this: can openly gay men be converted to indulging in the pleasures of a woman? The answer, I believe, is yes! Gay men connect emotionally with women, and women are universally desired. This is the basis for my idea."

He stopped for a moment to let it gyrate. It was certainly a touchy topic with a lot of popular substance. So far, Wink was still listening. "Naturally, *Conversion* will be the name of this social experiment. And no, not a religious conversion, but rather a sexual one. So now we have to find some guinea pigs for our experiment. We will need a laboratory. We will be observing two groups: one is a flock of women as yet to be chosen, and the other is a male gay couple I have in mind right now that's pretty much always in the tabloids. Essentially, we're going to see how gay these guys really are. That's our show, stripped down!"

It was certainly controversial, so Wink began his usual probing for the workability factor. "What women? What gay couple? What setting do you have in mind?"

"Famous and well-established women won't do it, but with a little digging I'm certain we could find some beautiful women ready for some real exposure. If they were a little desperate that would help. We'll hash that out, but as far as the gay couple, it's obvious to me. I'd say it's the hardcore rapper, Gay J, and the professional wrestler, The Buccaneer—or Tommy Bloom. He's also known as the Butt Pirate. These guys have been blipping on the radar for a solid year now, so this is by no means a fly-by-night thing. They have real feelings for each other, and I want to find out how strong those feelings hold up once we put them in the box. It could be the biggest gamble you take, Wink. But it also could be the biggest return. We've got to buy them all out. Just think of it as a re-investment. That's good business. I guarantee our viewership would be glued to this. Others would flock over for the mere controversy. It'll be a win, Wink. I know it!"

With his pitch concluded Wink was left pacing around the table, rubbing his prickly chin at the range of possibilities, while the others shook their heads of how Joshua Bannister had done it again. *Conversion…it's* perfect! We'll preview it without a clue as to what it could be. Is it about conversion therapy for gays or about religious conversion from different faiths? It's the juiciest thing I've heard in a while. Let's make this a reality."

"Yes, Wink!" JB egged on; the only executive that could call Mr. Winkelshten by his popular nickname.

"Yeah, how gay are these guys? We're going to see. This is not going to be just an American production. The whole world will tune into this one. The gay, the straight, the upright, the confused, the dumb, and the intelligent. It's not just entertainment—it's human nature!

"Can you hold your ground? Do you even want to? How much do you love and what are the limits of a gay monogamous commitment? Can you defeat the desires of the flesh? Is it worth it not to see? It's all one big—beautiful—boiling pot of disaster!"

"Yes, Wink!" JB nearly shouted, as an enthused church member does when the preacher says something good about the Lord.

Wink had walked back to the window where he looked out at the refreshed skyline with the vicarious vision of a general commanding distant armies. He was thirsty to conquer again. He turned back to the table, and stomping back towards them, declared, "Alright, you worthless bastards, do whatever it takes! Bribe, borrow, and steal! I don't care how you do it! I want the best on this! I want the blueprints drawn up, and I mean fast! I want the production quality shining like a diamond, and I want the promotional advertising in hyper-brainwash mode! Our ratings are going to soar into space on this one! It'll be the best thing we've done!"

They all started scrambling about in a kind of disorder Wink actually liked to see; a newsroom scurrying for the first crack at the hot story. He loved to see his people spooked into action. They knew it too. They all anticipated his ritualistic outburst where his head would shake like the blood was about to blast from the top of his head, and his eyes bulge with a growling façade. Yep, he was right there. "I WANT THAT FUCKING SHOW!"

**Silly Americans!**

## Sun-rae in Pyongyang

It was the 27th of July in the midst of her youth; a proud day as the streets of Pyongyang began to recede in the most orderly fashion following the conclusion of the annually held Victory Day parade. The masterfully orchestrated spectacle never failed to impress each and every year in the usual humidity; a short break from the harrowing winter which always seemed to be just around the corner. The sun was shining down on monolithic buildings of gray which were built as monuments of a world to last forever. The red of the Workers' Party pageantry with the olive drab of military uniforms and weaponry had all moved through in stunning synchronization. It was a proud display of national pride.

In the clap of marching boots and cheers for the Dear Leader, Kim il-Sung—deceased and alive at the same time—there was a pervading feeling they were born into the greatest nation on earth. The heir presiding over the festivities would one day be considered dead and alive as well, Kim Jong-il. A prominent billboard showcased a charming rendition of the two heads of state appearing as cute little chipmunks of gaiety and goodwill. It was a cartoon-like fatherly portrait capturing all the happy times in a singular moment. Underneath were flags hanging from nearly every building. Inside those were the shrines and plaques commemorating the Kim line, and those filtering through those places wore Kim lapel pins to individually commemorate the Kim line, whatever day of the year.

Between the billboards, buildings, shrines and plaques, and Kim lapel pins it was clear those reminders were not enough. The Kamsusan Palace of the Sun housed the remains of Kim il-Sung. The Arch of Triumph touted

Kim il-Sung's central role in ousting the Japanese to bring about independence. Mangyongdae Hill was the sacred ground where Kim il-Sung was born. Juche Tower served as a landmark embodying the political and social ideas of economic independence, self-reliance, and nationalism brought about by none other than Kim il-Sung. There was Kim il-Sung Stadium where the national fùtbol team played, and a stroll through Pyongyang might land one in the midst of Kim il-Sung Square. It was to be clearly understood the Kim blood ran through all Koreans—even through that of Sun-rae.

Victory Day, as she vaguely fathomed at the time, was just another way to keep the train rolling. It celebrated how valiantly the Korean Peoples' Army repelled the imperial forces of the United States, proving they were the real legitimate power in the world. It was all about their truth, their honor, and their identity. The threat of that imperial menace returning to settle the score was always looming, and so they were to be a society of constant readiness. Victory Day displayed that readiness. Sun-rae had been doused like everyone else. The imperials were holding the lit match. That's why the Kim line was so necessary. Those powerful hands existed to protect the people, and most importantly, to never let them go. It was assured.

Sun-rae's job following the parade was to sweep the streets, though in reality, there was not much to clean. All citizens, young and old, knew their places to get things done efficiently and without hesitation. It was understood these things were to be done voluntarily and with grateful hearts. With the intense national pride it was common to soap down and scrub the streets by hand as they were thought to be that precious. It was boasted as the cleanest capital in the world.

Acts such as littering were not a concern as one would never think to do so deliberately in the very center of the world. Even the most desperate drunks knew that. Sun-rae would be done with her duty shortly. As she scrubbed her grid of the street, she thought of other important matters.

According to traditional State agenda, following the conclusion of parade clean-up, families would gather together to bathe themselves in the history of the Glorious Revolution; a time marking the defeat of those who tried to ruin it in vein. In their homes they would enjoy one of a thousand ways to prepare kimchi, sing songs, and listen to a solo performance from each family member as all were proficient in at least one musical instrument. They would hum lullabies of the State; that proud father always looking down upon his children with enduring love. These fathers were of the Kim Dynasty. Even if they did not believe the entirety of the lore, it was still their culture. Just before bed they would all watch the State-run television glorifying on repeat, and let out a sigh of relief at the fact they were falling asleep as Koreans, waking as Koreans, and part of the greatest nation on the face of the earth. These were the permanent realities of the State.

Sun-rae had a different version of the way events should proceed. She was an introvert by choice, always keeping her thoughts inside. It was her treasure, and if she never drew a map, no one could get to them. At the time she was completely unawares, but she was to eventually become an enemy of the State. The beginning phases she was unable to feel. Yet, they were there on Victory Day, casing the scene with destiny recruiting only the best. Her path was set without her knowing. The rapacious curiosity of a child leading to the budding of a formidable intellect led her to the person she wanted to see most on that day.

She was not to be misunderstood. She loved, honored, and obeyed her parents. It was only that there was another time: one that was not owned by the State or her parents. It was her excruciatingly short amount of time. Her mother was volunteering as a traffic warden directing the populous from the orchestrated grandeur of Pyongyang. Her father was doing his part as a tour guide for those hand-selected by Kim Jong-il to view the greatest show on earth. His full-time job was a low-level civil administrator in the Party. Sun-rae would have exactly one hour to escape her family, Pyongyang, and the State.

Breaking rank during an official civic duty was highly noticeable due to the uniformity of Koreans as a whole. One communal characteristic setting Koreans apart from every other society was their seemingly innate ability to form straight and extraordinarily rigid lines. This was seen in everything they did as a collaborative and interactive body; a true vascular network of perfect flow to keep the heartbeat of activity going. This day, though, she would break rank and escape from the flow. She wanted to see her friend for the hour of freedom she had been fortunate enough to finagle. His name was Jing.

Where she intended to go would only take ten minutes to arrive, but it was not an easy stroll through the park. The destination would have to be carefully plodded towards as eyes were everywhere upon her. She could be easily derailed if an onlooker's curiosity became too great. When she arrived at the market district things would loosen up. The edges of Pyongyang were the places revealing the underbelly and private parts of the State beast. The perfect lines would become flimsy and then dissipate as people broke away in their own directions. Sun-rae's problem was getting through the lines. Were she to get caught up in them, it would shave a whole twenty minutes of her time with Jing. It would be another fifteen minutes home from Jing's. She would then beat her parents home by three minutes. If all went as planned she would arrive home safe with a certain glow from her time with Jing. There was something so exhilarating about secretive civil disobedience. She was now ready to navigate towards her mini-vacation destination, and only the nervous swell inside propelled her forward.

Infiltrating the lines of people was the way to cut her journey in half. Like a primitive computer game she would zig and zag between columns of people who were barely moving along. While pulling this off she always wondered why others did not do the same. She was glad they didn't, since it would have added more time to her journey. No one thought to take her approach simply because it would have been a thought of their own. Sun-rae went about things creatively. She would breakaway swiftly and move into another line before anyone could notice. As she executed her course she imagined herself as a ninja on an important mission, waving her sword, taking out the enemies in the shadows trying to stop her from seeing Jing. When moving into the next line she became a race car, revving her vocal cords to resemble an engine. She wanted to be everything all at once: a ninja, a race car, a little girl with the biggest imagination—but never ordinary. Blending in was what she had to do, but standing out was what she dreamed.

Entering the market district the swept and scrubbed pavement of Pyongyang proper ended abruptly. The rains from the night before made the outskirts muddy and slippery, instantly marring everyone's pristine garb for Victory Day. The city center was always lit up like a Christmas tree, but outside the city the people relied on the residual glow of the capital. The lack of adequate electricity they didn't mind. It became an unintended privilege from the State. They could be themselves and break away from the rigid order of things. Sun-rae constantly sought that break. As for her friend Jing; he seemed to be always on break.

Through the market district she strolled with a light foot, no longer cornered by the prying eyes of Pyongyang. She passed the many merchants getting ready for the end of the day. Their stands presented thrift garments, collectibles, assorted candies and chocolates, and Party paraphernalia. She was drawn to none of it. What interested her lied deeper than most children her age would go. Her seedy destination was smeared with grime where the dull glow of the capital was simply another distant celestial body; always there, but far enough away as to not dictate the course of life—only the conditions thereof. In those shadows, secret lovers claimed their stake, addicts found their solace, and those unfit in the official order of things wallowed in perpetual filth.

She was almost to Jing's. His space was walled off by dingy sheets held up by clothesline pins. There were hundreds of these behind the market district, but instead of residence numbers in a formalized order, the residences of the market district were designated by markers illustrating something about the person behind the sheets and makeshift huts. Nearly all of the markers were handmade, usually names of loved ones, scenes of significance on canvas, or abstract forms of sculpture leaving a distinct signature of character.

Jing had a marker that was a mystery in origin; an original all the way around. It was a jolly fat man felled in the deepest laughter holding a once-bitten turkey leg in one hand, and a mug of beer in the other. The jolly bloated statue was obviously enjoying life to its fullest. It was marked head to toe with random writings and drawings. Jing didn't mind at all. He liked it that way. People were making their own mark, however ugly or beautiful, and he provided the canvas.

Sun-rae peered into the shadow-drawn recesses of Jing's home. Always unafraid of the darkness, she called out, "Jing? Are you there, Jing?"

Her voice was soft and angelic in the most assertive tone, and it always brought a smile to Jing's face. Not only did he have bucked teeth, but they were gold-capped, which was the reflection she first saw, forming a wide smile of her own. "My favorite visitor! How are you, my dearest little friend?"

"Good now, Jing! Were you sleeping?" Sun-rae asked, chomping at the bit to manage her time wisely.

"No, no, no, just thinking." Jing said, sitting up on his wooden bed with only a soiled pad separating his back from the splintered boards. A weathered and cluttered writing desk sat next to the bed as he began reaching for the lantern. It was to be used sparingly, especially at dusk, but this was a special occasion. As he struck a match and lit the wick, he finished, "I was actually thinking of you on this Victory Day. I had a feeling you could break away. Too many people to watch. It becomes fuzzy for them."

"Fuzzy, huh? What do you mean, Jing?" Sun-rae innocently inquired, confused as to who *they* were, and why there would be too many people to watch.

Jing felt she was too young for such explanations. They were all downers anyways. Plus, carrying around any hint of those inclinations could lead to unintended consequences. He shifted the matter at once. "No need to worry, my shining. No worries at all. You don't have much time, do you?"

"Yeah, not so much. Are you feeling well, Jing?"

"Ah, enough about me! I have a story for you, but you have to promise you won't tell anyone else. Not even your parents. Promise me!" Jing firmly encroached with a voice of genuine concern.

Sun-rae knew to keep the secret. It was what all good Koreans were good at doing. Playing that role was national custom. "I won't tell, Jing. I promise."

The wick was flickering, twitching in the dull glow on Sun-rae's young face, bursting with curiosity and complete trust—interested in everything. The workings of the world had not robbed her of this short-lived wonder. Even in the deepest throngs of the market district she looked at everything, as a child, endowed with the vision of value. Even the mud squeezed between her toes held value. She was the finest optimist, and as her beautiful bold eyes sunk into Jing, he gladly began the story.

"There was once a girl, just like you, who lived on a farm in the middle of nowhere. Every day seemed to be the same. She became restless. She was not really alone. Her family was among her all the time, but still she felt alone. Her unbridled spirit made her want to leave them forever."

"What does unbridled mean?" Sun-rae butted in.

Jing smiled at how good of a question it was. She never asked silly questions. "It means something that cannot be contained, and so, cannot be controlled…like a wild horse. Do you understand?"

Her bold eyes had a vacancy sign in them this time, but she remained confident. "A little. Just give me some time."

He assured her with his gentle laugh, and continued, "You have plenty! That is for sure, but back to the farm girl now. This longing for a change made her very sad, and made her think scornfully towards those she loved the most. Her wish was to leave; running away into nothing. She ran away to seek answers, but found none which comforted her. She realized that all she had was her family. Then a storm blew through. You see, we get the cold winds out of the north, but none of these winds can lift us up and carry us away. That's what this wind did, and as the house she lived in swirled to pieces around her, flying through the night sky along with everything else she had known—she was struck and went into a deep sleep. When she woke, she opened her bedroom door to a whole new world. Her family and the farmhands she had grown close to were nowhere to be found. Her little dog had made the journey, though!"

"Were the others dead?" Sun-rae asked with caring reserve.

Jing was a man who pronounced himself in gesture. His skin would squiggle slightly in the creases as his weathered face would come to light. His smile glistened in rapture as if inspired beyond reason. Sun-rae made him feel and act in such a way. "The story must go on. You, and the story, will be just fine."

On he went into a magical landscape of color and glee. Everything was in its right place, imbued with meaning, inviting and luscious, strange and deliberate. The air was just right upon wrapping itself around the skin. There were no deep winters in this place. It was always a beautiful sunny day. She met all the friendly people of this place. They were like her—children. They danced and sang, all together, just like Victory Day. She joined in the song and dance with them, and became accepted among them naturally. The fabulous colors dripping off the horizon of an exotic landscape could not convince her to stay. She wanted to go home where things at least made sense, even if just the day before she was ready to be rid of her life on the farm. She was told by a good witch that the perfectly cobbled yellow brick road would lead her to the wizard. They saw her off skipping with joy. The journey was set.

"What's a wizard, and what's a witch?" Sun-rae asked, forgetting to let the story move along at Jing's will.

Jing would do his best to answer this one. The wizard meant everything to the story. His smile widened at the chance to introduce the real driving forces of life—doubt and truth. "A wizard can see all, knows all, and is everywhere all at once. The wizard solves all problems, and the yellow brick road leads to him."

"Why does she want to go see the wizard?" Sun-rae asked, trying to imagine why this farm girl would want to leave such a place of color, celebration, and magic.

"She wants to go home, just like you should soon."

"What happens next?" Sun-rae giddily begged as Jing realized more than her that their time was flying by. The last thing he wanted was trouble to befall her at the expense of a broken down old fool.

He gave her a soft pat on the head, barely grazing her silky black hair. With a loving smile, he said, "That will be for next time. You just think about the beginning of the story, my favorite little visitor. For the end of our time, which I enjoy so much, I want you to listen to something."

He pulled out from deep beneath his bed an ammunition box circa 1950's. It still clearly had the black block lettering of **US**. He flipped the top open, reached in, and pulled from it a black cassette player with mismatching headphones. Sun-rae held still as Jing fastened the headphones over her ears. He popped open the cassette player door just to be sure the right tape was set in. Sun-rae had seen them before, clearly knowing they were contraband and citizens were forbid by law to display any kind of separation from the State radio and television network. Despite that, she was eager to break the rules as the intrigue was too much to bear.

"Before you listen to this, you must listen to me, Sun-rae." Jing insisted, sitting on folded knees and drawing eye level with her. He lightly clutched her shoulders and his fixed goofy smile creased to sincerity. "You must never tell anyone that you listened to this song. Don't sing it through your day; don't even hum its beat. It's just like me; a ghost…not real. Do you promise to be mindful, Sun-rae?"

She nearly rolled her eyes that he was reminding her yet again, but instead smiled and reassured him. "I promise, Jing."

He returned the same. "Okay. After the song ends run along home. I will miss you and look forward to next time."

Her chubby little cheeks bounced with life as her eyes became exquisite slits accompanied by a smile seemingly on the brink of laughter. "Me too, Jing! And I promise I won't say anything."

He handed her the cassette player with his finger on the play button. He pressed it down until it clicked, retreated to his bunk, turned out the lamp, and simply watched. He personally did not like the music, but knew she would. Through her head flowed the American pop hit from the 80's which lifted Cyndi Lauper to the level of stardom. Sun-rae was instantly fascinated!

The fine arts and classical music was a significant aspect of Korean life. Structure, form, and presentation in perfect time gave reverence to the styles crystallized in the period of the Renaissance. What was constructed in woodwind, string, brass, and percussion was either soul-stirring symphonies or soul-zapping arrangements which brought about a lifeless monotony. None of this compared to the American hit which made her think of sunshine and playful exchanges in a carefree state of being. The chorus and title of the song said it all: *Girls Just Wanna Have Fun!*

The simplicity of the pop arrangement and the bratty voice of Cyndi Lauper, along with a tropical accompaniment could not help but to draw Sun-rae into a little dance. It was improvised, not like the graceful and precise mechanics of ballet. It was jerky and bouncy. Since she felt so safe at Jing's a little hum escaped the crack of her lips. Jing smiled as he watched her outline in silence, nothing making him happier than to see her pleased. He wished to know her the rest of his days. As for Sun-rae, she just didn't want the song to end—but it would. She would soon return home to eat kimchi that could be made a thousand different ways alongside the latest mystery fish. She would answer her parent's questions, watch State television with her father, and then go to sleep with the song playing in her head on repeat. She already craved their next visit, but for the next few minutes, she would be a girl having fun in the ardent search for something.

**The Stream begins...**

Johnston and Peg McCreeley entered a new life without regrets. It was easy given they had created the greatest work of living art—a baby girl named Madeline May McCreeley. Johnston fell in love knowing he had become a full-fledged man, holding Maddie in his arms; she wrapping her tiny hands around his beaten and weathered finger. For the short time he could, Johnston enjoyed the whiffs of innocence and purity that only a baby can vent. Now he knew what it was like to have a family, and not just a marriage.

As for Maddie, she was a dimpled-cheeked force in motion with kicking legs and seeking hands stretching out incessantly for growth. At first, her head was comically on a swivel. Her eyes did the same, eager to explore every facet of the world around her. During the rare times of relative quiet Johnston loved her cooing the most. He knew those squeaking sounds of warmth were to be as rare as the quiet times, and eventually gone altogether. Those sentimental times aroused a purpose in Johnston; that of protector.

It was all the more made solid as he oversaw the roll onto the belly from the back, which was a particularly scary process for Maddie. She then became his little animal on all fours, scurrying about on the hunt for new things. It amazed Johnston how much she could get into, but it would only multiply when she began to pull herself up on two feet. Instead of only the head in sway, so did her entire body as a drunk trying to think through their last action of the night. She would totter forth, and fall back down. Eventually, she would come to know it would be the most repetitive process in life, accompanied by the instinct to stand right back up. Then it was on to the walk. Running would follow soon after.

Words would be bundled together. Johnston and Peg were constantly taken aback by the force of curiosity never to be harnessed. They worked with her by way of teaching and interaction, since they had not been so fortunate to receive the same. Maddie was going to be different. She was going to be raised in love. Her cheerful and weightless disposition came as a surprise to both. They wondered if they had ever been that happy, overflowing with freshness in the twist and turns of living for the day. Maddie showed them who they were; a living mirror reflecting what they had forgotten, taken for granted, or altogether denied. For Johnston, he had never smiled and laughed so much in his life. He knew one could live in the biggest dump in the world so long as one received love from those who brought them into the dump. Her contentment was all he sought. Then, before they knew it, she was getting ready for her first day of school where she would be released into the wild.

The years leading up saw Johnston still at the rock quarry. He was no longer stacking rocks on pallets all day waiting for the next one to tumble down to the conveyer belt. He had become the foreman. His stubbornness—sweat and blood—had paid off. Maddie righting his mind was the vehicle to that destination. Peg was happily working part-time at the thrift store. She got to talk to people, share her home life randomly, and make some spending money. They had moved out of the trailer park and into a modest three bedroom home with a good school nearby, amongst other families with similar goals for their children. It was to be the place she could roam freely and explore without detriment. The plan was simple living.

Johnston and Maddie sat in the living room stuffing her backpack with school supplies, and Peg was glued to her television shows. Maddie was excited she would be able to play with all the other kids. With her high-pitched voice, there was yet another question for Johnston. "Daddy, why do we all go to school?"

Johnston always thought carefully before answering her questions. A child's questions are always straightforward, but the answers not so much. In her sponge-like state he tried to find the clearest path to arrive at the closest truth. "Because we have to learn new things and make new friends. If we're smart, that's what we'll do the rest of our lives."

She was rarely altogether confused, but always confident enough to play along. "I wanna be smart, daddy!"

She laughed wildly for nothing, donning blonde pigtails and shiny blue eyes. He lightly stroked his hardened fingers through her silky hair. All she felt was sandpaper pulling her roots taut. She had become used to that, instantly forgiving her father each time for the discomfort. "You're already smart, Maddie. I just want you to promise me that you're going to do one thing before learning and making friends."

She leaned in like it was a secret exchanged only between her and dad. The serious side of her cute little face waited patiently. He drew close to her ear, and finished, "Have fun!"

She laughed again and gave him a hug; those of which he never tired of getting. "Okay, daddy!"

They continued to pack for her first day as Peg watched over them affectionately. That affection quickly shifted to the television ringing out the instrumental interlude for Wink Broadcasting; a kind of dinner bell signaling it was time to eat. Even Johnston, an ardent despiser of nearly everything associated with television, turned his eyes towards the trademark theme. It held a universal appeal made all the more ominous by the blacked-out screen concealing the colors, motion, and message to come. A deep, penetrating voice began to bleed through the blackness.

"Something's coming…like you've never seen before."

The tempo of the theme picked up speed as the screen filled with spectrums of color and screen shots of the most hailed programming Wink Broadcasting had thus offered. It was the string of mini-series that were always edgy and taboo in content, concentrated on depicting those living at the fringes of society: old and new gangsters, maniac substance abusers, war machines, sex professionals, and prisoners strapped down by the system. It preceded a series of shots of Bill Doody aggressively confronting the camera, popular personalities as his guests, and finally a shot of him embedded with aid volunteers in South Sudan. Various shots of sport in play with the hoisting of extravagant trophies, scenes of celebration from ice baths to champagne showers amongst millionaires and billionaires. Then there was the different venues from a night at the symphony, to the punk show at the local dive, to the poppy halftime stage, to the honky-tonk in the boonies.

The theme began to peak as it went to the year-round holiday programming centered completely on innocent fairy tale viewing. The final stages of the montage ensemble saw the rotating of the different children's programming that spiked the attention of Maddie, along with the rest of the child population living under the stage of puberty who maintained interest in such things. The screen suddenly became silent and black after the litany of Wink Broadcasting's credentials was fully vetted.

"From the creators of 'Last Ditch Effort' and 'The Worst of the Best' comes Wink's next original programming adventure into how we react…in a state of reality."

The letters began to seep through the blackness of the screen, glittering in gold, outlined with diamonds, written in French script. As the letters came into full focus, they retreated, disappearing into the blackness to tease, and then like the hammering down of a gavel, were emboldened back on the screen to the company of a chilling organ chord. It read—CONVERSION.

Peg looked back at Johnston, investigating whether any hint of intrigue was written on his face. Yes, he had paid attention, but the only real intrigue and anticipation could be seen on Peg's face alone. This is what got her going; something open to speculation. Wink didn't provide one clue; only a word, which she guessed could only mean it was something big. Incessantly trying to drag Johnston into the orbit of what possessed her, she asked, "What do you think it's going to be?"

He continued helping Maddie pack. He knew indulging her would only make it worse for him. Saying nothing at all never went down so well. He did the next best thing. "I don't know, but I'm sure it's going to be the biggest pile of garbage they've put out yet."

*Why did she ask?* He was never going to be interested in what she liked. Not her figurines. Not her shows. Only Maddie. That was their common thread.

Her eyes unwillingly rolled back to the television as the commercials ran. It was one for Golden Motors. They had penetrated the Texas market with a whole new look. The bouncy house, petting zoo, and face painters were nowhere to be seen. The bright sunny day in Tulsa was replaced with the finely lit décor of a dealership at night, sleek and professional, moonlit and personal. Ralston Golden looked sharp as ever in a white suit as if he were about to preach from that shining city on a hill. He wore a jet black cowboy hat, only having one thing to say to the market now open for his consumption. "Howdy y'all!"

*zzz...*

For Ralston Golden, it was all going as planned. He began to stretch his auto empire without a snag, encroaching into the states of Colorado, Louisiana, and Texas. He was building a formidable brand possessing equal amounts of cunning and calculation. A training regimen was set in motion to bring the youngest minds freshly sprung from the vortex of college into a profit-driven environment offering so many incentives at the expense of their naïve souls. Like all seasoned enterprises the company philosophy centered on unrestrained growth. The culture fostered an identity which would tie them to the Golden name until one grew weary of the other. Regardless, the Golden name would be the ultimate benefactor of that relationship. Principally, the person of Ralston Golden riding home in his fully loaded luxury write-off.

In his personal life, the son he had hoped for had come, buttressing his master plan of carrying out dual purposes: the continued lineage of his bloodline and the indefinite survival of his business empire. The passing on of these responsibilities would not be articulated passively, much less with firmness, but more with a dominant sense of urgency. The traits he instilled would mirror that of his own self-perception: consuming as a force, meticulous as a savant, irresistible in persistence, and possessing the foresight to remain relevant through the finicky changes in society. Retreat, if at all necessary, would be strictly strategic. On that note, mercy would never be entertained. Emotions were the greatest weakness; a collaborator to personal defeat. Ages and stages of development were inconsequential. Even a motherly embrace was to be put in check. In the end, an unrivaled strength of character would be instilled in the person of Ralston Golden Junior.

Dinner was set on the table by Cynthia in the order expected. Ralston Junior had begun elementary education, but would not speak of it. He, like Cynthia, knew what was expected of them at the dinner table. Junior would listen, his father would lecture, and he would agree. Each night he and his mother would patiently wait for him to walk through the front door, hear his keys drop into the bowl, and listen to his footsteps press down the hallway as they sat upright to attention. He always made his entrances with a smile, accompanied by a nod of approval. They were his faithful adherents for which he provided all he believed they needed.

"Hello Cynthia. Hello son." He said, placing a simple kiss to each on the forehead in a gesture of vacant affection. He sat down at the head of the long table, which meant they were now ready to eat. Each portion was sampled by them all in unison, and after taking a drink the same, it signaled the time for a little family chit-chat to begin. "How was your first day of school, son?"

Ralston Junior knew to answer clearly and distinctly. "I liked it a lot, father."

"You liked it very much." Ralston Senior corrected. "Remember son, put your words in the best arrangement possible. You did not like it *a lot*, or *a bunch*…only *very much so*. Use a lot…and a bunch…only when you are trying to relate to simpler minds. Of course, always make certain they have something of value to gain before you stoop to their level. Do you think your father says *howdy y'all* on my commercials without apparent reason?"

"No, father." Ralston Junior said with a cracked smile, knowing it was his father's misguided stab at levity. Even if occasionally humorous, Ralston Junior was suspended in a constant state of petrification around his father.

"You see, son, you're already well ahead of the other children. What are the three pillars of a wealthy orientation of life?"

Without a passing thought to snatch, Ralston Junior answered, "Power, numbers, and will."

"How is power accumulated?"

"Through numbers."

"How are numbers multiplied?"

"Through will."

"What do these equal?"

"Wealth."

Ralston Senior nodded in approval with a near twinkle in his eye, but restrained the twinkle as it would have shown his son a softer side. He looked over to Cynthia who only showed a faint ripple of a smile as she looked down at the food she loved to pick at like a child. Secretly, she was avoiding having to bear another child at all costs. Not because of the over-powering influence of her husband; but that bearing children was painful, scarring, and worst of all, consumed all the free time she once enjoyed. The reason she was in the whole thing originally was for a meal ticket; not a 24-hour job. It pleased her that Ralston Junior was entering school. She could indulge more in the meal ticket lifestyle.

A boy was all Ralston Senior wanted. Hopefully, that would be all he needed.

"Yes son, this is the first step to a life of learning. This particular period of your life will last sixteen years. That's including college, which you will complete in four years. Your major will be finance and your minor, business. After that, you will begin working at corporate in accounting and quality control. I am the face, and you will be the details. You will be trained to identify any discrepancy, any loss, and then resolve the issue by any means necessary, always looking towards the pillars of power, numbers, and will. Before I die, as I surely will—

"Honey, don't scare him."

"Cynthia!" He declared loudly, startling both to a small hop in their seats with his eyes piercing into hers. The monstrous stare turned to a false shade of warmth as he softly reminded, "Honey, I'm talking to my son, the future of Golden Motors. Did you forget?"

She fell silent, taking another sip of wine, continuing to pick at her lukewarm dinner. Once she was done interrupting, he turned his attention back to Ralston Junior with another one of his warm smiles. "As I was saying before your mother spoke out of turn—is that I'm not going to live forever, but my brand will live on just like the lineage running through our veins. We will not be like other family lines, breeding generation after generation of workers with their noses to the grindstone, waiting on some skimpy retirement. The Golden line will be among the captains of industry, and what I mean by that is profits without limit. Right now, you are just a child, but you will inevitably become a man. You will learn how to operate in this society as a man, and I promise, it's not for the faint of heart. If you listen and follow my lead as you certainly will, I promise you will never be poor, and you will never be under the thumb of anyone besides the IRS. Son, my only hope is to see you one day with the title of owner and chief operating officer of Golden Motors from sea to shining sea."

His young face was vacant and expressionless. His mind had been trampled upon by adult concepts, and yet it was nothing new. It was something he had memorized, though he knew nothing of their inner workings or the ethical implications of those workings. A locked stare between them was his father's chosen path to showing affection, it never lasting too long. "Eat. Your food's getting cold."

Dinner ended quietly with each retreating to their separate quarters of refuge throughout the house. Cynthia's relaxation station was her bubble bath with the jets on low, wine glass in hand, and the tube rolling her favorite show; *Being Pretty*. The special weekly guest was the blonde bombshell Dallas Cowboys cheerleader, Bridgette Mahoney. There, she would blissfully soak, watching all the hardships a beautiful woman had to go through; something she could relate with completely.

As for Ralston Junior, he went in his bedroom to play and indulge in his favorite hobby, drawing. He loved more than anything to slide away into his imagination, which at that time, manifested itself on paper. He liked drawing horribly proportioned dinosaurs and box-like cars rolling on the street right alongside them; with the sun high in the sky and sturdy green trees that never swayed in the wind. He was trying to figure out how to draw wind. He was stumped.

For Ralston Senior, he retreated to his dark study where his maturated scotch awaited his company while viewing the nightly public broadcasting show moderately covering political, economic, and social matters. All that he fancied were subjects intimately associated with power. He plopped down on his studded leather recliner as the host of the show introduced Malcolm Grace.

"Now we will hear from the new voice of a party with many names: the Balance, the Ground, and the Shift. His name is Malcolm Grace. Mr. Grace, in your view, before we let the others weigh in—what is the most fundamental problem with the United States as you see it today?" asked the gruff and inanimate host.

"Credit." Malcolm Grace shot back nearly before the host had finished the question.

Malcolm Grace followed with nothing like there were no complications behind his answer. "Would you care to expound on that?"

"The US economy currently has the largest share of the world economy. All of it is based on a model of indefinite debt circulated by way of the dollar, trade, and the stock market. Of course, the government has proven its credit has no limit. It has ballooned it so exponentially that there is no way to break even, much less return to a state of surplus. Certainly, not in the coming generations, and certainly not until large corporations are brought to heel. You see, corporations operate on debt so they may expand their business into new markets. Their debt to income ratio, as a ballpark figure, typically hovers at four to one. This allows for aggressive expansion when the economic climate allows it. What happens when this expansion reaches its peak is a natural reduction. Let's say a chain that has to close a few stores, consolidate, merge or acquiesce, or the worst option—bankruptcy. How did they get this way? Probably a myriad of reasons, but likely it was mismanagement and dreaming bigger than reality allowed. The model is unsustainable at best, and disastrous at worst. Either way, the government is conducting itself as a business with unlimited capital and credit to needlessly expand at the expense of those they presumably work for—the sovereign—the people." Malcolm Grace succinctly summed up without so much as skipping a beat.

Ralston Senior scoffed as he took a sip of his scotch. Though perfectly alone in his study, Malcolm Grace forced him to utter something no one would hear. "Another idiot!"

**zzz...**

The modest studio based out of Washington D.C. was set to receive two more viewpoints on the state of affairs. Joining the discussion were two Senators in their seventies: one a Democrat and the other a Republican. They were both wrapped tight in dark suits with hair dyed and manicured to reach back twenty years in appearance. They wore big smiles showing off their pearly white veneers. Each wore a lapel pin: one of a donkey and the other an elephant. They were already briefed on the questions as well as the answers. Like touring comedians telling their best jokes, having been refined through timing and audience reaction; so would the Senators respond with what they knew worked best.

The Democratic Senator from Vermont was invited to go first. "I don't think the problem lies in less government regulation, but rather, I believe, more. Aggressive checks and balances is what makes our great democracy—

"It's a Republic." Malcolm Grace interjected, falling instantly silent afterwards, confounding the three present. He knew democracy was simply the institution that appointed the public officials to operate the government, which was a Republic. He tired of politicians constantly getting it wrong just because the word democracy sounded so much better.

After an odd look shot from the Senator, he continued, "As I was saying, responsible oversight is completely necessary in our great democracy, especially for those with the largest share of the pot. The money cannot be held in place; that place being the top of the financial food chain. What we need is meaningful tax reform to even the playing field, put that money in the government's able hands, and then plug it into the sectors that are not only struggling, but are also due for a bright future ahead of them. I also believe—and this is a vital piece—that we need to invest in clean and affordable energy alternatives. Energy from foreign sources—mainly oil—is an old burden that needs to be lifted. Once we really start trusting our government to do the job it is elected to do—and that's oversight—coupled with sound regulation, I firmly believe we as a country—

"You mean nation." Malcolm Grace interjected again, falling silent just as quickly as before. He also tired from politicians using fluff words like country to describe a nation like the United States. For Malcolm Grace, the country was a place to escape the city and urban clutter. It was the outskirts where nature still thrived and the oversight he so espoused was heavily deregulated, since very few there were keeping tabs. Both elements together he considered the nation of the United States of America.

"We as a COUNTRY!" He firmly pronounced, darting his defensive eyes in the direction of Malcolm Grace in exasperation. "We will—all of us— be back on top!"

Flustered, he crossed his arms over his chest and fell back in his chair with obvious disdain. The host dryly thanked him for what he had offered and reminded the unnamed present that everyone should be allowed to express their views without interruption. If that unnamed person could please refrain from interrupting, that would be great. He introduced the Republican Senator from South Carolina whose turn it now was to express himself in civil terms.

"Thanks for having me on. Always an honor. To address my colleague in the Senate, I believe the answer lies in less government meddling in the affairs of not only businesses, but individuals as well. Let businesses operate freely and let the people keep their money—

"Laisse-faire and trickle-down theory. Businesses are individuals now." Malcolm Grace violated once again as the sharp edge between them was now fully pronounced. He had been listening to the same argument since he had come to political realization, and he was tired of listening.

The Republican Senator chuckled softly as to dissuade the bubbling of his own frustration, and continued, "We all want to keep our money. We don't want to be taxed to death. In order to keep our great country strong we must continue to lead the world, keeping a strong foreign policy edge, since it's abundantly clear that we are invested globally. Protecting our most valuable asset—the people—and teach the tenets of democracy around the world—

"Policing, intimidating, and extorting weaker states."

*He did it again!*

Undeterred, but surely rushed, the Senator from South Carolina continued, "Delivering the great news of democracy to other countries for the betterment of the world as a whole is what our service men and women deserve as a testament to their sacrifice. On the domestic side, we need an agenda that promotes small businesses, instead of punishing them. Major corporations employ a great number of people, but we can enable full employment if we concentrate on small business growth. Adding to that, the outlandish debt we carry has to be brought under rein. Government spending has to be curbed, and a sustainable future for the coming generations must be realized. The snowball has to stop rolling down the mountainside, threatening to wipe us all out at the bottom. It is up to both parties. We need to stop harping on our differences and begin working on our duties, which is to provide the American people with the quality of life they deserve."

"Thank you, Senator." Said the host, peering over at Malcolm Grace who was to be given the last word, per orders of the producer. People were beginning to pay more attention to Malcolm Grace's truculent style that was structured to face off with the long established two-party system. They were all perturbed by his interjections, but none so much as the host. He saw what Malcolm Grace had done to the indomitable Bill Doody. It was the last spectacle he wanted on his own show. "Mr. Grace, final thoughts?"

Without the slightest lack of confidence, he began, "First thing's first, our fiscal reality needs to be completely re-formulated. For instance, regular people get turned down for loans if they're overextended. The government should be subjected to the same. People cannot print money at will. They would be charged with counterfeiting. There is no consequence for a government relying on a third party—by that I mean the Federal Reserve—to artificially ease an economy filled to the brim with depreciated assets, and then not having the conscience or couth to devise any kind of alternative. Obviously, only a few—and certainly not the many—profit from this crude arrangement. To hell with everyone else, huh?

"Secondly, it must be understood that big oil is not the enemy portrayed by those participating in the two-party configuration. We have all been complicit and hypnotized by the inventions of convenience, but it also seems apparent that oil and gas holds the keys to open the door leading us out of this mess. We must tap this *finite* resource in abundance and export it to emerging markets to get us out of debt; and then use it to fund research and development for cleaner energy, which we will also export to emerging markets when the time comes. Here at home, I'm all for nuclear energy. I'm not talking about weapons grade. That form of nuclear energy is useless to humanity. The threat of a global nuclear holocaust is not the only way to maintain a cutting edge. In fact, it is the most infantile position and should never be entertained as a reason for not aggressively pressing forward with this *infinite* fountain of energy.

"This leads us into the realm of foreign policy where we must stop playing an awful game of chess across the globe where the pawns are the only pieces being taken out, along with a dangerous geopolitical struggle of abstract ideals that effectively limits the flow of currency around the world, stifling growth and diversity by maintaining a desperate 'King of the Mountain' mentality that belongs on the playground; not the international stage. As for the United States; Canada is to the north, and Mexico is to the south. We are the only threat to us, and all of this perpetual fear-mongering must be paid for!"

The whine from Monty Lincoln's standing electric shoe shine machine barely muffled the airing of Malcolm Grace's commentary on the current state of politics. Monty Lincoln found himself amused by his reckless candor, and maybe even somewhat taken by the unflinchingly confident young man. It wasn't that he didn't have a filter: he just had the right one in place. His unwillingness to budge, his fearlessness of consequence, and his unique way of going off with an embittered style appealed to those that might have had enough of the status quo. His rhetoric was the unabashed debate in the salons of enlightened France, the taverns of colonial America, and the beer halls of Weimar Germany. It was the common sense stoked in flashes of exuberance and self-assured clarity among those common with the same ills. Monty Lincoln could see Malcolm Grace's bold and assertive character was a rarity to be had in the political gridlock. He was a rare bird, but Monty Lincoln fancied himself the rarest of birds.

While transitioning his admiration from Malcolm Grace back to himself, Margaret Buckey entered in her usual slumping and grumpy manner, though it wasn't always the case. She refused to smile, but she had very little to smile about. From the time of Monty Lincoln's introduction, he had concentrated all his energies in the Fellowship of the Enlightened. Margaret Buckey wished him gone since day one. People seemed to instantly respond to his allure of concealing some mystery never to be known. His charismatic and thought-provoking approach to metaphysical matters allowed a natural gravitation to his message. By contrast, Margaret Buckey's style was only needed in darkened sterile boardrooms behind a projector dictating thought through a lifeless set of frames, crippling her message into uniformed boredom. Monty Lincoln needed no slide show.

The demographics of the Fellowship had changed as well. Josiah the Jew, Tariq the Muslim, and Billy the Southern Baptist parted ways from the Fellowship; more because of one another than anything the Fellowship began to stand for. They were there one day and gone the next, very easily forgotten. The remaining founding members were Cindy the Buddhist and Baltasar the Wiccan. Then came some from the coffee shop Monty Lincoln frequented, and still others who simply came for a look-see. It was forced to become a congregation before long. While still in the initial throes of growth, those lost in life began to flock with an assortment of personal problems from addiction, to financial crises, to disabilities, to social awkwardness of the highest degree. Margaret Buckey had decided those who needed help would receive it with Monty Lincoln giving the nod. It would be the core element for growth within the Fellowship, along with the driving force of a staunch loyalty. Margaret Buckey did it for altruism. Monty Lincoln did it to swell the membership for legitimacy as only a student of Realism would do. Her grumpy persona had been culminating since their introduction for one single reason: she was losing her place on the center stage and was being written out of the plot by the magnetic force of Monty Lincoln.

"Interesting man, this Malcolm Grace. He's actually almost believable." He commented, planting himself in front of the standing mirror to apply the final touches to his delicate appearance.

"Why don't you vote for him?" She drearily suggested, completely uninterested in politics.

"He's not running for any kind of office. He seems to be forming a third party, yet to be another doomed failure. Their enthusiasm is refreshing when it comes around. Besides, voting is such a trivial civic exercise." He said, plucking any wild hairs from his bushy yet perfectly symmetrical brow line.

"Why is it trivial?"

Moving on to his moustache, he elaborated, "If I choose to vote for a candidate of public office I would cast my vote by funding their campaign. The real votes come from dollars. This is how I have voted in the past and will likely do so in the future. But, I'm like an artist. I must be inspired before I take action, and when I do take action, it's meaningful."

"I see." She blandly responded, evermore disenchanted by his know-it-all attitude. It was about to be transmitted in earnest for the first time in front of the Fellowship congregation. Prior to this day, he would just casually banter before and after the teachings of Margaret Buckey to the delight of the Fellowship, oftentimes taking them all to lunch or happy hour afterwards. Very few acts of kindness reverberate more than picking up the tab. His politicking and shoulder rubbing led to the Fellowship calling fanatically out for him to be the guest speaker. Margaret was forced to concede. After all, she was uninterested in politics. "So, what's your topic today?"

He was about to open the door to the next room where they sat awaiting his entrance, but instead turned back to face her squarely. Wearing a cocky smile and placing his hands atop her shoulders, he answered, "God."

With that, he opened the door to the next room with Baltasar striking the organ with an oddly fixed smile, hunched over the keys as if curled by a lifetime of bad posture. The congregation remained seated as Monty Lincoln situated himself behind the podium. Circling the room against the walls were standing lit candles to increase the ambiance of ceremony. Baltasar strung out the last chord and then retreated to his seat among the rest, doing his best to remain unnoticed. Monty Lincoln chuckled inwardly. "Thank you, Baltasar."

He looked out upon the congregation without cue cards or ancient texts to enhance his coming message. He felt this day was the true inaugural service of the Fellowship of the Enlightened. There would be plenty of adventures; all of them aimed at elucidating inner progress according to the formula devised by Monty Lincoln.

"God is a force. The animation of life. The far-off event of death, weighted in a feeble amount of time, daring us to waste what was so graciously given. God, the Divine, Providence, and even Fate—they are all the same things. They pull the soul apart at birth, scatter what is sacred to the winds, and along the path of life we spend the time trying our best to see where those pieces fit—so we may be whole again. On top of our impossible puzzle there are other souls shuffling by us, scattering the pieces we had already put in place, forcing us to start over. Strangely enough, this is the hallmark of our progress. One step back can lead to a few steps forward the next time. The past is our enemy, but we would still not have survived without the dualistic affair of protagonist and antagonist. This endless scuffle within each of us is why we press on each new day. What I say could be just reckless wonder. We all could be moving forward blindly without rest. But no! We have this insatiable lust for knowing who is at the levers, pushing the buttons, and marking the time from one experience to the next. If we choose to deviate from the path of knowing then we have numbed ourselves to complacency, and worst, acquiescence. This is the only true sin there is."

It was already time for them to take a breather, but his assured smile remained set. He fully understood what Margaret Buckey was trying to establish, which was a gradual climate of negation. Yes, faith in some form was innate, but it could be tempered into a chilled humanism devoid of any wonder. Her goal was to make the impossible intangible, setting out to embrace it as a hopeless excursion leading to full-fledged delusion. Monty Lincoln opted for a different approach.

"So, we are universal only in that we live in the same reality. Not necessarily in the same state of mind, but we all look to a power higher than our own, and typically not of this reality. We dream; therefore, we believe. But what is the character we believe in? What is the character of God? Is it the character of human sensibility that can viciously punish at one moment, and become a benevolent deliverer the next, according to personal preference? Is the character that of a parent who exacts fear and love until eventually all the children return home for the stay of eternity? Is this character formless and altogether disinterested in its creation, rather deferring fate to the forces of nature; a conscientious objector to the pitiful lot of humanity? Or is this character seen and unseen like the stitching of a finely woven garment, which is the true animation of all things? Or is this character just another debunked theory of wishful science that had once been showcased as fact?"

He paused again as his eyes traipsed over to Margaret Buckey leaning against the wall between two candles; the flickering light unable to conceal her scowl. He grinned and continued, "Who cares? Why waste time on the contemplation of fantasy, they say. I tell you why! Because every story handed down through the ages has character, and behind that, a lesson. So, I pose to each and every one of you—what is the character of your God? What does that character reflect? What does your God say about you?"

Margaret Buckey had slipped away into the next room in frustration as Monty Lincoln shoved the concept of God down their throats, which was a direct about-face from where she intended to take *her* Fellowship. She plopped down in the love seat like she was spent. The television glowed in front of her eyes, and now it was time to forget what Monty Lincoln was destroying. Although she was a woman surrounded by finer things and gifted with a finely tuned intellect, she found joy in popular culture, even when it took an about-face from her finer sensibilities.

"Welcome back to Inside the Frames! I'm your host, Chester Cali!" The slight and perfectly manicured young man announced, dressed head to toe in a loose retro shirt and jeans that kept the blood flowing only above his waist. He made a funny face and then followed it up with a laugh, which the audience reciprocated. He was such a chipper little fellow.

"We've all heard about this upcoming series from the media mogul, Frank Wink. It's been a couple years in the making. I feel like I'm waiting for the next Cher album to drop!" He goofily sputtered forth as the queue was sent for the manufactured laugh.

"No worries! Wink's gotcha covered—real soon. *Conversion's* theme is still in the shadows, and according to Wink's star creative genius, Joshua Bannister, it's an ongoing work in progress." Chester Cali said with a suspicious smirk as if to downplay the suspense, prompting an equally suspicious chuckle from the crowd.

"What has been released to our troubled and curious little minds is the location and its cast."

Chester Cali took on the role of voiceover as it switched to a full-screen panorama of a sprawling mountainous countryside bathed in luscious green. The canopy of trees droned over had some of the finest florets a jolly green giant may have made his bed out of on a starry night. Situated high in the midst of the green was a castle with steeply pitched roofs the shade of Georgia red clay, and stone walls the color of London's fog; a pleasant contrast. It had originally been considered a fortress, meant for defense and to be preserved through the ages. It was, in fact, timeless.

"The entire series will be shot at the most popular medieval fortress in the world—Bran Castle. Yeah, and if you're thinking of a blood-sucking vampire of gothic lore named Dracula, then you're spot on. This was the infamous castle depicted in Bram Stoker's novel which gave the vampire legend a lifeline that still exists in a big way, even today. It might even give some people the heebie-jeebies!

"Wink spared no expense in renting out the castle for the duration of the shoot, and we're pretty positive it was a pretty penny, considering it's owned by Archduke Dominic of Austria-Tuscany and furnished with Queen Marie's personal art collection. To put it in a single word—it's priceless!

"So it's safe to assume that Wink is pulling out all the stops on this one. Now that you can't think of anything to top the location, let's move on to a cast that's also going to be hard to top.

"First in line, we've got Monica Brooks. You remember this darling of the winter Olympics a decade ago in Antarctica."

A series of shots showed her with the smile of a beautiful young woman who was forever a champion, racing around the rink with effortless balance. She had porcelain skin on a delicately flowing physique. Then it was alongside her skating partner, Ricardo Antoline, who was also the picture of perfection glowing with all the subtleties of form and grace. They looked in love, but that had much to do with constantly having to skate beside each other in perfect time.

"After failing to land a triple-axle for the gold she came back home to lick her wounds with the silver, but the wound would only get deeper. A mere two months later she was involved in a car accident that took the life of Ricardo Antoline. She says those wounds have healed and she's ready for the spotlight once again; just not on the ice. She'll have her part in the latest Wink experiment.

"Next, we have the shyest girl in America, and there's a reason for that. Nearly three decades ago she—in what seemed impossible—fell into an eight inch well casing twenty feet below the surface of the ground for more than two days. Right then she became famous without even trying or remembering why. Everyone remembers her as a baby, but now she's an attractive full-time nurse and single mother of two. She has never granted an interview about the incident which captivated audiences around the world. Heather Douglas now appears ready to come out of her shell. No better place than Bran Castle on Wink's *Conversion*."

Grainy footage of her being pulled from the well, followed by stills of her smiling a year later were concluded by a photo of her in scrubs taking a patient's blood pressure. She appeared beautifully normal without all the pomp and posh of those reaching for the spotlight.

The next cast member was a hundred and eighty degree turn from any sense of shyness. The polished thin frame in glowing lingerie purposely accentuated her supple breasts. She exemplified a pharaoh god-king's exclusive mistress endowed with what men sought after: seduction, eroticism, and spurting lust.

"Now we're busting out the goods. But of course, this is Shonda Murano ten years ago. You know, the internationally renowned lingerie model who was once considered the most beautiful woman on the planet. Forget Miss America! But these days, she's a hair stylist in Beverly

Hills with some pretty high-profile clientele. She's going to take a break from the chop and get back on the main stage since her fall from the runway where age and appeal is the only package sexy can come in. *Conversion* may elevate her where she always wanted to be—a Nubian sex icon."

The roll of shots chronicled her glory days on ice ponds, under waterfalls, and on white sands. She made being beautiful so free and easy. It showed her in the salon still holding firm to the beauty she so naturally flaunted. She hoped *Conversion* would permanently lift her from the normalcy inculcated in the grind of everyday life. She was ready to return to her former glory.

The preview shifted suddenly to the opposite kind of sexiness that some would consider raunchy, and still others, outright nasty. She wasn't short of tattoos or piercings, and her pouty ruby red lips was the trademark her fan base recognized most readily. It was obvious she was a bad bitch. Her father was definitely not proud; wherever he may have been. If sex sold, it was all she intended to sell. Different from the other cast members, she was in her sexual prime at the pinnacle of her popularity.

"Oh man, it's who you don't want to bring home to mom, but dad might like just fine. Currently, there's no laws restricting the actions of this porn starlet who did over three hundred scenes this past year. In the interim, expect Barbie Red to sizzle on the screen in *Conversion*. Ladies and gentlemen, this a fierce sexual athlete that brings inhibition to an entirely new level. I'm sure you'll enjoy this, even if you hate it."

Barbie Red was portrayed in a macabre light soaked into the Libertine lifestyle of revelry, sadism, and a complete lack of decency according to those who had penciled in their sexual encounters weeks in advance. She wasn't the smiling and impossible-to-get gorgeous woman with a hint of mystery fueled by fantasy. She was the dead serious harlot from hell that was ready to fuck.

Gears shifted again as a pair of rustling pom-poms of blue and silver appeared on the screen. Then came the face emerging between the pom-poms; a wholesome face that could do nothing except smile and be cheerful with high kicks, hand stands, and the egging on of the perpetual pep-rally. Through her, and her notoriously bleach-blonde flock, the 'Boys were gonna get another win on Sunday.

"The cat was already out of the bag on this one, but as far as color in life, you can't beat ex-Dallas Cowboys cheerleader Bridgette Mahoney. In the years of Cowboy greatness she was just as popular as the players on the field who won the Super Bowls. As it goes, great things don't last forever, and with the decline of the Cowboy dynasty came an even steeper fall for Bridgette Mahoney. After a string of B-movie roles she fell headlong into the pit of booze and cocaine, becoming a groupie passed from metal band to metal band, culminating in a six month jail stint for possession of cocaine, valium, and marijuana just outside a Dallas nightclub. During her stint, she found Jesus, but quickly lost sight of him following her release. Now she's a novelty exotic dancer on the Las Vegas strip. It looks like she's shooting for a revival of fame on the set of *Conversion*.

"As you can only guess, more details are to follow about Bannister and Wink's new brain child that's adding to a growing family. Maybe one day, sometime in the near future, *Conversion* will play out in your living room. I only suspect you won't be able to peel your eyes away from the screen once it all begins. Join us next time on Inside the Frames—I'm Chester Cali!"

**ZZZ...**

*Inside the Frames* was finishing up through the lenses of Frank Winkleshten and Joshua Bannister from their dark room high in the New York City sky. A crystal decanter filled with aged Bordeaux sat between them on the conference table with two wine glasses waiting to be filled. It was always meant as an introductory celebratory sip, and there were very few days when celebration was not given its proper attention. Their top collars were unbuttoned and their feet kicked up. Wink felt as he usually did in his old age—reminiscent. His favored personal analysis and commentary was musing over their coordinated manipulation skills that never seemed to fail. *Inside the Frames* was also under Wink's dominion, solely intended to build the myth of how great upcoming programming was sure to be. This time was going to be better than the last, and these days, a little squirt like Chester Cali was the perfect mouthpiece to trumpet what was to come.

"Who's he fucking now?" Wink inquired, as natural as asking for the time.

Joshua Bannister had to think a little, but it came quickly. "Blake…uh…Blake, uh…Blake Temple."

It failed to ring one bell in Wink's head, which shocked him since he thought he knew everyone. "Blake Temple? What's he on?"

Casually, he answered, "It's his key grip."

Wink became confused. Why would Chester Cali be openly fucking a nobody? It wasn't Wink's life, but there was a clear difference between having a one night stand and publicly bringing out the one who was just meant to be a toy.

"Chester's a good boy. Does a good job. I just don't like the Wink and JB stuff. Like he's a part of the inner circle."

"Part of his act. Makes us look cool, I guess." JB said without apparent concern.

"What do you think of the girls?"

JB smiled at how well he thought it was all coming together. He loved watching his babies grow up into exactly what he wanted them to be. "It's going to be such a beautiful disaster. So ugly."

It's what Wink liked to hear. He was always thinking of the future, not only concerning the projected growth of his media empire, but the possibility of seeing the growth becoming ever fleeting. This was where reminiscence took hold as he pondered a legacy, which often kept him awake during still nights. What had he really brought to the table of lasting history? Sure, his children would spawn generations backed by concrete capital and ultimately change what he had built. He was only concerned about how he would stand alone. Would he be ridiculed? Revered? Worst of all, forgotten?

"When I began there were just a handful of shows, or even concepts for that matter. It wasn't like it is today. It's always been about the social fabric, and even more so, the human condition."

JB would listen once again to his redundant droning. Not only would he listen, but also show enjoyment of the ride down memory lane as he had witnessed it growing up. It was part of the job, and he knew every word that was about to follow. It was kind of like a ritual.

"I stepped in when the junkyard was being constructed. It was an old black man and his warm-hearted son, living in apparent squalor, but that's what made the pair so likeable. No crime scenes. Just laughs. Taking in and selling junk out of their own home. The company they kept was endearing. Nothing raunchy about it. It was about friends, family, and the heart. We had a few like that. Back then it was centered on the working class just below the middle.

"Of course, we had to cater to the other side of that coin. You had to have the old white grump with a cigar fixed to his mouth; barking all the time and only tolerable to those that loved him. He was the last white character who could get away with comedy centered around bigotry. All his antics just had to be kept in the family. That was when we could get away with basing a show purely on racial stereotypes.

"We moved from that by honing in on the popular saying, 'different strokes for different folks.' It showed that two black kids could come to learn from, trust, and even love the older rich white man who came to understand them after all, despite the distance between them socio-economically. The Man wasn't so bad after all.

"Then we went further by showing three's a crowd when it comes to dorky white people. They presented a zany side altogether cheesy and kind of weird, but in no way harmful. We followed that up with a nod to alternative lifestyles when two buddies had to cross-dress in order to get by during hard times in the big city, and that was just when Reagan ascended to his pulpit.

"Then we struck gold with the view of the black family as the Uncle Tom's. They could be doctors. They could be lawyers. They could be taken seriously. And they were damn funny! They had escaped the junkyard. They had used what they learned from the honest rich white man, and now they just had suburban problems. We had two shows like that; pretty much back to back. But if we were going to do it again we had to keep it fresh, and maybe just a little ghetto with a rapping Prince at the helm. That's when hip-hop was a real force to be dealt with. You had the funny black kid from the hood and the whitest black guy we could find who only wore outfits fit for the PGA tour or Wimbledon. It worked out just fine.

"The early nineties brought back the cheesy white people with all of their trivial problems. We put them in Beverly Hills, we had them being saved by the school bell, and saw them through their awkward wonder years. The dorky white people.

"And believe me JB, all of these shows would have stayed as pilots if it wasn't for spinning the social ills of society into the yarn of comedy. That's what made them work. Of course, without humor the human race would have killed itself off millennia ago."

Wink stared off into nothing for a moment as he made the clean break from sitcom history to Paleolithic theory concerning the self-extermination of the human species. Needless to say, at times, Wink thought about many things at once. JB was wholly accustomed to such behavior as it was just another sign the time was nearing for perhaps a handoff of Wink Broadcasting into more able and sensible hands.

"Those days are dead now. It might have all began with those no-holds-barred talk shows, or the first reality shows, or something we didn't even know existed. It's all actually been great for business. You don't need as many resources. Detailed and timed scripts are unnecessary. Plot is unnecessary. Technique of any kind is unnecessary. All you need is a set, a camera, a title, a simple premise, and people who have absolutely no dignity whatsoever. And the ratings just roll in. Who would've thought a big gay white guy could out-maneuver fifteen others on his way to a jackpot on a tropical island? You did, JB. You're a fucking scientist. Sometimes brilliance is so obvious."

The compliment marked the end of his rant; a token of gratitude for indulging again. JB was now expected to chime in and complete the circle. "People are obvious, and best of all, highly profitable."

Done retracing the breadth of his network and fulfilled to still do so, he poured them both a glass as was customary. He lifted the glass, and jubilantly declared, "To stupid people!"

"May they keep procreating!" JB followed as they took down the rare treat which was more like a sweet jam.

As they set their glasses on the marble conference table it occurred to them that Gay J and Tommy Bloom, otherwise known as The Buccaneer, or as the Butt Pirate; had been sitting there the entire time. Tommy Bloom held up a flabbergasted expression which mixed utter shock with a tinge of fear. He was also in show business, but these guys were the predators none saw coming, or would ever see for that matter. He tried his best to act like he heard nothing. For Gay J, headphones fixed, head swaying, eyes closed, with experimental beats and lyrics flowing through his mind; he was unawares and unconcerned with Wink and JB. To him, they were just a few more rich white boys. He would only pay attention when prompted. The two biggest dogs of the media landscape were coldly staring at them, and with a nudge of the elbow, Tommy Bloom snapped Gay J out of his zone to share in the moment he so naturally avoided. Gay J brought the headphones around his neck and returned the hardened stare as it was time for the game to begin.

JB began with Wink only chiming in to ensure it was all his own idea. "First off, thanks for coming in. I know you have your own shit going on, but we've got something to add to your plate. We'll see if you bite."

"Bite you will!" Wink nearly growled out.

Gay J nearly laughed, but Tommy Bloom sat still and petrified. JB continued, "*Conversion* is why we're here, and you two are the final pieces. Does either of you know about this upcoming production?"

"You been stretching it out so that no one gives a damn whether it drops or not. You got some pretty bitches with a past, and I'm sure you're just gonna turn on the camera, take the leashes off, and sit back to watch the ratings roll in. That's the usual." Gay J answered without a hint of reverence or awe with being in their presence.

"Yes, you're in the ballpark, but it's so much bigger than that!" Wink assured with swagger.

"Basically guys, we want you two to come aboard as the final cast members to be announced as soon as we have an agreement. The premise is unprecedented, the edgiest it can get, controversial to the core, and will be completely organic in composition. That is—what will happen once we begin shooting." JB followed.

"What's going to happen?" Tommy Bloom asked, wondering if it was going to be a show on hauntings and the supernatural; both things that terrified him.

Wink chuckled, looking upon Tommy as cute. "A natural progression of social interaction."

"As it stands right now, you're the most popular gay couple out there. I emphasize gay because this would not work at all if you were straight. That's why it's a perfect fit."

"Perfect!" Wink reinforced.

There was the usual silence accompanying an approaching build-up, but Gay J was quick enough to break its momentum. "So what the fuck is this?"

Laughs poured forward from the mogul and his deputy as they lauded his rawness which was reflected in themselves. JB cut to the chase as he leaned forward to close the distance between them, planting his elbows on the table with his broad shoulders pointed skywards. "You will be placed in Bran Castle for eight weeks with six beautiful heterosexual women who have one goal. They are going to convince you to hit for their team. Thus, they will attempt to convert you from being gay to being straight. That's it. That's the show."

They were both floored, but Tommy Bloom more so as he covered his wide open mouth with his hand, like blasphemy had been announced in the midst of a monastery full of nuns. He shot a concerned look at Gay J who remained lackadaisical and altogether apathetic. "That seems a little strange."

"The projections of our desires are strange. We're not asking for a lifetime. Only two months. Sixty days. It will turn out to be a very profitable time for the both of you. That, I can promise." Wink stated without doubt.

"What in yo sick minds makes you think we can be converted? Let me be straight up. I don't like the pussy!" Gay J laid out plainly without getting riled up in the least. Tommy Bloom nodded his head, standing by his man.

"You're missing the point. We don't care if you're converted. Experiments pass or fail the test. Watching the experiment unfold is what's entertaining. Either way, we'll win. There's too much personality enclosed for it not to be entertaining. You will not be forced to do anything. Like I said, it's an organic composition. We are merely creating an environment. It's yours to operate within. And, of course, you will be compensated handsomely. After the shooting you can go to an equatorial paradise for a whole year and talk about it. Shut it all out. You'll definitely have the money." JB shot back; his elbows leaving the table as he fell back in his chair to imply it was all that needed to be said.

Tommy Bloom heard enough and was growing frantic over the possibility that his cherished relationship—the only thing that brought balance—could be dragged through an unnecessary sludge simply for money. He turned to his lover for an appeal. "This can't be good. Why do we need this? When we're together there's no one else. The packed arenas. The stupid interviews. The assholes that make us do the interviews. The slimy paparazzi constantly snapping shots in our faces. We have each other so we can escape that annoying reality. What these two want is to see the destruction of this beautiful romance we've built, while they laugh all the way to the bank. Let's keep going the way we've been. I love it that way. Don't you, baby?"

Gay J placed his had atop Tommy's with rings around his fingers that may have made one think him a perpetual winner of world championships. They locked eyes as Gay J took in his heartfelt argument imbued with genuine feeling. It happened to be the same way he felt. They had been dodging the bullets that came with fame, finding solace in the moments shared alone. It was their private story. Their own script. It was the freedom to have their own beginning and the courage to know only they could bring about their own end. Gay J loved him dearly and could think of no other person he had adored more. He softly smiled for he knew it was what Tommy Bloom loved to see the most; melting that gritty street persona he kept on display. It was a look symbolizing they were one.

"How much you gonna pay us?" Gay J asked, turning back to Wink and JB, and tossing away the soft look.

Wink shot a quick look and JB was set into motion. He opened a drawer set into the table and pulled from it a manila file folder. He opened it up and presented it as a host does a guest at a fine dining restaurant. Both their eyes enlarged at what was set in front of them. Beneath their stupefied, iced expressions was the giddiness of a child the night before a trip to the waterpark in summertime. Wink and JB appeared content and patient in knowing their proposal could not be dismissed, even from the most inflexible heights of moral ground. The two lovers looked at each other as they held each other's hands tightly, preparing to bear the brunt of an oncoming force.

Tommy Bloom would ultimately make the final decision. He was the dominant partner to whom the recessive would have to gain approval for a decision that affected the entire household, or deal with an interminable amount of scorn for not properly consulting the dominant. His final decision felt more like a question, but it would be firm. "It'll be fine. We'll make it through, baby?"

## Back in Pyongyang

Though the days seemed to be constantly gray it was still bright outside to Sun-raè. She was lost in a daydream, an often interrupted slip rarely able to fully blossom. Geography class made it easier. She knew full well the dividing lines of nations on the crust of the earth. That was not the primary focus. She was now in the Higher Middle School of Six Years. She had bypassed the general school system intended to keep the agrarian-minded purely agrarian. She could have been admitted to the Special Purpose School; a destination for those especially to be groomed for a revolutionary education consisting of the Party and the power it wielded. Her parents decided it was too much of a man's world. The Continuing Education System right in the middle would suit her just fine. It was still designed for political education, but left out the emphasis on Party power as an overlord, and replaced it with a socialistic humanism which would find her a fitting place in society amongst her comrades in the daily march. Following her Higher Middle years her ambition was to attend the Pyongyang Medical College where she could eventually, and quite simply, help others. For now, she would sit through another geography class where Korea—specifically the northern half—was situated not only at the center of the world, but that of the entire universe. Fortunately, she could answer any question thrown at her out of the blue, which is why she felt comfortable slipping into a daydream.

She drifted off to many places. Her mother and father stood prominent. She loved them dearly. The warmth and understanding of her mother put her childish fears at ease. With a stern exterior, yet playful intuition, her father brought in the concepts of devotion and respect that were to be long-lasting. As a family *cell*—the term used by the State to designate a household—they filled their time with activities like a game of Chang-gi (Korean-style chess) between father and daughter. It was not who won or lost that stuck in her memory, but win or lose, her father always held up the same proud look of love. She had neighborhood friends who played many games, but she specifically liked the Nol-Ttwigi. It was a Korean see-saw where a child would be seated on one end, and one standing on the other end. The one standing would jump on the seat of their end, catapulting the seated one so they landed on their feet like a cat thrown through the air. She was growing out of that simplicity, but still formed a smile at its innocence.

Still another cherished time was helping her mother prepare dinner for a father returning from the bureaucratic machine of the Democratic Peoples' Republic of Korea (DPRK)—a hopeless bore of repetition. Their soft faces of clear complexion always cheered him up. But her favorite was the time she and her mother designed her own Yon (kite) down to the dye and stitch. It flew so well against the gray sky. She remembered her mother's free expression and how she shared her own bit of daydreaming when she said it was her fantasy to fly high with the kite above Pyongyang. To feel what it would be like to float above it all. In life, they were all to be so precise. So perfect. Daydreaming was a social norm.

That was where her daydream flipped to her dear old friend Jing. All the precision of Korean life subsided when she gave Jing the controls. She was a well-tuned and proficient violinist, but the orchestra and symphony arrangements lacked a certain flair filling her ears once the headphones were fixed around them. As a younger girl she loved the poppy sensations of Cindy Lauper, Madonna, Michael Jackson, Whitney Houston, and Paula Abdoul. But then Jing introduced the classic rock: Beatles, Stones, Hendrix, Zeppelin, Doors, and her favorite of all—Janis Joplin. Jing omitted their back-stories, but she was accustomed to music standing alone without a face. Like much of the world, she fell in love with their riffs and the rules of life they made on the fly. By way of the moving picture she fell in love with animation as Jing was able to round up The Jetsons, Heathcliff, and Scooby-Doo. As she grew, so did her tastes. She liked Alf and Family Ties. With each new introduction, Jing just happened to pick right. It was not only the media Jing picked which touched her sensibilities, but also his mere presence. He was such a carefree entity in apparent squalor, and didn't have one problem with it. He had friends, not comrades. He made people happy. His was the unusual ability to remain content in the underbelly of society. There were no secrets. No rigid uniformity. No stoic faces lined up without a crease of error or humor. Jing was actually the yon flying above them all as her mother mused, and the stitched design was Jing's jubilant wrinkled face with his bucked teeth shining down on a sad city. Our Dear Leader and procurer of infinite joy— all hail Jing!

She was snapped out of the deep by the movement of chairs and the closing of books. Class was adjourned for the day, and to her delight, she could now be refreshed by another one of her visits with Jing. Though they all were, this was a special visit. She would finally see the end of The Wizard of Oz. Jing had deliberately and patiently stretched out the movie as if it were a study. She would finally find out who the wonderful wizard was. His omnipotent wisdom and bountiful kindness would get Dorothy home, the Scarecrow a brain, the Tin Man a heart, and the Cowardly Lion some courage—or so she expected. They had already been sent on the mission to get the Wicked Witch of Wests' broomstick in exchange for their wishes being magically granted.

This was what she looked forward to seeing as she ran through the market district, vendors smiling and waving at her, drunks too slow to react, and strays keeping pace with her for the moment she was in their space. Then came the curtained dwellings and the uneven ground where Jing resided. She only looked for one marker; the fat jolly man with a once-bitten turkey leg and a mug of beer. There it was! She flowed through the curtains and Jing's old face lit up with cheer. It was their time again.

The Technicolor danced on her face in the dark of their cave a short time later. To her dismay, the Wizard would not fulfill what he promised to deliver. He proved to be powerless when Toto began pulling back the curtain to reveal the backstage elaborate production. The Wizard was simply another man pulling levers, blowing smoke, and playing silly little games at the expense of hope. They believed this Wizard could deliver upon his promises, since they must be trivial to an all-powerful force as he pretended to be. Very little grief did they give him for his falsehood. His finality of wisdom was the revelation that all they had to do was believe in themselves, and when Dorothy finally succumbed to this, she awoke back on the Kansas farm where she ultimately belonged. Sun-raè was happy for Dorothy who remained stout in her convictions. What a great story!

She and Jing began to walk through the shanty neighborhood which she felt was her own. Jing was flushed with apprehension about what he wanted, and felt needed to be said. Who in their right mind would understand him, much less a young girl who knew nothing else except what constantly danced before her eyes. "What did you finally think of The Wizard of Oz?"

"I didn't expect Oz to be a regular person. I think he may be a liar, Jing." She noted, as it was exactly where he wanted her to go with her thinking.

"What do you think of Dorothy? Special girl, huh?"

"Yes, she was. I really liked her ruby red slippers, but the whole time she was in Oz she could never take them off. Her feet must have smelt really bad."

Jing laughed at her observation, which he would have never considered. It was those things inside her he did not want to shatter. As they strolled to a familiar spot between them where a creek ran softly across solitary stones in view of Pyongyang, packed with monumental buildings; the most prominent among them all was the Party billboard with the laughing, almost clown-like face of Kim il-Sung, benevolently looking down on his forever faithful populace. From this setting Jing would propose what he felt would be the best for Sun-raè. He felt a storm coming. Power had just switched hands in the Kim Dynasty of pure Roman nepotism. Death and even deeper subjugation were certain to follow. Pyongyang was not the only life to live, and was the center of absolutely nothing. It was important she understood this state of affairs. It would be the only time he would touch upon the matter, but he wanted it charred into her memory so she could use it when she was stronger. He was to spark the reaction, and how it would spawn from there was entirely up to her.

"How is the family?" He asked with his usual mixed tone of curiosity and compassion.

"They are well." She recited automatically, but after further contemplation—"Now that I think about it, they have never been bad."

His next inquiry was sadly enough a trap, but she would have the correct answer. He believed it. It was their most important secret. "I would be just fine with you around all the time. They are fortunate, and so are you. Do they know about me now?"

"No, you are still a secret, and my favorite one."

She wrapped her arms around his thin waist and closed the grip down affectionately. He returned the same. The love between them was nothing either wanted to ruin, but life was happening and they were growing older. She was leaving the realm of a child and was walking through a door labeled YOUNG WOMAN. Priorities were going to change, either on her own accord or abated by other forces. Soon she may not have any interest in a secret friend. The State, her peers, and the confliction of her personal dreams would soon be pressing in from all sides. Much to do! Much to think about! She would be brought into busier times.

"Do you remember at the beginning of the movie when they talked of being young at heart? How the work of the fully grown can rob the happiness of youth?"

In Kansas, as farmhands, they worked the land as must be done. Dorothy wanted another reality without the grinding effects of repetitive survival. "Yes, I remember.

Father says work is a product of the soul. When we grow up, he says, the soul is fed all the time. He says to be a child now because I cannot be a child forever. I will deal with the soul later."

Jing smiled at how she was guided so well, with such delicate reserve, so as not to break her little heart or spook her to a mistaken action. She was guarded, but her imagination was set to run free. That was behind the smile. "We are all children. We become grown. We work for food, clothing, and shelter. But we do not stop being a child. A child has wonder on its side. An adult is different. They hit a plateau, and submit their wonder to the will of the machine: the State, industry, or just pure fantasy. As you grow, remember to never lose the wonder. Never live to work. I believe you to be more creative than that."

In her mind, only one question popped up. "Is that why you do not work, Jing?"

He laughed aloud as she made it so easy to do. But he had to get down to the business of the matter. It was not about his walk. "Never mind me. You know the Scarecrow wanted a brain. Dorothy wondered how he could talk without a brain. He said people did a lot of talking without a brain. Is he right about that?"

All she could remember was his flimsiness, his jerkiness, and his song. "Yes, he was so funny! He did not seem so scary."

He always gracefully led her upwards. "Do you remember he said that other people would think he was scary if he had a brain? Why?"

She thought for a moment, and then she fit her usual mold of being pleasantly surprising. "Because then he would be useful?"

A hammer could not have hit the nail harder on its head, but he would stay on course for the deep. "Good…what about the Tin Man? He is a worker too, but all he really wants is a heart. If he had a heart, he would feel emotions, and those would lead him to new interests. Of course, he would still work. It would only be so much better if he had a heart to go along with the work. Do you understand?"

The pauses were merely rehearsals in her head. "I think so. Work is not really worth anything unless you believe in it? Unless you can get some kind of fun out of it?"

She followed along so well, but digging through concepts and being generally astute, was a national tradition. "And what about the Cowardly Lion? He came out so tough, did he not? And why? He is the King of the Jungle! Who would dare test the wrath of a lion?"

"Dorothy would! No doubt about that!" She announced, delivering a slap to the open air. "Dorothy put him right in his place."

"She shattered the reputation he had built, did she not?"

"All too well!"

Most adults in the market district could not follow along this well, but Sun-rae was different; a product of finer education in North Korea. "Okay, so on we go down the yellow brick road to the all-powerful and wonderful Wizard of Oz to ask for a brain, a heart, some courage, and a one-way ticket back home to Kansas."

She would skip to the chase without skipping a beat. "But the Wizard is not a Wizard at all. He is only a man."

"Right! He is only a man, so keeping promises is quite difficult for him. What does he offer besides what he could never deliver?"

It was fresh in her mind, and became all the more disappointing as he nudged her intellect to the analytical. "Scarecrow was given an honorary degree."

"Though he had not opened one book, taken one test, or entertained even one field of study. Go on."

"The Cowardly Lion was awarded medals for courage."

"He was scared of every waking moment, and defending himself was out of the question. Go on."

"I think the Tin Man got the worst of the deal. He was given a heart-shaped clock on a chain, and was told all he needed was kindness and love."

Jing smiled down at her again. "He pretty much already had those things, huh?"

"I thought he was kind and loving, and shiny. He sure was not mean." She confirmed as the great hoax was brought further into the light.

"You see, Sun-rae, the Wizard was useless. A seeder of fear and doubt…simply another human."

Quiet blanketed them in the sanctity of their secret spot. From then on, Jing would feel the responsibility for altering the perception of the dominant world around her. There had to be other ways to live. Jing felt he had always lacked the brains, heart, and most of all courage to carry out what he was about to suggest. In more ways than one, it meant one's life. The smiling clown-king on the billboard measured the value of each life. No more!

"Tell me, Sun-rae, do you ever think and dream of other lands other than the one we live?"

There were so many. They were vibrant, blended in spectacular color, flowing along by magic and impossibility, with the common thread being that of a lifetime of joy. Yes, something like that, out of grasp. "Sure…but I cannot go to them. There's nothing worse than betraying the Fatherland. This is all there is for me."

It made Jing so sad to hear it, but it was something he had always heard. The pang of despair and hopelessness was so much greater when heard from the young. Fools who were fully grown he dismissed without a second thought. They were past lost; only slaves to the order. His affection for Sun-rae compelled him to steer her off the track of blind servitude. Neither did he want her to become anything resembling his own being. That reality was also a lost cause. In the deepest sincerity he only wanted her to live a life with some semblance of variety and choice. A life where her spirit could be let loose and fed heartedly. A life of virtual worship to one family, one ideal, was the grandest heist of the soul. Hers was much too beautiful.

"You should go South."

Thinking it was one thing. Saying it was another. The promised consequence was torture and death; those promises being not at all empty. The regime had the Bowibu state police to sniff out dissension, and once found—real or imagined—administered a barbaric form of punishment void of any human decency. Jing had barely escaped power changing hands many years before, and he knew it was only a matter of time until the new Kim would exercise his divinely-appointed force in a statewide sweep of strangling brutality; a simple reminder of who remained in complete control. These were Jing's fears for his dear friend, Sun-rae.

As they looked in each other's eyes it was clear an unspeakable line had been crossed. Yet, they could only move forward from then on. "You should leave the North. This place is not for you."

A frightening sensation swept over Sun-rae like some evil force was leering down upon her, waiting for the precise moment to consume her whole. She was to revere her Fatherland! Never doubt those granted with its preservation! It was the rule of Kim, love of country, work, and family—in that order. That was the program!

"But Jing, this is the greatest country in the world with the finest leader, the finest people, and the finest military. This is the best place to live. The report came out again this year."

The report was presented annually by the State news agency. The recurring theme was that Korea sat confidently at the top of the global quality of life index, and that the United States' quality of life sat at the very bottom of that index. The report had not one shred of viable research backing up its claims, but who would know anyways? The only message accentuated was that Korea was 1st place in all matters of the world at large.

"I sure hope this is not the best place to live." Jing quipped, as Sun-rae fell into further shock over the conversation taking place at all. "This is Oz, my dearest friend. A great fraud. Without color. Without wonder. A dead dream. That man on the billboard is the one behind the curtain, pulling the levers and blowing the smoke. We as proud Koreans have been robbed of our brains, of our hearts, and the courage to put an end to it all. He hands you a brain from Kim il-Sung University, a heart of Juche, and courage behind the People's Army. You do not deserve any of it, Sun-rae! Your destiny is not in service of the Party! Your destiny is solely your own! Gather yourself. Remain a ghost. A plotting criminal; until you carry out the act which will save your life and begin a new one. If there is anything I wish for you—is that you dream big and follow through using your brain, your heart, and all your courage. You will need every bit of it."

It was the dormant motive in the back of most minds, concealed behind tired eyes. This was the first time these forbidden thoughts were brought to the fore so boldly, and from then on, she would be able to see it in the eyes of many. Reacting on this motive in any way, shape, or form was futile. She would merely store it away, and like a rare jewel, let its worth grow until she could no longer ignore the value. She now knew the jewel was in place.

They both gazed at Pyongyang like it would be the last time. Jing put his boney arm around her shoulder, and softly said with sad foresight, "I will miss you, my dearest little friend."

**Back in the States…**

The political panel of the Jagorgin Group had been going back and forth as usual for their weekly commentary, and were naturally running out of steam. Their ages were definitely a factor. The host, Murray Jagorgin, was an old man fixed with a permanent scowl. Although, behind his black frames and thick lenses was a nice enough man. He was joined by Doug Turin; a failed former presidential contender turned pundit out of necessity. Deborah Miffin was an older lady with the coveted Ph.D. and a tenured honorable fellow at the Institute for a Perfect World. Mark Williams was one step away from a breathing machine and already fitted with a colostomy bag, but his regal beard lent evidence to his life as a prominent historian. They all wore ill-fitting nice suits, but it had very little to do with their political libido.

Murray Jagorgin hacked violently into his handkerchief as he transitioned to the closing topic of the show. He glanced at what came out of him, shook his head in disbelief, stuffed it back into his coat pocket, and carried on; "One final thing this week: Malcolm Grace and the Civics. They have a political foothold all over the country now and it doesn't seem like they have any intention of pumping the brakes. They have used a grassroots approach by first concentrating on municipal boards, city council places, and mayoral seats. They went after the congressional district seats in state legislatures, moved into a few governor's mansions, and now command a presence on the national level in Congress. The next natural step, and with the general election looming, seems to be a shot at the White House. Malcolm Grace, of course, is the founder and ideological headpiece of the Civics. He does not hold public office and hasn't shown any interest in running for public office, but his party has other ideas in mind. They want him to run for the Presidency. Whudya think?"

"He has mobilized those disheartened political stragglers into effective public servants. He's all about the structural organization of the Civics, and this is a party with everyone, it seems, on the exact same page. Solid foundation. No cracks to be seen." Deborah Miffin stated, chiming in first to get the fresh round going.

Doug Turin reached out his hands, blinked his eyes, and tried his best to recall what he was going to say. He winged it instead. "They're hard-nosed. All about business…I'm sorry…all about proper governance."

"Yeah, don't let Malcolm Grace hear that." Deborah Miffin joked, referring to Malcolm Grace's insistence that government should not, at its heart, operate as a business. They all laughed at the obvious reference.

"But seriously, he's revived a political pulse and consciousness that has garnered plenty of mass appeal. In effect, he's made the dominating two-party system seem like a boring two-sided coin. The only choices—heads or tails—after it's all said and done, it's still just one coin." Mark Williams gruffly added.

"Sure does seem so. We'll end this week with some footage of Malcolm Grace at work on the issues. Hope you enjoy. Have a great week and we'll see you next time. Goodbye!" Murray Jagorgin closed with an exaggerated wave of his hand as he reached for a bit of levity.

*

Malcolm Grace was standing on the stage at a Civic rally in San Antonio. Before him sat a throng of people on blankets and lawn chairs; picnic-style like they were about to take in a concert. It certainly was a show and Malcolm Grace was in full stride.

"The Republicans say to build a wall, put more boots on the ground, and keep on deporting. Make it as difficult as possible to become a resident of this state, a citizen of this nation, and a legal contributor to the well-being of society—a tax payer!

"The Democrats say this nation was built on the backs of immigrants who held this undying vision of prosperity that could never be exhausted. They want on-the-fly legislation of brisk executive action to address isolated matters, but all that does is pave the way for more money to be thrown into the pit of bureaucratic dysfunction that both parties have soundly built for generations. Amnesty is not the answer! Fair and measured assimilation and naturalization is!

"It must be plainly said that the United States is no longer this inexhaustible land of plenty. Yes, there is still opportunity, but we are hurting as a nation in all respects. Remember, natural-born citizens graduating from college are stuck in the same economic sphere as a majority of illegal immigrants. Wages are stagnant, cost of living has doubled, and resources are frighteningly stretched. The Civics will ensure that the immigrant population gets the respect it deserves, but the legal citizenry of the United States deserves the same in return. We don't need a fence, we don't need more boots on the ground, we don't need handouts, and we don't need velvet gloves to handle this dilemma we all face. We need mutual understanding, mutual benefit, and most of all, accountability based on realistic expectations. The bureaucratic machine that seems to always have their wheels spinning in the mud, going nowhere, needs to get going on the road that leads to some kind of humane orientation. A culture must be established—not a mandate! This nation is not to be exhausted! It is to be grown like the relationships we should all be sincere upon building!"

*

The scene switched to a cloudy day in Philadelphia amongst a crowd of predominately young people with rainbow flags in tow. Malcolm Grace sat in the middle of them without being elevated, completely vulnerable to the passions of a collective body with something in common. They had all seen his unrelenting style. Now it was time to view it live.

"At present, there are two strong movements streaming through society: LGBT rights and fair wages for women. Those of you in the lesbian, gay, bi-sexual, and transgender community are finally able to wed legally without any barriers. Congratulations!" He stated, as the crowd gathered around him erupted with cheers and applause. He nodded his head, acknowledging their fierce persistence that had led them to victory. It was something he could unequivocally respect.

"Your fight!" He exclaimed, bringing them back under his spell. Once they all hushed down, he continued, "Has not been won. Believe you me, it has just begun. Now you will experience, if you so choose, the inherent pitfalls of vowing to tie yourself financially to another individual for what is presumed to be the remainder of your lives. Approximately fifty percent of first-time marriages end in divorce. Those married multiple times, sixty percent. Your opponents offered the reason for their resistance to your constitutional rights as being based on the social fabric of the family itself. Their argument was that a straight man and a straight woman are the only households that can raise a decent American citizen. They are wrong. Only love and discipline can raise a decent American citizen, and human being for that matter. But now you have been bestowed with this great power to raise a family, and as the old saying goes: 'With great power comes great responsibility.' Just remember; should you choose to raise little ones, don't fall into the trap of bitterness and attrition stemming from the wars of love. The only real victims are your children, and the suffering that is hoisted upon them, has nothing to do with constitutionality. It has everything to do with your personal constitution. I wish you all the very best on that heavily tread and underestimated winding road.

"There's that other issue as well. Apparently, there's not enough women in executive positions. Off the top of my head, I don't know how many chief executive positions are filled or available, but it seems to me that we're talking about the top one percent of the socio-economic ladder. CEO's are hardly a representation of the whole. Those working on the first step of the economic ladder have always been the drivers of productivity; whatever gender. I think the real problem is the curving away from qualifications. If a person is not qualified, then they should not be in a certain position—period! The Civics will not adhere to the practice of telling businesses whom they should hire. We will as a governing body promote equal vision, which means you are not male, female, black, white, Hispanic, Native American, gay, straight, disabled, old, young, are something else as yet to be classified. You are simply another citizen and human being that must earn their keep to responsibly maintain what is most important: yourself and your family!"

*

He was then in an auditorium in Detroit among high school students wearing hardened and distrustful faces who had heard it all, but there they were that day to see the fiery and unapologetic Malcolm Grace. His grim demeanor was somehow magnetic beyond their collective resistance. He was not there to placate. He knew the school administration and some of the teachers did that very thing to them every day.

"I know, I know—just another suit coming in with a big smile, talking of how bright your future is going to be. Don't worry, I didn't forget my crystal ball!" He said, as a rare chuckle tumbled forward from the student body. He quickly pressed on as they granted him passage, "As I've stated before, the Civics will not do promises. We only have goals just like every one of you, and none of us can achieve them alone. From what I can see, our educational system needs a new vision. We have just tried federally mandated standardized testing with the scores serving as a marker for how much funding a school receives. These tests are based on recitation and memorization, lacking in applicability in the real world. I can assure you all that you are not meant to be robots shuffling through the arteries of a computer program! You are meant to be creative, innovative, and fully able to pursue your own interests on your own time!

"That's why we came out against homework from the outset when it comes to public education. We stuff your heads with loads of information during the school day, and then cram them again when they go home to friends and family. They are barely given time to soak it all in, much less think of it in practical terms. We're wearing you out to just like we are wearing out ourselves. Parents are told to leave work issues at work and home issues at home. Why not the same for all of you? At work, at school, we pursue what must be done. At home, we should all partake in what's best for our personal morale. We must encourage the imagination, and tone down the rigors of the formula. I think we could learn so much more about ourselves and where we belong in our lifetimes."

*

He was seated in a chair under a harsh spotlight in front of a graduate student in the library of the John Hopkins School of Advanced International Studies in Washington, D.C. The young woman about to conduct the interview was considerably nervous as he calmly waited for the opening question. He personally disliked the one-on-one exchanges, as it lacked the energy generated by an in-the-flesh live audience. "Um, Mr. Grace…what is your view on the future of foreign policy as the Civics see it?"

"We see it in real terms. Specifically, we as a nation are clearly despised across the globe, and if not despised, at the very least, ridiculed. The reasons behind that run deep through recent and far-flung history. The most recent examples are the war in Iraq, and Vietnam before that: two wars that could have been completely avoided altogether. Yet, as a world power with the largest share in the global economy we are expected to intervene in certain situations that could disrupt the ebb and flow of that economy, whether other powers want to accept it or not. Remaining on the sidelines is impermissible. However, engaging in senseless bloodbaths without a clear victor is even worse. For our military, readiness is of central importance. We must always be well-rounded. What I mean by that is we have to maintain our capacity to fight on a large-scale conventional basis just as well as on a clandestine one. We must openly share our secrets, tactics, systems, and hardware with allies to bring about standardization that will amount to effective execution, and present real results as a global acting body. We must also come to terms with the fact that the world, much like the laws of nature, are not at all passive. Peace is not an enduring and fixed state of being. It is transient. We must always be ready for its departure. The course is ours to chart, and until we formerly relinquish this role which is generally understood, we have no choice but to be proactive in foreign affairs. In all honesty, I would prefer we lead the way."

She had expected his bombastic and grating style. He was instead calm, legs crossed, hands resting docile on his knee. There was no crowd to lure out of their collective shell. He knew that style was not at all attractive in the near Stoic world of high academia. She shifted in her seat, and continued, "Okay, so that's the hard power approach. What about the diplomatic approach for the Civics?"

"Cold professionalism." He said plainly, as the unalterable finality of his answer was conveyed in his confidence. "No more of these smiley-faced, glad-hand photo ops for the public, and then a mere moments later we're back to where we started. We don't always have to be breaking some new kind of ground that isn't even there. Diplomacy is built on trust over a long period of time, culminating in a long history of one's word holding up. I can say that our diplomacy will not be based on stunts and choreographed displays of common culture and interests. It will be all about workability, and that means we either merge likenesses for mutual benefit or we do not. Time is precious. I don't expect ours to be wasted, or any other player for that matter. What's most important to understand is that the Civics refuse to fake it just to, at the most, garner a targeted public perception built on columns of dry sand."

*

He was walking down the street amidst the bustle of the high-rise city without guards, without party members; when a woman of paparazzi appeal approached him with a cameraman anchored to her side and a fuzzy-headed microphone gripped in her hand. Like most agitators of a professional grade, she was in a rush and always welcomed with open arms incessant confrontation. "Mr. Grace, what is the Civics view on abortion?"

He kept walking, without looking at her, answering evenly, "I would recommend to never vote solely on a single issue alone. It is an issue for those who cannot expand their political thought past a personal moral viewpoint they see embodied in the person they choose to vote for. Sex is legal. The most common outcomes are babies, STD's, pain, and pleasure. Cigarettes are legal. For that, it's cancer, bad breath, pain, and pleasure. Alcohol is legal. For that, drunkenness, liver disease, pain, and pleasure. Abortion is legal. For that, you may earn a kernel of doubt in your conscious, a load off your chest, and an experience you might not want to go through again. All personal liberties carry with them adverse consequences. The Civics view? It's your life. It's your call. Choose wisely."

He turned into the entranceway of the Civics headquarters in New York City, leaving her with a smile and the feeling she had just received some great unscripted material. "Vote Civics!"

*

The air was whipping around the Rugby wind farm in North Dakota as the microphone he held hissed like a snake and pounded like a heartbeat. Looking strangely at the temporarily obnoxious device, he jokingly asked, "Check, check, is this thing on?"

Laughs tumbled forth as he returned a rare smile. "But really! I assure you, this massive and impressive wind farm is only a part of the future face of energy as we all may know it. That future will consist of an independent trifecta that includes wind, solar, and yes—nuclear energy. Oil, gas, and coal are indeed—dinosaurs—but there is still an abundant amount of all three on this continent, and elsewhere. The wisest move would be to export it all, supply emerging markets at an applicable rate that, quite frankly, edges the competition out so they are no longer necessary. The competition becomes the dinosaurs themselves. We then invest these massive profits in the grand-scale infrastructure of the trifecta, which will in turn fuel the future of how we get from point A to point B: nationally and globally. There will be networks of trifecta-powered bullet trains connecting every major US city. Aerial rail systems within the heart of those cities, paneled highways for solar-powered cars, and the continued efficient-driven refinement of mass aviation. If we don't begin thinking about getting people out of cars and off the shifting pavement then the dream of energy independence will ultimately not materialize. The alternate sources of energy need to be thought of as oil, gas, and coal. The primary sources of energy needs to be thought of as the trifecta. We have to fool ourselves for a while until this frame of mind sets in. Just like we've somehow set in our minds that oil and gas will last forever. And remember people, we're not even talking about water!"

*

The final scene on the string was at a rally in Chicago where politics and crime have a long history of bedding down together. A place where murders occur like clockwork and some of the finest food on earth is served. Donned in a thick black overcoat on a day that gave the city its nickname, Malcolm Grace was especially fired up. "Make no mistake! They are going to throw the kitchen sink at us. They will show no mercy. This only means they are taking us seriously now. Remember that we started at the bottom. Our message will remain sincere. We don't govern for love of power, or love of title, or for any other kind of ego-driven purpose. We don't bend to the buck and we don't change the game for special interests. What we do is operate professionally, work tirelessly, and do what is only the very best for the people who depend on our sound discerning which stands impartial, so that it can truly be allowed to work for all. From the local level to the executive level, we will—

It was the synchronized thunder from the assembled crowd that stopped him in his oratorical tracks. Their message was clear. "Run! Run! Run! Run! Run!"

Standing to their feet and pumping their fists, it was the first time the camera caught a humble blush drawn on the face of Malcolm Grace. It was an adamant showing. Running for the highest office in the land was what they unanimously demanded. With everything drowning out as the moment seemed to consume him, only hearing the thumping clamor of his following, he resigned to a bashful submission and exited the stage with a smirk that harbored hidden intent, goading them all to want it even more.

Johnston thought he would never live to see it; a politician that wasn't just another well-adjusted actor. He viewed politicians as touring comics using the same material in different places, taking in the reactions, and adjusting the delivery as needed. The difference? Politicians were never funny, but he didn't expect them to be. They were to speak on serious matters in a crazy world. What was ever going to be funny about that?

"These Civics are making a march for it, Peg." Johnston said, knowing she liked politics as much as he liked the opening episode to *Conversion*—he hated it. "Hell, I might even vote."

Peggy was on the couch, with Maddie sitting between her legs on the floor, enjoying the comb pressed through her silky blonde hair. Maddie liked watching television with her parents and was curious about the energy showcased by Malcolm Grace, though everything he talked about failed to concern her completely. "He seems a little angry, daddy."

Johnston smiled at nearly everything she said. "Well, maybe it's because he is. I think everyone's a little angry, except the people sitting at the top. They're always pretty happy. They certainly do make sure things go right for them."

"Are you happy, daddy?" She asked, as Peg swung him a look, saying he should answer correctly without hesitation.

Smiling again, he answered correctly. "As long as I got y'all under the same roof as me—that's all it really takes for me."

Peg loved it when he showed his soft side from time to time. "Would you vote for him?"

"I don't vote in the general election, honey."

"Why not?" She inquired, already knowing the answer; one in which she did not comprehend all too well.

"Because we live in Texas. It's a red state—for now. Our electoral college will keep it that way. In the presidential election they cast the vote that really counts." He explained as it flew over their heads.

"Who are the people from the college? What are they learning?"

Johnston liked how she always seemed to ask the right questions; ones in which adults would shy away from to avoid appearing foolish, though they would ultimately remain ignorant. "Honestly, baby, I don't know. I think only they know who they are."

She was confused yet again, but did not become frustrated. It only allowed openings for her honesty to get through. "That seems kind of stupid."

Peg ceased combing her hair, reminding with a stressed grunt not to say such things. "I'm sorry, momma. I meant it seems kind of silly."

"That's better." Peggy admonished with ease.

Maddie came to her feet, throwing her hair over her left shoulder, ready to fulfill her plans on a summer's day.

Talking about the Electoral College with her parents was not on the agenda. The day had not a cloud in the sky and she had free reign to move about it as she pleased. "I'm going to meet Ral. I'll be back for supper time."

"Okay, have fun. Be safe, baby." Johnston said. She gave them their hugs and kisses; a healthy habit both parents hoped would never come to an end.

Out the door she went without a worry on a steamy July afternoon. She hopped on her bike and started peddling. As the chain cycled to propel her forward, so did the thoughts roll through her mind. Home life was her centerpiece and she could not have been more content. Her home was a lasting refuge. A warm place in the winter and a cool place in the summer. Johnston was the stone set in place—implacable. Their fun was as easy as a kitten pawing at a ball of yarn. He took her down the Guadalupe, scaled Enchanted Rock, canoed at Broken Bow, fished in the Gulf, and hunted in the eastern woodlands. She complained about none of it. He would tell her; "Kids are raised soft these days. Their faces stuck to screens pumping a bunch of garbage in their heads. Not you, Maddie. Not you."

Peg, for her part, loved the garbage he steadily scorned. Mother and daughter watched droning talk shows putting on exhibitions for the confused, disillusioned, and clearly uneducated of society. It provided a pleasant reminder that their lives were not in the same disorder. Peg gave her first lesson in make-up, took her along each and every time for family shopping, navigated her way around the kitchen, and encouraged Maddie in her artistic endeavors. She had been scolded and punished on the rarest of circumstances. She had never been spanked. Life was good! She could ride her bike freely on the way to her favorite local spot where she could take a dip to escape the summer heat. Home was always going to be there. She knew not all were so lucky.

She took a path cut through the woods to reach the watering hole which boasted what she thought in her youth to be the biggest tree in the world. It was a secluded attraction for the young and old alike; a rope hanging from its sturdiest branch. She was meeting Ralston Jr. whom carried the flattering distinction of best friend to Maddie. As she emerged from the woods Ral was in his usual spot, perched on a large rock in the shade. When their eyes met, they shared smiles of gentle recognition. As they relaxed in each other's company they would feel the mushy silt between their toes and the bright sun on their shoulders. The warm embrace of the clouded water was the summer ritual they sought after. It had been gifted to them again.

"Summer's almost over. Back to school."

It was not an enthusiastic observation from Maddie, but in general, reality had a way of dodging enthusiasm altogether. "Middle school. Jeez, it's going to be a lot different."

Maddie agreed, yet she seemed to worry much less than her friend. "Do you remember when we were in second grade, Ral? We were in Ms. Beatty's class. That seems like such a long time ago."

"It was a long time ago. My father says to just wait. When we grow up we'll get old and die before we know it. Pretty scary, huh?"

Maddie pondered this assumption a moment, but with her usual introspection, she became a little skeptical. "But your dad's not dead yet. How would he know?"

"My father knows everything." He reminded her with childlike innocence.

"My dad says that nobody knows everything, and no one ever will. It's impossible." She said with gentle reproach, slowly moving through the water, paying attention to every wrinkle on the surface.

Ral could not quite piece together what she meant, but neither did she. It was an existential concern which did not concern them at present, but was a piece of wisdom that would remain in the corner of their psyches until they eventually expired. It made Ral think about Johnston McCreeley as a father. With assets and expenditures compared side-by-side Johnston McCreeley was the pauper and Ralston Golden Sr. was the prince in a pure Machiavellian sense. Ralston Sr. owned a thriving multi-faceted business, and in many ways, the people that worked for him, since their quality of life depended on the very success of the business. Men like Johnston McCreeley were fed and sheltered by captains of industry. Men like Ralston Golden Sr., as well as Ralston Jr., had heard this with the repetition of a rising sun. The message was clear and forceful—always be the owner. Always have faceless dependents carrying out the breadth of your personal schemes and dreams. Never be a Johnston McCreeley. There was no money in it. Of course, Ralston Golden Sr. knew everything, so it was completely unnecessary to consult outside sources. Ralston Golden Jr. always heard his father's voice bouncing between his ears: 'Just listen to me, son.'

"I wish I had your father." Ral's confession took Maddie by surprise as she dunked her steaming head underwater, bobbing back up refreshed. She was incredulous to hear such an admission from her best friend.

"Why, Ral? Your dad's rich. I think that's great!" She optimistically pointed out, though she instantly felt guilty for downplaying her own father in a sense. "I mean, don't get me wrong. I'll keep my dad. But what's wrong with your dad?"

Ral found Maddie a disarming force in his young life. He felt he could tell her anything. As they grew up, he began having brand new feelings that were on the rise and foreign to his being. They shared a closeness he desired beside him indefinitely with the covetous nature of a true believer. "It's the logs I have to keep. Numbers, and more numbers. Budgeting, tracking, percentage growth, projected growth, targeting, overhead, margins, income, revenue, tightening up, trimming the fat, squeezing the lemon—every last drop."

He lost her after logs, but instinctively chalked it up as one of his many peculiarities. The grand meaning behind it all was none of her concern. She listened and found a way to relate as a friend is expected to do. "Then the profit. Always the profit. Never enough. Never too much. Supply and demand. The only way is to supply the demand, and never work for the supply because that never leads to ownership. There is always a way for more consumption. It's all through pure will."

She was barely listening at that point, merely nodding with some show of complicit approval. She did notice he was doing this odd recitation more often. She felt a chilled darkness at his expression which was devoid of any kind of feeling. "And everyone is to be manipulated. Real wealth is never built on honesty. It's through a secret and a smile. Always move forward. Tell them it's what they need, even if they don't need it. Even if no one needs it. Take ownership of them. It's all that people respect."

It finally dawned upon her that these were the lessons of his father. Not only did Ral have to maintain a stellar performance at school; he was expected to be even sharper at home. When did he have time to imagine? He brought his near diatribe to heel and left the door open for her to probe. "Is that what your dad says?"

If she only knew, he thought. His sleeping dreams seemed to be his only solace, besides his precious time with Maddie. "Like I'm stupid. Like I'll never understand. But I understand! How could I forget? He won't stop! That's why I said your father is different."

In her eyes, Ral had everything he wanted. He had a theatre room in his house with leather recliners, a popcorn machine, and a slushy station. His big back yard housed plenty of room for him and his golden retriever to run freely. He had a fresh water pool fitted with a yellow slide and a bubbly hot tub for the winter months. The tarmac court could accommodate both tennis and basketball, paired next to a silky sand volleyball court. Ral's luxurious lifestyle clearly eclipsed her own, but Johnston had once told her that being rich came in many ways. She had a room with a door that could be closed, a backyard, a dog, parents that loved her, and the comfort of knowing none of that would change. Each day they woke up together as a family in a cycle of safety. That's what made them rich. It wasn't only tied to their bank account.

"He might be a little different, but your dad still loves you." She said, handing her best attempt at reassurance. His vacant stare showed her it was falling on deaf ears. It left her to think there were even darker scenarios in the background. "Does he hit you?"

He was not deaf any longer as the reel of his mind began to roll, uncut. Flashes of harsh discipline for leaving his baseball glove in the hallway, his hat on the dining table, his shoes in the theatre room, or the bathroom mirror stained with toothpaste splatter. Under absolutely no circumstances should urine splatter on the inner edge of the toilet bowl. A slip of the mind or an unintended accident would never be permitted. If Ral did not retain his rigorous business instruction, Ralston Sr. coined it an intellectual crime. Never was a belt used. It was a pegging slap to the back of the head, a forceful grip around the back of the neck, or simply a condescending verbal lashing which made him feel smaller than an ant. It was coldly meant to build him up, but really only served to break him down. Maddie could see her friend was programmed to flinch. It saddened her to know someone could have so much, yet still carry around such dark pain. She disliked the symptoms of growing up just as much as he did. A little kidding around was now in order.

"Do you want my dad to beat up your dad?" She smilingly offered, as a smile finally swept across his face. She couldn't see that he was imagining the rough and tumble blue-collar Johnston McCreeley pummeling the dapper Ralston Golden Sr. with a life lesson. Maddie was wrong to think she had pulled him out of the darkness, but she had been convinced. "Come on! Let's see how high we can get on the swing!"

They walked up the rocky muddied bank to climb the trunk of the bigger-than-life tree where a thick knotted rope hung from its sturdiest limb. Both thought about being grown up one day, which they equated to being free. For Maddie, it was to travel and explore the world, leaving a piece of her heart in the house she was raised. For Ralston Jr., he would no longer be at the mercy of his father; a shadow too large to escape. Neither had the slightest clue there was very little mercy in the world of grown-ups. In that moment, on a summer day, they would swing from the rope as high as they could, let go, and crash into the murky water. And one day, if they grew up, they would long for the innocence of the swing that sent them soaring freely through the air.

***ZZZ…***

Monty Lincoln's Fellowship of the Enlightened was thriving with new members; all of whom were enamored by his ambiguous and esoteric message centered on self-recognition in the present. It was no longer a congregation at Margaret Buckey's city estate where he first spoke on the character of God, subtly deflating the myth that God and humankind were to meet at one time on any dimensional plane whatsoever. God was not at the ticket stand granting admission to the splendors of eternity exclusively for those special persons who had adhered to a strict regimen of stylized morality throughout their lives. Neither was God to be limited to so narrow a reality as being the perpetual teller at the Department of Motor Vehicles—'now serving 200,369,245, 123, 666.' What a waste!

It was obvious to Monty that God lived without limits. Thus, so should the lot of humanity. Fully conscious of the fragile timeframe of human existence, it perplexed him to see people content to follow the order of manmade morality with all its rigid disgust for the carnal pleasures. That was to be the sacredness of the Fellowship of the Enlightened, which is why Monty had to purchase a property northeast of San Francisco where they could privately invest in the exploration of this carnal existence. Monty was not in it for the money—only the movement.

He had lain the foundation by putting forward a simple set of tenets. The first was INSIGHT: the ability to look inside, outside, and all around, gripping good and evil, knotting them together to extract what was needed for the moment at hand. The second was the keen OBVSERVATION of others: learning the credible responses when engaged with different personalities so as to induce the reaction most favorable to one's own ambition. The third was the advanced use of the DIALECTIC once engaged in debate to effectively refute what one thought irrefutable, thus humbling the engaged so it appeared they were naturally below one's own intellectual grade; and in course, would do one's bidding. The fourth was recognition and complete ACTUALIZATION of the finer senses. Sex was to be a transcendental natural art as it undoubtedly was the animator of their very beings. The natural appetite was never to be suppressed, but unleashed with an unbridled passion that reverted to forgotten times when decency didn't exist between creatures of the same species. That was where heaven resided. Finally, all of this led to LAUGHTER being the healer of bruised emotions and the natural lubricant of social harmony, accompanied by the spirit of music. The ethos put in place an individual among the collective with advanced knowledge, few personal restrictions, and all of it culminated in the lifelong pursuit of pleasure. It was these concepts that embodied the character of their God.

Monty Lincoln's designed procession was in stark contrast to the traditional church, synagogue, mosque, or any other place erected for worship. The procession was a feisty, far from dull body that formed not out of duty, but out of pure craving. They would file into the main foyer of what had once been a Mormon outpost, fitted with a large dining table topped with a panorama of delectable eats. Three-tiered towers of summer sausage, cheese, and crisp sesame crackers. The ripest batch of grapes from the Sonoma Valley were surrounded by a cornucopia of other fresh fruits. Nut mixes, moist vegetables, and pita bread to be dipped in fresh hummus. The center of the table housed silver-plated trays topped with Atlantic oysters on the half shell, stone crab, tiger shrimp, and slices of Sea Bream sashimi beautifully contrasted against the light-emanating ice. Closer to the end of the dining table was sliced prime rib presented in a wheel formation with some warm au jus and butter sauce in the center of the wheel. Sliced tenderloin was drizzled with a fire-roasted tomato and garlic sauce that gave it a succulent deep red hue from skin to skin. Roasted quail rounded out the meats sitting in a silky Port wine sauce. Servers dressed in black rotated around the Fellowship, making certain everyone was handed a shot of whiskey once appetites were satiated. It was meant for the toast they knew was soon to come from Sir Monty Lincoln.

No, it was no ordinary church. Children were not permitted under any circumstances. There was no clapping, smiling, uniformed choir backed by a band to usher in the praise and worship as lyrics to the holy jingle were projected on the wall. First-time visitors were not singled out as the Fellowship was only attended by members and their carefully chosen guests. There would be no solicitation for a tithe sandwiched between the worship and the sermon. Only a life-sized ceramic piggy bank was placed in the corner of the foyer. Above it hung a sign that read 'At Your Leisure.' There was to be no pressure. Only a release thereof.

Monty Lincoln listened to the bustle of his Fellowship as he adjusted his manicured appearance to emerge as the host with the most. He was to lead in the celebration of life, liberty, and the pursuit of happiness among like-minded individuals who wanted to find heaven not in the clouds, but in the very spaces with which they tread. He swung open the doors to a round of cheering and clapping. He strutted up to the dining table, plucked a tasty piece from each section with relish and arrogant delight, quivering over a joy only meant for the night. He fancifully snatched a shot of whiskey out of seemingly nowhere and held it high to bring proper attention to the matter at hand.

"Dear Fellows! I have not the faintest doubt that merriment and pleasure are the finest qualities life has to tout. Never be convinced this joy must remain at a distance, intermittent and constantly interrupted by weaker forces. Take comfort in knowing that in these hours, in this place, we fly above the flock!" He belted out as the loose skin from his chin jiggled with intensity. He spun around as if to connect with each of them through the eyes. "To our revelry! To our recovery and eventual mastery of the realm we call Reality! May we make it our own! Do what thou wilt!"

They took down the spirit with ease as it initiated the release. Quickly they abandoned the foyer, spilling down the back steps of the homestead onto the pebbled torch-lit pathway leading into the redwoods where interwoven energies of nature and fire would spur them to an indulgence that was to be characterized as sinful, deliberate, and excessive to some eyes.

*

It was certainly the view of Dane Shavers within the foliage on the outskirts of the property, based in a rental car for his operation. This night, he was determined to infiltrate the Fellowship of the Enlightened to expose their conniving and wicked ways. He was a pudgy middle-aged shock jock, journalist, documentary filmmaker, political activist, and self-proclaimed revealer of a secret world order bent upon subjugating the breadth of humanity under the rule of an elite and wealthy few. He paid his cameraman well. Only a select few could withstand the ferocity of his convictions as the weight and application of them over time would eventually tilt the balance of power to exclusively serve the unseen many. Or so that was the applied theory Dane Shavers employed to achieve that lofty end.

The camera was rolling in the darkness of the rental car so as not to compromise their position. Like children hiding in a closet, spying on their parents, Dane Shavers began in whispers; "Here we are in front of a compound where diabolic and secret processions take place. The group calls themselves the Fellowship of the Enlightened, but really they're just another ritualistic cult having grand designs for bending the world to their will. Of course, we were denied access. So now, I, Dane Shavers, will once again risk everything to expose the truth. Here we go again into the belly of the beast." Dane Shavers said, never having asked for access in the first place.

Trespassing onto the property could not have been easier. The flimsy wired fence failed to follow down a ditch line, so crouching and crawling under constituted the extent of the daring infiltration, which Dane Shavers ordered to be cut from the official version. They began to make their way through the dense redwood trees, and it wasn't long before they could see the shadowy glow of figures in motion as the blaze of the fire pulsated through the night. The closer they drew near the more they could hear the festive Fellowship's music, laughter, and spontaneous howls of unabashed banter.

With eyes centered on the approaching scene, disregarding where they stepped, they were both suddenly tripped to the ground. Adrenaline rushed through their bodies, believing they had been discovered. The camera kept rolling as they looked over frightfully to identify what had sent them tumbling to the ground. To their consternation, it was a man and a woman fucking very hard; she on top and he on bottom. The tumbling trespassers failed to make them skip a beat as Dane sheepishly whispered, "I'm so sorry!"

Without the slightest acknowledgment of their presence, or even remotely wondering who they might be, they simply cackled in the warmth of their sexual embrace and continued to fuck away the pain in a tingly state of ecstasy. Dane Shavers bewilderingly moved on, surprised they had not even flinched. He turned to his counterpart, eagerly asking, "Did you get that?"

A simple nod sent them forward, but now special attention would be paid to what might be at their feet. Steadily they approached the flames where they heard music being played. They set up their position crouched down at the edge of the wood line just a stone's throw from the blazing bonfire. Situated around it was the Fellowship engaged in a delightful soirée. All were drinking, some were smoking, and the whole lot was bathed in excitement. For a solid hour Dane Shavers recorded their antics. An impromptu band had formed to one side of the fire: a mountain dulcimer, a harp, bagpipes, a chime board, a wooden flute, and a bongo drum were played in unison which soundly permeated a haunting rendition of what Dane Shavers would have placed in a time of barbarism. The cameraman, in his view, thought it was pretty damned cool. Women danced around the unusual ensemble like mystical woodland nymphs in Dane's mind, but the cameraman just thought they were hippies on a high that he wouldn't have minded joining in the least.

Men were kissing men, women on women, and men on women: friends, lovers, or nothing at all. They would rotate to a new partner without the slightest apprehension, leading Dane Shavers to speculate whether they were all gay, or if it was one big game of dare. Some were in elaborate costume like Egyptian royal garb, resplendent in serpent headdress in the real tradition of the Pharaohs. There was a Druid in full cloak, methodically circling the fire with a single lit candle in hand. Then there was the Native wrapped in buffalo skin, sprinkled with turquoise, donning a headdress of feathers from a mighty bird, stomping and chanting his way round the fire. In the shadows of the woods men and women relieved themselves without care. While the cameraman devised ways to eventually join them once this job was done, Dane Shavers remained fearful as he wildly imagined himself being tied to a stake and mounted atop the flames as a sacrifice to some demonic force. He had never been much of a partier.

"Can you believe this? I wonder what they're planning." Dane Shavers whispered, as his paid accomplice could not have cared less, seeing nothing nefarious in the scene. Dane began to focus on identifying a single member. "Who is the leader?"

His eyes ceased scanning when they naturally locked on Monty Lincoln, who appeared to Dane Shavers as certainly an advocate, if not the incarnate form of the Devil himself. Perhaps it was the red breast coat with the black satin collared shirt underneath, with arms folded across his chest, looking strangely stately. The yellow and orange of the fire drew sinister shadows upon his twirled mustache, pointed goat-tee, and slicked-back silver hair. Most eerie was the feeling that Monty Lincoln was staring straight at him, holding a menacing grin, effectively freezing Dane Shavers to the spot. It ridiculed, 'I see you. There is no place for you to hide. We will have dealings one day.'

The stare-down, whether real or imagined, was finally broken as a Fellow handed Monty Lincoln a bull horn. He placed the tip to his lips, tilted it up to the night sky, and blew a sound that travelled through the thin air, serving as a call to unite at the foot of the fire. This was the display of organization which Dane Shavers wanted to see. Tumbling out of the woods next to them was the couple they had stumbled over, still fastening their clothes and giggling along the way. Dane Shavers would now hear this man speak, and then would make a run for it himself, for he felt more afraid than he could ever remember.

As he watched them all gather at the base of the fire, Monty Lincoln patiently waited for them to settle with a smile. It was not a condescending 'sit down children'—but rather—'gather round my friends of the same mind.' A server in black approached Monty Lincoln with a white candle standing erect on a golden stand. From his breast pocket he pulled a match to light the wick. Once the flame was healthy the server shuffled away. Monty Lincoln's smile held steady as he began to address the eager and anticipating congregation.

"Hear ye Enlightened! It appears our God has a sense of humor. How fortunate the world is to have us. The character of our God is bountifully benevolent. It is not the character of a jealous benefactor expecting sacrifice after sacrifice, and the constant recognition through worship for its very existence. How could we ever be relieved of God's debt? Only in the final moment when you finally return to God, of which you never knew in the first place? Take comfort! Here is your heaven! Here are your friends! Here are your lovers! Rejoice!"

He paused as they sent out hoorahs, hoorays, and the like; blissfully lost in their inebriation. They primed him to continue. "This joy you feel in our present intercourse is not a fluke only to be summoned when we gather in this place. You are on the ceaseless hunt to find it in the monotony of your work, the gnawing spirit of your boredom, and the influence you wield through all you meet. Do not reveal the secret. Steer them to the source, and let them drink of it on their own. It is the only way we can truly value the gold we discover in our lives. Your lives are not meant to be spent from season to season, grind to grind, just to escape once a year and return to continue dying in the same place you were born. No!

"You are to scale the mountain to take in the Divine's work, sail the oceans where Father Time has no place, and draw deep into the past for the knowledge to face the fear of death—that wretched spoiler of a good time—because the more we know, the less we fear the unknown. What is free from our control, let it be! We will shine through the dungeons of ignorance until we finally burn out. This our calling!"

Dane Shavers could hear every carefully chosen word and every deliberate gesticulation which had them spellbound. For a fleeting moment, in one of his many times of self-doubt, he wished he could become one of them. However, he bore a clear responsibility and an other-worldly mandate to bring ruin to those who could only plot the perpetual benefit of a selective few. It was their exotic lust for power and the ultimate immunity from law itself which brought Dane Shavers to a place where he was putting all the pieces together. Monty Lincoln had already given him ample reason to classify them as the usual suspects, and he would give Dane Shavers just a bit more as he lofted the candle into the night sky.

"This represents us all. We burn. We flicker; just as the stars. We are made of them, but we are not like them. A star does not consciously know it will eventually expire. It just knows to burn bright and shine through the recesses of space until the light falls on our simple eyes. We do not shine like that. We radiate our inquisitive pathos to envelop our entire being. Steady as this solitary flame stands on this wick, so must the knowledge we acquire and use to the greatest advantage. This is something exclusive to our creation. If this wasted potential were ever to be quantified; it would be the most disturbing proof of our primacy. But not us, Enlightened! Not us!

"We see the forest from the trees, deeply feel the pangs and pitfalls of the moment, and hear the echoes of history calling us to reach further into the dark where the precious light of knowledge hides from our groping and desperate hands. We have a limited time to act. It is not our duty. It is our fate! This flame represents you all as individuals, ruled by time, and sucked back into the fold of this mysterious universe—just as that of a star!"

Monty Lincoln blew out the candle as the smoke wafted and disintegrated into the night air. He looked over them all as it was brought to bear how truly small they were. He turned his back to them, tossing the candle into the fire, and raising his hands to the sky. "You alone were that single flame, but we are this raging fire! Consume! Drown! And in this lifetime, burn bright until the final exhaustion—DEATH!"

As the firelight danced off Dane Shaver's eyes, and the Enlightened spun back into their revelry, he had the distinct feeling this was something more than just a cult. It dawned upon him that the Fellowship of the Enlightened would now be his chief concern. "Did you get that?"

"Yes—I did."

Accommodations were none too shabby. Not only was there the aristocratic grandeur to behold, but also the natural world as the castle was neatly nestled within the deep green of the Carpathian Mountains. The medieval relic had been preserved through ages of lore, mostly left untouched by the violent stages of humanity. Its original purpose was a defensive fortress, but nowadays it was purely an estate museum for the eyes of paying tourists. A two-lane highway ran alongside the castle as those of modernity arrived one-by-one to take in the grounds. They would inhabit Bran Castle for twelve solid weeks.

The knocker on the front door was a smooth face of human royalty wrapped tightly around by coy fish and the tentacles of what seemed to be some kind of mythological sea monster. When each of them used it they could feel the hollowness of the inside. When the heavy oak door creaked open—no matter what level of intelligence—the same mysterious force slapped them in the face. The castle's timeless allure provided the ambiance that would produce the desired results for the experiment called *Conversion*.

Bran Castle had been purchased and renovated by the Hapsburg Dynasty: that of Queen Marie and Ferdinand I. Art collected by the Queen the world over had been strewn across the walls, but any trace of that class had been safely removed to a secure location for the filming. The timeless estate, which was the inheritance of Archduke Dominic of Austria-Tuscany, was to be refitted under the direction of Joshua Bannister. He turned to sharp colors that nearly seared the unsuspecting retina. In came the neon pop art of Warhol, and the splattered paint on canvas resembling Pollack. The movie posters rounded out the gross transformation from one age to another. The furniture was squared off and easily assembled, resting on bright shag rugs meant to protect the classic hardwood floors. Gone were the handcrafted antiques never meant to be buried in the sands of time, original paintings from a time when form and likeness were paramount, uniquely lifelike sculptures of all sizes, hand-carved thrones of intricate design never to be replicated, heavenly-inspired canopy beds, and the displayed weaponry and battledress of defenders and conquerors alike at a time when the fortress had first been completed in the year 1388. For twelve weeks its royal lineage would be completely desecrated. Frank Winkleshten had the bankroll of the present royalty in existence within the borders of the United States. Archduke Dominic of Austria-Tuscany was going through some hard times, and with his nose pointed high in the air, he was to be complicit in the defilement so long as he received a slice of the American royalty.

The castle had been gutted of its decorative character, but the luster of its significance had not been lost altogether. They had their own space and their own view, which was an impressive first for them all. Joshua Bannister felt the Romanian late spring was the perfect setting to get the juices flowing. It didn't take long for the camera to start rolling and the introductions to be made with a few choice questions.

Gay J was getting situated in the Tea House erected on the castle grounds as a spot to view the estate pond in comfort. The question was simple and straightforward. *When did he first know?*

"I don't remember when I started liking dudes. It just happened. When straight dudes go through the phase of being scared of the pussy, I guess that's when I was scared of the dick. Just like they got over it, I did too."

Tommy Bloom was setting up camp in Princess Illeana's house on the Estate Gardens. He was pinning pictures of Mindy, his beloved Yorkshire terrier, to a piece of particle board. Pinning up pictures of Gay J had been forbidden under the direction of Joshua Bannister. The same question was posed. *When did he know?*

"Gymnastics…and the locker room. Especially the locker room. But, officially, the Swedish foreign exchange student named Bjorn Togelid." He confessed with a big, warm smile. "Gosh, he had a big secret. He was a lot of fun."

Gay J and Tommy Bloom were used to sleeping apart when both were on tour, but never in the same proximity. In fact, Joshua Bannister considered it imperative they were never to cross paths with one another, and if so, they were to be hustled away. It would undoubtedly put the experiment at risk of falling apart. The imperative was to isolate; then infiltrate. As they continued to settle into their quarters another essential question was posed. *How had they come to this point?*

"Momma worked hard. Daddy nowhere in sight. Grew up on the streets, studied the hustle, pen and pad, plugged in the mic, and followed the beat. The rest is history." Gay J quickly summed up without a misstep.

"Mostly failure got me here. I wanted to be an Olympian, but I guess it's not so bad. I have J. I hope we keep striving for the gold medal in our hearts." Tommy Bloom mused, already showing off his cheesy and genuine personality with another big smile.

Joshua Bannister had a different question for the ladies who were also settling in for the twelve week haul. Bridgette Mahoney had landed King Ferdinand's personal dining room. The competition aspect and the gauge of their attraction would come out first. Technically, and even more so contractually, the ladies were to distribute their energies equally to both Gay J and Tommy Bloom. *Which of the two did they favor?*

"First off, I'm going after Tommy. He seems to be a softy. He's built the way I like—bulky—and he has a warm smile. Those are the same attributes I have!" Bridgette Mahoney answered, as bubble gum popped between her perfect white teeth. She swung her hip out unconsciously as was customary in her former profession, always meant to charm on the sidelines of a Sunday football game.

As for Shonda Murano, she landed the music room housing a cozy fireplace beside an open window looking down into the castle courtyard. She was also a professional strutter-of-her-stuff, with fine almond skin, carrying herself as a delicate beauty that gravity somehow could not take hold of. Now it was time to strut her stuff for *Conversion*. "J-E-R-E-M-Y Boland! He's not going to be Gay J with me—just J. I think we'd look good together. He's got some star power. That's what turns me on."

Monica Brooks was setting herself up in the Biedermeier drawing room where plans were once put to paper for the defense of the boundaries stretching out over the lands buttressing the fortress. "It's hard to say who I would choose. Elegance and grace sometimes only happens on the ice. I don't know if either of them skate. I guess I'll just have to pick the better dancer."

"I'm fucking them both!" Barbie Red bluntly stated with grounded conviction, setting up her things in the Logia where all the royal contemplation was once burrowed through. "It's what I do. These other bitches are going to hold out, pretend their pussies are so special, and then play like prudes in the sack if they even get that far. I'm a professional. That's the difference."

Heather Douglas was looking out the window of the yellow room, a.k.a. the Castellans' room, housing vaulted ceilings. It was big and empty; kind of like the way she felt. She turned to the camera with almost fearful eyes which were certainly anxious. "Why did I come on this show?"

They were all set into place. The question came back to the guys. *What did they think the progression was going to look like?*

Gay J smiled wide. "A wild time that's gonna be off da chain."

Tommy Bloom shook his head; more than a little concerned. "It's going to be a big mess. That's for sure."

The degrees of artificial separation were dialed in. The women would stay in the castle where they would also dine together, meant to hasten the competition and draw them into a flourishing gossip feast. The men were set on the Estate Gardens where they would exclusively play host to the princesses in the castle. The microcosm of illusion was about to begin its gnawing debacle of forced interaction.

Shonda Murano was the first invited to Gay J's tea house for an introduction. Once inside, they sat together on the couch and talked, attempting to discover the similarities existing between them. Both were celebrities in their own right—that was one. It was the common thread between them all. Joshua Bannister knew it was all he needed.

"The beats is tight. I'll give you that." Shonda Murano complimented to signal that criticism was coming up next. Looking down on her painted nails she was sincere in her liking of his beats, but she wasn't a fan of the lyrical content. The graphic and often demeaning sexual aspersions was reason enough, but it was also something else. "It's just…"

He waited patiently for her to finish, and though he failed to give a damn what she thought either way, he probed, "What? Tell me. I wanna know."

Shonda Murano had not been born a lingerie model. She was raised in Oakland to a low-income family in a neighborhood having plenty of foul-mouthed ghetto boys flapping their gums. Gay J was lengths ahead of them in smarts, but he constantly used the word most popular among the flapping gums.

"You throw around the word nigga on every track."

"Yeh, so?" He tossed back like a hot potato.

His truculence took her aback as she realized they had veered onto the wrong road. That didn't stop her from making her point using a careful voice of pleading. "Can't we just move past it? It's just so hood."

Gay J nodded his head and licked his thick lips, knowing all too well where she was coming from. It still surprised him, that coming from the wrong side of the tracks, she could not understand the reasons as to why the word stuck around with such staunch stubbornness.

"Only a select few still use that word. Hood niggas like me, and racist white motha' fucka's like them.

"*We* say it to reduce the power of the word. To take over ownership of it. To kill the negative effect it has on our psyche.

"*They* say it to convince themselves and others that we're not as human as they are.

"*We* use it to show them that we are human, and they don't have ownership over that word. We're not afraid of them, or the word. Believe it or not, somebody, somewhere, is calling your pretty ass a nigga right now."

Her cause was instantly shaken with both thoughtless on where to go from there. After a momentary slough through the wreckage she wisely decided to just have another cognac and change the subject. She had gotten the first crack at Gay J. It had been a bumpy introduction, but so would be the rest.

*

On horseback and slowly exploring the Estate Gardens was Tommy Bloom and Bridgette Mahoney. It was an overcast day delivering the chances of an afternoon shower, which was only one of the worries on Tommy Bloom's plate. He was riding on an animal he had been introduced to once as a boy of nine years. Even as a full-grown adult the confidence to handle such an animal had not been given legs. Bridgette Mahoney, on the other hand, was completely at ease atop her steed. Not a surprise since it was her idea. Tommy Bloom only hoped she didn't have the need for speed. The horse at the time of nine years-old went fast, and the ride ended with a nice knot on his head.

"Have you ever ridden horses?" She asked.

"Once when I was a kid. It was actually a terrifying experience. As you can tell, I was never a country boy—or a country man for that matter." He blustered out, as his hulking frame swayed in the saddle. He did his best to appear natural, even brandishing a shaky smile, but she wasn't buying any tickets to the show.

"You don't have to *be* country to *get* country. Either way, I still like the look of a well-built stud in the saddle. It's my favorite!" She pined with a wink and a smile as the bubble gum still clacked in her mouth. Truthfully, she thought her well-built stud in the saddle with his long blonde mane looked more like the hero on the cover of a grocery store romance novel. However, that wasn't the matter at hand. She had a job to do.

"Well…" he nervously began, sensing the flirting flung his way. He wanted to have fun, but the results-driven expectations instead made him divert to awkwardness. With cheesy uncertainty, he continued, "I try my best…uh…to look my very best!"

With a cringe of embarrassment for him she broke eye contact to look off at the clouds that seemed to rest on top of the green mountains surrounding them. He ridiculed and criticized himself while waiting for the page to turn between them. Her attention came back from the clouds after the dust settled from his verbal flop. "So how are you taking it in so far? It's beautiful, isn't it?"

"It's breathtaking!" He burrowed forward with full enthusiasm, which really wasn't there. She could see it went beyond awkwardness. He was genuinely bothered. It was their second day and the jitters were everywhere. "It's just that I feel a little boxed in."

"I understand. People like me and you are always on the run. It feels weird to pump the brakes and stop—quite literally—in another place and time. Just relax, Tommy. Enjoy yourself! That's what this is all about!" She offered with an upbeat tempo meant to boost his spirits as only a leader of the cheering section could do.

"Yeh, I guess you're right." He conceded in a defeated tone. He was doing his best to feel more at ease. The real problem was that he couldn't stop thinking about Gay J.

She was ready for something drastic to break his mold of awkwardness. With the team down and only a few left on the clock, it was time to get motivated. "Hey! Just got an awesome idea! Let's see how fast these engines run!"

Yes, there was a clear path running in front of them for a good stretch, but in no way did he want to get behind her terrifying idea. With his face filled with panic, he pleaded, "I really like this pace."

She could not be diverted, enthusiastically yelling, "Come on, Buckaroo! Live a little! Yee-haw!"

As her horse darted off and his followed her lead, he felt he had to correct her misnomer before disaster struck. "It's Buccaneer!"

In a full gallop he knew to hang onto the reins, tuck his heels to the body, and just go with the jerky flow. The only problem was that he wanted none of it. Bridgette Mahoney was just ahead of him, glancing back like these were the best moments in life. He looked like it was one of the worst. His gallop was not going to change into a stride, which made Tommy Bloom recall a time he rode a giant wooden roller coaster. It was when he threw his back out while simultaneously vomiting. It had been impossible to dismount from the roller coaster, but this horse was a different story. Like opening the door to a car heading towards the edge of a cliff he had to jump and tumble into the clear as best he could. He swung his leg over to achieve the half-saddle position. It was going to hurt, but that failed to serve as a deterrent. He attempted to leap off the galloping horse to safe and stable ground, but instead his stout frame pegged the ground and stuck to it like a javelin. The short fall stole all the air he had, leaving him gasping. The good news? He was off the horse!

Incredulously, Bridgette Mahoney circled around and came upon his motionless body as he kept his eyes to the sky, recapturing his breath. "Gaw-lee, Tommy, are you okay?"

"Need a minute." He grunted.

"Why didn't you just pull up on the reins?"

The obviousness of her question irked him, as it mixed the physical pain with the sting of humiliation. All he could do was wish for it all to be over. Of course, not without the promised booty. "I don't know, but what a bad idea!"

*

While Tommy Bloom was gingerly coming to his feet and limping away from his laughing horse where Bridgette Mahoney pretended to be genuinely concerned; inside the tea house Gay J was finding his groove. He was enjoying it so much more than his life partner. All he knew was that his phone was resting on the nightstand in Atlanta. He was given license to completely be himself without having to deviate for the sake of anyone: knit-picking producers, brand-powered sponsors, or wacky fans. Though he was in front of his biggest audience thus far, he couldn't feel any eyes upon him. There were no throngs of people packed tightly together, waving their hands and bodies to his beats as they reverberated off the walls. It was precisely why he blew up another line that wasn't going to get him any higher. It was cocaine's winning strategy. One was never enough.

"That's some real shit!" He confirmed, tapping his nostril as he sniffed it back for the drip. He swiped his finger across the surface of the silver tray and numbed his gums; just to get the full effect.

His guest was Barbie Red. They stood together in the bathroom with the door closed, only because it felt appropriate. She had smuggled in the drug to get a leg up on the competition, surmising a mutually shared dopamine dump would allow them to by-pass the shaky introductions. She had been right.

Her black leather pants wrapped tightly around a solid bum which had been conditioned by years of intense sexual intercourse. Her enhancements were precisely set in a violet blouse. Her jet-black hair was up in a bee-hive; the old-fashioned way. What she offered would be lain out crystal clear for the immediate taking.

"You do much white girl?" She seductively inquired, mainly referring to the cocaine, though she just happened to be a white girl too.

He got the hint, but wasn't taking the bait. "Naw, I'm into blunts. T-Bloom would never let me do this shit."

She edged closer to show off the plumpness of her glossy ruby red lips. Swaying over his lips like a magnet teasing the opposite charge, she softly said, "I would let you do anything you wanted. Does he let you do anything you want?"

She was a pro at innuendo, but he wasn't bucking just yet. He was just a man after all. "I'm daddy. I do what I like."

She was a mere inch away from him, poised to strike or be struck. She would be fine with either outcome. "And what do you like?"

"I'm gay and black. Naturally, I like dat ass."

"What do you think about this one?" She spun around, while maintaining eye contact as she backed it up for an open invitation. "Touch it."

It did look good wrapped up the way it was, feeling not a bit of shame as he gripped both hands around it. He was merely verifying its impressiveness. "You sho' is built right."

She rubbed her rump up and down on his crotch professionally. She could feel his manhood, but it lacked any reaction to her stimuli. She spun around to face him, intent upon pressing her tantalizing sexual abilities. She stared intensely into his eyes as she stroked his soft member that remained unresponsive; something she rarely encountered, even with supposed gay men. At times, a little soft-spoken dirty talk could arouse the most spooked of them. "I can make you cum, too."

Sexy was not her deficiency as he was undoubtedly turned on, but none of it was going to manifest itself physiologically. It had nothing to do with being gay. "Maybe so, but that's why T-Bloom don't let me do this shit. I just end up a wet noodle. Especially on *this* white. Woo…way too pure."

Having confessed that, he put his nose to the tray once again. She turned away knowing how true it could be. With cocaine, it was either the night of your life, or the night of nothing. The in-between was hard to come by. With her initial plan backfiring the only sensible thing left was to remain in the bathroom until all the blow was gone, which is exactly what they proceeded to do.

*

A hot tub churned on the backside of Princess Illeana's house where Tommy Bloom and Monica Brooks were taking in a crisp night for the first time, sipping champagne from crystal flutes. The gay wrestler and the former ice queen were finding it hard to loosen up. Tommy Bloom was just glad to dip in a vat of therapeutic comfort with his back was still sore from the fall. As the water bubbled and fizzed about they pretended to look at other things besides each other. When their eyes intersected a sheepish grin was exchanged, only to continue scanning a lot of nothing, while both searched for something to break the ice.

"How's your back feeling?"

The concern in her voice, whether phony or genuine, had to put a little crack in the block of ice. "I've had worse, but in the ring I can control the fall. This one wasn't rehearsed."

The crack failed to spider web. Flashes of Gay J kept popping up in his mind to utter annoyance. It was the times they were naked and nestled in the warmth of their bodies. A cool fan circling above in the cherished silence of a bedroom all their own; with the moonlight sticking to the wall from a cracked window on a night teetering between winter and spring. That was where he wanted to be for however long. Monica could sense the detachment as he cupped the foam dancing on the water with his hand like a child. Rightly so, the crack in the ice filled back in.

"I know how you feel." She sympathized as he somewhat snapped out of it, wondering if his drift to another place had been so obvious. "I see it all over you. You just want it all to be over."

A slight feeling of ease came over him as she seemed to relate in some way. With the recognition of a feeling unspoken, he could sense her kindness. The ice quickly began to melt. "Wow! You're actually spot-on."

"You were a gymnast, right?" She probed, as her facial features began to pronounce themselves in his eyes. She had the delicate look that if dropped on a hard surface, would shatter to pieces.

As she pressed further into the fray of his core, he cracked the door for her to look inside. "It was my dream. I wanted to be what you are. It never happened."

His honesty framed in defeat brought back her own shortfalls. As he cracked open the door, she would open a window. "Oh, it's not as great as you think. Your whole life becomes only about medals and podiums. The only one that ever mattered to me was the gold. I never got it—my obsession."

He decided to dig deeper, falling even further beneath her stature. "I was never even close to qualifying, much less competing."

He was crouching ever lower, hunched in inferiority. She had no plans to be the one to boost his spirits, but she decided to offer him a hand to bring him back to her level. "I can imagine you were good enough. A lot of people are. Sometimes the pieces just don't fall into place. They did for me until I missed that triple-axle. One piece out of place and it all falls apart."

Their shared moment of failure prompted Tommy Bloom to grab the champagne from the ice bucket on the ledge to fill their flutes. He had enough of the sullen and downtrodden exchange. Shedding the throw of defeat was what had to be done, and so a commemoration via toast was the best thing he could come up with. "To all the pieces falling into place just how we planned!"

Enthusiastically she met his flute, but the carefree enthusiasm was thwarted by the face of Joshua Bannister floating through her mind, demanding her to take further action. "And to us!"

Before she said it, just for a fleeting moment, Tommy Bloom had lost sight of why he was there in the first place. After all, it wasn't to make friends. The ice they had melted somewhat returned to block form. All he could do was meet her glass with a fake chuckle and an empty smile. "Right."

*

On a fine Romanian morning Heather Douglas was walking up to Gay J's door carrying her usual anxiety over the fiasco in its beginning stages. She was beyond timid; like a child uninterested in social interaction through fear of the unknown. Perhaps those suffocating days in the well left a lasting impression. Stepping out of her safe zone became a dark realm where forces could gobble her up until the light of rescue shined down on her stained face. Either way, Joshua Bannister could not have cared less. She was on contract. Inaction of pursuit was a breach of that contract.

She lightly knocked on the front door as it creaked open. There in the living room wearing oversized pink headphones resembling those worn by an aircraft controller, plaid boxer shorts, a wife-beater, and knee-high baseball socks, was Gay J. He was shuffling around in the process of running through some new lyrics over some fresh shock-soaked beats, putting a new puzzle together for his next LP, completely oblivious to her presence.

*Fuck-a-butt, what?*
*Fuck-a-butt, who?*
*Push it on through when I hear the sound of the boom*
*Rip away the fruit that comes from the loom*
*J got somefin' fo you ass comin' real fuckin' soon*
*Gettin' so deep, make Sinatra wanna croon*

His head suddenly ticked sideways when she came into his peripheral. She stood there like she had just been pulled from a well: shocked and disoriented. Attempting to crack a smile, only a look of fear came through. Gay J was used to that. Not every day did people come across a big gay black rapper lacking femininity in every outward way. He had always taken it in stride. Looking her up and down he judged that if Shonda Murano was the epitome of glitzy runway class and Barbie Red of sexual abundance sliding down a pole; then Heather Doulgas was the hard-working single mother letting her beauty shine in moments only she would allow. She was the woman at the grocery store walking slowly down the aisle, but highly noticeable to every man walking down the same one. In awful places like the DMV, or waiting areas in general, she was the mysterious focus for a man trying to pass the time with a pleasant view. Despite the simple warmth she exuded, Gay J still liked fucking with people.

"You gonna stand there looking crazy, or pour us a stiff one?" He asked, bringing the headphones around his neck, knowing for sure his brainstorming session had come to an end.

She had just woken two hours beforehand. She was not a drinker, much less one that enjoyed stiff ones. "It's ten o-clock in the morning."

Her recognition of time fell on deaf ears as his routine was set in stone long before he came to Bran Castle. He threw her a smile, and said, "I like a solid buzz before lunch. It makes my afternoon nap better."

She inwardly admitted there was a tangible shred of reason behind his proposition. She had been there nearly a week, practicing avoidance, and saying almost nothing. She was told that approach had to end. What kept her going before she came on the show was the constant routine of work, home maintenance, and the raising of her child whom she missed dearly. With these strange new developments that would ultimately lead her and her son to a more comfortable life, she supposed a morning cocktail couldn't hurt. With a shrug of her shoulders to shake off the inhibition motherhood so staunchly upheld, she said, "Oh…why the hell not?!"

zzz...

"Not bad. Not bad at all." Wink said, pulling on his suspenders as they snapped back onto his chest. With so much programming to plow through it had become his unbeknownst tick relating to boredom. "How are they gelling? You think we'll eventually see some fireworks?"

Joshua Bannister was staring at the map projected from his brain, and approximately, they had gone a quarter of the way. "We're steering in the right direction. It will happen, and when it does, it will be live and uncut."

"We're taking a lot of flak for this one. We've got the Evangelicals screaming on one side and the gays on the other. And—of course—women." Wink noted with apathetic disdain, though Joshua Bannister knew those elements were the best kind of criticism for the show.

"If something is hated it's all the more likely to be watched by those who hate it." Joshua Bannister assured with plenty of experience in peddling useless entertainment consumed by the masses. Controversy was the main ingredient with human tones of either sex or violence. Wholesomeness, or any relic thereof, was wholly unattractive. Staying relevant meant measuring popular fervor and tipping the scales to the extreme. Conversion ensured that relevance. The only real problem Joshua Bannister faced was planning the next orchestrated chaos streaming into households. For inspiration, he usually just turned on the evening news.

"Didn't used to be like that. It's why I have you around, JB." Wink admitted, trying to remember what was next on the day's agenda. Yet another reason for having JB around. Wink simply couldn't keep up anymore.

"Are you ready for Doody?" JB reminded, as a look swept across Wink's face like a skunk had just sprayed the room.

"Today? No! The last face I wanted to see! Dammit!" Wink lamented, thinking of Bill Doody as he was: a spoiled and spiteful pundit on the wrong side of nearly every issue. His delivery was coarse and shallow; the minds of his viewership the same. The size of that viewership—massive. He thought the self-proclaimed master conservative must seriously be shaken if he was requesting a meeting with the top brass. Wink made it known to Bill Doody himself how he preferred never speaking to him under any circumstances, so this had to be important.

"Unfortunately, he's about to walk through the door." JB said, pressing a button on the digital switchboard. "Send in Mr. Doody."

Bill Doody walked in with a film of sweat over a pale, wrinkled face, nearing seventy years. The thin strands of hair studiously stuck to his scalp were dyed a golden brown, which was not even the original color from the days of a youthful Doody. It was meant to fool his audience, but the effect was also for his own self-perception. "Good afternoon, gentlemen. I won't waste your time. JB, if you want to hit play, we'll just dive right into this."

Their eyes flew to the screen as Malcolm Grace stood alone on a stage with a backdrop of people sitting and listening, holding up signs reading: CIVICS—FORWARD. He was laying out his macro-vision, methodically dialing up his personal fervor and charisma. Wink and JB had been fans of Malcolm Grace ever since he made a mockery of Bill Doody on his very own show some years back. It left Bill

Doody with a comically paranoid complex concerning Malcolm Grace, as if he were the absolute worst thing that could happen to the nation—some sort of apocalyptic nightmare.

"The principle difference between the Democrats and Republicans is the irreconcilable feud over the symbiotic relationship between the federal government and the state governments. It was exactly why the two parties came into existence, and remains the fundamental element of their continued survival. Division is the apex of their appeal and reasoning.

"The Democrats claim they want to take care of everyone. The Republicans feel they should only take care of their own. Re-distributing wealth for socio-economic balance in the utopian ideal on the one hand—holding the wealth close to home so it builds through the bloodlines for generations to come on the other. All of this is based on land valuation and property ownership. The common God they both worship is money. Both insist this is all in your best interest.

"Civics!" He yelled, cutting the flow of his reflection upon history off and snapping the crowd assembled before him, and those watching from wherever, back to modernity. "We wish to look people squarely in the eyes, and say, 'I am one of you!' In this age and in this time we should prosper together, because after all, like a partnership of mutual devotion, it one day dawns upon us that money cannot be the most important thing. It should be loyalty and trust! It's high time for a true relationship between the people and its representative government that has become the biggest business in the world. We are not its consumers! We are its citizens! This is the new era the Civics will usher in!"

The signs flapped behind him as the people smiled and clapped, but they knew he would not return the adoration as was customary. He was serious; filled with confidence built from enduring a long period of dysfunction. He was fed up, and showed it. Wink sat impressed, looking over to JB as to suggest, 'Wow, this guy may be the real deal.' JB simply nodded back as Malcolm Grace stood alone on another stage without the possibility of interruption or recourse on his views.

"Do not be fooled by the structured deception of the politically correct and how both parties attempt to wrap explosive and detrimental subject matter into a nice package, fitted with a shiny bow on top. Once upon a time—long ago—people spoke plainly with one another in the absence of smoking mirrors and fear-mongering aspersions. These days! Our days! Those same explosive and detrimental matters should be drug out into the open. Like those rambling in the bars and coffee shops, in the boardrooms where deals are struck, and in the beds we roll in! The Civics will not pander for the desired response, but will instead govern to the response of the people as was presented thoughtfully, without organized deceit!"

Another crowd erupted before him as he remained reserved and stoic, seemingly unmoved by their collective enthusiasm. JB was steadily garnering an edge of concern as he continued to watch. Malcolm Grace was striking a chord well beyond the tactics of a shrewd salesman. He was actually calling out the salesman's technique without selling his own definitive alternative. He was merely insisting they should no longer buy what was being peddled. In effect, he was calling for a boycott of the pervading political culture which kept people swimming in a pool of absolutes where only two options existed—good and evil; right and wrong. He continued to press his point outside under the sun of a cool fall day.

"What an embarrassing sham our political system has become. How conveniently it has been hailed that progress can only be achieved through the endless bickering of two—supposedly—diametrically opposed forces. Pick a side is what they insist!

"The current *modus operandi* is the machinery of two gears rotating, locking into one another, creating energy through controlled friction. The lubricant? Money. But what if you add a gear to the existing gears?" He offered, playing out the concept like he were placing the said gears in motion where he stood. "It is assured the controlled friction of three gears would generate greater positive force for greater efficient purpose. And make no mistake, this efficiency could not be generated without the reciprocal action of all three gears. The Civics aim to be that third gear to perpetuate a forward motion, which is exactly what the people of this great nation deserve!"

As Wink and JB grew all the more amused, further did Bill Doody slide into an existential funk. He had never forgotten, much less forgiven, when Malcolm Grace splashed on the public scene at the expense of his show. Malcolm Grace had to be stopped, but it seemed his little montage was not helping his case according to the amusement lit upon Wink's face. In the final scene Malcolm Grace's Civics had just wound down another round of applause. All that was left to do was punch it the rest of the way home.

"For too long there's been puppets in the White House, dinosaurs in the Senate blind to the disaster looming around the corner, a part-time House more interested in throwing barbs than devising meaningful legislation, and a tenured un-elected Supreme Court that is only a collaborator to the whims of this money-driven outlandish farce.

"Take heed! We are coming! The Civics are coming!" He shouted with a shake of his fist as the crowd raucously erupted, standing to their feet and displaying the reverence he aroused within them. "We will judge impartially at the peak of our wisdom, and then stand aside to usher in fresher perspectives! We will legislate full-time for optimal effect according to the specific needs affecting all of us, and we will lead from a base called the White House with tireless sacrifice until we are broken-down and miserable from carrying out our solemn duties for the general betterment of present and future generations! We're here to stay, people!"

Bill Doody's head sagged in panic as he dismissively waved his hand towards the screen, pleading, "Oh, turn it off! It's just a disaster!"

Wink and JB were puzzled at Bill Doody's wildly overt inability to bear the existence of Malcolm Grace. It was rewarding to see someone so flippant in his own spotlight regress into a full-blown fluster, driven by the most stubborn pride. "Oh, come on, Bill. What's so dangerous about this guy?"

Wink's question without any trace of concern forced a double-take from Bill Doody. *How could they not see it?* "Gentlemen…you must understand…he is the worst enemy to all of us. He's telling people to grow up, to think for themselves, to change the existing order! That existing order specifically benefits everyone sitting at this table. We dictate public opinion because we pit good against evil, right against wrong, conservatives against liberals, Democrats against Republicans. Without the public's blind obedience to this order, not only the Doody Report, but a large chunk of your programming will have to be re-thunk. I mean, re-thought. I don't know about you, but I don't like the looks of that playing field."

Wink could always spot Bill Doody's flawed and repugnant logic with its expectancy of an imminent doomsday. His concern for his own show was legitimate since Wink secretly was content to facilitate that downfall. His sinking into obscurity would be accelerated so that a youthful and energetic voice could be put in place to cleverly espouse the same winding confrontational rhetoric; only with a twist that catered to the likings of the up-n-coming generation. Bill Doody's days were naturally numbered, but as far as the threat he described weaving its tentacles into other aspects of Wink's programming universe; Wink failed to see any immediate danger.

"Listen Bill, this guy isn't going for the head of the snake. That snake is me. He's giving soft body blows. This is a monster guys like you created. As it goes, now you want me to destroy what you've created." Wink despaired as a mafia boss handing out tough love, intended to humiliate and belittle, just to watch them cower, before conditionally answering their prayers. "Maybe a little change is good, Bill."

Bill Doody couldn't see it, but Joshua Bannister had been cued, and summoned to settle the matter as they both concealed their joy at watching Bill Doody's blatant sulking and apparent hopelessness. His loyal viewership would never see him so soft. It had only been that one time. It was Malcolm Grace who was trying to make him a disgrace. Wink and JB let the silence between them stretch out purposely. JB was about to take over. Wink had heirs to the throne, but in the end, Wink Broadcasting was going to be Joshua Bannister's empire one day.

"Grace would never attack us. He needs us. Right now, survey says that fifty percent of the voter universe is interested in the Civics; no matter which way they politically lean. He's going to have a major advantage with all of this accumulated media exposure should he decide to run for the White House. The real problem is if non-voters fall in love with him, and decide to actually go vote, it will transform the existing political atmosphere into a display of how the two-party system is outdated, overrated, and unproductive.

"Bill's right. That will not do us any good. It's always better if they stay aimlessly dredging through the mud, instead of flying freely above it. They will take flight if Grace and the Civics snag that humungous pool of non-voters out there. He will undoubtedly poison our well, which is the very conscience of our viewership. I think the current status-quo is the most favorable to our continued growth. Things are going so well. Grace would disrupt that for certain, and in all honesty, he may attempt to systematically dismantle this great machine we've built. It's better to find a way to destroy him now rather than later. Otherwise, he may become king."

Wink's saggy eyelids lifted as his forehead rolled up in suspicion as Joshua Bannister struck the nerve necessary to stir him to action. Frank Winkleshten alone was the king ruling from the top, and no barking politician was going to circumvent that natural arrangement. Only death, which Wink felt unlikely, could ultimately dethrone him. None of the living stood a chance. As Bill Doody hung by a single thread for some shred of good news, and JB sat with a face of stone; Wink nonchalantly made his way into his private office, fitted with a feudal throne gifted to him by Archduke Dominic of Austria-Tuscany.

Before closing the door for some private reflection, he assured, "I'll get someone on it."

**Meanwhile…back in Pyongyang**

Before dawn was a quiet time when the world stood still. Soon the sun would rise on another day in a home that, for all intents and purposes, was on the up-and-up. She was swirling in the confusion of adolescence where the carefree naivety of childhood was being affronted by a new hardened awareness. Adulthood was on the way with all its complicated modes of uncertainty. To sooth those oncoming insecurities, she found solace in strumming her violin.

At present, she was intent on mastering the melody of George Gershwin's An American in Paris. She was granted the pleasure of hearing it performed a year prior by an orchestra that her father, mother, or pretty much anyone else had not quite expected: that of the prestigious New York Philharmonic Orchestra. The extremely rare exception of their Dear Leader permitting such an injection of fine Western culture with which they were forever at war was rarely seen. The exquisite precision of the orchestra itself and the incredible exception left an indelible mark on her memory. If a note had been obstructed or a time missed by the visiting orchestra, her hearing failed to pick it up.

They had performed at the East Pyongyang Grand Theatre to a live audience of the Party elite. All the faces present were solid without the faintest shimmer of emotion as both national anthems were played; both national flags flanking the orchestra. It all had such an official air. When the white-haired conductor announced they would play Gershwin's piece, and that he only hoped someday, someone, somewhere would compose a piece entitled, *Americans in Pyongyang*—he was met with a polite, unified chuckle.

Sun-rae was unlike every other Korean kid that evening. Children were forbidden to attend such an official function, but in a rare moment of exceptions handed down from on high, her father had wrenched out just one more. His rise through the Local People's Committee within the DPRK paved the way for her attendance to experience the magnificent resonance which no television set could ever boast. They were stuffed in the back row of the third tier. Though her father's face was to remain placid, he would still glance down at her in smiling approval, shifting his hand atop hers so to let it be known he was having a great time in her presence.

The performance had danced along with deliberate grace and theme. Among her favorites was Czech composer Antonin Dvorak's *The New World Symphony*. The Native American folk song was from the 1st movement and resembled the entrance of a conqueror returning from a great adventure out of which any number of tales could be told. It was all up to the imagination. Sun-rae marveled over how it must be true that music was the universal language. In such fantastic and rare moments she only hoped Jing was watching somewhere. He certainly was.

Just as the selected assemblage thought it could not get any better, harnessing their collective gaiety like fortified monks, the orchestra struck a chord which chimed through the soul of the entire Korean peninsula: North and South. It began with the gentle plucking of a harp, lifting them off into a familiar dream. The sounds conjured a path cut up a misty mountain, reaching all the way to the peak where two lovers were caught in a swirl of longing and loss. The piccolo set them on a lonely journey, undertaken with a stubbornly sad conviction—a journey that had to be done. The violins came rushing in to divide the lovers against their wishes, opposed to their will. The crescendo reminded them that even though the forced separation had to be endured; there was still comfort in the hope of being reunited. She was saying, 'I still think of you, my dear…our love so deep it transcends space and time…never to die. Arirang! Arirang! The battle cry of love!' When the pain was at its zenith, and the longing could no longer be endured, the solitary piccolo gently called him back home where his love still remained—patient and resolute.

It was an encore unlike any other the audience had expected. The standing ovation saw the austere and suspicious faces turn to waving hands and broad smiles of mutual acceptance. Enemies had suddenly become friends. Truths unmarred by human toil had been exchanged. The Korean folk song was *Arirang*, which brought about a euphoric allegiance that inextricably bound North and South. The interpretation veered many ways in many styles, but the core theme remained the safe return of lover to lover. It was said to have originated in the late Josean Dynasty towards the end of the nineteenth century, gaining mythic momentum during the colonial Japanese occupation that saw unified Korea under brutal rule until 1945. During that time it signified the longing for independence. The lost love was a nation of their own again. Following the Korean War the song symbolized the longing for unification of the peninsula: North to South, South to North. In that moment, those in the East Pyongyang Grand Theatre shared a special feeling that happens either once in a lifetime, or not at all—indivisible oneness. Sun-rae felt that oneness as she and her father applauded along with all the other jubilant smiles of contentment.

*

THE SUDDEN BANG at the front door jostled her from her early morning daydream, strangely dousing her with a splash of formidable fear. She heard her mother open the door, but as far as words exchanged, she could hear none. Then her father's shoes began to slowly clap down the hallway. They seemed to halt at the doorway. Then she heard a thunderous stomp. It meant he had executed a drill maneuver as if playing a part in a state ceremony.

"Greetings, comrade! Today is a fortunate day for you. And look! You are dressed for the occasion. Let us go fulfill the Party's glory—through you. Your prize is infamy!"

As the front door shut she recalled when she heard the same words at the same exact time in the morning several years prior. Then it had brought forth an entirely different sensation of a brighter future to come. Now it was inexplicably dark without warning or explanation. She darted from her bed, put on her clothes, and went out into the hallway to face her mother. Sun-rae's eyes pleaded, 'Tell me something good, mother.' But her mother shared the same sense of desperation.

When her husband had entered the upper-echelons of the Party machine she never wanted to believe him when he cryptically said, 'So close to the snake, we will be squeezed to death or poisoned. Enjoy this while it lasts.' She could offer no consolation to Sun-rae. Everything had already been finalized.

"Go get ready for school."

She did as she was told, solemnly closing her bedroom door, acquiescing to the feeling of utter defeat. Her mother knew neither what to do, what to think, nor whom to blame. Their Dear Leader had made a decision. They had ultimately been spared from the bomb which had been dropped on their content existence. Her ears were ringing. Her heart was pounding. The dust caked her vision. In the home they had made she was suddenly confused as to where she was. Disoriented by the uncertainty of their future she knew she had to gather herself. Somewhat dizzied, she stammered down the hallway and burst into Sun-rae's room. It was empty. The window leading outside was open; drapes flapping hauntingly about in a rare early morning breeze. Stupefied, she could not help but think that all would be lost. It was now possible they would not be spared.

*

Sun-rae was swift in stride as her sights stuck to the bumper of the black luxury sedan her father had been placed in. She was now playing a high-stakes game of hide-n-seek. The streets were still cloaked in darkness, aiding in the concealment of her movements. She was adept at following the string of shadows between buildings. Her heavy heart was beating overtime, but what persisted even stronger was an intuitive foretelling of an unthinkable reality. What kept her moving forward was the desire to know this reality; validate or refute it, with her own eyes. *How else would the feeling go away?*

She darted along as May Day Stadium imposed itself in her line of sight. As she kept her eyes glued to the bumper the car drove under the stadium archway. The same archway they had passed under each year as a family to watch the national futbol league in action. She stayed tucked to the dark edges amongst the manicured trees and brushes, maintaining a safe distance. She secured the view of a lonely entrance to the side of the stadium. It passed up the main entrance where Party members were filing in, each face consumed with the same dreadful intuition she felt. This was official Party business, and they were convening for a deep purpose.

Squatting and concealed, she watched as all the doors opened to the sedan. A lone man stepped from the shadows of the side entrance. She immediately recognized his uniform. He was a member of the State security apparatus in charge of seeking out dissension—the Bowibu. The single red star centered on his peaked officer's cap explained it all. Four of his fellow officers tumbled out of the sedan and saluted him accordingly. He coldly nodded without returning the salute; hands firmly clasped behind the small of his back with his shoulders pointed outwards to emphasize his natural rigidity.

Then her father's head popped out from the car, and as the four calmly walked him into the recesses of the side entrance, she could see the silver hue of the cuffs that bound her father's hands behind his back. Right then, her heart flopped out of her chest and hit the cold ground like a dead weight. Her intuition was confirmed as reality.

STARTLED AND TACKLED to the ground with a firm hand clasped over her mouth, Sun-rae was suddenly eye-to-eye with her mother. She sharply whispered, "I have you! Settle down now!"

Frozen solid in fright, it was the most relieved she had ever been to see her mother. The wrenching feeling in their guts sent them both into a frantic embrace. "What is happening, mother?"

She stroked Sun-rae's smooth face without alluding to an outcome contrary to the worst. In her own mind her husband was already gone. It had been around the time Sun-rae was born when May Day Stadium was last used for such a purpose. Back then, the second installment of the Kim Dynasty had sniffed out a military coup with rumors swirling that the conspirators—a set of generals from the Peoples' Army—had been burned at the stake like witches following the phoniest of show trials. Of course, those were just rumors, though the generals were never seen or heard from again. The third installment of the Kim Dynasty had now settled into place. It was once again due time for a re-education of what allegiance meant in the Democratic People's Republic of Korea.

Ultimately, it was a confirmation they both tussled with internally. Could they handle knowing absolutely? Beyond the myth, the nation, and the Party; a unique toughness embodied the Korean. It was time to tap into that awareness. They had to know. "We are going in there. Stay close to me and do not say a word. Promise me you will obey!"

"I will." Sun-rae quickly affirmed, also desiring the definite form despite how ghastly a display it might turn out to be.

Summoning the greatest will within, they stood up and walked out into the open as the black sedan motored away, leaving the Bowibu officer to remain in his chiseled implacability. He immediately noticed them walking his direction and patiently awaited their introduction. Her initial intentions were to get into the stadium, but upon approaching an agent of all that could be considered evil, she retracted from her foolish decision. What have I done? Get home! Just get back home!

"Good morning, comrade! We mean to cause you no trouble. I am Moon, and this is my daughter, Sun-rae. She has made a silly mistake this morning. She escaped out of her bedroom window when her father, Kyong, was picked up for official Party business just a short time ago. So as not to waste any more of your time, I just wanted to make you aware that we are leaving here now. We are going home where she will be punished harshly for disrupting Party business. We beg your forgiveness and understanding, comrade."

The new plan in place of a non-plan was just to get out of there, admitting their wrongdoing and securing safe passage back to the house where Sun-rae would not be punished in the least. Between them would flow a river of emotion at the erecting of a memorial to be forever observed. Then there would be the long slow crawl back to normality after the loss of a loved one. It was not at all what Sun-rae had in mind, but she quelled the defiance in her heart in favor of honoring her promise to remain quiet, although she did not find it necessary to look the Bowibu officer in the eyes as she stood straight; stiffly upright, exuding dignity against a man who was well above the laws governing herself, her mother, and her father. He took notice of this showing as he had seen it so many times before, yet rarely from the young.

"Thank you for listening, comrade. We will now be on our way." Moon said, walking off to abruptly conclude the botched non-plan as the duties of a mother had taken her back to what was most important—the care of her daughter.

The officer's face had been without expression, but that was about to change as he saw the opportunity to hand out a lesson to the defiant Sun-rae. "Stop!"

Moon's protective nature turned to trepidation as she turned to face him. Sun-rae, on the other hand, was energized by his command as she considered it a glimmer of hope to find the truth. He slowly stepped towards them, planting himself directly in front of Sun-rae, leering down upon her. It was the first time she had faced a man who had destroyed the lives of many and even killed in the service of the Dear Leader. He was the consummate professional. The part he liked most about his job was the interrogation. Brute force was the last resort, but always the final outcome.

"How old are you, Sun-rae?" He asked in a surprisingly soft voice which failed to match his exterior.

"Thirteen." She answered confidently as her mother grew tense to the point of snapping in two. She could not lose both in a single day.

"You saw your father being taken in, did you not?"

"I did."

"You saw that he was bound?"

"Yes."

He paused momentarily as her responses, though wholly evident, were lightning fast without any pretense of showing respect for his position. "Why did you come here by openly defying your mother, and as she put so well, to disrupt Party business?"

She stared up at him boldly as his gaze transfixed to reflect the darkest part of the human soul. She remained unaffected. "He's my father. What else is there to say?"

"Sun-rae! You disrespect!"

He quickly snapped his hand up to attention as a motion for her to shut up, which Moon fully complied. His face turned sinister as he fought to hold back the forces wanting to teach her a lesson in pain. At thirteen, it was time for her to understand exactly where she fit into the scheme of things. "I know a place inside where you can see and hear everything without anyone being able to see you. It's actually my favorite spot. Would you like me to take you there?"

"Yes!" She responded in strange excitement.

He donned a slight grin at her steadfast assertiveness and then shifted his attention to Moon. "And for you, mother? Would you like me to take you there?"

Moon hesitated with an inner shudder of terror before answering, "Yes, comrade."

"Then it is settled! We will view this demonstration of Party glory together! There are only a few conditions to this offer. First, you must not make a sound. Second, this is between the three of us. Third, this actually never happened. Assure me this is agreed upon. Any confusion at all?" He outlined as they shook their heads in acceptance.

"Should I state the consequences for violating these conditions?" He pressed further as his smile widened and his eyes brightened. The threat was implied and very much received.

"No, comrade. We are fully aware and wish you no discomfort. We thank you for your generosity, and of course, that of our Dear Leader." Moon assured as a slave would her master.

The Bowibu officer turned and began walking to the side entrance as they trailed in tow. Upon entering the stadium they followed along a dark corridor that wrapped around the building, gaining height. The only sound they heard was their own footsteps pressing upon the glossed concrete. Moon and Sun-rae keenly sensed the danger as light began to creep around the curving corner. Without warning the corridor opened to the interior of the stadium: bright green on the playing field, gray seating, and hanging from the rafters a giant red flag emblazoned with the yellow hammer, sickle, and writing brush of the doctrine of Juche. Situated beside the flag was an equally imposing portrait of the revolutionary Kim il-Sung in military garb looking out into the distance; not to be mistaken for the Kim il-Sung wearing a suit and surrounded by children, donning a benevolent smile of compassion like a modern politician. This Kim il-Sung was not in office quite yet. He was the General in a time of war.

On the opposite side of where they stood sat several rows of Party officials dressed for a black-tie affair with their Kim pins glistening from their lapels. Moon placed her hands atop Sun-rae's shoulders to symbolically hold her in place. Their eyes went to the center of the field where a wooden platform stood. Three solemn men were bound with ropes around their necks. They stood atop the medieval stage while adhering to the whole process. One of those men Sun-rae knew as her father and Moon knew as her husband. It felt like they were going to hold their breath forever.

Not a sound was made as lone steps were taken on the field by the enigmatic head of the Bowibu; a man only seen when atrocities were sure to follow. Sun-rae had never seen or known of the man, but Moon knew. He was the great flood, the plague sweeping through every home, and the pale rider bringing an end to it all—man, woman, and child. Blood raced, spines stiffened, and throats began to tingle at the sight of him. He stood erect as a regal being, facing those seated with a scowl drawn which invoked a certain brand of presence. It was official—not a breath was to be taken in or released. They were all underwater now.

"You have forgotten, comrades!" He shouted, grimacing in a way which meant he felt betrayed and ultimately hurt; almost to tears. He was a father about to spank the bottom of his first-born child. *This is going to hurt me a lot more than it's going to hurt you, but you have given me no choice!*

"It has come to this. Somewhere along the way you began to lose sight of our purpose—our course—our victory. This divine vision was gifted to us by the one who still looks down on us from atop Mangyongdae Hill—our great warrior—our Dear Leader—Kim il-Sung!" He thunderously continued, pointing up to the picture of their hero. "This divine wisdom is to be streamed through the generations without dilution—always replenishing—always pushing us along. We must never go against this current. It is within us. It is who we are. Forever!"

His voice, shrill and vile, brought about a paralyzing nausea none of them would ever admit to feeling. Their bodies were reacting to a pain yet to be administered. Kyong, standing on the platform with hands bound, did not feel it as much as those seated. He knew he was dead. Everyone else still had some kind of chance.

"And where does it begin? Where does our national worth lie? It is not your idea. It is an idea tried and true. You are here today only because this idea was carried out before you by those who birthed the Fatherland. The greatest on this very earth.

"Comrades! Listen to me! We are still at war! You will know it is won when the evil forces of the West are consumed by fire, reduced to ash, and scattered to the seas of time without a trace they ever existed! We will win through our iron *will* found in the doctrine of Juche! Have you forgotten? Have you chosen to forget?"

He shook his fist at them, grinding down on his teeth, with tremors convulsing his being at what he knew to be the undeniable truth. He pointed at the red flag hanging from the rafters with a twitchy finger of psychotic design, and explained, "The hammer and sickle signifies our industrious and tireless work to preserve the Fatherland through self-reliance. We do not need anything from the outside. Everything we need is already here.

"The writing brush signifies those sacred facts—not ideas—penned by the greatest of revolutionary minds. Betrothed to us, it is our duty to remain revolutionaries until we are complete. One organism! One blood! Running through the veins of all! No impurities! Divine engineering, which our Dear Leader exemplifies!"

By this time, tears were flowing amongst those seated. The tears rolled to show they were touched to their very core by the majesty having brought them this far. With rectums clapped shut and nerves shredded to bits it was well understood their collective emotional reaction was a product of fear, which was just as acceptable as a product of pure joy.

"And how do we remain endowed with this divine biological functioning? It is simple. It is done through blind, obedient, and steadfast faith in the Party under the guidance of our Dear Leader. There is no other way, and there will never be any other way! Those whose faith falters; whose heart and mind is not forever flooded with Juche; they will be called to account for their weariness and cowardice. They will pay with their lives!"

If Sun-rae's shoulders had been a board her mother would have snapped them in two. They saw it coming in the distance. A wall of dust on an empty plain. A wall of water stretching to the sky off the coastline. There was nowhere to go.

"So here are the ones who have lost heart. Here are the cowards unfit for a life of Juche. They are the highest traitors because they have shamelessly collaborated to denounce our self-reliance laid down by the hammer and sickle of present and past generations, and by the revolutionary code written by the greatest minds. Let it be known! Let it be seen! With one voice! With one body! We will cut away the cancer so that our Fatherland may flourish forever! Long live the Democratic People's Republic of Korea, and long live our Dear Leader!"

He pulled down the lever that dropped the trapped doors under their feet. In the precious and brief time before the rope snapped his neck, Kyong was in the sunshine of a rare summer day showing Sun-rae how to fly her first yon. Then he was rolling with Moon in the bed they first made after marrying. In the lasting moments of clarity he was

moved to chills by the defiant refrain of *Arirang! Arirang!*
And then the composer brought the orchestra to a close with
the final wave of his baton.

There was pure silence as the three dangled to their
deaths. The head of the Bowibu slowly walked back from
the same place he emerged as those seated began to
decompress, letting out and drawing in deep breaths. Some
held hands. Others embraced one another for having been
spared. An unwavering and unquestionable brand of loyalty
had been reinforced. None held back their tears of joy.

Sun-rae looked back at the officer who had let them
inside. His grin manifested an evil in its purest form, but it
failed to frighten her. She was beyond fear. Beyond anger.
She was ready to become one of them. To kill. To take away.
To play God.

They were escorted out the same way they had come.
Moon was exhausted and traumatized, only taking solace
that they were going home now, though their home had been
shattered to pieces. Reaching outside and released from the
grips of the officer, Moon was only looking to console her
daughter. Like a new nightmare beginning after the worst
just ended, Sun-rae suddenly darted away once again.
Confused and only knowing to follow in pursuit, Moon
yelled, "Stop, Sun-rae! Please stop!"

The rolling tide continued within Sun-rae. It
propelled her in the direction of the market district to find
her dear friend, Jing. She had to know where everything
stood. It wasn't long before she was speedily passing by the
dejected and dismayed faces of the market vendors, ashamed
they had stood by and watched what Sun-rae had just missed.
She pressed on into what was once Jing's mud-laden tent

city—torn to pieces—everything unrecognizably scattered and dislocated. The few sheets remaining were stuck to the muddy ground, stained red with blood. Random possessions were strewn about; some on fire. In no way could she know where Jing's tiny space could have been.

As she spun around again and again, it finally caught her eye. It was resting on its side, wounded like everything else, but miraculously still intact. She walked to, and stood over Jing's marker—the jolly fat man with a beer in one hand and a once-bitten turkey leg in the other, covered head-to-toe in graffiti. It was all that remained of Jing's existence as she knew it. The loves of her young life had been taken away in one fell swoop. She became numb all over. *Not fair…not fair.*

She heard her mother panting from behind. Nothing was to be said. It was time to go home. Sun-rae knelt down to the statue and stroked the jolly fat man's cheek. She pretended it was Jing's. It was the only closure she would be allowed that day. With their death, out from her sprung another being, who could one day be willing—all too willing.

**Back to the Land of the Free...**

Ralston Golden Jr was walking to school as he did each morning, dreading the entire process anew. It was always the question of fitting in. His face was riddled with puss-filled pimples, and his frame was slight by the standard of both sexes. He was non-athletic, a sub-par student, and lacked the desire to change any of it.

The hippy kids had their long hair, hacky sacks, and suspect hygiene. The jocks had their muscles and a mastery of whichever ball appropriate for their sport. The brainy nerds had consistently high scores and could find part-time work by doing the jocks' load of weightier schoolwork. The class clowns had little chance of becoming successful in the real world, but at least had comedy on their side. And the weirdo minority were just odd enough to be left alone entirely, flying under the radar until it was all over.

In the throes of a prolonged identity crises, at an age when the focus was on setting oneself apart, Ral was to stay hidden in the fray on the fringes. He was considered the rich kid. His future was funded and money would never be a worry. The heir of Golden Motors was unconcerned with such matters. He was viewed as spoiled, already having it made in the shade. When would he ever have to earn his keep? So thought the hippies, the jocks, the brainy nerds, and the weirdoes. Maddie McCreeley was the lone exception.

Ralston Golden Sr had lain out plainly why Ral was not going to private school. The unearned sense of entitlement lacked in public education. In order to profit from the normal person it was necessary to learn their desires, their weaknesses, and where their loyalties stood. The ultimate goal across the spectrum of commerce was mass manipulation based upon the quirks and eccentricities of the target audience. Habitual consumption was the thing which would keep the Golden's line of wealth alive and kicking. Once the high school experiment was completed, Ral would attend a private university. There he would meet other rich kids to participate in the grand social engineering scheme to keep the old money at the top where it belonged.

It was indeed lonely at the top, but absolutely necessary. Riding high and smiling down at the carnage below made one a leader. Getting away with it all until the last breath; that made one an icon. Learn to despise them, Jr. *It's the only way you can take everything from them. Don't trust anyone, Jr. Just me, and I promise, you won't ever be like them.* Ral found no enjoyment in any of it. Only in the times with Maddie.

She was the healthiest soul he knew. When she walked, she floated. She worked a room in slow motion, everyone falling for her charms. Her smooth face was genuinely lit with an eagerness to engage whomever had the pleasure of being awarded her attention. She loved and helped people naturally like she were the patron saint of a higher good. She was class president, a shoe-in for Valedictorian when the time came, and popular enough to one day snag a homecoming queen crown. Maddie had a future that she was going to earn, which Ral knew would make it all the more sweet. To him, she was already the sweetest. It was why he considered this part of the day to be the very best. He was going to walk the prettiest, most special girl in his life home. It was their tradition.

*OH SHIT!*

He stopped dead in his tracks at the sight of the most disgusting beasts known to the animal kingdom. He was king of the junior class and would soon be king of the entire school the following year. He stood over six feet. His physique was big muscles wrapped tightly in skin. He held the school record for seven touchdown passes in a single game, and was the biggest dickhead Ral had the displeasure of knowing. He established a reputation of talent mixed with an attractive grade of dangerous stupidity. It was always about that damned nail-biter against a bitter divisional rival where he threw that Hail Mary pass to win the game in the closing seconds during a rainy night. He would eventually end up a fallen football star who preferred hanging with those on the path towards a criminal record.

It was all he would ever need to get away with everything. Other than his athletic exploits, he also headed the hazing department. So amused was he by his thoughtless actions: the wedgies, locker stuffings, battering verbal abuse, theft, extortion, welshing on bets, vandalism, and even a little arson. Ral had been personally subjected to at least three. It was well understood through clear demonstration that physical violence would be exacted if people failed to mind their own business about his antics. It was nowhere close to an idle threat. Nobody wanted the mug he could deliver. Of course, his usual prey were the undesirables, which Ral was head of the pack. He effectively had everyone fooled for the time being, but Ral hoped he would see the day when big bad Toby Self would walk into Golden Motors with bad credit, a fat gut and a bald head, pig-like kids with a pig-like wife, to buy the cheapest thing he could fit them all into at thirty percent interest.

That day was a fantasy. This day was real. And there they were; laughing and flirting like there was a legitimate reason to do so. All pretend. All fake. It's my walk! *It's my time with Maddie! All you want to see is her boobs!*

Ral walked up to them with the pent up intensity of a bottle rocket. The laugh they were currently sharing he wanted to scream over and drown out. He felt it was time to stand up without regard for the consequences. Just as he was about to take decisive action—Toby—with a chummy voice completely out of character, like his body had been snatched up by some alien force, happily greeted, "Hey Ral! What's going on, buddy? Good to see you!"

"Hey Ral." Maddie acknowledged with a timid indifference which made Ral feel like a pebble on the ground looking up at them. He sensed a shift, leaving him excluded, which was his greatest fear.

"Are you ready to go, Maddie?" Ral asked with an edgy tone of desperate jealousy. Without saying the specific words he was pleading with Maddie not to break their tradition. She just looked around in every direction besides the condemnation set in his face, as if dodging the truth under interrogation.

Toby Self slapped down his meaty hand on Ral's shoulder with threatening implications, and politely suggested, "Ral, I really wanted to talk to Maddie about something. I know you two do this every day. It's just that I got this brand new truck and I want to give her the first ride. You could come along, but it's only a single cab, and since it's a chilly day, I don't think you'd be comfortable riding in the back. Sooo…if it's cool?"

It wasn't even close to cool. It was steamy and boiling. Ral shot one last look at Maddie to seal in the guilt for breaking their honored tradition, especially for a low-life like Toby Self. She countered the look with one of her own which was meant to assure him there would be other times, accentuating it with her warm smile that always melted Ral down to butter. Toby's intimidating glare was abandoned when he noticed the bond between them, carrying the force of time to prop it up. It was now Toby's intimate goal to break that bond through whatever means necessary.

"Trucks are cool." Ral said as sarcastically as possible. He turned away from them quickly and walking away, said, "Have a great time! Hope you can talk over the engine noise!"

He was walking the opposite way of where he needed to go, but it was okay. He would find a crevice. A place rarely tread. A hole where he could give it a good cry. The tradition he held with Maddie would not be his only loss of the day. Upon arriving home he would have to deal with his father. Report cards were in. There would be a talking to.

*

Maddie walked through her front door as Toby Self's truck rattled away like a residential garbage truck. The household mid-sized mutt met her at the door with his trademark wagging tail and tongue. "Hey, Mitzi girl!"

With frisky Mitzi at her feet she walked into the sunlit kitchen to see her mother chopping vegetables and watching a talk show bent on pseudo-psychology and a forceful display of collective judgment. "Hey, mom!"

She peeled her eyes from the small television for just a second. "Hey, sweetie. Who's got the loud truck?"

"That's what I'd like to know." Johnston McCreeley said, walking out of the bedroom still caked from head-to-toe in rock dust. He folded his arms across his chest and stood upright as if Toby were present in the room with them.

Maddie dropped her book bag on the stool and got on her tippy toes to place a kiss on her father's cheek as was customary. Still, she knew the question soundly stood. "He's just a boy from school. He just got his truck, so he wanted to give me a ride."

"What's his name?"

"Toby."

"Full name?"

"Toby Self."

"Where does he live?"

"I don't know."

"How old is he? What grade is he in?"

"He's sixteen. He's a junior."

"Does he conduct the party train on the weekends?"

"That's enough, Johnstie." Peg interceded, knowing the questions would roll on indefinitely if not put in check. She threw a wink at Maddie and returned to her chopping as the audience on the talk show hooted about something that was really nobody's business.

"Okay, I'll stop. It's just surprising not to see Ral. It's a change. That's all." Johnston defended, unfolding his arms and loosening up as he lovingly ruffled the fur atop Mitzy's head.

"Straight A's again, daddy!" Maddie bragged, pulling away from the topic of Toby Self.

"Well, there's another line of credit. Figure out what you want." Johnston said, referring to a full day of splurging on whatever she desired. He always extended the line to Peg as well. He was wise enough to know that keeping the women happy kept him happy.

"So what are those edu-crats up to these days at school? What's next for doing what's best for the kids?" Johnston asked, quickly scooping up a carrot from the cutting board as Peg playfully slapped at his hand.

Since Maddie was an involved and high-performing student she was often swayed by the politics of the school administration and their grand designs. Johnston, being one of those Texans who couldn't trust the government as far as he could throw them, always wanted to remain in the know.

"They want to build three more schools." Maddie answered, as she joined her mother in watching the antics of the talk show.

"Three more schools?" Johnston barked. "This city is only twenty square miles with thirty-nine schools. There's one on every damn corner. How are they going to pay for it? Another damn bond?"

"I think they said that's what it's called. Not sure, but they're talking about it a lot. They gave me some flash cards that read *Vote Yes for our Kids*. Oh, that reminds me! I'm supposed to give some to you and mom."

Johnston's eyes widened and his blood quickened. "Those sons-uh-bitches are at it again! We're already a billion dollars in debt from the past four bonds, which we haven't even begun to pay off. Property taxes rise each and every year. Now they're pimping our kids out to get the vote? Do we need another multi-million dollar bond on public debt so they can build another Taj Mahal? You know, because kids can only learn in a big fancy building. As soon as the ribbon's cut it's already at full capacity, which only means they have to build another one. Yeh, it's all for the kids! I tell you who it's for. It's for the contractors, the architects, and for the school administration to keep their six-figure incomes, and whoever else has their sweaty palms out. Bullshit!"

Peg and Maddie shared a smile and a giggle at Johnston's expense. Nothing could work him up more than something a vast majority of the local populace were not interested in or knew very little about. Peg and Maddie certainly could not have cared less as the bald and suited talk show host was about to reveal the results of the DNA test establishing paternity. "So I guess you don't want a yard sign, huh, dad?"

Johnston knew she was teasing him, which served as a signal to cease his rant as no one was listening anyways. Peg and Maddie were paying close attention to the announcement at hand. It wasn't going to be best picture or album of the year, but the DNA results would suffice for the time being until awards season came along.

At the revelation the crowd unleashed their despicable outrage. The young white man wearing a ball cap turned backwards and tilted on the side of his head, with an oversized football jersey, and pants strapped around his knees, was still going to deny the scientific certainty of his coming fatherhood. His three-hundred pound black counterpart continued to bawl her eyes out as she lambasted him for being the most deceitful of losers. The only thing the audience lacked in their outrage was heads of lettuce to chunk at the stage. At the peak of the obnoxiously loud buffoonery, Johnston winced at the volume it kept.

"Peg, can you turn down the idiots, please?" He requested as kindly as reason would allow him.

Peg turned it down just a hair for artificial appeasement. Jokingly, Johnston added, "Maddie, you shouldn't let too many boys take you home. You might end up on that show."

"Johnstie!" Peg lightly admonished, as Maddie glanced back to roll her eyes at the suggestion.

"Hey, it's the stuff y'all like." Johnston played, snatching another piece of carrot and following it up with a loving pat to Peg's bottom. He moved in to give her a peck on the cheek as she pulled away, merely to extend the play. It was how their afternoons went: easy-going, honest, and warm.

*

The short walk home was in stark contrast to the days Ral walked with Maddie. It was well out of his way to walk her home, but he always thought if he kept the small sacrifice going she would eventually recognize it and reward him with what he fantasized over obsessively—a kiss. He had put in the work. In his lonesome reflection he tussled with the thought that Toby Self would instead capture the prize. The injustice would crush him.

He walked into his expensively adorned home housing the lighting of a dingy cellar. There was no pet to herald his arrival and no hint of aroma that dinner was on the way. His mother had just taken her afternoon dosage, paired with a martini. On the leather couch she sat, yet to change out of her silk nightgown. Ral simply liked that she never gave him any grief, much less said any words. "Hi, mom."

There was an indiscernible response he couldn't make out. Perhaps a grunt. That was the usual, but he always wondered if she ever got bored sitting on the couch in the darkness, staring off at nothing. Branching out from the foyer was a long hallway stretching to the rear of the home where he heard his father laying down the laws of business. Ral moved towards the voice, as always, with flinching apprehension. The walls of the long hallway were a genealogical record of the Golden line all the way back to the Gilded Age. It was a line stacked with entrepreneurs from all walks of industry. They postured the same way in each portrait: filthy rich, finely dressed, and none showing a hint of happiness in their ghostly faces. At least they weren't faking it, Ral always thought. It was a line of achievement destined to endure. The only light in the home came from his father's study, which he was about to dreadfully enter. Ralston Sr. was wrapping up another all-too-important conference call.

"Like taking candy from a baby! I'll be talking to you soon, Councilman!" He nearly yelled with a devious laugh of pretension as Ral plopped down in the chair facing his father's imposing oak desk like another client, another partner, another employee.

Senior opened the cigar case at the edge of his desk, snipped the appropriate end off with a gold-plated cutter, and dipped it in his glass of bourbon. He tasted the sting of the bourbon as he lit a match, rolling the cigar between his fingers to even the burn, wafting the smoke which never failed to make Ral's stomach curl. Senior sat on the edge of the desk, intently inspecting every aspect of his son's appearance. Each day he was to be pressed and sharp. Not by the cleaners, but by his own iron, starch, and personal precision. He noticed his pointed collar was a little crumpled. "Why does your collar look like you put that shirt in the drier?"

*Always something. Never satisfied.* "I don't know. Probably from just moving through the hallway at school. It gets really crowded. What's like taking candy from a baby? Is that good news?"

His question was only a diversion. Whatever Senior had to say, Ral was wholly disinterested. "We're going to break some new ground. But first, we have to clear what's there."

"And what's there?"

"Low-income housing and abandoned businesses for the most part. I was just on the phone with one of the city councilmen. They're going to present another proposition on the next ballot. These propositions are approved by the voter. The only catch is that we have to convince the voter that their money is going to be spent wisely. Since it's a local election, no one is really paying attention. Those that are voting on it will be the ones standing to gain the most from it, and the ones who have been fooled into believing their tax dollars are going to capital improvements: like city services, parks and recreation, and whatever else sounds peachy. In reality, it opens the door for developers to develop, and guys like me and you to open shop. The price tag is huge and the windfall is assured. Everybody wins!" Senior explained, always for future reference, sliding the cigar from side-to-side in his mouth.

"Who loses?"

The cigar ceased its slide, signaling to Junior that he had struck a nerve. He was particularly courageous for the day, like he had nothing to lose. He always thought about those trampled upon by the vast fortune he was to eventually inherit. What about the families displaced who had called it home for perhaps decades? On one fine day the ride was over against their will, being scantly compensated, and lacking in the resources to defend their lot against the partnered forces of the government machine and the private sector. It was those specific perspectives which made Ralston Senior want a different son.

"You insist on being weak, don't you?"

Senior shook his head at his son's lack of proper reckoning according to the dog-eat-dog configuration. No amount of leniency for the consumer would ever allow the aggressive expansion that Senior's plan envisioned. "You wanna make a difference with people, Junior? That's what charitable contributions are for. Right now, Golden Motors donates to over forty different charitable organizations. You know why we do that? Because it brings us in new business. We do good things. We're the good guys. Come on by! We got that same goodwill in your vehicle-buying experience! I'll do charity all day, Junior. You know why?

"It doesn't cut into my profit margin. I won't do it unless I can write it off. As for these poor people you're worried about having to relocate, I don't care. They will be compensated. We turn an area of poverty into one of prosperity, and that means progress in the common welfare.

"So there it is, Junior! There's your justification for curbing the cost of expansion. I swear, sometimes I'm completely convinced you'd rather be doing something else in another family. What that could possibly be is a mystery to me. Everything is being set up for you! What's the fucking problem?!"

Ral knew it was about to get worse as Senior fumed, lighting his cigar again so he could pull it harshly and fill the room with an even greater cloud of bitterness. The last thing his father exclaimed was actually a statement, but Ral tried to answer the question. "I don't know. I just don't know."

It was time to move on for Senior. He flicked the ash of his cigar in a silver tray on the desk, and said, "Report cards came out today. So…report."

"Four B's and one C." Ral answered without delay, flinching as the silver ash tray flew to the wall, bouncing from it and crashing to the hardwood floor.

"Goddammit!" Senior belted out, smacking his free palm on the desk. The outburst had momentarily stirred his mother in the front room, forcing her to glance around in confusion. But after a small sip of the martini she had forgotten about, she sank back down. Ral sat still, looking down at nothing. It was time to turn into a sponge and soak it all in. "What's so hard about school? It's just memorization! So easy! Am I calling you lazy? Yes! Am I calling you stupid? Yes! They're both the same things! They both yield the same results! Failure!

"Listen, I could get you into a top-tier university with mediocre grades. That can be done. The problem is that I don't want to do that. It's embarrassing. I was at the top of my class. You know why? Because I wanted to be the top guy! Your little hillbilly friend Maggie knows that—

"It's Maddie." Ral inserted, fixing a stern expression that stunned his father. Senior wanted to strangle his son to death, but was held by the spark of likeness in Ral's expression. It was a look he utilized in high-level talks when things were not going his way, and when moving forward, they had better start going his way—or else. Noticing this likeness calmed Senior to a point. Even if only a smidgen, he saw a little something of Senior in Junior.

"Maddie…right." Senior slowly acknowledged. Ral oriented his eyes downwards. He knew his father would always have the last word. "I assume you have homework, or something to memorize? Get out of my sight."

Ral stood and turned to leave, but Senior had one last thing. Always one last thing. "Junior?" Ral turned to face him with a deflated posture. "You will conform. You will be what I tell you to be."

Ral walked out of the room back into the hallway of memories. His hate for his father grew stronger with each portrait he passed. For Senior, the hate was mutual. He regretted not having one more child, being that this one was such a waste. The problem was that he disliked children. They were so helpless—so needy—so unfit.

He had put the television on mute for his conference call. Now his interest was spiked enough to turn up the volume. This guy continued to amuse him, and that was only because Ralston Golden knew he didn't have a chance in hell.

***zzz…***

The restless rustling on the other side of the door could not help but birth a special and rare anxiety within Malcolm Grace. He took pride in viewing himself as a person of unflinching fortitude. His public persona up to that point had led him to a destination of his own choosing—to form a viable third party option which posed a genuine threat to the long-standing two-party American system. His role was ideological headpiece and chairman of the Civic party. Not once had he come close to entertaining the notion of running for public office, much less the highest office in the land. What the future held was favorable. Perched at the top of the Civics his efforts concentrated on fixed interests expressed through the voters, expansion of the party, and the full absorption of controversy so those actually holding public office did not have to deal with the distraction. After all, they had real things to worry about—like executing the duties of their office.

Now he was being pushed in a new direction by the general will of not only his constituency, but that of the wide body politic. The former was pushing him to arrive at the pinnacle of governing power; to quite literally, seal the deal. The latter was yelling to put up or shut up; meaning the continued life of the party rested on Malcolm Grace's practice of carrying out what he preached. He assured his constituency that he would maintain honesty and transparency among them throughout the ordeal. As for those rustling on the other side of the door waiting for him to deliver the announcement, they would always be held suspect.

"I'm scared." He admitted, as a shockwave rippled through the room like he suddenly confessed he was an entirely different person than he led them to believe. They had never known him to express doubt—only conviction. It took the wind out of their sails for the time being. It was a clear deviation from the Civic culture he had fostered: no fear, no compromise.

"They're going to tear me apart. That's the whole nature of the job. That's why they age so rapidly. They're owned in all ways. A modern American slave. Staying who I am, and who I have built myself into will be the biggest challenge of my life. My identity will be consumed by the identity of all. It's inevitable. Once I enter the bubble I'll never get out. I'll become a museum piece of what was once scorned, laughed at, and maybe even loved. I'm alienating myself for the inalienable. Lately, it's what's been keeping me up at night."

He scanned the room to see indignant faces feeling the same fear they assumed he would never acknowledge. His hidden layer had been exposed like splitting open a cadaver, only for the reason that it had to be done for the livelihood of all. He wanted to show continence stripped down and void of any illusion. It would be the one time they would see such a sight. Slipping on his blazer, making certain it was squared on his frame, he nodded at them with the deepest gratitude, knowing they were the reason he stood at the edge of the precipice.

"You know why it keeps me up at night?" He asked without expecting a response; only their singular attention. Smiling wide to remind them of his usual swagger, he continued, "Because I'm going to win this damn thing. All ye Civics…let's go get it!"

Shedding his apprehension and going into full attack mode he led them out into a room full of microphones, cameras, and faces eager to print the first story. It's what always confused Malcolm Grace. Why were they all there? Why all the hoop-lah? How many devices had to record such a rehearsed moment? He knew why. It was to shake him. It was to catch the moment when he would appear weak, and then point their fingers at him to call it out.

"Get ready for something different!" He blaringly declared, captivating them to instant silence. He allowed a moment passage to let it all set in. "Because there's not a chance of it staying this way when the Civics take the helm!"

*There he is*, those flanking him like disciples thought. All of the press assembled, with dangling necklace badges like they were backstage at a concert, were dialed into Malcolm Grace's infamous thousand yard stare. It was especially distant this day. "We're not going to take sides. We're not going to look out over the people, seeking approval from the loudest group, all carrying the same signs. We're not going to bathe the downtrodden in a wash of perpetual victimhood. We're not going to privilege the wealthy as if they were above the laws governing the downtrodden. We are the forerunners in a new practice…a new association. Let it be known. Let it be willed!"

There was no teleprompter, no flash cards, no tilt of the head downwards; only a scan from side to side, saying, 'Are you listening? You better be!'

"We don't make promises!" He nearly yelled, leaning forward over the microphone. This time he was serious as death snatching away the final heartbeat. "Promises are made to be broken. We only have goals. We will solve problems through the imagination, and not the formula. Policy will not be established through the fear of what is to come. It will be through the aspirations of what we will become. We are among the people—not above them. It is time to govern for all the people—not just a few people.”

Only a few clicks were heard as he let the defined attitude of their leadership style set in. It was now time for a rundown; a reminder, of the ways things are, the way they were, and the way they should be. “Our great Republic was born from rebellion against tyranny. It didn’t take long before the liberating principles of democracy took hold to carry out the hallowed purpose of the very document that secured our Republic’s future to this very day—the Constitution. The forces necessary to keep that document alive are healthy divisions, fruitful debate, and insightful interpretation. Nothing is meant to be clear-cut in this kind of system. It’s not meant to just be. It’s meant to *be* earned. Nothing worth anything is attained without a fight.

“We as a nation are at a crucial moment when the tide must turn. What I mean is that this two-party flip-flopping of power must come to an end. Historically, our options have principally been between Federalists and Anti-Federalists; Republicans and Democrats; liberals and conservatives. The parts were put in place for operation: the legislative, the judicial, the executive. How would the machine run from there? People either forget, or they simply don’t know that both these camps have been dead wrong. They are both historically responsible for what haunts the American consciousness. Both were proponents of manifest destiny, which resulted in the displacement and annihilation of the American Indian—whatever tribe. Today, the Democrats say they stand for equality of the sexes and the races. It was quite different at the dawn of the Civil War. The Confederacy was the bastion of the Democrats and the Union under Abraham Lincoln was the bastion of the Republicans. After that horrid affair we had to reconstruct, which brought about the age of industrialization, the robber barons, and the introduction of an unsustainable money system built upon boom and bust. Both parties allowed this to happen. Then came the consequences of the grand illusion—The Great Depression. Franklin Delano Roosevelt came in to save the day by expanding the government with a New Deal for the American people. The bones of his policy was that future generations would pay for the economic doldrums of the living generation. Those who had not even been born would be saddled with the debt. It is true, he did not have a choice. The lords of finance had already bought the machinery of government. The heisters were granted consent. Then came the worst war in the history of humankind—the Second World War. The immense amount of blood shed in that affair was the proverbial hand that pulled us from the roaring rapids which were sure to drown the nation as we know it today. For that brief period in our history, the American people forgot they were Democrats, Republicans, conservatives, liberals—they were one. Following our victory over the forces—once again—of single-minded tyranny, we were given another chance to set things right. It was the rise of the middle class family. We fell in love with the home, the job, the car. As difficult as it may be believed, in the late fifties and early sixties the Republican Party was not the standard-bearer of the South as it is today. The Southern Democrat was very much an active presence, exemplified in the person of Lyndon Baines Johnson. What changed all that was the signing of the Civil Rights Act of 1964. That's when LBJ famously said, following the swipe of his pen, that he had just signed over the South to the Republicans. He was right. The Party which had once led the charge to free the American slave under Abraham Lincoln now found a new base in the very lands where the fields were worked without wages. The roles reversed, but the names stayed the same. Today, these two parties have consorted to completely sell-off America as the true reflection of history tells us; not to mention the realities on the ground. The government, like the majority of Americans, are living paycheck to paycheck without any substantial savings. It's time for some fresh leadership which does not come from an outdated model that has exhausted itself.

"The third option—the Civic option—must not be a fly-by-night, organized in haste with the only clear motive being a distraction during an election year for the advantage of a Democrat or Republican. We are not the Whigs, the Bull-Moose, the Green, the Reformers, or the Libertarians. The Civics are not a distraction! We are an active and permanent participant. Our clear goal is to break the two-party stranglehold and swing open the door to a fourth, fifth, sixth, seventh—whatever number it takes to shake this mold of endless gridlock and sluggish responsiveness to the will of the people as a whole. That's why it is our time to lead!"

He took a moment to gather himself as the room digested his words. He looked to the ground, re-situated his posture behind the podium and took a quick look back at his constituency to see all their heads nodding. Malcolm Grace looked out to the faces in front of him, solely concerned with the quality of their recordings, as they performed one last tweak of their gadgets before receiving the big news. In them, he saw the people as a whole. His stomach twirled.

"Notice that I'm not referring to myself as an individual extended from the body of the Civics, or maybe even detached. There is no establishment. There is no faction. There are no neo-elements bent upon the extreme. There is no ideological separation. The Civics are all on the same page, and we all have the same unifying spirit of the founding peoples who swelled up against the lack of options, which was the source of their tyranny. We are not revisionists. We want our honor back! And it will be my greatest honor to serve the people in the most sacred of public offices.

"Therefore, I am announcing my candidacy for the office of the President of the United States. The Civics are the head and the people are the body. Both listen to the other and move forward accordingly. We will always be in touch. Thank you for your time!"

He stepped away from the podium as the press exploded in a rant of activity. The platform had been laid out in the usual ambiguous manner, but Malcolm Grace knew the rest would come later. He and the Civics filed out of the room without any celebration in their stride. They held back from congratulating or flattering him with the supposed inevitability of his victory in the future. That was against Civic etiquette. The fighting was never done. They would wait. Yet, he had to say just one last thing in their presence. Following that, they all could sense there would be an evolution within the Party from that point on.

With a confident smile, candidate Malcolm Grace said, "We're in the fold now. Let's go the rest of the way."

*zzz…*

"Why doesn't Mr. Grace have any kids? No family of his own? I assumed those were prerequisites to be taken seriously as a presidential candidate. That would make for an awful empty White House." Said the anchorwoman in a slim and sleek red dress. A string of pearls hung around her neck. When she lifted her delicately manicured hands to emphasize her point; a gold watch and a platinum wrist bracelet dangled from her pure complexion. Her lips were full and glistening; her hair shaped to a fine shine.

Her co-anchor was always smiling, and for no apparent reason, but he sure could wear a navy and polka-dot bow-tie with the best of them. He was there to agree and add a little splash of cheesy humor. "He could get a few dogs, Tara."

They both snickered at how true and clever it was.

*zzz…*

"What are they?" He fired forth in a microphone which had been sprayed with his spit on a regular basis. The spit-ter was a pudgy man past his mid-life who had already suffered one stroke and was surely headed for another. It was all about the radio waves—his voice—unopposed. The outrage. The distrust. He was the extreme product of a Cold War kid.

"This is a question yet to be answered. They say they're the alternative. What does that boil down to, Chairman Grace!

"There's been plenty of chairman's in political parties, but only a few come to my mind: Chairman Mao,

Chairman Lenin, Stalin…the man-child at the helm in North Korea. Is this what we're heading for? LISTEN TO ME!

"He won't do Q&A sessions. He used to do a few interviews at the beginning of all this; now he does none. He's accountable to no one. At least the quack on his way out knows he wouldn't be able to get away with that. Everyone answers to someone. Smells like a trail leading to the rule of a dictator. Is this really where we're going?!"

*ZZZ…*

The backdrop from where he was sitting displayed a lavishness fit for the annals of Roman lore. The old man in his designer suit had been in the business of evangelical broadcasting for so long he actually believed he was the undisputed messenger of God. There was proof. The prayer requests never stopped pouring in and the donations remained steady. He was to make certain the medieval Catholic practice of Indulgences was kept alive and well.

"I have not heard this Malcolm Grace make one reference or acknowledgment to the Almighty in any of his speeches. This is the only thing that troubles me about his movement. It leads me to believe that he is an atheist. And listen, believers, we all know who's behind that disorder of the mind.

"He was cast out of heaven, thrown into the bottomless pit of hell where he awaits his destruction at the hands of Jehovah Jirah. He is called Satan, the Devil…Beelzebub. We can only hope that Mr. Grace will clarify the state of his faith, if any exists at all."

*ZZZ…*

He was wearing a Red Sox ball cap and Bruins hockey jersey. His mustache was full with age and so was his belly. He was about to chomp down on a bratwurst when he was popped the question on a sunny day in downtown Boston.

"Hey, I like tha fuckin' guy! Heard he's a Patriot's fan. That's good enough for me." He roughly answered, biting and tearing away on the juicy piece.

**ZZZ...**

She was stridently moving through the rush hour crowd as always; in a hurry, with razor-focus and an unyielding will. She was the power woman with a leather briefcase, trench coat, and black heels. The only way to stop her march through the day was to peak her interest.

"Umm...I admire his direct, no nonsense approach. Does he have my vote? I really want to see how it all plays out. My final decision will likely be made at the polls." She stated, hopping on a ringing phone and moving on to the next conquest.

**ZZZ...**

He was walking through the massive parking lot of the auto plant where he had worked for twenty-nine years. He was a black blue-collar man who was happy with life and ready to go home to eat some dinner with his wife.

"Ya' know what? I like this government being colorblind thing. That's a good idea. He said somethin' else 'bout being a victim. Don't quite know what he means, but he's got my attention. I'm listenin'."

**ZZZ...**

The grisly old host of the Jagorgin Group was in the final comments phase of the program, and as always, he got in the last word. "The big question this week is Malcolm Grace's past. What we know is that he was an orphan, abandoned by those who brought him into the world. As a child he bounced from foster home to foster home, never really knowing what a stable home felt like. Yet, he never fell into trouble with the law, was an exceptional student wherever he went, and this upbringing has obviously made him fearless. In reality, the only parental guardian he's had is the State.

"Mr. Grace does not talk about it; has stated he will never write about his past, and contends his story will be laid out in actionable policy. Regardless, as a literal son of the State, will he endeavor to punish or honor the parent that raised him? We shall see. Till next week, breath it all in. Goodbye for now!"

*zzz...*

Dane Shavers was catching the end of the Jagorgin Group as usual on a Sunday. The piece on Malcolm Grace-elect only brought about a few passing thoughts. Mainly, he questioned whether everything Malcolm Grace said concerning history was true. Not that he cared much. They were all a bunch of liars clawing for official power. The conclusion was fixed in his mind. His mind just happened to be on something else.

It had been quite a surprise when Frank Winkleshten procured his services vis-à-vis Joshua Bannister to pull up as much dirt on candidate Malcolm Grace as possible. It was proving a difficult task. He had already sprawled out his personal life without shame. There were no extra-marital affairs; he had never been married. There were no legitimate or illegitimate children, which at least meant he had been careful in his sexual life; and so far, his financial portfolio had no stains to rub out. Nothing was juicy about Malcolm Grace with which to mar his image. To Dane Shavers, he was a devout ideologue of his own design. It just so happened that Wink was throwing a substantial amount of money behind this muckraking campaign. Wink expected results. Dane Shavers was starting to think he would just have to make something up in the end. It certainly wouldn't be the first time he had done so.

Dane Shavers was interested in another personality, and that interest was entering a realm of obsession. Wink's funds were being diverted to the further examination of Monty Lincoln's Fellowship of the Enlightened. The Fellowship was becoming more established, more reclusive, and increasingly up to no good in the haunted mind of a power conspiracy theorist like Dane Shavers.

The Fellowship, sunk into the northern California redwoods, had erected an ornamented archway straddling the entrance gate with the initials FOE on the front. Hung from the keystone of the archway was a golden owl; alert and upright. A red-pebbled driveway snaked around the tree-line where it opened up to the compound itself. Resting in the center of the circled driveway was a fountain of veined granite. The fountain showcased the sculpture of a single tree. A glistening silver snake was wrapped around one of its branches, looking down upon a naked woman holding a golden apple in her hand.

During his surveillance Dane Shavers could see no one was coming in and no one was going out, save the trucks delivering goods and services. A couple of times he heard shots fired in the distance. It all smacked of his staunchest obsession; the art and practice of the occult. In his personally-driven investigation he found his work at an impasse. He needed an insider. Someone who knew anything about the illusive gentleman who had spoken at the foot of the bonfire the night he breached the fence for the first time. She was to arrive any moment.

The buzz from the intercom was on time, which meant this Margaret Buckey lady was already on a credible footing. Dane Shavers released the lock on the door to let her in. She walked in with a soft smile with her hand extended in greeting. "Hello, Mr. Shavers. I'm Margaret."

He accepted her hand with kindness and motioned to the chair in front of his cluttered desk, covered with misguided evidence of a plot by the powers that be of global domination, and ultimately, enslavement. "Hello, Margaret. Please have a seat. Would you like a water or something?

Don't have much. My personal assistant hasn't made it to the store in a long time."

"No thank you. I'm fine." She answered, unable to catch his humor. She was only concerned about settling her old body in a foreign chair properly.

Dane Shavers threw her a faint smile, already suspecting this older lady could know Monty Lincoln through unbecoming past associations. "So Margaret, tell me a story."

She kindly returned the smile, and began; "I was the original founder of the Fellowship of the Enlightened. I intended it to be a breeding ground for theistic myth-busting. I being an atheist, it was my goal to dispel any belief of there being a higher power in any form or on any plane. I was to scientifically prove this in a tone of compassion, and then demonstrate it through virtuous action. I did not seek out fellow atheists. I only wanted believers from all different walks of faith. It was moving along just fine until Monty Lincoln walked through my door. He took it over almost immediately. There was nothing I could do."

Dane Shavers was already bored. "Is there anything you can tell me about his past? I've tried to dig up anything. It's like Monty Lincoln is a stone-cold nobody."

She shot a cross look his way. "Oh, he's not a nobody."

"I think you're right. I mean, obviously, he has money to burn." He pointed out, as she shifted in her seat at the discomfort she felt by simply speaking of Monty Lincoln.

"He's a dangerous man. For all."

Dane Shavers leaned in. It was the direction he wanted Margaret Buckey to lead him. "Now why is that, Margaret?"

It would not be much, but it was all she could offer to help along Dane Shavers in his mission to expose Monty Lincoln's Fellowship of the Enlightened. "He's not a traditional theist. He is certainly no atheist. He's not an agnostic. He's…a Luciferian."

Dane Shavers had heard the classification beforehand many times. He delighted in what he had already suspected. Hopefully it was more than a cult. Rather, a death cult. Nevertheless, he wanted to hear her version. "And what exactly is that, Margaret?"

"Everything's real fuzzy." Cindy said, lying down on the floor in a room packed with her fellow Fellows. The setting could have been mistaken for an opium tent in an Old West boomtown; bodies on top of bodies, groping and rubbing, with time forgotten. Yet reality and time waited patiently for them all to return from the wispy mountaintop, the deep wilderness, or the barren desert. Monty Lincoln, lying next to her, knew very well he would have to return from that period of reflection and tell his followers what he had learned in his self-induced exile, brought about by copious amounts of narcotics. His message had fermented long enough in the drowning effects of a prolonged succumbing to the basest desires.

The *fuzzy* Cindy referred to was not the dragging symptoms of the mind and body recovering from the continual saturation of the five senses. It was about where the whole thing was going. As she saw it presently, they were all becoming gorging addicts without self-control. All the faces around her looked worn and noticeably older. They all wanted to know the same thing. Constant revelry had proven to be not enough. "We've given you everything we have. It's been a long time. People are getting tired, Monty. Where do we go from here?"

Monty Lincoln knew all too well the sentiments of his following. The internal grumbling was becoming more endemic in the culture he had crafted, but they were unawares he had led them to the threshold. Looking at the ceiling, lying next to her, Monty Lincoln knew they had arrived. "Ye of little faith; my mother would say when I doubted her judgment, her assurances, and my own abilities. She was the steadfast optimist. It was the only attribute I took from her to cultivate for use in my own life. I questioned and doubted her like a child does…and a fool much later. She always pointed out the pitfalls. I have always willingly jumped straight down into them. One thing I have learned for certain is that the only proper starting point in any successful endeavor in life is from the rocky bottom. Nowhere to go…but up. I believe you are there, Cindy. I believe we are there. It is time for our steady climb out of the pit…ye of little faith."

His hair was disheveled from scalp to jowls. His fine clothes had the sopping look of someone on their fourth day in dress, putting in chemicals and sweating them out without pause, shrunken from the dehydration. It was by far the worst he had looked as he dizzily stood to his feet, nearly stumbling on those lying about. He was raptured in that fuzzy haziness, but it was high time to pinpoint their destination. He was to be loud and boisterous; for he knew they would not hear him any other way.

"Can you see, Fellows?!" He yelled, breaking their trances and bringing them back to the here and now. Their heads ceased to sway and their eyelids to sag. They all thought, *what now?*

"The entire world is confused. Sensitive to the touch. Clawing at the virtues of a repugnant child. Resistance to this desperate state only goes so far as the random jabbering behind a digital wall and the rare demonstrations completely unrelated to the fact that all are being sold off—equally. Their only concern is the trends streaming into their eyes like acid blinding them. All it amounts to is a collective identity crises.

"The masters of wealth are encouraged and content with this state of affairs. All they have to do is keep screaming—freedom, equality, optimism, happiness! These masters use these illusory words to enslave through endless distraction and petty toiling over inconsequential matters. They want you to remain children. When I say they…the masters…I mean a body unseen; also behind a wall. This wall…this façade…is called the free market: a behemoth of world dominance that few can escape and few have the patience to understand. It is the direct mastering and manipulation of this marketplace which brings about what not only buys freedom, equality, optimism, and happiness; but also unbounded prosperity with impunity. It is unrecognizable to the hordes pulled along blindly by this system lawfully set in place."

Monty Lincoln stopped so they could perhaps see the progression of his framework. First, he had lured them all into the redwoods to separate them from the bustle of urban life. Once that was accomplished, the next phase was to disconnect entirely from the outside world by having them willingly hand over their smart devices, as there were to be no distractions. Finally, all financial assets were to be compiled in a collective pool that Monty Lincoln would use to be grown, instead of spent. The cycle of earning from week to week, or month to month, for the span of one's life was the bitter reality of employment. Monty Lincoln said they could live without working. Eventually, light monitoring was all that would be needed. He created a living atmosphere of real freedom, void of consequence. Their Fellowship was to become a societal avant-garde.

"And what is their religion—these masters? They are not the Christian, the Jew, or the Muslim worshipping a jealous, reactionary, and demanding God that promises a life when this life is no more. The Supreme Toddler! The Supreme Deceiver! They are not the Buddhist or the Hindu lying prostrate to a life of passive resistance; the breaking down of the body to channel some immortal soul that may be their own. They are all afraid of death! These masters! These manipulators! What is the character of *their* God?"

He was nearly twirling in place as they all began to emerge from the fog he had intentionally enveloped them in. They were listening, and now that he held them once again, he would temper his tone back down. After all, he was an understanding man. "A hedonist. A gorger of pleasure, pain, and experience. A keen observer. A seeker of knowledge that puts it to work in this lifetime; for the benefit of one's self and one's fellowship of like-minded friends that know something the distracted multitude does not. It is a club, a fraternity, an order, a mummed society. They are a Fellowship enshrined with one Supreme Being alone; the bearer of the ultimate wisdom."

Above each door throughout the compound hung a golden owl just as there was one hung at the entrance of their domain. He pointed to it, and continued, "The owl can see through the dark while in flight. Along their path, any trace of light from the moon and the starry sky can be used to illuminate the darkness as if a spotlight from the heavens was set before them, affording them the ability to avoid the dangerous traps of nature. This naturally endowed wisdom is innate, highly evolved, and indestructible. The owl is our symbol of this eventuality—to penetrate the darkness.

"Yet there is one wiser who is above and apart from nature—rather, universal. It tells us to be merry and free from pettiness. Free from chains. We are to eat of the forbidden fruit which unlocks the knowledge that the God of sacrifice; the God of perpetual ignorance; the God that peddles the lie that life never ends—does not want revealed. Our God of Light is benevolent, uninhibited, and merciful.

"So, Fellowship! There it is. These masters know that the only way to have paradise on earth, in this lifetime, is to rule on the backs of those enslaved by the God of Abraham who prefers blindness to the light of vision. Knowing is the centerpiece. Secrecy is the pulpit. Now we will let the light stream in, Fellows. The light of Lucifer!"

**zzz…**

He was ready to absorb all that Frank Winkleshten was undoubtedly going to hurl at him. The report Wink was flipping through had been slapped together with the same hastiness of a middle school student's book report based solely on Cliff notes. Dane Shavers had slacked to the point of personal shame, but the worry over Wink's reaction affected him even more. In Wink's vaulted high-rise office with reading glasses resting on his bulbous nose, he kept shifting his eyes upwards from the paper as Dane Shavers pretended to be fixated on random objects sitting on the desk. Wink's eyes would draw back down on the paper, deliberately turning each page like he was trying to look deeper into an otherwise placid document. His eyes would flip back up, and they seemed to beg Dane Shavers; 'You're joking, right?'

Wink closed the stapled report flat on his desk, slid it back towards Dane Shavers like a casino-dealer would a playing card, removed his reading glasses while setting them down carefully, and then interlocked his fingers to a resting state. Dane Shavers ceased his avoidant stares into nothing and faced Wink who was scaffolding a condescending smile. Wink had been handed the wrong answers. They were the ones he already heard.

"You must have been up all night putting this together, which must be the only plausible explanation for this resounding piece of shit. You could've just handed me a note that read; 'What everyone already knows about Malcolm Grace.' At least that would have wasted less of my time. So, let's go over again why I brought you under my employ. This time pay attention. You're obviously not getting it yet.

"Dirt!" Wink yelled, crumpling the report into a ball and pegging it off Dane's forehead. "Who does he fuck? Where's the misappropriation of funds leading to an official inquiry? What extreme political associations has he had in the past? Who are his biological parents? Drugs I don't even care about. These days, he'd be a weirdo if he hadn't, and who would believe him anyways? Why no wife? Why no kids? Why no desire to have either? We used to be able to play the gay card, but the whole world's going gay these days. Better yet! Does he hate the gays? That would actually be a better way to smear him these days. You have to inextricably tie him to something seedy with moral implications, and it's to be found somewhere in his past. You have to make him deal with his past!"

Wink stood up from his chair and turned away from Dane Shavers to face the city. He was frustrated to find Malcolm Grace so squeaky clean. "Anyone can be ruined in the public mind. Even me. But Mr. Shavers, the difference between you and me is that you're under my thumb. The next time I see you there better be some credible results, or else our association will come to an abrupt end. As you can likely foresee, you would be the loser in the course of that exchange. I prefer mutual benefit. It's not wise to waste my money. I would never forget it. I would never forgive it. Now go get me my fucking dirt!"

Shooing him away like a fly at a barbeque, Dane Shavers stood up and gladly walked out without a word; tail between his legs, somewhat dismayed he still had the job. Joshua Bannister was entering as they brushed past each other with a quick nod. Joshua Bannister made a face describing what he thought of Dane Shavers—a joke. Sitting down where Dane Shavers had just been blown in place, he said, "I don't know about keeping him around. He's a whack-job."

Wink wholeheartedly agreed with the assessment, but also knew the public mind was a whack-job. Dane Shavers was a man who jumped to conclusions and appealed to the fear-ridden, suspicious corners of the psyche. Wink just needed him to get motivated, or more necessarily; catch a break in the story. "We'll give him a little more time. Either way, I'm going to cut him to pieces when it's all said and done."

Joshua Bannister quickly moved on to more pressing matters. "The ratings just keep on inching up for *The Boland-Bloom Partnership*. It's almost like there's no ceiling. A cow that never runs out of milk with these two."

It was time for Wink to ask a stupid question—stupid because of all people he should know the answer, but as the head he could pay less attention to the details of what lain in the stretches of his media empire. "What season is that on?"

"Third. It looks like it's going to be the final season." Joshua Bannister hinted, licking his lips and bobbing his head, indicating the news was about to get better.

"Final season?"

Joshua Bannister's new concept was in pre-production, inching towards public consumption, and he knew they would gorge on this one. "Our lovely couple has agreed to terms on *The Big Switch!*"

Wink was happily reminded of the evolving concept which constituted the natural progression of their exclusive association. Wink never thought something like it would ever be popularized in his lifetime, much less on his very own broadcasting network. But the world was moving fast, and with that blinding acceleration, it was perfectly acceptable to be a man one day and a woman the very next.

*

Tooting another line up his nose was becoming more difficult. He was losing suction and his natural filter was being smelted away. The bodily bulk he once boasted had also melted away and every day was exactly the same. It had been that way since his days on Conversion. Though wildly popular and personally profitable, it put in motion a locomotive whose wheels he wanted blown off the track. Then he could run away, leaving the wreckage behind, only looking back to see how it was all so stupid.

Following the initial awkward introductions during *Conversion*, it moved along in the same direction to the delight of the viewership. Bridgette Mahoney became Gay J's natural enemy as she pursued Tommy Bloom. She chose what she knew to be her most effective approach—putting sexy on. She felt the best spot for a little impromptu romance was around the wishing well in the castle courtyard. There she would make her move.

"Do you believe wishes come true, Tommy?" Bridgette Mahoney asked, nudging her elbow against his to purposely close the space between them.

"Only if you have a coin, I guess. And I don't have one on me." He said, nervously patting his pockets while she laughed like it was so irresistibly amusing.

"Oh, you're so funny, Tommy! And you're right! Even a wishing well comes at a price." She noted, looking up at the big night sky, drawing in a deep breath to demonstrate her fondness for the crisp Romanian air, and then placing her hand atop his. She acted fast before the awkward stillness fell upon them. "Look!"

She pointed skywards, declaring, "A shooting star!"

"Where? I don't see it." He said, scanning the cosmic expanse for a glimpse at the otherwise rare occurrence. He eyes fell upon nothing of significance.

"Aw, you missed it!" She exclaimed, feigning disappointment at what she had not seen as well. She only used the imaginary shooting star to create another opening. "Now that's a free wish, Tommy. It's given to us by the stars…only by chance. Do you want to know what I wished for?"

Their faces were the closest they had ever been to meeting, and her pull was apparent. He conceded internally that she was beautiful, but all it did was further amplify his anxiety. "You're not supposed to tell me, because then it won't come true."

"It's coming true now." She seductively whispered, crashing her lips into his to provoke the arousal of a suppressed attraction which she assumed had no choice but to bow to the authority of her beauty. Her eyes were shut; his wide open in terror. She strung the kiss out, looking for the eventual transition to the French-style. As she eventually pulled away without it going any further, she optimistically felt it was the first step to achieving her goal to convert him. Barring that, she felt she had just kissed a lifeless mannequin.

In the final assessment, she had failed to convince him to bat for the other team. Never having to deal with rejection from the opposite sex in the record of her life, Bridgette Mahoney then became bitter and reclusive. She snapped back when spoken to for no apparent reason, often digressing into a hissy fit. In short, the beautiful Bridgette Mahoney became ugly. Joshua Bannister simultaneously being the architect and enforcer of his own design had only one direction for her to go, which was to shift her attention to converting Gay J. Her reaction was more than candid. "Eww, you're gross!"

Barbie Red, for her special part, kept the hunt going for the both of them; unrestricted by any hint of discriminating tendencies. In her relentless pursuit it became violently apparent her aim was to knock off the competition. Her means to that end was the use of blatant intimidation through targeted and unveiled threats. Her favorite target was none other than Bridgette Mahoney who epitomized all the qualities Barbie Red despised throughout her youth and beyond. Bridgette Mahoney was the goody two shoes with a permanently fixated smile and a birthright of entitlement. She was a real *daddy's* girl who actually did have a *dad* to take care of every little thing. Cornering Bridgette Mahoney out of the blue one day, Barbie Red made it clear. "Listen here, you bleach-blonde spoiled-rotten bitch! Stay away from Tommy or you might wake up missing something that makes your whore face look so pretty!"

Her other attempts at edging out the competition were less daring, but still quite effective. She would sneak into Shonda Murano's bed chamber and hide some key accessories which enabled her to look her best for the day. This not only frustrated Shonda Murano, but also wasted her time so that when she came into the presence of either Gay J or Tommy Bloom, she seemed to carry an air of irritability.

She was always seeking out the culprit to these non-crimes which would lead her to make false accusations, though her main suspects were always narrowed down to either Bridgette Mahoney or Barbie Red; feeling they were the closest to the level of her own devious nature. Barbie Red's multiple orchestrated attempts at subversion and conversion ultimately came up short. She digressed right along with those she conspired against. When the game was finally up and there was no hope for getting either Gay J or Tommy Bloom, she resorted to the ultimate slur hitting below the belt, screaming about them both; "Fags!"

When Shonda Murano decided to out-maneuver the culprit of misplacement by hiding her own things, she was then able to present the product once strut down the runway. Violet lace covered her most treasured parts with a matching silk blouse draped over glowing caramel skin that could make any sentient being take another look. The package was tightly wrapped and the accentuation of her form lent to the impression of professionalism. Unfortunately for her, it was just not enough to sway Gay J to the other side. Like her competition Barbie Red, contempt at the lack of his desire for her manifested itself in a high-charged exchange. In her response to rejection, which never happened, she returned to the hood she had risen from.

"Yo' dumb ass is just anotha' one of those old school fools wanting to stay street the rest of dey lives!"

"Oh! So yo' triflin' ass is on a different street?"

"Actually, miles and zip codes away from yo' ass, nigga!"

"Nigga?! Looks like you pullin' back into Compton! Welcome back to da' hood, ho! Ya' see, you think yo' ass is so special. That's the last thing that turns my nigga ass on!"

They never got on the same level; street or otherwise. This left room for someone like Monica Brooks who was undoubtedly the most passive of the womanly bunch and a front-runner for the sweetest. So sweet, in fact, that Barbie Red could only glare at her without considering one of her private cornering consultations of intimidation. Monica Brooks became a soundboard for Tommy Bloom after their first time in the hot tub where a hint of relative sentiment was found between them, allowing a friendship to naturally form where they could both take pleasure in each other's company. Tommy Bloom saw something in her that Gay J rarely offered: an understanding warmth in contrast to his dispassionate persona stemmed from the extreme circumstances of his youth. Gay J grew into being guarded and suspicious of sentimental overtures. Monica Brooks had grown up in a sheltered existence in the same socio-economic category, saddled with similar delicate sensibilities, and shined as an athlete in the more graceful sports. Likenesses tended to lead them both to seriously consider the ridiculous premise of conversion.

"We should just try." She said, playfully crossing her legs on the bed to clearly signal the flirt.

Tommy Blooms' elbow propped up his hulking frame lying next to her, receiving the signal clearly. "What if it ruins something? I love our conversations. It's actually the only thing getting me through this."

"You'll never know till you try." She pressured, cocking her head to the side, wearing a smile slathered in cuteness. "Listen, just close your eyes and trust me."

It was the confirmation he needed to follow her lead—trust. He nervously drew in some breaths like he were about to leap from the top rope in the wrestling ring. Closing his eyes, frozen in darkness, he awaited her move. *Should I pucker? Should I leave a slight opening? Should I scream like a little girl and put a stop to this whole thing? I'll just stay still.*

Suddenly, her moist lips were upon his in a subtle and easing manner. With her eyes closed she pressed into him as the warm breath escaping their nostrils danced about. She put to task the tip of her tongue as a jousting match ensued. Yet, it was as far as both were willing to go. Pulling apart to resume the usual space and opening their eyes to see the reaction, it was clear they were clutching at thin air.

"What do you feel?" She softly asked.

"Absolutely nothing." He replied, dismayed and awakened at the same time. She smiled at his deer-in-the-headlights expression, but was disheartened by the fact that she had indeed felt something. He obviously viewed it as further confirmation that he was—indisputably—one hundred percent—gay.

Then there was Heather Douglas who often found herself as Monica Brooks' counter-role within the castle boundaries, being that her attachment to Gay J was just as equal. What Gay J saw in her was a much-ado-about-nothing attitude leaving the impression of a laid-back, drama-free persona, which he fancied. The emotional output of Tommy Bloom was endearing to a point, but at times, it was downright annoying. Heather Douglas was a dogged realist unafraid of experiences leading to new perspectives, but never advertised the trait without constraints. Of the other women in the castle she was the ghost posing no immediate threat to the living, which afforded her the luxury of being present while simultaneously being unnoticed, and ultimately forgettable, just so long as she didn't make a peep. Her illusive style made room for a daring proposition to be taken quite seriously.

"We should just get naked and give them what they want." She nonchalantly posed, pointing to the camera nestled at the top corner of the wall.

At her suggestion it was Tommy's face that came flashing through Gay J's mind as the pangs of separation served as a reminder of what he still had. It was not enough to back down from an obvious challenge. He could not have given less of a damn about who he was entertaining on the other side of the camera. It was all about accepting the challenge. In his world, any perceived weakness was a personal failure and a major character flaw. After searching Heather Douglas' eyes for the sure signs of sincerity, he calmly responded, "Let's do it."

Moments later they were rolling in bed, skin clashing against skin, lips wrestling for position, and bold intentions being acted upon. They had taken nothing to lubricate their base senses, aiding in the liberation of their sexual energies. No blow. No drink. No smoke. Ultimately, nothing Gay J could point his finger at to explain why he carried around a wet noodle instead of a big black stick. There had to be only one explanation.

Rounding first base and heading towards second was when he frustratingly began putting his pants back on, wondering aloud, "How did I get this gay?"

All of it spelled the closing act for the show itself. Once the possibility of a successful conversion had been fully exhausted the only trajectory was downwards for the homesick cast. The contracts were nearly fulfilled and the itchiness to depart from the aristocratic castle nestled in the majesty of the Carpathian Mountains was acutely palpable. A begrudging selfishness began to consume them all.

Tommy Bloom was nearly taken over completely by his want for an end to it all. He would cry, cry out, and pathetically wallow in his longing to re-unite with the man he found most attractive to all other human beings. Gay J just upped his alcohol intake to bring about as much sleep as possible to pass the time without any effort. The women, being isolated to the castle proper, were reduced to a whirling frenzy of vile insults, half-baked physical entanglements, and the complete disregard for spatial courtesy. What prevailed was a highly entertaining meltdown for the viewership just as Joshua Bannister had envisioned as a contingency outcome. Conversion or no conversion, he knew the failed experiment would be just as entertaining as a successful one.

The whole idea never meant to serve any particular party entirely. Those outlets leaning politically to the right of societal matters hated it because of the cast, but not necessarily the experimentation of conversion therapy. Those outlets leaning left hated it because it presented a stage for conversion therapy itself, which they viewed as the most preposterous of all premises. The slanderous gossip columns were giddy and grateful, as it provided them with a subject matter to bark about incessantly, never running short on material. The middle-grounder majority simply shook their heads and laughed without any kind of spirited commentary. *Conversion* became the highest grossing show in the multi-decade history of Wink Broadcasting.

It left Gay J—at present—in the bathroom making sure the blow had went all the way up, leaving little trace of his real condition. Following personal inspection, he emerged from his fifteen hundred square foot bathroom into his equally-sized bedroom, and then into his stepped living area overlooking the flat expanse of Los Angeles proper. Perched in the Hollywood Hills amongst the royalty of the industry their mansion was the proverbial heaven on earth. It was true. Their lives had changed drastically.

The power couple were no longer who they once were. Gay J was no longer behind the mic and the Buccaneer was no longer leaping from the top rope. Following the wrap-up of Conversion it was Joshua Bannister who began pushing for the natural progression of their highly profitable association. The next concept revolved around the tested and strengthened bond between Jeremy Boland and Tommy Bloom. *The Boland-Bloom Partnership* documented their engagement, marriage, and lavish nesting in the Hollywood Hills. Their riches grew to unimagined heights as the personal talents they once rigorously exercised drifted into the obscurity of their memories. Now they were just celebrities in the public eye. Their daily lives became the performance.

With all the glitz and glamour fueled by a cornucopia overly satisfying the human frailty of want and need—there was still something missing. In reality, they only had brief moments with each other, and even less with themselves. It was usually when they slept, but even then they were being watched. Going out in public was like entering a wasteland filled with flashing bulbs, invasive and mocking questions, and a certain profound dread at undertakings 'normal' people would never understand. With the world at their feet all they could feel was the most enduring misery.

As Jeremy Boland slipped open the glass door leading out to the unused Olympic-sized lap pool, he noticed his partner sunbathing in a pink speedo, wearing white-rimmed sunglasses. He sauntered over and sat down on the netted lounge chair next to Tommy. "What's new, baby?"

"Have you talked to JB?" Jeremy asked Tommy, clearly flushed of all enthusiasm.

Tommy looked down at the haze hovering above the city where the hysteria of popular culture had them both squirming in its fickle grip. Jeremy had never come close to considering a gender transition. Tommy, on the other hand, had always felt completely comfortable in his effeminate sensibilities. The only part that scared Tommy was the actual surgery, and then the rehabilitative recovery. Besides those crucial factors, Tommy could not find an immediate reason not to pull through with the third installment on their odyssey with Wink Broadcasting. Sexually, Jeremy had always been the pin and Tommy the cushion. It was the reason The Big Switch would not be that much of a big change at all.

"Yeh, I did. I guess it's something to think about." Tommy answered with clear hesitation and even less enthusiasm.

"Then a kid?" Jeremy followed, looking out over the city he was well on the road to hating.

Everything was pre-planned. Nothing they ever did was spontaneous. One would remain a man, and the other would become a woman. They would bring a child not into the world, but into their world. If it was really all going down then Jeremy wanted to go on with his private interest, which had always brought him a discernable amount of grief, inexhaustible in its nagging. The mystery had always been who his biological father was and what had become of him. He knew the same nagging question would eventually ail the child they chose to adopt, and down the line it would go.

As they kept their eyes to the expanse, Tommy placed his hand atop Jeremy's. Their fingers devotedly interlocked as they remained in the same accord. "Yeh, baby…then a kid."

## North of the 38th Parallel

The Pyongyang skyline had become increasingly bleak since that fateful morning when Sun-rae lost her father whom she revered above all else, and the dear friend who had shown her so much. Jing had provided a glimpse into a world outside her rigidly insulated one: all order, all obedience, and all consuming. Her father, apart from Jing, had been an entirely different man in societal stature and personal constitution. He had willingly adhered to the conformity demanded by the cult of personality which had no appetite for deviating from the rule. He decided to go headlong into this conformity once he found her mother, and then became devoutly obedient to it when Sun-rae came into the world. Though they went opposite directions in their walks of life, it still seemed to Sun-rae they were somehow one in the same. Both had smelt the rottenness and stagnation their reality was wading in. Though in differing degrees, both had plotted secretly against their masters. This same natural outgrowth of defiance began to stretch from her being in all directions as she reached maturity.

Sun-rae had not lost contact with the Underground that perused the market district prior to the purge. It took a while for them to coalesce again, due to the existential fear the purge naturally kindled, but in time their fears diminished. The primary object of defiance had always been the soft power of outside media influences, and sure enough, she again found a hidden spot in the midst of harsh officialdom where she could indulge as she pleased. Her interests had grown apart from the innocent portrayals of Western values, and the free-wielding way of life she admired. The deep losses handed to her crushed the amiability of childhood, leaving a crystallized disposition desiring to feel more of the same. Only this time, she would be the one exerting the force to effect.

In her thirsty search for a new stream to the outside world she had stumbled onto the many Westerns of Clint Eastwood; his name alone invariably reeking of a fully-armed frontier loner without want of love, sympathy, or mercy. It was all in the eyes, announcing the arrival of death in measured breaths as the hawk circled above and the ominous whistling bounced off canyon walls between two deeply entrenched foes. The duel had been set in motion by destiny. Official justice had nothing to do with the proceedings. They were outside of the law according to their own law, crafted among bad men and harlots riding their chariots into Hell.

She was also introduced to John Rambo; the Vietnam veteran who had killed entirely too many people for his conscience to stomach. Sure, it had been sanctioned by the powers that be, but the effects of duty only left him with the habits of a drifter: endless wandering, no attachments, and self-imposed isolation in order to cut away the past that was brought to light in the bustle of society. Who was to make ruin of his seemingly harmless travels? None other than the authorities with all of their impunity, selfish enjoyment of their mandate, and the overseeing of injustice dealt to those not fitting into their narrow profile of what a person should be. After rattling the hornet's nest which was John Rambo, it became a complete surprise to the authorities that he would be so bound to a counterassault of methodical execution, resplendent with various gateways of gunfire and strategically placed explosions to make those cackling uniformed clowns wish they would have killed him when they had the chance. Bloody, unleashed, REVENGE!

Of course, there was a classier and less roguish way to kill one's enemies. Preferably, it was to be done in a formal tuxedo following a martini—shaken, not stirred—on the wing of an airplane in flight, on the roof of an international bullet train, or in pursuit behind the wheel of a rare classic automobile. All the hi-tech gadgets and special operations training utilized to scrupulous efficiency rendered all international terrorists bent upon the destruction of civilization—in the end—powerless. The executioner of these high-level deviants was none other than Bond—James Bond.

Sun-rae mused about being constantly submersed in a world without law, typified by the old Westerns of Clint Eastwood, the one-man army delving out vigilante justice on the establishment of authority itself, and the intelligent assault imbued with class in the tight package of Sir James Bond. She fantasized of combining all the characters and their traits into a single unified force, under her command alone, to burn and destroy the effigies responsible for taking away her dear friend and loving father.

She always thought of what she would say to the Bowibu officer who allowed them entrance to witness that fateful morning tragedy, and the high ranking Party official who pulled the lever to hang her father until dead. It was a lighter piece of cinema which catered to her ethereal side, but evenly maintained realist tones without becoming something else entirely. She loved *The Princess Bride* with her favorite character's lifelong quest to avenge his father's death at the hands of the six-fingered man. She easily memorized the character's vow when he found the killer. "Hello. My name is Diego Montoya. You killed my father. Prepare to die!"

Her renewed association with the purposely unnamed Underground network brought her into a more impactful role where she was able to build her physical strength and temper her mental edge to withstand the fear of being discovered as a traitor. No longer was it about the procurement of outside media, hunched in dark corners or in shanty spots of repute, to view what was forbidden; attention always broken by the slightest sounds. It was now about personal action. One question always resonated within her: *What are you prepared to do?*

There were many avenues of service to the ghost effort against the powers. Naming it could help identify, locate, and forcibly squash the movement. With such a disproportionate playing field it was necessary to pretend they were all just playing a game, but no one would know what they were playing. Thinking of it any other way would lead to certain death, or even worse; the continuation of life in a penal camp. Those who took part in the treasonous activities were only known by the number of their specific role. Like any organization, legal or illicit, communication lines had to remain open and flowing to achieve operational success. Every part had to know what the other was doing. Any static in the transmission could sink the effort into a quicksand never to be pulled from. That's why role #29 (courier) was so widely revered and yet so scantily volunteered for. The operations impinged on the accurate and successful dissemination of information. Without a central command base, underground tunnels, caves embedded in mountainous terrain of unforgiving topography, or places like the market district had once been; operatives like Sun-rae were imperative to building a plan without holes, to be executed at a time unknown. Springing into action was not just a concept. It was how they were going to get their point across as soon as the State showed a crack—an opportunity. And what kept circulating through their thoughts? *Arirang! Arirang!*

In Sun-rae's able hands the messages were always received. Knowing every nook and cranny of Pyongyang, along with most of the passing faces, aided her task greatly. She delivered to many recipients covering a wide range of positions within society and the State itself. They were court clerks, police officers, professors, shop directors, street vendors, bus drivers, and even others with jobs unknown. Arriving home each night, it became clearer that it was all a big game of chance; out of her hands once committed to the mission.

Her mother could tell she was always someplace else in thought, but she was the only one who could notice. Sun-rae's studies had not lagged and continued to fluctuate between the top three spots in her class. She was never a busy socialite, only doing so when it was obligatory. She had the natural reclusive behavior of diligent and smart people whose passions are driven towards the future. Putting one's head down amidst the distracting social fray was the only path to something near that end, and she never stopped thinking about that end. All of these character traits curbed the suspicion which could bring it all crashing down in one fateful swoop.

While Sun-rae waited for the dinner call from her mother she poured over some blueprints in her room, trying to figure new routes to break up the routine of her rounds, and remain unnoticed. Her concentration was broken when she heard the distinct sound of boots knocking down the hallway. They brought chills, freezing her for the moment. Those were State-issued boots; the same ones that had taken her father away. She heard them stop outside their front door. She hurriedly folded down the blueprints and stuffed them under a loose floorboard in her closet. She then sat on her bed to await what was to come. She looked at her trembling hand which was a symptom of primal urges blended with the human penchant for killing. She was feeling it ever more as of late.

Moon opened the door to a face she had once seen whose eyes gleamed with the same penchant Sun-rae was dealing with in her bedroom. It was the Bowibu officer who had led them to the viewing in May Day Stadium where her husband was hung from a beam. The Bowibu officer's smile was the same as on that day. A sickly nausea brewed within her instantly, but she would never hand him the pleasure of knowing it.

"Hello, comrade. Please come in." She humbly invited, moving to the side and stretching out her hand as if welcoming the most distinguished guest.

Holding his peaked officer's cap in one hand, and with the other snug to the small of his back, he slowly entered as she closed the door behind him. He looked about at the décor, which amounted to pretty much nothing. The bare walls accentuated the way the home felt—empty. She had stripped the home of the things serving as a reminder of her husband, which was pretty much everything. All that remained was a line of three framed portraits hanging above the front door. It was the glorious succession of the Kim Dynasty from left to right: Kim il-Sung, Kim Jong-il, and Kim Jong-un. The Bowibu officer smiled back at the smiling faces above their heads.

She walked past him into the kitchen as he continued to lovingly gaze upon their chipmunk faces. "Would you like some tea, comrade?"

Like snapping out of a trance he whipped his head around to face her, nearly seeming agitated that she had interrupted such a precious moment. His smile strangely resurfaced as he answered, "Please! That sounds so nice."

Motioning to the chair tucked under the table, she offered, "If you would like a seat, comrade."

She turned away to prepare the tea as the legs of the chair scraped across the hardwood floor. She racked her mind for the purpose of his unannounced visit. It had been quite a long while since she endured the displeasure of his company, and the only pleasure she gained from this round was that he had come alone. It meant it was not an official inquisition, or even worse: an arrest leading to a re-education camp, or the even more brutalizing Yodok labor camp for the remainder of what would then become her short life. Never had she so carefully prepared a single cup of tea, and never had she so desperately wanted to spike it with a dose of poison.

"We have been watching you." He informed in routine fashion, as was customary. "Not only after your late husband's unfortunate death, but also at your very fortunate birth."

She believed it. She felt it pulsating around her each day, buzzing at her ear like a petty fly. The Bowibu officer carried the habit of reminding people where they stood in relation to his employer, and in his mind, he meant absolutely nothing by it. "But you are not like him. You are much better than him. His heart was too wild…unable to be tamed. An untamed heart cannot be put to proper use for the good of all. You have a heart of goodness."

The churning nausea inside her failed to subside. It was spraying the walls of her insides as she turned to face him with a cup in each hand. She set a cup in front of him and sat herself down across the way. She took a sip with eyes drawn down, slowly set the cup on the face of the table, and then did what she had to with all the dread raked into a giant heap—looking him straight in the eyes.

"He was a lucky man." He complimented, letting the tea sit idle in front of him. "His wisest decision was winning your favor among the many poor decisions he made. He did you a great disservice. Wouldn't you agree?"

Her answer would be a lie, yet it had to be framed in sincerity. "Knowing what I know now…well…I can see your point, comrade."

She was sipping the tea too quickly. Her eyes were darting. Her foot was tapping. None of it could be helped. Interrogation was at the core of his official duties. Bringing doubt to its knees was his specialty. Here he would so kindly, as was his daily good deed, attempt to put her at ease. With the tea losing its steam setting idle in front of him, he had still not taken a sip and his eyes had not darted once.

"Moon, in all honesty, his death served the nation well. He was a man on the inside looking out. He began to have feelings for what he was looking at on the outside. What he forgot was that whatever remains on the outside can never be allowed to enter what was built with blood. It is not because these outside forces will defeat us. That's an impossibility. It's about keeping the blood pure—free from the pollution of foreign diluting. Because they will make it thin and weak—no longer ours. We will cease to be one nation, one people—invincible—indivisible. We will become a Mongrel race without identity, without purpose, and without a history written by our own hands. These outside forces that not only seek our Mongrelizing, but that of the entire world, want to do it without firing a single shot or sacrificing any of their own blood. They want us to spill our blood, on our streets, in our homes; so they can eventually walk in, pick up the shattered pieces, and put it all back together according to their own design. They must not succeed in this! We must survive!" He concluded, erratically waving his index finger and pounding his balled fist on the kitchen table just hard enough to rattle the tea cups.

He still had not taken a sip. Hers was long gone. She needed a break from looking at him. Standing and turning away, she asked, "Would you like me to heat your tea, comrade?"

Oddly looking down at the cup, he forgot it was even there. He had no intent to drink it, but happily replied, "Oh please! That would be lovely."

She reluctantly scooped away the cup, imagining it was the water bowl of a mad dog. The mad dog really wanted to reach her in some way and was fully aware of the tension he brought to the setting. It was true he had another motive concerning Moon. He was not after information. He was after something else. She set the warmed cup back in front of him and then sat herself back down. She went for her cup again, and when she did, he went for his. It was his way of showing they at least had something in common. He kept his sights drawn to the way her thin and smooth lips puckered in anticipation of the hot tea. All she did was look at his forehead; it being normal, featureless, and nothing special. He set down the tea and pretended to be satisfied. It was time for one of his charming allegories.

"Speaking of the outside; there is a game called Jenga in the West. Have you heard of it?"

She had indeed, but in this particular situation she would remain clueless. "I have not, comrade."

He did not believe her answer for a second. "It's a simple game with simple rules. You see, there is a structure…an elongated cube: whole, sound, and complete. The players take turns, pulling pieces from the body of the structure and stacking them on the top end. As you can imagine, this makes for a very shaky foundation, as the objective is to gut the very core of the structure. As with all games there is a winner and a loser. In Jenga, the winners are all the players that did not pull the final piece to bring the whole structure crashing down, which was inevitable as soon as the first block was pulled. Despite how very silly and pointless this game seems to be; do you know how to never be the loser in such a game?"

He cracked a smile as if the punch line was about to be delivered regardless of her answer. He just needed her to give it a little a push. She decided to push in the opposite direction. "The law of averages, comrade?"

His smile tumbled into a dishonest laugh. She was using sarcasm. He hated it, though he conceded it was a perfectly acceptable response. "That's clever—but no. So, again, do you know how to never be the loser in such a game?"

She made a misstep. She knew clever was the last thing she needed to be. Humbly, she answered, "I have no idea, comrade."

He leaned in on the table, moving his head forward like a crane. His face wickedly lit up, he revealed, "Never play Jenga!"

She wished her minor chuckle would have been about courtesy. Fear compelled her to gush forth as the shame swelled within her from doing so. His laugh was more pronounced, but had much more to do with false courtesy, as there were clear intentions behind it. Just as suddenly as he began—so did his laughter stop. "You are so beautiful."

The last time she had been told so was when her husband lived. Then again, it was the first time in a long time she had been so disgusted. The blushing warmth of embarrassment did not flush her cheeks and no chord of any kind was struck within her. Never in her life did she want to be so repulsive and undesirable. As he suddenly stood to his feet, straightening his attire, and clasping his hands behind his back; she realized she had not responded. "Thank you. Very kind of you, comrade."

She felt the mood change as he deliberately began strolling around the kitchen table. His intentions were unfolding. Her dignity was not to be stripped in one of the camps. It was to be stripped right there in her own kitchen. She wanted neither, but would choose the latter in a life and death situation. "I understand how lonely it becomes. I had a wife. She died as well. I didn't see it coming. She was here one day, and gone the next. I think that's something we have in common."

It was true he had lost a wife. She had succumbed to a brain hemorrhage, never returning from her coma. And true, her husband had been there one day and gone the next. Yet, with these supposed commonalities she still felt light years away from him, though they occupied the same space. His wife had been taken by the laws of nature; not of the State. In her mind, there was a stark difference. The distance was felt even more as he placed his hands atop her shoulders, prompting an immediate desire to slip into a coma of her own.

In a whisper, he put it all out there. "We can help each other. We can feel good again. Don't you want to feel good again?"

Every nerve in her body was holding back the violent twitch of self-preservation as he leaned over her with his lips headed for the valley of her smooth neckline. Feeling his hot breath rapidly approaching she held her own breath as if underwater. She tried to detach; to go to another place at the onset of his violation. It did not work as the violent twitch won out against her will, and took up the duty of denying him the pleasure of a willing body. "Please, comrade!"

Only a faint taste of her skin was had as she jerked away from him. She nearly fell from her chair, but his measured speed and strength stood her upright, whirling her around to face him. With his free hand clutching her face to emphasize the inner severity her rejection had aroused; all Moon could feel trembling through her was the march of an impending death.

"You are a brave woman, but dangerously stupid! Choose your end now! Two choices! I'm sure you've heard of Yodok? Hwasong? It would be one of those! That I can promise you! You've heard the stories—horrible stories! Walking skeletons! The unmarked pits of the dead! Treasonous bastards picking through cattle shit for kernels of corn! Babies cooked to be fed to the dogs!"

The ease with which he put her in his clutches sent a good enough message, but the growling evil tones forced her to digress into an uncontrollable sob. Option number two, whatever it was to be, would have to be the lesser of the two evils. Though equally abhorrent to her dignity—quick and bearable.

"The second choice." He said, lowering his voice and quickly pinning her hands behind her back. With a face red with fear, survival, and fury; she had already guessed his verdict. "I take you now. And at least do me the honor of pretending you like it!"

Groping his free hand between her legs she clasped them shut and attempted to swivel away from his probing fingers. As he rolled out his tongue and pressed forward, her hands came loose of his single grip. She began crashing them down on the rack of medals pinned to his breast coat. In doing so, she was vying for a third option: biting, scratching, and kicking—dying right then if it had to be. But she did not want to die! She wanted him to die!

Just as the scuffle was spinning out of control, taking on a mode of its own, they were both pulled back by a voice like that of a ghost. "Mom, are you okay?"

They pulled apart mutually at the sight of Sun-rae standing in her bedroom doorway. Moon assumed Sun-rae had already slipped out the window. It had strangely slipped the officer's mind that she could have been there. Sun-rae's voice resembling his daughter's was the only thing that snapped him out of his rapist will. He fixed his uniform to its original polished state, righted his posture, and returned to his demeanor of creepy official kindness mixed with a sinister professionalism. Sun-rae wielded a surprising magnetic power which left him suspended and dumbfounded. He was not used to such an effect on his being.

"Sun-rae, you are doing well in school. So well, in fact, that you're at the top of your class, I believe." He cheerfully noted, stepping towards her as she stood implacably in place. As he loomed over her, she showed not the slightest sign of flinching. "What are you going to be when you grow up?"

Her answer was programmed and utterly insincere. Even those who had engineered the answer knew the difference. What was said was the most important thing. "To be everything I can possibly be for the Dear Leader. I intend to make up for the shame my father brought upon my family. What a disgrace. What a dishonor."

Still awed by the ice running through her veins at an age of certain uncertainty, he patted her on the head, looking back at Moon with a smile. "How cute! You must be so proud."

He walked past Moon with a threatening glance reserved for her alone, foretelling of another time; another place—without a doubt. He picked up his cap and stuffed it under his armpit. Opening the front door and turning back to them, he had one last thing. "Until next time, comrades! May you both continue on the path of Juche."

Moon and Sun-rae did not need words to share the feeling in the room. Moon was trapped, unable to even dream of a different life full of new experiences and a clean slate. The existing motions of life forced her to conform until she finally expired. Sun-rae, in the defiance of youth, thought the exact opposite. For her, this was the corner turned, the final straw, and the deciding factor all rolled into one. Moon knew her well enough to see that bold decisions were about to lead to fantastic outcomes; whether leading to a telling of the tale at the end of a perilous journey, or a story never to be told as the voice would be silenced in the darkest heart of a supposed civilized world. Moon nodded with a loving smile, saying with her eyes—*Go find out. Be free. I will always love you.*

Within the hour Sun-rae was in the shuffle among the Connectors. They were the ones who planned and facilitated escape routes for those who had the best chances of success. The drawing table before them had maps overlapping one another. They stood around them pouring over different contingencies, bickering over the best ones, and adhering to a fierce desire to inevitable action. There was nothing to make any of it light. These were life and death plans, but unlike the pristine generals of war buttressed by the State; all of their individual asses were teetering directly on the line.

Number 4, who was a stoutly built man with a pudgy face, busted his way through the tumult. "Please countrymen! We must let Sun-rae speak! After all, it is her journey!"

They all fell silent, turning their eyes exclusively to Sun-rae amidst the billowing smoke of cigarettes dangling from the creases of their mouths. The lead Connector placed his hand on her shoulder, and calmly asked, "Which way will you go, Sun-rae?"

They made way for her as she stepped up to the drawing table where the most obvious options were laid out. The route most used was through China. The first leg would be crossing the Yalu River from the west into Dandong, with a group, to meet up with the Snakeheads: a smuggling outfit known just as much for their bad deeds as their good ones. From that checkpoint there would be a trek of several thousand miles through China proper with the constant threat of deportation and repatriation by the only traditional regional ally of the Kim regime. Once through China they would enter Laos with the final destination being Thailand. Once there, if they had not been discovered along the way or trafficked for profit by gangs far seedier than the Snakeheads; the official policy of Thailand was to deport them safely to South Korea. Though at a glance daunting in time, distance, and pure luck; it was the most popular of the known escape routes.

She moved her fingers on to the next map outlining an escape route to the north, crossing the Tumen River into China, but then slipping into Mongolia to eventually reach the capital at Ulaanbaatar where the local authorities would hopefully deport them to South Korea. What discouraged her from that plan was Pyongyang being situated so far from the exit point at the Tumen River. Once they crossed the sliver of Chinese territory they would have to go through one of the most parched and brutal climates on earth—the Gobi desert. Depending on the current diplomatic relations between Pyongyang and Ulaanbaatar it would become a crap shoot as to which Korea they would be sent to—North or South. She saw no favor in those odds.

She went on to a third map, which she only took a look over to give all the options equal attention. On the eastern edge of North Korea was the Sea of Japan. A makeshift and unsound vessel would have to be constructed once they reached the departure point. It was then left in the hands of Providence. The myths surrounding such a feat were regional lore of the most epic proportions. The Mongols under the rule of Kublai Khan had attempted the journey twice to defeat the Japanese on their own soil in the latter half of the thirteenth century. Both times their fleets were swept away by typhoons, which became known as the source of the divine wind—*kamikaze*. Apart from that trinket of history, Sun-rae as a Korean had been aggressively taught about the atrocities of the Japanese occupation which had a hand in birthing the divine revolutionary person embodied in one Kim il-Sung. She had been programmed, against her will, to hate the Japanese. It was nearly equal to her detestation of remaining under Kim rule. The swirling ethnic and national bad blood was too tainted for her to even consider such a route.

The Connectors took turns explaining the pitfalls along the way. She took it all in as a leader does among numerous advisors. However, a completely different idea floated to the top of her mind. It was an idea none of them would entertain, even in a dream. Hers was definitely a dream. It was bloody, violent, and completely irrational— just as the Kim regime had proven itself to be. Her plan involved embarrassing the regime not only at home, but also abroad. If she were to pull it off, it would show a striking crack in the effigy of such a despotic State. If she could beat them, then it would be clear that anyone could beat them. The probability of certain death was secured, but so were the rewards.

Number 4 saw she was off in another place. He wanted to see exactly where that place was. "Sun-rae, what will be your decision? I know it is a difficult one."

Her stern expression panning their hardened faces silenced them. It was time she veered off the beaten path into the unknown. "I will go through the demilitarized zone…straight into the South."

A few of them chuckled; a few it did not register with; and a few more were enraged with dismay, as her lunatic suggestion seemed like an insult to their intelligence, and more importantly, an egregious waste of their time. Number 4 was baffled at how she said it with such finality. The DMZ running along the border separating the two Koreas was one of the most heavily fortified zones in the world, despite its name. Defectors from the Peoples' Army had slipped across the border to the South, but that was only possible due to the proximity and precise knowledge of the inner workings by the defectors themselves. The Connectors could count on one hand the number of successful escapes from the DMZ. It was impossible for a plain civilian.

"Sun-rae, this is a joke, right?" Number 4 proposed, offering a way out from her ridiculous proposition. She stood her ground without responding. "How would you expect to succeed? From the gates to the border with the South is a considerable distance. That's filled with heavily armed soldiers on high alert twenty-four-seven. Perhaps you're not feeling well?"

"No, I'm feeling just fine. My plan is not simple. One flaw, one mistake, one detail overlooked, and I will be dead. But it can be done, and I'm going to do it!" She confidently posited, centralizing them into a raptured focus, reined in by her reckless courage. They were hearing it as a train wreck—impossible to turn away from.

"When will you do this impossible feat?" He pressed forward, unable to fathom any reasonable window for such a suicide mission.

"During the annual military exercises between us."

It was roundly agreed that was the absolute worst time, but then again, none of them could contribute a better time. No time was favorable. "Sun-rae, this is crazy. The entire Peoples' Army will be in motion, readying for war, and most of them hoping it will happen. It's pure suicide!"

"Yes, they will all be there, but they will also be distracted. All of their attention will be aimed across the border, and not what's happening on this side of the border." She explained without bombast like it was something already achieved, tried and true—proven.

"How do you expect to cover the distance, deal with the manpower, and slip across the border undetected? How are you going to get through the front gate much less? Have you lost it, Sun-rae?" a Connector urged, who had laughed, not quite registered it, and was equally enraged with dismay.

She didn't harbor any of their doubts. Her will was greater than their doubt. The hate had consumed the fear whole, and now she was ready to live or die. Nothing more. Nothing less. Her life would no longer be in anyone else's hands. In her mind, it was already done. Looking into each set of eyes with the unlikely grit of a life-long warrior, it was all too clear for her. "I'm going to kill through them to the other side."

**Back in the Great Old United States…**

She so enjoyed her late-night snack; strawberry wafers dipped in low-fat yogurt. In her advanced years the things with which she consumed had to have a healthy spin, even if superficial. Few moments she had all to herself in the confines of an assisted living community, popularly coined as the Projects. The walls constantly vibrated with the sounds of crying babies, booming rap music, and loud verbal exchanges of all kinds. This was her time to tune it all out by tuning into her main man—that cute little crazy white boy— Dane Shavers. As his show was about to begin Loretta Crowley shifted in her recliner to make sure her massive bum was situated just right. She grabbed her 64 ounce diet soda sitting next to her on the floor and readied herself to learn something new about the "Conspiracies of the Illuminati and the New World Order."

Dane Shavers was in his usual mode of paranoia and outrage concerning those fixed in the highest peaks of societal power. Unfortunately, he could only afford a thirty-minute 3 a.m. time slot catering to insomniacs, or those perpetually on uppers. No matter. It was still an audience.

"The New World Order is a method—a system conspiring to an end. Believe me folks, there is an end game. Dangerous and powerful people are at the levers. They're the politicians, giants of commerce, and the privileged from birth. The Bush's, the Clinton's, economic pirates like George Soros, the Koch brothers, and royalty of any kind. I've exposed them all!

"The big players are important, but we can't ignore the up 'n comers. You saw how I blew open wide the truth behind the pagan Bohemian Grove where members of the

Illuminati go to release the burden of having to rule their specific spheres of power. It seems the California redwoods is a popular spot. The Grovers now have a neighbor. It's the Fellowship of the Enlightened led by a man named Monty Lincoln. He may not be running for the highest office in the land, taking down the Bank of England, or sitting on a throne in a castle of yore—but—he is in the process of building a cult that couldn't be up to anything, but very bad things. So let me introduce you to this new lover of evil and deception…one Sir Monty Lincoln."

Dane had received some pictures from Margaret Buckey during the time of their association. With a little touching up, shading, and sizing of what he was given, Dane went into a little more depth. "Not much is known about this man of mystery, but a source close to him reveals that he has always been in the higher rungs of power in some capacity. He's said to be a polyglot, and well-adjusted to unique cultural customs that may suit his agenda. His wealth is not known, but his mastery of global markets and currency exchange trends is formidable. At the compound he has purchased deep in the redwoods, he is engineering a new society that seeks to expand the systematic deprivations of the Illuminati and its eventual goal of a New World Order. You know what it is? The usual: debt slavery, population control, and one-world governance.

"Everyone worships something, and the God that Monty Lincoln—and those promoting the same agenda worship—is none other than the fallen angel, Lucifer! That's right! The bearer of light that blinds the inhabitants of the earth to be ruled not by grace and even-handedness, but through the deceitful accumulation of power into the hands of a select few. All of this is done with a handshake and a smile. There is now a sister base for their operations in the person of Monty Lincoln!"

Loretta Crowley had shifted forward in her chair as her mind flipped back to a point in time she thought had been buried so deep, as to have decomposed without leaving a trace. Yet, there before her eyes was the revenant; that awful part of her life which occurred so long ago. Her psyche had so magically repressed it, but it was the curled ends of his regal moustache and the way his eyebrows came to a fine point at the edges of his temples. His dress was immaculate with all the personalized adornments set in place: the tie pin, the cuff links, the pocket watch, the belt buckle. Surely, it could not be him!

It was now imperative and pressing beyond resistance. She had to get in touch somehow with Dane Shavers, especially if this Monty Lincoln was exactly who she thought him to be. If it were so, then it was no empty conspiracy. He was an incarnation of Lucifer. He was the white devil who at one time wielded full command over her body, and complete dominion over her soul. As Dane Shavers pleaded for more information to bring this villain of the world into better light, Loretta Crowley quickly jotted down the website running at the bottom of her screen. She felt excitement. Other than her late-night snack, she would finally have a purpose.

**ZZZ…**

In a dark room; a strip of neon green lights scrolling along the top half of the wall—changing numbers, decimal points, pluses and minuses, ups and downs, in real time—what did it all mean? Baltasar was beginning to understand, if only modestly, the method to all the madness. Cindy was still in a fog about what it all meant, but she was content with being the Queen to a living King; ornamental and forever observing. Monty said daily events were invariably married to all those symbols running along the wall. These events—ultimately the course of economic transactions—set the mood for the marriage. The reading of the symbols was the relationship actualized. It was to be preferably optimistic. Indifference created nothing. Gloomy and anxious nail-biters left things up in the air and volatile. There was one constant in the marriage, and that was moodiness. Sometimes it amounted to nothing at all; an empty suspicion. Still, one had to make sure by asking the appropriate questions. As many a husband knew through the battles of marriage—a happy wife meant a happy life. The secret was to keep the market happy.

"Oh my, another shooting." Cindy noted, pointing to one of the screens which had the story breaking. She clutched at Monty's elbow to convey her distress and sympathy to people she would never know. "Sixteen dead this time."

Monty shook his head as if to convey he felt something. He would show it only for her sake. He knew random mass shootings never rattled the markets. Prime infrastructure had not been destroyed, shipping lanes were not disrupted, flights had not been grounded, and political upheaval had not brought everything to a standstill. For

Monty, it was an inconsequential hapless circumstance. Those true feelings failed to deter him from patting the top of her hand lightly, saying, "Poor souls. Stamped out too soon."

He allowed a few moments of silence to pass in false reverence until he moved onto more important matters. Thirty minutes remained before the closing bell; a time when money was lost, made, or remained static for the next day of trading. Monty was going to make at least a few moves. "Baltasar, how is that push option ticking with Feather Airlines?"

Baltasar was steadily transforming ever more into a decrepit shell of a man, yet his service and dedication was beautiful to Monty. Cheerfully, he grunted forth, "It's spot on. Ding, ding!"

"Sell it, my gorgeous savage. Put two-thirds of our winnings in crude and keep the remaining in Feather…but this time…put it in a call three above the mark at one week. I do not know how prudent that decision may be, Baltasar. This recent volatility is quite wearisome, but as those blonde-haired surfers ride their waves, so must we. The difference? They shall fall off the board. We shall not."

Baltasar giggled with delight at Monty's comparison, turning back to his computer screen to execute the commands. "Yeah, we're not falling off our boards!"

Monty looked at Cindy with a smile as Baltasar ended his comment with a snort. She smiled in return at how truly quirky Baltasar had always been. She and Monty were about to exchange one of those kisses couples do when only a glance suffices as grounds for a shared notion, when the bell from the front gate rang, swinging their necks to the security monitor hanging from the corner. Deliveries always arrived in the morning. Outside were two men in dark suits, donning dark shades, with hands propped on their hips to blatantly display the gleam of their badges. Dismounted from their blacked-out SUV it was no secret as to the reason behind their sudden and unannounced visit. The grip at Monty's elbow was tightened by Cindy.

"My love, see these gentlemen into the library. Graciously welcome them with open arms."

Not long afterwards the agents entered Monty's lavish vaulted library with their usual uniformed swagger of high-end justice. Both were over-the-hill, but could still pass a physical test if brought to the challenge. However, their action days were over. Their roles were sequestered to an introductory phase, signaling those of action were lying in wait, should any part of the process break down. Introductions and handshakes were robotically exchanged as they all sat down. Monty offered refreshments of their choosing out of formality, but they declined as he knew they would.

"Mr. Lincoln, you must be wondering why we have paid you a visit." The one acting as the lead began.

"Not really. You are the bearers of unsettling news." Monty said with a whiff of self-assuredness and a little disdain for their authority, yet remained without emotion.

Agents like these were never really taken aback by bluntness. It only signaled they could get to the point much faster. "There have been several reports of repeated gunfire within the grounds of your compound."

"Compound?" Monty threw back, showing his displeasure at such a negative connotation. "I prefer to call it an exotic estate."

"Regardless of what you think it is…the fact is…that repeated gunfire has been consistently reported. Can you explain this?" The other offered forward in a more obtuse tone.

Monty was not in the least confused, but still appeared to look that way for his own amusement. "Yes, we have guns. We shoot for recreation, for sport, and sometimes randomly for no particular reason when the pleasures of the night seem to get away from us. All of it is done within the confines of our exotic estate."

The agents knew this encounter was about to come to a close. It had already served its purpose—putting Monty Lincoln and his Fellowship of the Enlightened on notice. The lead would deliver the rest of the message. "Monty, there is also concern that people are being held here against their will. You know…the fact that nobody goes in and nobody comes out? We would like to take a look around, talk to a few people, and really just make sure everyone is in fair condition…and of course…under your supervision."

"There are…and have never been…any children at this estate. Each one of our Fellows is a fully grown, independently thinking adult, which maintains all the faculties necessary to make personal decisions for themselves. As for their condition, you can simply look around and see this is not a haven of squalor. Knowing that, I believe, is the only assurance you will need at this point and time. Is there anything else, gentlemen?"

Monty knew full well his approach would anger the bureaucratic messengers, but he also knew blind compliance would in no immediate way lead to the ATF forever disregarding their existence. The inquisitive machine had been set in motion. In the end there would be two options: pack it all up quietly and return to society, or brace for the showdown. Monty had never desired a family of his own. He had always been a man of the moment, frolicking in the waters of wild spontaneity. This Fellowship was his way of settling down. They were his family to raise as he saw fit. He would protect that family. These men would never understand that. It was too utopian of an ideal for their boxed-in and rule-driven world.

He saw the agents to the door and they wished each other well. Monty walked past the library and down the hallway framing all the appearances of order, form, and instilled class. It was the first half of the exotic estate—the tamed half. When he opened the door to the other half it was a passageway to an alternate reality; precisely the one he wanted to shield from the prying eyes of the agents.

There the Fellowship was gathered around a rectangular pool of clear water sunk into the floor where a naked pair of those original wretches from the coffee shop days were half-submersed. The bearded and tattooed man was holding his lover's hand as she drew in machine gun breaths and pushed hard at measured intervals. A celebration was at hand around them. There was a clown forming balloon animals of different colors, and once they were speedily assembled, he would toss them into the pool for a float. A kid—that is, a young goat—was there just because someone thought it was a great idea. There was cake and ice cream, and a punchbowl spiked with vodka. A glittering banner hung from each corner of the wall, sagging down over the center of the pool. It read, *Welcome to the Fellowship!* The gaiety and anticipation flowed freely through the ruckus audience. Monty had built it up as the next step in their evolution. This day was to be marked and never forgotten. All of the partying suddenly halted when the clear water turned red below the expectant mothers' waistline. The swaying deep red cloud and her horrible screams froze them all in time.

It was real. Their first natural-born citizen had arrived!

Monty, still fully clothed, walked into the pool as the newly-appointed father fished through the cloud of blood for the fresh life. After one last howl of agony and one last push, up bobbed the stained and wrinkled newborn. The father scooped the child up in his anxious arms. The child drew into a fit of frantic crying as it shook violently from the shocking transition from a warm and cozy world to a blindingly cold one. The mother took her child from the father, and the tears of agony turned to ones of joy. She knew she had done well.

Cindy had followed Monty into the pool carrying a towel and a blanket. Monty handed them to the glowing mother who hurriedly wrapped up the child, holding it flush to her bare bosom. Monty rubbed the child's forehead with his thumb and smiled down upon the doting parents. "What do we have there? A boy or a girl?"

The mother, still uncontrollably weeping, announced, "It's a girl!"

The *ooh's* and *ah's* filled the room as Cindy attempted to hold back her tears. Monty smiled big, and asked, "What shall be the child's name?"

The mother glanced at the father, and both again agreed. "Lilith!"

*Brilliant*, Monty thought. Such a perfect fitting. It was time to acknowledge the significance of the moment, so he lifted his head and began. "This is the first-born member of a new society. Our society!

"Lilith was the name of the first woman, created not from man for man's use, but created for her own sake to seek her own way. She is the free spirit beholden to none, never chained to guilt and shame. She is the rarest—the priceless—the most natural. Through her, human will knows no bounds. She is a pure reflection of our society. Now we grow and leave it all to the winds. Welcome, Lilith! You will be madly loved!"

The room returned to their celebration with even more earnest as Monty turned around to Cindy. He rubbed her belly, thinking about his full life which had felt like such up until then. It was only going to become fuller. He was tickled beyond what any vice instantly delivered. Cindy was with child, and soon she would be wading in that very water. Monty's only selfish hope was that it would be a boy.

No 'likes' on his latest post. It was another one completely ignored. Ral thought it was pretty witty; one of those general observations that is supposed to be relatable to anyone, thereby inducing the reply, 'I know what you mean…feel the same way about that.' Ral supposed no one out there knew what he meant. It probably didn't bode well that he ended his observation by stating, 'Just a thought'; which signaled he really didn't have much confidence in the observation himself. In all honesty, he really hated *Bookfaces*. No true friends were on there, but now he was on his way to see a *real* friend—Maddie.

The summer before they climbed on Maddie's roof to take in the cloudless night sky filled with twinkling stars. Maddie had explained the amazing energy of a star, and how there were theories saying the universe began from an exploding star, and because of all of those fragments, it meant everyone was made of stars. She even went so far as to say the entire universe may be just one big, bright, burning star—and they just didn't know it. Maddie was not only dreamy in the eyes of Ral, but she was also a dreamer. That's what he loved about her. All of it gave him the inspiration to pluck her heart strings with his original birthday present.

He had crafted it with his own two hands: along with some wood chisels, sand paper, stain, and gloss. He carved a star into a block of wood, which could have been mistaken for the Lone Star of Texas, yet he was still confident she would know the real meaning behind it. Below the star he had carved the word *Precious* in cursive script. It had been his secret pet name for her, and though she had never been given the chance to react, he believed she soon would. It had taken him months to craft, and he had done a fine job if he had to say so himself.

He rounded the corner to see Toby Self's truck in the driveway to his unwavering disgust. It wasn't going to matter. Nothing was going to deter his special delivery. He strutted up to the front door, and just as he was about to ring the bell, the door opened to Toby and Maddie in the entranceway; both startled at Ral standing in the way with a wrapped present in tow. It was obvious she was walking Toby out, concluding their visit to Ral's delight. Toby quickly got that look in his eye which meant he was about to stir up some trouble. In one decisive move he threw his arm around Maddie's shoulders, and pivoting so his beefy back faced Ral, swallowing up the slight Maddie; he landed a kiss on her—long and hard. It wasn't a harmless goodbye peck. It was meant to fire Ral up with jealousy, which is what it superbly accomplished. Toby hadn't thought it through all the whole way, though. It had also fired-up another person sitting on the couch watching Sunday football with a beer fixed in his hand.

"Bye, babe!" Toby said, shuffling past Ral with a smirk only meant for him to see.

Johnston followed him outside as Ral and Maddie watched on: one hoping for a showdown, and the other nervous one might break out. "Hey Toby, what the hell ya' think you're doing?"

He wasn't loud. He was plain and even. Before turning around to face Johnston, Toby said in his head, *Ah, old timer, don't get in over your head.*

Maddie wanted to see none of it. She pleaded in vein. "Dad!"

Toby turned to face him with a faint smirk for the sake of showing slight disrespect. "Sir?"

"I've never laid down any rules for how you handle my daughter under my roof, 'cause I only figured it'd be understood, and I wouldn't have to spell it out." Johnston laid out.

"Spell out what, sir?" Toby pressed on, acting oblivious to where he was headed.

"Dad!" Maddie called out again on deaf ears.

Ral's eyes were wide with a matching mouth. He said in his head, *Get 'em, Mr. McCreeley!*

Johnston took a step forward to square-up the bigger young man. The look Johnston shot him was only brought out of the vault on special occasions. "Listen to me, Toby. I'm not the edu-crats you dodge or the coaches you flatter when you used to be worth a damn on the football field."

It struck Toby deep as only the reminder of a personal failure can do. The faint smirk was gone, and Johnston leaned in. "I'm much…much…worse than them." Johnston let a moment pass for the soaking effect before he continued, referring to the kiss that had just been placed. "Not like that. Not in my home. Have we come to terms?"

"Dad!" Maddie nearly screamed. She knew well enough to remain where she stood.

Ral was still begging for karma to intervene. *Oh please, Toby. Do something stupid.*

Johnston's eyes never blinked, and neither did Toby's. One had the capacity to kill. The other was just a bloated bully. Strangling his desire to rebel against perfectly good reason as he customarily did, Toby conceded without apology, "Yes sir."

At that, both turned away from the other as Johnston returned to his couch, grabbing his beer and kicking up his feet. Toby started his obnoxious engine, revving it up, since it was his only release-valve in the situation. Maddie led Ral inside and closed the front door behind them. She propped her hands on her hips, and in a snotty way, said to her father, "Dad, you embarrassed me!"

"No I didn't, honey. I embarrassed him." He stated evenly. It was always plain, simple, and direct with Johnston.

"You sure did, Mr. McCreeley!" Ral enthusiastically interjected as he always did—without welcome. Father and daughter both shot a look his way, saying, 'No one asked you.'

Maddie knew continuing on the subject to her advantage was useless. Besides, she was about to receive a present. "Come on, Ral. We'll leave grump-a-potamas to his football."

As they turned to leave the room Johnston knew what to say. "All we need is this field goal to win the game!"

"I don't care." Maddie blandly quipped as Johnston very well knew she really couldn't care any less about football. His slight chuckle kept it playful.

Ral followed behind her through the hallway, watching her pony-tail slightly sway from side to side; one of the many little things which drove him wild about her. It also presented the opportunity to check out her hiny, and how it set nicely in what she wore for the day. Entering her room it always smelt so nice. Ral figured probably because it was always clean with everything in its place. She shut the door behind them, plopped down on her bed, crossing her legs beneath her, and waited for her present.

Ral was too young to realize he would be getting on the path to souring the moment he had planned for months, so he went ahead with it unawares. "Why do you like Toby so much? He's such a jerk."

Puzzled he had decided to agitate her instead of make her day, she crossly responded, "Actually, that's what you're being right now. But to answer your question, I really don't know. I just do."

Ral's oily face kinked at her inconclusive answer, but he decided to further accelerate her frustration. "Are you in love with him?"

He immediately regretted asking it as her pretty blue eyes incredulously squinted at him. "Ral, I'm sorry, but that's really not any of your business. Who I love is only between me and that other person. Nobody else really matters…so don't worry about it."

That hit him hard. It was further proof his fantasy of one day sharing the thing called love with Maddie was just that—a fantasy. He thought she was growing colder as they grew older. Yet, he was going to deal with it as long as she allowed him to deal with it. After all, he was the one in love. It was funny, after he thought of it for a split second, that she was kind of right. He had never told anybody he was in love with her. He could only express it through the wrapped present in his hands.

A silent tension fell over them, and while Ral thought she was becoming colder, she simply thought he was getting weirder by the day. Ral held out the present to her, breaking the tension, and declaring, "Happy birthday, Maddie!"

She turned her frown slightly upside-down as she grabbed the surprisingly well-wrapped present—for a guy. It had some weight to it, which intrigued her even more. Cheering up was on the horizon. "Ral, what did you do?"

He sat down on the bed to watch her open it. He loved sitting on her bed. The torn wrapping exposed the face of his artwork which had an immediate impact on her. What struck her most bluntly was it being handcrafted in amateur fashion, which could only have meant Ral most likely had made it with own two hands. To Maddie, it was painfully obvious this was a first attempt at the craft of wood carving.

"Do you remember last summer when we were on top of the roof and you told me that story about the stars, and how we're made of them, and all?" He asked, as her eyes could not leave the glossed block of wood. "Well, there's your star."

Yes, he had carved the crooked star, sanded it smooth to the crevices, stained it dark, and glossed it to a high shine. All for her. "And the word below the star. It's how I—

"Precous?" She suddenly questioned, as tragedy instantly befell Ral like the opening of a dam. *Oh no! It was true!* How could he have missed it? Precious was how he thought about her, but he had left the 'i' out of the word itself. It was official. He had ruined his own moment; so, so long in the making. The cursive form carving of the now non-word had been slow and tedious. Talk about poor planning and bad spelling. He knew his present was now only good for a laugh; the laugh of Toby Self, further solidifying his terminal weirdness. She was supposed to love it, finally gaze into his eyes, and fall in love with a gentle kiss. Now her face was turning blush as his turned white. He wanted to rewind, disappear, and perhaps even die. None of those things would happen. He could only endure the crushing embarrassment at the fact he had misspelled a word scrolled for months in advance.

Barely audible, he finished, "—think of you."

Sensing his freefall without a parachute, Maddie shot up from the bed and headed for an empty spot on the wall. "I love it, Ral! Do you think it would look good right here?"

She was being polite, and he appreciated it. The only problem was that his longed-for moment was already ashes in the sea. It was yet another grave disappointment, but he would still play along. It was still Maddie. Always Maddie. "Yeh, it's going to look real good right about there, Maddie."

*

He was dejected walking into his home later that evening. He could usually mask it; at least somewhat. He was used to his mother being swept up in the delusional psychosis of alcoholism, and a father even more oblivious to the systematic meltdown sitting right next to him. Even the billowing smoke his father failed to notice as she coughed and coughed. This time, Senior was doodling on his tablet when Ral walked through the door with an exaggerated mope. Why he wanted them to take notice of his moping Ral did not know and would certainly soon regret.

"What the hell has gotten you so down in the dumps?" Senior rudely inquired, engaging with both his son and the tablet, but far more with the tablet. The tablet was cool and useful. His son was not.

Junior was still too young to understand that people who regularly displayed apathetic dispositions were unlikely to develop a capacity for sympathizing, no matter how much one wanted to be cared for. Into the trap he would fall again for just a shred of what his father could never deliver. Ral's deficiency? Honesty.

His mother emerged from the fog for a moment to sloppily fain interest. "Yes…sweetie…what's…matter?"

Though she was incoherent, he could still recall the mother he once knew when he couldn't remember at all, but knew for sure had once existed. It made him answer his father's question. "I made Maddie a present. I carved a star out of a block of wood. It took me three months to make."

"Did she…like?" his mother asked with closed eyes and a grin which had no business being on her face.

"I messed it up. Below the star I carved the word 'Precious.' Somehow, I left the 'i' out of 'Precious.' I didn't even notice it until she pointed it out when I gave it to her. It was so embarrassing." He slowly confessed, still in shock from the massive blunder.

His mother's grin had turned to a crooked open mouth, but her eyes remained shut. Senior belted out a laugh and shook his head, thinking in enormously broad terms how stupid teenagers were. His mother tried to slap at her husband in her only child's defense, but fell way short. Senior began, "So you had three full months to realize an error so simple, but you say it didn't come to mind at all? The whole time it evaded you? Beyond that, if you actually read it without the 'i' it doesn't even…well…it's not even close to a word. I bet you were embarrassed, but I just can't see how it happened? How your mind found that acceptable?! Precious, spacious, auspicious, conscious, delicious, ferocious…"

Junior had already moped back to his room and slammed the door on a father that reminded him more of Toby Self hammering a grating style which chiseled under his skin, peeling it back from the muscle. An unwarranted and cruel method he understood less than his father's inconceivability concerning his belting out of 'cious' words. How would Ral cope with it all? Sit down at his computer, put in the ear buds, and continue binge-watching season four of *Dead Island* about a cruise ship swallowed up by the Bermuda Triangle and then shipwrecked on an island of human-devouring zombies. Ral knew none of the vacationers would survive, but he still had to see it all go down. It was infectious.

In the corner of his desktop screen was the breaking news window. The headline read, "Shooter kills six at coffee shop, then turns gun on himself."

*How could somebody do such a thing? What had people done to him? Could it be worse than what was being done to me? Surely—it had to be.*

**ZZZ...**

"This big switch is turning into a giant disaster!" Tamara Bloom-Boland lamented, wearing a frilled pink day gown with fluffy red slippers on her feet. The Buccaneer, or Tommy Bloom-Boland, originally known as Tommy Bloom, or the Butt Pirate—was now Tamara. She was a full-fledged female. *The Big Switch* had been undertaken by the most prestigious Beverly Hills sexual re-assignment surgeon. However, like any tinkering with anatomy, unwanted and unpleasant complications sometimes arise.

"I had a package! A huge, beautiful package! They said I'd have the same sensitivity. That was a lie! They said nothing could go wrong. This vagina is collapsing! I would say it's mine, but is it? I guess! I don't know! We're all supposed to have two sources of pleasure. That's what I was born with. Now one's closing up shop completely. I can't go back now. I miss playing with it, putting it to use, standing up peeing, all of it! I'll tell you something right now—I'm not going back to that butcher!"

Gay J was sitting on the carpeted steps leading into another huge room with no assigned purpose. He watched Tamara's movements, which were unsuccessfully attempting to appear feminine. He wondered out of nowhere if he could still consider himself gay at all. These days he woke up next to a woman. Wouldn't that make him straight? Tommy—he meant Tamara—had always been feminine, but now he—he meant she—now played an exaggerated role. The slim cigarettes, Spanish white wine by the bottles, air ball perfume spray, and the uber-expensive customized hair brushes were all of the in-your-face indicators. He was waiting for the artfully shaved poodle to appear, nipping at his heels with the same flippant tenacity Tamara now dealt out without a sign of nearing exhaustion. It all left him seeking refuge, yet again, in the bathroom where he snorted blow like a pig. He had completely melted away his creativity, along with his ability to recall what he was trying to say from one moment to the next, which greatly frustrated Tamara. All he could remember to do was go to the bathroom, which was where he was currently heading.

He still knew Tamara required some kind of response. He delivered one like someone under hypnosis. "There's a void."

"What the hell does that mean, J?" Tamara called out, but could only hear the closing and locking of the bathroom door, followed by the overhead fan being turned on. "Taking another shit, huh J?"

"What's shit?" Dillon, their adopted four year-old son asked, as he bounced into the room. Dillon was a master at catching them off guard with his ever inquisitive personality. Gay J and Tamara had been pressured to import their son like an artifact, only to be found as far away as possible from modern Western civilization: the leading ethnicities being Asian, Middle-Eastern, or African. They decided on a half-white, half-Mexican baby out of a hurricane ravaged trailer park deep in the woods of Mississippi. They really loved him a lot.

"It means poop, sweetie, and mommy shouldn't be saying it. I'm sorry." Tamara said, stamping out her cigarette, but downing the rest of the wine to substitute the unfinished slim.

"Daddy—I mean mommy..." Dillon said, still getting used to the transition himself, which was recent. He only knew he always had two daddies. "Can you read me a story?"

Tamara shook her head about how the confusion always seemed to be magnified in some way. Tamara just made it a habit to quickly expel it from her thoughts. "Of course, sweetie. Just go to your room and wait for me there. After we read, we'll eat some lunch."

"Okie dokie, mommy!" Dillon said, bouncing away in a trot whcih only a child can pull off convincingly.

"Annnd…cut!" Joshua Bannister commanded, standing in the corner of the room with the camera crew, oddly startling Tamara, as their presence was more like a fixture set in the home for display. Each time she was surprised by their presence; she thought she lost a little more of—*herself?*

JB was in his usual sheen of a designer suit and devilishly manicured good looks. He always appeared so pleased and content when he stopped by, and that was for the most obvious reasons: $$$! Sending a thumbs-up Tamara's way, he praised, "Wonderful work everybody! Keep it up! I'd like to stay longer, but I have a very important meeting to get to. Until next time. Continue killing it!"

He strutted swiftly out of the room, always with urgent purpose, checking the time on his Rolex. Tamara's eyes followed him out. When the door slammed behind him, Tamara lashed out in her man voice, "Yeh, fuck you!"

The camera crew pretended they heard nothing as they began to tinker with the maintenance of their equipment. To varying degrees, most everyone beneath Joshua Bannister felt the same way as Tamara just exhibited.

She swiped her silky blonde extensions from her face and lit another slim. She walked to the bathroom door where Gay J was numbing himself on the other side. She lightly tapped it, and said, "J, are you okay? What's the void?"

She waited for his response, but none came. "Dillon wants a story before lunch. Will you join us?"

Still no response. She really needed a response. Right then, she felt she could stand at the door forever. They could talk about it all through the door. That would be good enough. She would begin. "J, I don't want to do this anymore. I don't want to live here anymore."

Tamara paused as it all began to bubble within her, summoning tears to her eyes; the hand of raw emotion clasping around her throat. She sucked in a few rapid breaths to subdue the gushing. "I don't want to make any more mistakes, J. It's all gone too far. Let's just throw it all away. You…me…Dillon…we could just take it easy. Make it all worthwhile again. Our way…in our time…for us. Doesn't that sound great?"

Still no response. On the other side of the door J was leaning over the sink, looking in the mirror with his own eyes filled to the brim and ready to spill over. The same hand squeezing her throat was upon his. It had been a long time, but now they finally agreed on something. Now J truly saw himself in the mirror and could only come up with one description of what he looked like—disfigured. In the realization, he forgot he had been asked a question he wanted to answer.

Tamara decided to go back to the original question, since it was more grounded and pertained to the day they were living—not a dreamed of day. "Will you come read with us, even though we know the story a hundred times over?"

Still staring into the mirror as the levy of his eyes broke, his voice broke through the cracks. "I'll be right there."

Relieved and able to move on with the rest of the day, she released herself from the door. J decided to wash his face and hands, symbolic as it was hygienic. He took the baggy of blow from his pocket, flicked it twice to confirm how much was left. It was enough for another lock-in sit-down. Knowing he would regret it right after the story, he tossed it into the toilet and quickly flushed it away before he grew the urge to fish it out with his clean hands. He could already feel the agony to come. He opened the door to go be what had never been shown to him—a father.

*

Ah, the limo ride through downtown without his own hands on the steering wheel, not even seeing the driver; and best of all, everyone on the other side trying to look in, but never seeming to learn that the passenger windows were the darkest tint possible. It's the way JB liked it—behind the tinted glass. That's the way he liked to view everything.

He was on his way to the exclusive country club done up in the same exclusionary illusion. Bright green golf courses, carefully constructed ponds and gardens, and in the clubhouse; certain sections cordoned off from certain types of members. JB liked the all-access membership. Thinking of all the success and profits from the relationship between Wink Broadcasting and the Bloom-Boland's, it was spinning in his mind where the next opportunity would come from. Where was that next piece of bubblegum to suck dry the fruity juice, and once becoming bland, spit it out on the ground? It would come to him. It always did. If it didn't, the mania of populism would hand over some new material, no matter how silly.

Upon his arrival he made his way to the "executive" conference room where Wink, unable to escape the pruning of his entire being, facilitated the advance by blowing plumes of cigar smoke, drinking single malt scotch, and playing poker with his fellow pruning moguls. Following their shared bout of unnecessary and raucous laughter; like a mob capo bringing down to size an associate, Wink remarked, "There he is! Baby genius! Remember when we looked that pretty, boys?"

They all laughed in agreement as the bald portly one commented, "I was never pretty. Didn't need it. All I needed was this." He rubbed his index finger against his thumb, signifying the almighty dollar. They all nodded along. "And maybe a few sprays of smell good."

"Yeah, these days it's getting a little harder to cover-up." Said the other, looking like he had unearthed himself that very morning from the grave, took a shower, and put on the most expensive suit he could find.

"No worries! You just add a little bit more of that." Wink added, rubbing his own fingers together to bring it back around to what made them truly attractive. Again, it wasn't that funny, but they thought they were hilarious.

A television was constantly on around Wink. It was his business. What was actually happening on it rarely caught his undivided attention, but on the screen popped the catcher—Malcolm Grace.

He immediately began to grumble as a heated viciousness stirred inside, doused in scotch. "What the hell is keeping this guy around? What the hell are the Democrats and Republicans doing? And what the hell is a Civic, anyways?"

The portly one affectionately stated, "I like him."

Wink shot him a dirty look, grumbling some more. He took the television off mute to hear what Malcolm Grace was going to say at the Civic National Convention in St. Paul, Minnesota.

"He sure is a good looking son of a bitch!" The one that unearthed himself from the grave that morning pointed out enthusiastically. Wink shot over another dirty look, but inside he secretly agreed.

The Party faithful were layered in rows around the lone figure of Malcolm Grace, cheering him on as he took the microphone in hand. At the peak of their applause, he suddenly blurted out, "We're going to lose!"

Boos beat against his ears, but were the kind knowing he wasn't serious. He waved his arms, reiterating, "It's true! We don't have a chance in hell!"

They began to settle down when they realized he was probably being serious. Defeat was stenciled on his face. He continued, "Popularity or sheer numbers is simply not enough. It's enough on the local level…the state level…even on the national level; but on this level it means very little. The Founders had an idea about this level, the Presidency. In regards to the highest office in the land they were careful not to let direct democracy do its job. Why?

"They feared the people would, knowingly or unknowingly, elect a despot who would undermine the core values of our Republic—liberty and the pursuit of happiness. It was instead decided by men of higher ideals, higher intelligence, and a certain brand of patriotism. With these views in mind, they constitutionally constructed the institution that is the Electoral College system. Essentially, a ghost organization made up of—who knows? In theory, this voting body does not have to be seen because they are blindly trusted to place the right vote. One for either a Republican or a Democrat. All the College does is seem to validate the two-party system with its revolving door for people to lead from the same societal class—a ruling class. I believe this to be an accurate examination, and not in the least a conspiracy theory. The proof is all around you, yet in the shadows.

"So about our plight? I will not win. I am not allowed to win. I am fine with that. The Civics are not about revolving doors. We are about new passageways and frontiers. The perversion of our political system has been a long process, but it's wearing itself out. That's why we now exist. Strange as it may seem, *we* are *their* creation.

"We started out not from the lobby level, not from the parking garage, but rather from the storm shelter. The worst passed over, and so we emerged to pick up the pieces of the wreckage. To re-build! To forge indestructible structures impervious to the winds of big-money interests, reactionary populism, and a dualistic approach to democratic participation.

"I, Malcolm Grace, will undoubtedly lose this particular fight. But…the dog will remain. We will not be killed. We will be made stronger. They will not be able to eschew, or ignore our advance forever. We are young and time is on our side. It's not our time to win, but that time will come. With enough Civics in Congressional seats we can begin to change these distrustful laws against the people themselves.

"Do not think for a moment that I am abandoning this fight. I'm seeing it all the way to the bitter end on pure principle. I am with you all!" He loudly concluded, as the crowd gathered around threw themselves into a tizzy.

Wink quickly stamped on the mute button. The portly one again enthusiastically noted, "Guy's got balls!"

"Shut up!" Wink shouted, but not in the manner they were used to. There was darkness behind it. Not just flared banter. They didn't understand the reaction. Malcolm Grace was talking about shifting the power paradigm; the same one Wink enjoyed and used to the fullest. He also thought the Civics were disguised communists, and once you started talking about fidgeting with the Constitution, then another freedom could be adjusted—that of the PRESS, which Wink had the stranglehold of monopoly. He glared at JB, wondering where the dirt was that he had asked for.

"You haven't delivered my dirt, JB." Wink said, slowly standing to his feet. He moved face-to-face with him. JB would never admit it, but Wink's breath was hideous, mixed with decay and every other odor permeating the room. "This might be the first time you've failed me. Let's hope it's the last. Because all the ratings, all the riches, all the great ideas could invariably be provided by another. You are just like everyone else. Dispensable."

JB wanted to head butt him in his old nose, but instead showed that he was cowering. He didn't say a word.

Wink drew his face even closer. "Give me what I need to destroy him, so I don't have to destroy you."

**ZZZ...**

Dane Shavers set the double mocha with extra caramel frappe in front of Loretta Crowley, and lit a cigarette. Surprisingly, it was all she had requested for the sit-down. He still expected she would want something more at the end. "Tell me the whole story."

Her swollen fingers wrapped themselves around the cup as she pulled from the straw. Setting it back down in front of her on the table between them, she began, "Believe it or not, Mr. Shavers, I was once a stunner."

"Call me Dane. And I can believe that."

"I wasn't even twenty yet, but that was when I fell into the wrong crowd. I was living in D.C., which was by no means cheap. I was stupid. You could convince me to do anything back in those days, and putting some dollars behind it made it all the more easy for me to do. I worked for a high-end prostitution ring. It catered to business and political types on the Beltway. We did a lot of sex shows. A lot of scripted stuff. It paid a lot. I really didn't do much one-on-one work."

"Okay, yeah, uh-huh." Dane said, as he waited for her to suck down some more of her drink. So far, he had not detected any storytelling.

"But one time, the price was right for a little one-on-one. Monty Lincoln was the one. British accent, fly dresser, lots of swagger, and didn't seem to have a care in the world. This was right before the big AIDS scare. He wanted to do it raw dog—

"Raw dog? Is that a kind of sexual position?" Dane asked, quickly jotting down the phrase itself.

"It means doing it without protection." Loretta answered, only thinking of two words—*white boy*. He quickly squiggled over the words on the pad.

"Go ahead."

"I told him it was possible, but the initial offer had to be doubled. He agreed like it was nothing. I told him he had to pull out, though. Again, he agreed. We did our thing, but he didn't pull out. He was a real asshole after that. He barely gave me any time to get my clothes on before he was pushing me out the door. Before all that, I actually thought he was charming. Boy, was I wrong.

"Anyways, I ended up pregnant. Being a Baptist raised in Georgia I would never consider having an abortion, so I had the baby—a boy. I gave him up for adoption and went back to work; this time with a new rule. Protection always. I never saw Monty Lincoln again until I saw your show."

"Are you certain it's him?" Dane pressed.

"Yeah, that's that old white devil. My heart skipped a beat. The past gave me a good slap in the face. I thought I had forgotten. I guess not." She finished, as some tears welled in her eyes and she slurped on the drink through the straw, making the obnoxious sound of a drink already drunk.

"Well, that's pretty interesting stuff, Loretta. I just want to see if you know about one more thing. The boy? Do you know where he's at? Who he is?"

"Yeah, I do. His name is Jeremy Boland. He's a rapper that goes by the name of Gay J." She said, as Dane put his pen to pad once again. He acted like he didn't know who she was talking about.

"And you've never tried to contact this Boland?"

She shot him a sad look. "How could I?"

It didn't matter. Dane had the material to add to another one of his shows. Not only could he throw more spotlight on Monty Lincoln and his Fellowship of the Enlightened; he could throw some more spotlight on himself. The greed of fame on any interminable level ruled all. Even lonely old Loretta Crowley. *Conspiracies of the Illuminati and the New World Order* was getting some more teeth. He handed Loretta an envelope with a little more, knowing their relationship would not come to an end so soon.

"Thank you, Loretta. Thank you."

The locker door slamming on his hand was so sudden and quick that Ral barely felt the pain from it. The locker room was a dangerous place, like shark-infested waters. Here was the shark standing before him, showcasing his rows of pointy teeth—Toby Self. He had two hammerheads with him, grinning on the outside and frowning on the inside. They wanted big bad Toby Self to like them so much. Ral wasn't scared of them. He just hated them. Hate squashed the fear. Hate was so much more useful.

"Ya' know, Ral, we just can't seem to get on the same page. Ya' see, I don't want your oily pock-marked mug at my girlfriend's house anymore. You haven't been getting the hints, so I think we're going to have to resort to other means." Toby said, as his hammerheads began to move into position, reminding Ral of clowns without the laughter, left only with the evil.

Then a foul stench began to fill the room, which was not all that uncommon; but this one was special. "You get a whiff of that, Ral? Maybe something fried? Maybe some onions? Last night's beer?"

From around the corner leading to the bathroom stalls and the showers came the near 300 pound center for the football team—Larry Packett. He folded his marshmallow arms on the bridge of his man tits, appearing pleased with himself. "As you requested, good sir!"

"Good going, Pack! Smells ripe. I owe you one, man." Toby said, as Pack left the scene of the unfolding crime.

"Don't think nothing of it, bro!"

Just as he left they jumped on Ral with all their might, but Ral had every intention of sending it back. A foot stomp. A chop at the thigh. A bite on the hand. It forced them to change their approach. The violence escalated. The harm was compounded. "Fuck that! Strip him down!"

Ral was wearing a white t-shirt and boxers. They were torn from his body like a bandage. Toby pointed and laughed at what it revealed. "Oh my God, you have such a little cock!"

It was now the pig-carry the rest of the way to the stool of Larry Packett. The smell became more and more concentrated. There was no further resistance to be had. Ral drew in one last breath, closed his mouth and eyes, and braced for the experience. He felt the turds bumping into his nose, cheeks, and forehead. He just needed to last without taking in another breath, but that all depended on how long Toby wanted to draw it out.

"Listen here, Ral! You stay away from Maddie! She doesn't like you! Will never like you! She likes me! My girl! You are, and will never be anything to her! Next time, you bleed!"

They brought his head out of the toilet and carried him towards the showers as Toby turned one of the knobs. Ral had avoided internal contact with Pack's refuse, but on the way to the showers he needed to draw in a breath, and some bits were sucked into his nose. They threw him in the shower bay where he was met with ice cold spraying water. The hammerheads cackled, flipping him off, and fleeing. The only thing Toby added before doing the same was a loogie shot from his mouth in the direction of Ral.

"Lay low, Golden boy!" He warned with a point of his finger, and then left with an insidious cackle of his own.

Ral was sitting on his naked bottom while the cold water pelted his pale skin. He slowly came to his feet, turned the knob to hot, and took a long shower. He thought, 'How could Maddie have even the slightest interest in a brute like Toby Self?' It was typical. The usual. The absolute worst. *Where is my breaking point?*

How much could be endured before the animal bared its teeth and sprung into lashing action, leaving an unprecedented amount of devastation in its path? What were the signs? Did it start with anger and end with nothing; no feeling; no emotion—a tsunami, tornado, a plague? *Yeah, a plague!* That took longer. The suffering was more. Lasting.

The entrance door to the locker room swung open, snapping him out of it. Lathering himself up, nothing came to his mind. Then the answer fell in like a coin into a vending machine. *Love did it all. Love was responsible. But how?*

**ZZZ...**

The news choppers were circling overhead. The news vans were lining the sides of the road. At the entrance to the compound was the slew of federal law enforcement personnel and vehicles: ATF, FBI, and Homeland Security. The stand-off was on its fifth day, becoming quite the popular news story, 24 hours a day, seven days a week. Continuous coverage—continuous speculative debate— continuous.

Bill Doody had someone on the ground among the muck. "Leslie, how is it down there?"

Leslie was the prettiest field reporter in the world, yet eloquent and serious about ambition. Those less attractive may have been eloquent and serious about ambition, but they just lacked the full package. "It's relatively quiet for now, Bill. It appears a lot of preparation is taking place. Perhaps this is the calm before the storm."

"So you think there's going to be a storm, Leslie?" Bill asked, leaning in like he was going to hear her better that way.

"Situations like this are unpredictable, but Monty Lincoln and his Fellowship of the Enlightened have three distinct things going against them. One—federal authorities feel people are being held against their will, perhaps even children. Two—this land has recently been declared a national conservation site. Three—cooperation from inside the compound is non-existent, and authorities know for a fact that the group is heavily armed. Put all these factors together, Bill, and the likelihood of this ending without the use of force appears dismal."

"Shut in, my dear. That was my dream. Locked away by my own accord to prosper among those I chose to love. No longer having to learn anyone new." Monty Lincoln sadly noted, peering out the window with Cindy by his side. She stroked his bristled cheek with the back of her hand. She was now noticing his age.

"Why don't we just leave, Monty? We'll explain the whole thing. They just don't understand. We can make them understand. This has all been so much fun, but it has to end. Please! For the sake of our child?" Cindy pleaded, placing his hand on her bloated belly which was about to come to term.

He stood to his feet, moving towards the fireplace. He was in the most awful conundrum. The world was the last place he wanted to return, but it appeared the world was not going to leave them be.

"I have never been a grounded man. This was the most recent development in my life. There is no starting over for from this point on. There is only a haunting re-visitation…a ghost in limbo. We are always bitten by the past. It's coming again. Coming to bite me."

His trailing off into the mystic was never comforting for her. It only meant he wasn't thinking right. He was doing that a lot lately. There was nothing to be said. He suddenly returned, but remained hunched in the darkness of his own being. The light from the flames below danced on his tired face. "You must all leave me. I will only be taken by fire."

**zzz…**

"Welcome back! Bill Doody here. We have an exclusive breaking story that you're only going to see on this show. We have two special guests: Mr. Dane Shavers and Ms. Loretta Crowley. Thanks for being on the show!"

"Thank you, Bill."

"Thank you kindly."

"Okay, let's just get to letting this cat out the bag. Dane, you've been investigating this Fellowship of the Enlightened since they withdrew into the California redwoods. What are they about? What's their end purpose?"

"Bill, I would say they are a devil worshipping, sex, death cult. Their leader, Monty Lincoln, is perhaps best described as a shadowy figure with secret society connections all over the globe. He has lots of money, knows international finance inside and out, and should be designated as an unsavory character at best."

"Okay, so you've seen this with your own eyes…this devil worshipping…this sex…this death cult?"

"I infiltrated their compound in their early days. Upon entering I witnessed wild sex orgies, devil chanting around a fire in pagan garb, and heard gunfire on several occasions during my investigation. I just call it like I see it, Bill."

"So, Ms. Crowley, what is your relation to this Monty Lincoln? This should be real enlightening." Bill turned, smiling at how clever that little quip was.

"Well, Mr. Doody…"

"Bill, Bill, Bill, please."

"Well, Bill...some...I guess it was close to thirty years ago now. You see, Bill, as a young woman I was a prostitute in DC around the Beltway. I looked a lot different back then. Monty Lincoln had been a client of mine. I bore a child. His child."

"And who is your son? Anyone we would know?" Doody asked, already knowing the answer. He paid a good price for the exclusive.

"Ah yes, he's very popular. It's Jeremy Boland, or I guess Boland-Bloom, otherwise known as Gay J."

*

They were suddenly ambushed by flashing lights as always. Airports were the worst. They were returning from a secluded family vacation they only thought to be secluded. The pictures had already been published, but it had still been a fine time. Now it was over. Back under the knife and microscope of the mobbing paparazzi. Along with their flashing lights, they also had oodles of questions.

Holding a snoozing Dillon in his arms, Gay J would be the target. He was sober. He felt good. "Gay J, are you going to meet your father?"

"My father?" he snapped back.

"Yeah, the devil, sex, death cult leader, Monty Lincoln?"

Gay J was beyond puzzled. Not about the name, but the resume behind the name. "What da fuck you talkin' 'bout?"

"Honey! Language!" Tamara insisted, covering Dillon's ears with her white-gloved hand.

"Who's saying this?" Gay J insisted, continuing to move along as fast as he could to the SUV parked in waiting.

"Your mom."

Stopping in his tracks and turning towards the beggars of celebrity dirt, he was now exasperated to incredulity. "And who is that? Man, y'all trippin'!"

She was almost there. Tired enough to doze off and put the smartphone down for a consecutive six hours. She liked leaving the bedside lamp on. The glow of it would wake her later. She would then turn it off, knowing she would then fall deep until it was time to rise. The rain was tapping at her window. A good night's sleep was about to be had. She liked these particular nights: peaceful, warm, and sure to be rested for the following school day.

Right as she was slipping away the tapping on her window became more pressing; out of rhythm with the rain. Out of step it made her believe someone was outside the window, and fear came over her in a hurry. She held suspicions as to who it might be. It was the only reason she blindly pulled up the blinds.

Company was not what she wanted, but especially not the soaking wet company of Ral. He knew the rules; no boys after nine allowed in the house, period. Still, she opened the window. "Ral, what are you doing? It's late! You shouldn't be here."

"Sorry, Maddie, I just had to talk to you. It's important." He said, not really having a thought-out plan for his being there. Maybe he was warning her? Maybe he was whining? Maybe both of those sandwiched together would lead to their first kiss? He was utterly discombobulated.

"Alright, climb on in. But just to dry up, and then you gotta leave." She insisted, fetching him a towel. She remained standing as to let him know this was going to be a short encounter. "I had just fallen asleep, Ral. What is it?"

He found the reason. He came to ruin Toby's good standing. "Maddie, Toby's done something to me. You need to know who you're dealing with."

She folded her arms across her chest. She was already beyond irritated. Disinterested, she said, "Okay. What?"

"In the locker room the other day Toby and his crew attacked me. I was changing, so I was naked. They had Larry Packett take a shit in the toilet, and they dunked my head in it, but they didn't flush. He told me to never come back around, or the next time, he'd hurt me really bad. He'd make me bleed." He explained in drawn out, wounded tones. It was true. He was wounded, but believability was all that mattered.

Ral had been so dramatic for so long, to the point of weirdness, that Maddie's usual sympathetic buttons were not being pushed. Ral, the childhood friend, had now become a harassing nuisance. "Listen Ral, it's late. I really don't think Toby would do something like that."

"Maddie! You've got to believe me!" He cried out.

"Ral, keep it down!" She insisted, whispering harshly. "It's time for you to go."

She pointed to the open window where the rain continued to fall. He glanced over to the spot on the wall where she had hung the star he carved for her. It wasn't there. It was just an empty space. "Hey, what happened to the star I made you?"

He caught her off guard. The truth would send Ral over the edge. It was ugly. She didn't like it one bit. It was creepy that his pet-name for her was *Precious*. It was beyond amateur that he misspelled the word without noticing. There was only one thing she could think to say. "Listen, Toby took it. It really bothered him. I kind of don't blame him."

Now he was mortally wounded. Getting his head dunked in piss and shit wasn't worse than this. Now she would know, whether she liked it or not. "Do you know what that was a symbol of, Maddie?"

*Please don't say it*, Maddie thought.

"It's a symbol of our love, Maddie."

"There is no love!"

"Now, hold on." He begged.

"Ral, love has never existed between us! If we had anything, it was friendship. It's looking like that doesn't exist anymore, either!"

He shrunk into a whimpering whine as he placed his hands atop her shoulders, desperately clinging; "Maddie, please stop. I'm sorry."

She bucked his hands from her shoulders, and pointed with even more zeal at the open window. "Get out, Ral!"

Her bedroom door swung open with Johnston standing tall in his white cover-all pajamas, holding a pistol to his side. He was actually relieved it was the harmless Ral. "What the hell is this? Ral, get the hell outta this room!"

Johnston grabbed him by the elbow like a bouncer leading out a disorderly drunk. Before Johnston closed the door behind them, Ral looked back at Maddie one last time.

She was mad, but felt a shade bad, too. Both looks transmitted—*Why?*

They went to the living room where Johnston sat him down, placing his pistol on the coffee table. Peg came out from the hallway in some pajamas of her own, asking, "Is everything alright, Johnstie?"

"Yeah, it looks like Ral got a little lost tonight. Everything's fine. Go back to bed."

She did so without a second thought, leaving the two to sort it out. Ral eyed the pistol for a moment, admiring it. Johnston began his questioning. Was he on drugs? Did he realize he could have been shot? Ral remained respectful as he always did with Johnston. He told about what Toby did to him. That he just wanted to warn Maddie about what she was truly dealing with. Johnston listened, but all he could come up with was that Ral had been in love too long without any hint of return on Maddie's part. Johnston's purpose was to lay down and enforce the law pertaining to his own. It couldn't be avoided.

"Did you stick up for yourself? Did you at least get a few hits in?" Johnston pried.

"Yes sir, I did."

"Good. That means you still got some dignity."

Ral's head sagged in humility, but his eyes remained drawn to the pistol. He would just say what he felt. "I wish I could just kill Toby."

Johnston thought nothing of the admission. It was a phantom punch; a teen's silly fantasy. He still had to deter him, as he felt an adult should when faced with the hot air of an extreme intention. "We all want to kill sometimes. And sometimes…be killed. That's why there's the law…and that's why there's tomorrow. Tomorrow's fairer. Today? You just chalk it up and move on. I know you have feelings for my Maddie. You'll get over that. Like I said, tomorrow will be kinder than today. Day by day it will get easier. I know the history, Ral. I know how you feel. But you crossed a line. You're not going to be allowed over here anymore. Do you understand?"

There was no give in Johnston's eyes, and his voice sealed it with evenness. Ral knew it was done, but answered as he was supposed to. "Yes sir."

"Okay, I'll take you home."

The rain poured down heavy as the wipers went back and forth violently. Not a word was exchanged; only the embittered weeping which Ral was unable to stifle. He kept his head nuzzled in the darkest corner of his side of the cab so that, at least, Johnston wouldn't see it—only hear it.

***ZZZ…***

"Mr. McCreeley! What brings you here this morning? Always good to see you as usual. I know this isn't about voting down a school bond. Nothing on the slate there." Principal Livingston said, walking into his office, shutting them in, and planting himself behind his cluttered desk. He was a middle aged man of mid-height, with an easily breakable structure, already sporting a comb-over, wearing a short-sleeve oxford dress shirt, tucked into khaki pants, with black orthopedic shoes on his feet. The two men were from different universes. The gap was never going to be bridged.

"Hell, Livingston, I know y'all are drafting another one. Is this one gonna be more than the 175 million last election cycle? Some more Taj Mahal's for our kiddos to learn in, because it's all about the décor, right? Get the architects, the consultants, the construction companies to overbid the contracts. Instead of spending what you already have in your coffers, y'all leave it up to the parents, pledging it's all for the kids. They're suffering. Don't you love 'em? Don't you wanna help 'em? You get it all passed through with guilt and shame. All to over-develop. All to bloat your salaries. Everyone's pockets get fatter except the present and future generations of taxpayers. But hell, the State raised me. What do I know?"

Principal Livingston hated dealing with Johnston McCreeley. He was anti-everything. Nothing positive ever came out of him. One of those paranoid types scared to death of progress. Yet, Livingston felt for him. It must have been heartbreaking to be an orphan—to be thrown away.

"Are we here to talk about something that's already done?" Livingston politely asked, but with a shade of strain.

Johnston remained standing, surveying the walls covered with posters of inspiration, and in passing, thought, *'Nothing worse than blind optimism.'* He went back to Livingston. "In a way, why I'm here has already been done. It's about that terror, Toby Self."

"Ah yes, I see him and Maddie together all the time." Livingston pointed out with a smile, only to rattle Johnston; but he would follow up the jab with an act of kindness. He slid a jar on his desk towards Johnston, offering, "Sucker?"

Johnston glared at him, but took a sucker all the same, unwrapping and tossing it in his mouth. "It's not about him and Maddie."

"Okay. Then what?"

"It's about Ral Golden and Toby Self. Ral told me a story last night. It's pretty troubling. Toby and a few others attacked Ral, dunked his head in the shitter, and then told him it was gonna be worse next time if Ral didn't leave Maddie alone. What I want to know from you, Principal Livingston, is why exactly Toby Self gets to run around this school to reign as a bully with impunity?" He dug in, taking the sucker from his mouth and twirling it between his fingers. "Now why is that?"

Livingston leaned forward, placing his elbows on the desk, while interlocking his soft fingers. "Johnston, first off, I'm not a psychic. Nothing's been reported."

"I'm reporting it."

Livingston sputtered out a facetious chuckle; "What's this have to do with you? What's your affiliation?"

"Concerned fellow citizen."

"I can appreciate that, but it's just not good enough. If, and when this supposedly happened, it is obviously well after the fact. Where's Ralston? How come he didn't report it?"

"Listen, Ral doesn't have anybody who has his back. His mother resides on the other side of the Milky Way, and his father is too busy building his empire to take notice of what's going on in his son's life. Because of these things, it's leaking into my household, and you know I won't have any of that. I want disciplinary action taken against Toby Self, and whoever was with him for the attack on Ral. That is, of course, after you get both of them in here—right now."

"Johnston, I'm just not going to do that. There's still no grounds, and it really doesn't seem to be a concern of yours. I *can* assure you we will monitor the situation. You've given us a glimpse. That's the only place this can go from here. I'm sorry."

*Smug*, Johnston thought. What a waste of a trip. How foolish to think it was going to turn out any different. *Bureaucrats*—the worst. Puppets of the system. Dead inside. Executors of thought; of directing all to monotony, to weakness, to dependence—

"Are we done here, Mr. McCreeley?" Livingston asked, growing increasingly uneasy in his presence. If anyone was considered a loose cannon, it was Johnston McCreeley. That time at the town hall meeting when the ISD was pitching the bond to the voters. Johnston had broken the

Superintendent down without compromise, and when those in the audience came to the Superintendent's defense, Johnston turned his wrath to them without abandon. It was a gory display of free speech on an issue that should have been cut and dry, without controversy. Johnston didn't see it being for the kids. No one was ever going to change his mind about it.

Johnston's eyes darted at Livingston. It was the same ones he had seen once before. They meant some serious business. Livingston's attempted conclusion was still floating in the air, unanswered. "Not yet, Livingston."

Johnston finally took the chair, sitting back in it, folding his own arms across his chest. There would be a little more to discuss. "Ya know, there's this pacifism y'all push out there that only relates to certain people. You talk down bullying, but don't do anything about it when it happens. You want everyone to have a disorder of some kind…an insecurity…something wrong that only y'all can fix. There's this new one I heard about. Ral might have it. He's got the symptoms. It's called Affluenza? You've heard of it, you know the story. That poor rich kid plowed into some people on the side of the road, drunk as a skunk…killed a few of 'em. He got off easy because he was a minor, and his lawyer welded two words together. Life was so damn hard for the little son of a bitch, because he came from a dysfunctional family of affluence, which I guess gave him flu-like symptoms—Aff-luenza. It's actually pretty funny to think about until you find out he got off the hook from some phony-bologna psychological disorder. What he really had was a substance abuse problem, a lack of respect for authority, decency, and the lack of healthy fear that anything was going to happen to him. What kind of disorder do you think Toby Self has?"

Livingston desperately wished for an end to another session of interminable rambling from Johnston McCreeley. "I couldn't tell you, Johnston."

"My point is guys like you are letting it all happen. Pushing your pacifism. You're telling these kids that everyone wins all the time. Nobody loses. Just as long as they lift a finger in participation. They don't have to appreciate or earn anything, much less experience consequence until it's too late. Until someone gets hurt; all because it would be so inconvenient to throw a pebble in their pond of delicate sensibilities. You're molding weaklings, and letting monsters like Toby Self rule over them."

Livingston wanted to punch him in the face, but wouldn't dare. This redneck hillbilly was blaming him alone for social ills completely out of his control. He was academically trained not to hate, but he was there now. He wished for someone to bust in the room unannounced, the phone to ring, the fire alarm to go off—*something!*

"Are you gonna get Toby Self in here?" Johnston stubbornly pushed forward.

"Johnston, it's not going to happen. I believe we're done here." Livingston bravely insisted, but Johnston was implacable. Livingston stood to his feet to leave the room. Johnston could stay if he wanted. He extended his hand to be met by Johnston's. "Thank you for coming in this morning, Johnston. Have a nice day, sir."

Johnston wasn't going to meet him half-way. He was going to get relaxed instead; settle in for the long haul. He propped his elbow on the top edge of the chair, which hiked up his untucked shirt, revealing the revolver wedged in his pants. Johnston never noticed it. It was like a man with a fully grown beard, without sensation—a part of him. However, Livingston noticed it like a shiny bar of gold in the black mud of a mine.

"Is that a gun?" He asked in disbelief.

Johnston got into his eyes, and tried to hold them. He knew a big mistake had been made on his behalf, but he wanted to make it clear that he was walking away without incident. Livingston had to call it in. No doubt at all. Johnston had meant to leave it behind in the truck. He felt stupid now. This stupidity was going to lead to a felony. Both were frozen, unsure what course to take next. Their eyes continued to talk for them. Crucial life decisions were on the way, and one of them was going to buckle. The quiet couldn't have been thicker.

A gunshot suddenly rang out, jolting Livingston as he tried to gather what was going on. Johnston cocked his head slightly to the side towards the closed office door. His expression wrinkled into one of immediate concern. As they were both coming to the conclusion that it was a gunshot; another followed—and then another. It was then that they both realized it was going to be no normal day at school.

## Training Days

Cold. Hard. Wet.

That's how it had been for a solid month. The cold was in the concrete. The lower the temperature dropped the harder it seemed to become. The wet was the agitator; something to push her over the edge. It was maintained that way for the desired effect. The creature discomfort was brought to new levels. The constant shivering and teeth-chattering wasn't the worst hazard. She could fall ill without a break from the harshly created environment. Regardless, there would not be another chance. The training was a trajectory whose path could not be altered. Should illness or injury befall her, it was agreed Operation Sunrise would be altogether abandoned. Her reaction to the training would say it all. It was precisely why her cell was cold, hard, and wet.

Sun-rae was at the end. She knew it had to be close. Her time submersed in the training had not been kind; feeling and thinking each ticking moment. The cadence was given life by a deliberate drip within the walls, never to be plumbed. Where it was hidden only the wicked would have known. That first week it was a special kind of nuisance, driving her to imagine wielding a sledgehammer to bring down the walls. The second week saw her solitary nights bring about a loneliness she had never known. The drip began to transform from nuisance to a welcomed sort of company. But now so close to the end, she wondered if she would miss the drip and its gnawing repetition.

She sat cross-legged in the center of the cell when he entered that first day. There was nothing particularly striking about him. His prime physical years had passed. The quickness in his limbs had faded, but nothing had befallen the nimbleness of his mind. It was filled with experiences whose lessons he would impart in the young who were still strong and inexhaustible; lusting after revenge and glory. Slowly he paced around her cell with hands clasped at the small of his back. His stoop was slight, but enough to show the run of his years. They had all been hard. They had all been about war. Thus, there would always be legend swirling around Master Chol.

No number was needed to conceal his lofty name. His was a mythological brand for the Underground. He had never toted bureaucratic, military, or Party clout. His family had been rice farmers. The legend went that the regime arrived one day, announcing they were confiscating his family's winter food stock for unpaid taxes. Master Chol's father had put up a fight against the order, but only through an impassioned plea to reason and decency. It was said the officer in charge stood silent and listened until Master Chol's father had finished. Without a word in return the officer pulled his pistol and shot his father dead on the spot. Master Chol, a young boy, was arrested alongside his mother and sister. It was off to hard labor at camp Yodok. There his mother and sister would eventually die from the cold—the wet—the hard labor. Master Chol maintained himself as useful, but it was more than the Bowibu at Yodok could have realized. There was no way of knowing how it had leaked from the hell trap that was Yodok. The tale could not have been any taller. The young Master Chol had escaped, killing his way to the other side, never having been seen again. Now the older Master Chol, gently settling from his pacing in her cell, stood over a young Sun-rae who was intent upon the same path. Her training was set to begin.

"Not a word, Sun-rae." Master Chol uttered plainly. "You may grunt. You may grimace. You may scream out in pain, but not a word. Not a statement, a question, a concern. You are only permitted to listen, to do, and to endure. I have the way. I will show it to you. Not a word, Sun-rae."

And so it went—not a word. Yet, the beginning phase was nothing but words. Master Chol delivered them with a dry frankness as she followed him through the winding paths of the secluded mountain. With hands clasped at the small of his back and feet shuffling forwards in slow deliberation, he let her in.

"It was long ago, Sun-rae. For five hundred years the Joseon ruled our people. Over those centuries they built a unified and majestic people who held fast to this hard land. Like all peoples they wished to live in peace, but to live in peace is to live by the grace of another. It has always remained true: only a few protect the many. When the few fail, the many suffer. These few were a warrior class. These warriors were held in higher regard than the Joseon line in the minds of the many. All knew, without them, peace would not sustain. They did not war exclusively for those in the royal palace. They warred for truth and justice in all its forms, which was the heartbeat of the people. Now *you* will be that warrior for truth and justice. The price will never be paid so long as our people exist."

When the winding path ended it opened back up to her cell resembling a forbidden sepulcher. He would politely shift to the side of the entrance to allow her passage. She would enter and take her place at the center of the cell, always sitting with legs crossed beneath her. Master Chol would follow in after her, and it was always just one last thing.

"You are of a select consciousness, Sun-rae. You are the one out of the many. You have been selected through your suffering. It is not destiny. It is natural selection. But this does not come from the method. This natural selection comes from the highest divinity, only realized through injustice. It forces you to act, to make right. Now, suffer more. You must feel every bit of it."

Days went by as she followed and listened; a brisk and constant wind swirling Master Chol's words through the air. They were of fear and doubt; the forces that impeded the warrior's conscience when moving forward into danger. The fear of death. The doubt of success. It had to be overcome. It would be so by a brutal surprise. An insertion of speedy chaos. Once accelerated forward the momentum was not to be broken. If broken, defeat would surely follow. There could not be any space of adjustment for the enemy, as the unthinkable became their reality. Relentless trajectory until she burst through to the other side.

Master Chol kept on it, purging the fear and doubt from her mind. Anger was never to be used as a propeller. Anger was the root of fear. Tempered *will* would be the driver, fully justified without the need for an alibi. They did have it all coming; even those of so-called innocent association. Nothing was innocent. Not even Sun-rae. Nature had no opinion of any living thing. When the volcano erupted, when the flood drowned, when the wind uprooted, and the fire consumed—she was to harness this dispassionate force. On she listened to Master Chol in the day, and to the drip at night. They were preparing her well.

The next phase to be instilled were the *motions*. Maximum flexibility had to be achieved, accompanied with an unshakeable center of gravity. The warrior's body had to be acclimated to the unpredictable twist and turns war so ungraciously introduced.

"The motions will help you get in and out of tight spaces. In battle the body must be able to withstand any position that confronts it. You will bend. You will fold. You will slither. You will leap. You will be flung, and you will fling. In all instances, you will have to stand upright and ascend to the occasion. The body must be given some inkling of what is expected when faced with impossible times."

They would come in to stretch and bend her to form. Tissue to ligaments she became like a wire. Then came the balance, finding her center where implacability could be sustained. Then the black clad figures would trot in to place themselves along the walls around her. Each of the figures knew their point of insertion. She would have to run on instinct and decisive action.

The first motion was side to side. Out they would dart from the wall to penetrate her space. It was shuffling left, and shuffling right in a continuous circle. The pressure would ratchet up. They were sent in from odd angles. It was getting high, getting low. Jumping over one only to get down on her stomach at the other one leaping forward. In the shuffle, Sun-rae was far from perfect as she collided at times, but it was met with a steadfast insistence from Master Chol, "AGAIN!"

She was sent out on the mountain to find her own way. Up she would scale the ancient boulders that hid trickling brooks. Her forearms ached from the climb and her lungs wheezed from the thin mountain air. Once she hit what she thought to be level ground, down it would slide at her feet. Down she would begin to tumble as the mountain's surface followed. Losing her center of gravity altogether she clawed at the earth for stability, ripping nails out from the seats of her fingers. Just when the panic was beginning to take hold for the worst, her hands would clasp to a jutting branch. Everything continued their descent around her, but she held fast to the saving branch. Then Master Chol's voice would ring out clear, and closer than she could ever imagine. "AGAIN!"

Late in the evening they would place her back in her cell. Exhausted she would flop on the cold, hard, wet slab. Her heart would settle and the tightness would set into every part of her body. Then there would be the drip, counting time and slowly denting whatever surface it splattered upon. When she woke from the little sleep she could get, which was more of a doze, her body felt like it was wrapped in a tight cast restricting any type of meaningful movement. She did feel broken, but as they pushed her, the body responded in kind.

They began working in the intricacies of the martial arts. None of it was meant for her to square off in an old fashioned exchange of pleasantries. The only point to prove was that she could strike and move through whatever obstacle—human or material. The *motions* had given her the base for moving through these obstacles. Now they were going to add more tools. Hand to hand combat was an essential component to moving through the close-quarters she would encounter. Master Chol kept in her ear.

"There will be a point in the mission when you will finally have to face the numbers. They will be thrown at you in waves. You will have to strike past them quickly, lest they seize you and the mission fail. You must not look behind you until the attack comes from the rear. It is always forward. Not even a glance back to relish over the dead in your wake."

She felt the weight tossed back and forth from the locking up of two competing forces. Locking up was the last resort. If she did find herself in a stationary clinch there was only one response—to kill quickly. Master Chol threw her into the grappler's world where drawing tight to the body and cinching in the incapacitating hold was the order of the day. The goal was to smother or break. Smother around the neck. Break at the joint. Her newfound body went exhaustingly through all the *motions*.

It became time to move forward to the next phase of training. The weapons would propel her forward to deliver doom to all she encountered along her impossible journey. Master Chol kept his instruction swiftly rolling along. "A weapon means nothing without a wise operator at the helm. The blade will not cut through, the bullet will not enter, and the bomb will not annihilate. All of a weapon's effectiveness is about timing. Nothing of it is about chance. A weapon will only bring the desired outcome when the technique is precise. You will be made wise with your weapons, Sunrae."

The symbiotic relationship began in earnest. She was handed the knife and shown how to properly slash and stab. She felt the weight dispersion of the throwing blade. She watched it bounce off the bark of a tree until she grew frustrated, but when it did finally stick, she grinned in delight. She felt the hand pistol bucking in her small hands. She held the assault rifle tight to her shoulder and felt its discharging force—and to her surprise—much more manageable than the pistol. She was schooled in the putty bomb and its kill radius. She heard the sound of its booming detonation and the strange force it emitted from such a tiny package; like a great wind of destruction. Once she had been properly initiated they put her on the run, firing from all angles and positions. The surprises came. They forced her up and down and through. Slash and burn would be the order of things. The personal relationship blossomed between the able weapon and the wise operator.

The progression was building her confidence concerning the attack. Yet, Master Chol knew an intimate execution of the attack could be extinguished effectively by the introduction of the elements. They could arise at any point, but they would be drawn out in force should she run into a scenario assumed worse than death—capture.

"There are forces still much greater than you, but you must feel them. They are all present at the highest degrees of war."

The first was suffocation. All the *elements* had that specific characteristic in common. And so it went as the cloth was tightly wrapped around her face. Struggle she would in vain as she felt the manufactured departure from consciousness. It would be restored by a slit at the mouth by Master Chol. Precious air would rush in as she hacked greedily for it. Then it was underwater she went, slapping and attempting to rake in breathable air. When her struggle slowed, up they would bring her as her gasps became greedier. When she came back to normal levels and all of it seemed to be over, Master Chol would command, "AGAIN!"

They stretched the smothering *elements* into her basic need for water. They increased the physical exertion, expecting her to perform on less. With wrinkled tongue and chalky inner linings they decided to turn up the heat. It was not to be a welcomed departure from the cold, hard, and wet. To a corner of the cell she was placed. From the middle of one wall to the middle of the other a line of fire was manufactured to enclose her in a wall of flames. On the other side of the wall of fire was Master Chol.

"A flame is not dense, but it is devouring. Our first fear. Who will be broken first? You, or the fire?"

The lack of oxygen began to choke her. The heat pressing upon her skin convinced her she would soon begin to melt. Balled into the corner to shield herself away, she thought to cry out, 'Put it out!' But from the beginning it had been understood—not a word. The suffocation was becoming too much with all the *elements* in play. What scared her the most was the feeling of being trapped.

"Stand up, Sun-rae! Leap through the flames! To the other side!" Master Chol implored.

She slid her back up against the wall as she came to her feet. The soles of her feet began to feel the burn off the slab. There was only one way to go; and that was out and through. As her eyeballs dried wide open and the back of her throat began to choke her, she mustered all that was left to leap into the wall of fire. Out she came through the other side, collapsing into Master Chol's arms in maximum exhaustion. He dragged her from the cell and laid her down on the cool dirt in the fresh air of a mountain night. As she gathered her senses and everything was brought back to balance, Master Chol knelt down on one knee over her in the moonlight. The uniqueness of the *elements* phase was that they were all presented the same day in horrible succession.

Having not buckled, Master Chol's promise came forth. "NOT AGAIN, Sun-rae! Now we move on."

From there on it was all a sharpening of the edge. The fear and doubt had been vanquished, replaced by unshakable confidence in abilities only known by those with unshakable resolve. It was there in the center of the cell with her legs crossed where the days of her training were being reflected upon. They were surely solitary days, but she looked back on hard days fondly. She had no team, no escape route, and would have no communication. Sitting there so serious towards the end of the ordeal with such heavy thoughts, she decided to lighten her surroundings. Her only company, as usual, was the drip. She felt playful, so it was time to get a little silly.

"Do you want to see what I can do now, Drip?" she asked, springing up to her feet in giddy anticipation. The soreness no long ailed her. She was spry and unrestrained.

She threw punches. She threw kicks. She changed the levels: coming high, coming low. She spun in place, delivering the back fist, changing direction to deliver the elbow. The flying knee came out, followed by the head butt and then the roundhouse. She executed a back flip and then a front flip until she stood at a fighting stance for the next challenge from the shadows. There was still the drip. No change. In her boredom, she would have to give it life.

"Were you not even looking, Drip?" Sun-rae stopped to ask, propping her hands on her hips. She wanted to make pretend this last night of loneliness. "You're not impressed? Fine, I'll show you more!"

All of her weapons were laid out on the floor against the wall. She hadn't named them. The relationship wasn't going to last that long. Like when playing her violin there came a time when everything was grooving and the effect was maximized. She had become harmonious with her weapons. First, the weight of the throwing blade had been brought to scale. She shuffled sideways to align herself with the entranceway to her cell. Not far from the foot of the entrance stood her large target; a thick-trunked tree.

"See if you can take your eyes off this, Drip!" Sun-rae said, throwing the blade through the entranceway as it did its own flips through the air. It quickly found a sticking place in the trunk of the tree. She stood straight up, thoroughly pleased it had done so at her masterful command. She haughtily folded her arms over her chest and leered over at the side of the wall suspected to house the drip.

Her hands switched back to her hips to protest the dismay she felt from the drip being unimpressed. Still feeling quite playful she would confront the drip's apathy. "What do you mean, no big deal? That one was right between the eyes!"

As she pointed towards the entranceway to urge the drip to take another look, she was suddenly stopped in her silliness by Master Chol standing in the way. She immediately snapped to attention, though it was unnecessary. Master Chol stood in the moonlight, solemn as ever. He turned his head around to look at the precision of her placement and the distance covered. He turned back toward her with what she thought could be a smirk. "Nice throw."

He had obviously heard her talking to herself. She went back to not saying a word in regard to his compliment. He strolled back to the tree and removed the blade from the trunk. He walked back, entering her cell with an expression of kindness, and handed the blade back to her. He was to bring her his last lesson. "You have come far, Sun-rae. The rest of the way is now before you. Where are you at with your fortitude?"

She did not answer. Not until he said so. It could be one last trick. Holding fast to the original command was the right answer. Master Chol could see her steadfastness, which answered some of his question already. "You may speak, Sun-rae. Tell me, how do you feel?"

She hadn't thought about it. Feelings meant emotion. Emotion was the entrance to weakness. She learned that in the indoctrination phase. "I'm ready, Master Chol. I know the time is near. I'm just waiting to be called."

He smiled at her matter-of-fact delivery. "And called you will be. These are the last moments here. I, or this cell, you will never see again. Your mother, I don't know. I wanted to tell you she was handed over to the Snakeheads as of this morning. She is off through the China way. May fortune be with her. May a happy reunion be in your future. I know it is possible."

He turned around and sat upon the slab. He did it rather gingerly, which drew concern from Sun-rae, though she would never reveal it. "Thank you for the good news. I am hopeful for a reunion in the future."

All he saw her exuding was strength, and what she needed most—a sense of certainty at victory. Unwavering was what one had to be. "We have similar walks in life. As you know, I lost my father when I was very young, and later on, my mother and sister. I was in the camp five years before I gathered the nerve to bust out. I meticulously planned it, timed it out, and when the day finally came—I will be honest—it was easy. I had become a very efficient prisoner. I listened to every order, never wavered physically and even befriended some of them. So, it was a complete shock to them when I went on my rampage. The one I had befriended the most, I slit his throat and put on his uniform. His rifle in hand I knew the guards liked Sunday nights for getting together and playing a few games. Opening the hut door and spraying inside was instant gratification. From there, I walked towards the front gate where the guard tower was manned. They hit the horns and switched on the lights. It was perfect. I could see them and take them out. I killed the guard in the tower, shot a few more of them on the way out, and then became a ghost. I've lived in hiding ever since."

She was dumbfounded on how he told the story like it was nothing. It was definitely something, but it only made her think—*if he can do it, I can do it*. Master Chol continued, "The difference between our journeys is that upon victory you will be inserted into a different world. I escaped hell to enter purgatory. You will escape purgatory by entering hell to get to heaven. I actually envy you. You will be free."

A silence fell between them that was none awkward in the least. They were admiring each other with their eyes and posture. She had the deepest respect for Master Chol, and he had the same for Sun-rae. He knew she would feel the same fire he had once felt. They would eventually become one in heart and mind through that fire. She put on a smirk of her own, and finally replied, "I will be free."

He smiled warmly and the round rosiness of his cheeks reminded her of the jolly fat man statue Jing once had. That memory triggered everything. It was Jing's smile, her mother's smile, and her father's smile—interchanging through her mind. Unknowingly, Master Chol had just reinforced an already stout fortitude. Being reminded of *why* one was doing something was the orator's most effective approach.

Master Chol would now knowingly place hope beyond what was immediately before her. "Tell me, Sun-rae. Once you have made it across to the other side, and perhaps one day in the future, you are able to find and embrace your mother once again…what would you tell her?"

Sun-rae didn't have to think long. She got into position for another throw of the blade. "I made it!"

At that, she threw the blade even harder. It stuck deep into the tree to the delight of both. She came to a resting position with her hands on her hips. Like the way she had been busted being silly, she asked him, "Did you see that? Right between the eyes!"

He smiled, and nodding in approval, answered, "I sure did."

## Back to the American Spiral

He had pulled an all-nighter, and what a long night it had been. He started it by finishing a good cry, but that was only temporary. He busted into his father's gun safe, pulling from it a chrome-plated .45 caliber pistol; a gift from a fellow high roller in the world of business. He busted into it many times before, knowing where his father hid the keys. He always returned them to their proper place in precise dimension. What he liked most about the pistol was how heavy it felt in his hands. He liked loading the chamber with a round to hear the click-clack effect. That's what the bad asses did in the movies to let it be known things had gotten really serious. He imagined Toby in front of him, shitting his pants.

The rest of the night he would be in complete control, with controller in hand. Level by bloody level he would rise to the challenge by pushing the buttons. He would collect the intelligence, sort through the clues, talk some trash to master_destroyer01, and get sucked into a world resembling nothing of the uniformed upscale regularity of suburban life.

There before his eyes was a post-apocalyptic wasteland. The schools were shelled to ruin. No football, no basketball, no baseball teams. No prissy, stuck-up cheerleaders. The women in this world were sharp-edged beauties who only wanted to help the cause of survival, but once that was done, it would then be time to get laid down by a real man—pure frontier romance. The roads along the way were gutted, filled with the debris of a society plunged into violent anarchy. Those disfigured from the nuclear fallout were exceptionally hard to kill, but they were still going to die in the most gruesome fashion. Outfitted with a weapons cache of guns, knives, bullets, and bombs—life only continued if they were constantly expended and replenished. Sleep was for the weak. There was only the mission—to the death. Ral could only think to himself; *What a wonderful world!*

"Did you break into my safe?" Ralston Senior belted out, breaking Ral away from the digital landscape of carnage that erased time better than conversation imbued with drugs and alcohol. Ral realized he had forgotten to put up the pistol. Senior stood over him, waiting for his son to snap out of the trance. "You little shit! Have you completely lost your mind?!"

Senior moved for the pistol, but Ral was still caught up in the digital valor. Ral snatched it up, standing to his feet, facing his father squarely, pointing the pistol at him like the amateur he was. Senior looked incredulously into his son's face. It was shape-shifting from seriousness to playfulness, and between the turns of those two was the underlying hate grown as old as Ral himself. Senior felt it all to be dangerously genuine, but regardless he was going to stick with his usual methods.

With a daring expression, Senior said without mercy, "You *have* lost your fucking mind. You break into *my* safe, take something dear to me, given by someone dear to me, and now you're pointing it at me?"

The shifting in Ral's face seemed to pick up speed— I'm serious, I'm playing, I hate you. Senior took a step forward. "Give me that gun."

Ral took a step back in kind. He generated a grin out of the shifting expressions. He was in another game, but this time there were no levels. Or, maybe there was? He just didn't know the direction he was going. Senior was looking for the game to end, which is why he made his sudden move of grabbing the barrel of the pistol to wrench it away from his hapless disappointment of a son. Senior found his son much stronger than expected. They began to wrestle for control. Senior became enraged at the stalemate. Ral's laughing, like it was some kind of playful exchange between father and son for the very first time, only escalated the situation. Ral felt tickled to be putting up such a good fight against his old man.

Ral even grew so bold as to mock. "Come on, dad! Whatcha' got?"

Senior had enough. He was going to end it. Releasing his strong hand from the tussle, he cocked it back, and delivered a backhanded wallop to the face of Ral. The sting brought instant tears to Ral's eyes as they were jarred apart; Ral crashing into his dresser and Senior taking a few steps back, pleasantly surprised by his own strength.

Ral lifted the pistol with eyes shut from the sting of the slap. His rational decision-making faculties withdrew for just a moment, and in that moment it tumbled headlong into a place of revenge where it was okay to pull the trigger. The pistol bucked clean out of his hand and fell to the floor. His ears were ringing from the blast, but then he heard a loud thump. As his senses began to bounce back, he looked down on the floor at his father in a heap. It was unbelievable—a head shot. A lucky shot that couldn't have been real. But it was real—very real.

He leaned over to make sure. Blood wasn't pouring from the wound. There wasn't any splattered on the walls. It was just a dark hole towards the top of his forehead where only a minimal amount oozed out. It felt anti-climactic.

Video games and movies put so much more into it than reality. Ral started flipping through thoughts, feelings, and scenarios. Should he call 911? Should he go on the run? Should he start digging a hole? Where? Nobody would know what happened, besides him. *Wait!* His mother was in the house. Maybe she was too bombed to notice? How was he going to move the body? Why was he not affected? Why was he not begging for his father's life back? Why was he relieved?

He paced the room without letting go of the pistol. No one would ever believe a head shot like that to be an accident. He was in big time trouble now. He was still a minor. Yeah, that was it! He had mentally checked out—a lapse of negligent lunacy. In this lapse, he could finish the job. Two birds—one stone. He'd go to jail, but not for that long. After all, he was just a kid. He had a disorder. No one knew about it yet, but he could get it diagnosed. He had been bullied, ridiculed, treated like a complete nothing. Wasn't that reason enough? And then! No more obscurity! No more being ignored! Attention would be directed towards him exclusively! Who would miss his father? Who would miss Toby Self? NO ONE!

He stuffed the pistol in his pants, stepped over his father's body, and went to his office to rummage for the keys to the Benz. Something he was never allowed to touch would now be used freely at his own discretion. He grabbed the keys and swiftly made his way down the hall past the framed faces of his lineage. They meant nothing to him; had no effect on him. They were just pictures. He never met a one of them. He turned out of the hallway of memories to see his mother bewildered that she had been ripped out of a deep, self-induced stupor.

"Ral, honey, did you hear that loud bang?"

"Hear what, mom? I'm headed to school. I love you." He said, placing a quick kiss on her cheek, and moving on without allowing her time to think.

As he drove towards the school in class and luxury, it was he who was the big shot now. He was going to make the big splash. Turning up the radio loud and sliding back the sunroof; it was the freest he had ever felt. Turning into the school parking lot to conclude his joyride, he decided to shoot for a faculty parking space. He figured right about then the football team would be heaped in the locker room following practice. Larry Packett was not the target, nor the other cackling hammerheads at Toby's disposal. It would just be Toby, and then he would give himself up. Then he would explain why. Then society would understand.

There was a clear path to the locker room. Ral opened the door, walking in to the consternation of all changing into their clothes for the day. They had been cutting up, but as Ral swiveled his head about, they began to take notice. After all, it was one of the school's biggest dorks in the presence of gridiron greatness, and he wasn't there to squirt water in their mouths or hand them sweat towels. He was there to even the score.

His eyes locked on Toby, standing among them with a towel hung around his hips. Ral jerked the pistol from his waistline as all their eyes bugged. He pointed towards Toby and fired. The lucky shots were over. The tight end standing next to Toby wearing only his jock strap took the shot in the shoulder. Ral loved how some of their screams were like little girls. Toby joined the attempt to escape into the adjoining locker room where the shower bay was housed.

They were all taking a big chance. The exit to that section of the locker room was sometimes locked, sometimes not. They were all caught in an hourglass effect, trying to stuff themselves through a limited space. Toby was in the middle of the fray. Ral pointed and fired again; this time striking the leg of the cornerback still in pads. Ral remained undeterred by his poor marksmanship. He was focused.

Those Ral walked past in his murderous trance were making their escape from where he had entered. Now there were only those in front of him. They all began to scream even louder when it was discovered the exit door was indeed locked. They then retreated to stick tight to the walls, to the corners, begging for their lives. The intended target became clear to all of them, and steering clear away from the target became a uniformed goal.

Toby quickly became isolated, and upon seeing this, screamed out, retreating into the shower bay with no way out. "Ral, chill out, man! I'm sorry!"

Ral was thoroughly enjoying the terror he inspired; it being long fermented and ready to be served for the special occasion with which they were now in. He turned into the shower bay where Toby stood naked, losing grip of his towel to put up his hands, wishing he had the strength to punch his way through the tiled wall. No such thing was going to happen. He could only belt out at the top of his lungs. "Come on, Ral! Be cool! I'm so sorry, man!"

Ral took a look down at Toby's genitalia, scoffing, "I'm not impressed, big guy."

He pointed the pistol as Toby contorted himself into a guarded pose like in a game of dodge ball where one turns away from the impact, though it wasn't going to hurt in the least bit. Neither would the two shots volleyed by Ral. The first hit Toby in the gut. The second hit his chest. Toby wrinkled his face like he was on the verge of crying, and before his body crashed face-first onto the shower floor, he let out a desperate whimper.

Ral turned the cold water on, adjusting the spout so the spray landed directing on Toby. He was surprised to see these body shots were producing more blood than the lucky headshot to his father. As he watched Toby's blood swirl into the drain, it began to dawn upon him what could be waiting. Turning the gun on himself was considered, but quickly rejected. He thought of remorse, but that was only concerning the punishment sure to come. Then there was the wild possibility of somehow escaping punishment altogether, going out on the lam, just so long as people knew it was Ralston Golden II who finally had enough. Once all of those thoughts passed, he only felt the deep uncertainty which shook his greatest fears to life.

Those fears then knew the fear of life itself when Johnston McCreeley suddenly entered the shower bay with his own pistol held up at the ready. He was not expecting to see Ral, but seeing him then, Johnston's own fears flourished. His look told Ral something else. It was fierce with self-preservation, especially when looking down at the lifeless body of Toby. Johnston didn't make sure if he was still alive. He knew he wasn't.

Ral crumbled into a raging sob as the weight of his crimes were put to scale. Just as Toby had nowhere to go a few moments earlier, so was the fate of Ral. The ugly head reared up, laughing and saying, 'Why did you listen to me? You idiot!' Facing the music was enough, but Mr. McCreeley? After all was done, could he bring his dad back?

Toby back? Why was Mr. McCreeley here? Was this the punishment? *Maddie!*

Victim or no victim, Ral held his grip with the pistol. "I'm sorry, Mr. McCreeley! I don't know what happened! It all happened to me! Why did it all happen to me?!"

His face became so distorted, he became unrecognizable through the wailing. He even stamped his feet at the cold water running around him. He used his free hand to clasp it over his mouth like he was about to vomit. Nothing came. "I killed my dad! It was an accident, though! I really just wanted to kill Toby…I mean, it just happened like this…because of Maddie, Mr. McCreeley! She doesn't love me! Who loves me? What am I going to do now?"

The gunshots were being responded to as the moments passed. Johnston knew it wouldn't be too much longer. *They* were en-route. The pistols they both held had to go before they posted up to end the tragedy. "You gotta put that gun down, Ral. Once you do that, you can work on a new life from here. If you don't put that gun down, your life will be over. I promise."

Ral wasn't ready to give it all up. The resident victim inside him waited it out. It always had. "Don't you get it? How it's not fair? Everybody's so mean to me!"

The last was the scream of a child, which Johnston countered with a man-shout of his own. "Ral, I don't really give a shit! Put the gun down!"

The forcefulness seemed to neutralize Ral's reaction to the unthinkable, but he still held to the pistol. Facing the music of the tune he violently blared was still not clicking in his psyche. He thought he might be able to go somewhere else; beamed away—erased and never thought of again. He was still there, though. It wasn't going away.

"This is the police! Come out slowly with your hands up! We don't want this to end badly, but there's not a lot of time! If we can't talk, then we go the other way! Make the right decision! No one else gets hurt!"

Johnston's fears grew ten-fold from where they had been when he first heard the gunfire in Principal Livingston's office. Entering the shower to see Ral, the fear dipped even lower, but now a new beast was to be dealt with in Johnston's own psyche. Everything known was that two male assailants—whom by now *they* knew by name—were conducting a rampage on school grounds. One had just threatened Principal Livingston in his office. The other was the weird kid at school, and it wasn't a big surprise at the most recent development. Johnston knew he was wrongly implicated; that age old saying, *wrong place/wrong time.* Who the authorities sent in was not the patrol cops with radar guns in their hands. This was the legal hit squad. He also knew they were no longer interested in prolonged negotiations with *terrorists!* In front of Johnston was no longer the kid who always came around. He had just killed two people, and wounded two others. For a man like Johnston McCreeley, sentimental overtures from any direction were easily blocked out. A decision had to be made. All he could think was that it was not going to be him on this day, in this way. Not because of a kid named Ral.

"We know you're in there! Come out with your hands up! This is the final warning!"

They weren't saying anything. What was there else to say? Going down was all that was left. Johnston thought it could end in a flurry of bullets, or in a controlled manner. Unlike Ral standing before him—flirting with annihilation—Johnston was an innocent man. Those lined up on the other side of the wall, packed tight to each other, were not affiliated with the justice of a courtroom. When the clock ticked past a certain amount of time, the rush would be quick, decisive, and deadly. Itchy trigger fingers, another heroic story of civic duty, and Johnston—the father, the husband—would be no more. Maybe? It was a possibility. The heart took chances. The mind disregarded the heart.

The lead of the stack on the other side of the wall, transfixed by his call to duty, looked back at the officer in command. He willingly gave the signal, which was the beginning marker for a countdown synchronized into each one on the stack. Once that amount of time expired, first tear gas would be thrown in. That was only to push them out so the target would be less deadly, and their position all the more deadly to the trapped shooters. Just like the *terrorists*, it was also a shoot-to-kill plan of action in their minds. The lead on the stack unhooked the canister of tear gas from his waist belt as the time was about up. The only sound that could be heard was the pitter-patter of the shower. The humans were dead with silence. Seconds were counting down for the first wave, followed quickly by the second wave that was going to end the whole ordeal. A single shot rang out. The hardened faces flinched. It was easy to do— even for the most hardened.

zzz...

Another beautiful morning in America! Another hour to gossip about what happened yesterday. The studio audience was mostly from out of town. Those who stayed locally were of the obsessed. They had all watched from their living rooms, waiting rooms, and fast food joints. Now they were part of the live scene; they could laugh and clap along when prompted, and be part of something *special*. It was their time to bask in the glow as they passed through the shining city; only to return to their worn lives, in their own cities of dull sheen.

*Chatter Box* was a success. It was a roundtable of women whose opinions ultimately mattered the most. The transition for them was a no-brainer. There was a little jockeying initially to determine who would front the show, but Joshua Bannister already knew it was going to be the prettiest of the bunch—Miss Bridgette Mahoney. Flanked around her was the rest of the female cast of *Conversion*. Shonda Murano had gained a little weight, sported tight corn rows, and turned up the street dial in her diction a bit. Heather Douglas was still the most reserved of the bunch; just kind of there. Monica Brooks had convinced herself that she was now a lesbian, which delighted JB, since he wouldn't have to find another lesbian to fill the spot. Diversity, at whatever cost, was crucial. Barbie Red rounded out the table, blanketed with even more tattoos, and pierced with even more holes stretched to the specifications of an African tribeswoman. They were all back together—making a killing.

Bridgette Mahoney had her trademark gum clacking in her mouth as she began the show with her ever-fixed cheerleader smile. "Good morning all! We've got a lot to chat about today. So much going on, but we're going to take it all in. We've got a special guest today, but I want to play a little guessing game first."

"Oh great, another fucking game." Barbie Red chided. The editors always knew to be on guard with the regulatory BLEEP.

"I hear you over der, Red." Shonda Murano agreed, as the severely hung over Barbie Red shot Shonda Murano the finger for no apparent reason.

"Girls, girls, girls, let's focus. I'm going to give you a couple of clues. First one…he's tall, dark, and handsome." Bridgette read from a notecard in her hand. She was so excited to ask the question.

"Really specific." Barbie Red quipped.

"Tell me it's that new black James Bond. He fine as hell. The only thing is…he talks so damn white." Shonda Murano chipped in, seemingly confused.

"Well, I think that's because he's British." Heather Douglas blandly noted.

"Who are we talking about here?" Monica Brooks offered.

"Okay, okay, okay…second clue coming up." Bridgette moved on. "That was an epic fail on the first clue, girls. Here's the next one. Remember, focus. Each one of us has worked for him."

"Is that the clue?" Monica Brooks quickly asked.

Bridgette threw her a condescending smile. "Yes, that's the clue."

"Wink's pasty old butt ain't comin' out, is it?" Shonda Murano said, as the audience released a giggle.

"No, I don't think it's him. He's not tall, dark, and handsome." Heather Douglas murmured.

"It's Joshua Bannister, you dumb bitches." Barbie Red wearily announced, while her face fell into her folded arms like a student passing out in class.

Bridgette laughed it off unconvincingly, executing a weak transition as the audience's applause beat her to the punch. They began clapping as she tried to keep up. "Let's give it up for the uber-talented, Joshua Bannister!"

Out he strutted looking like a million bucks, which he had well over sitting in the bank. He gave a politician's subtle wave, and the smile of a deviant getting away with everything all at once. He embraced Bridgette with a peck on the cheek. He moved on to Shonda Murano, then to Barbie Red who slapped at his bottom as he walked away. She had always wanted to ride him, only because he wielded so much power. She thought the same of old Wink, too. He made his way back around the bend, barely acknowledging the boring, yet necessary duo of Monica Brooks and Heather Douglas. The audience beamed with applause as JB took a seat between Bridgette Mahoney and Shonda Murano. *His* show was about to begin.

"Oh, this is great! Joshua Bannister, the one, the only. How are you, doll? You look so great as always!" Bridgette gushed.

JB unveiled his pearly whites drawn against his tropical tan. "Thank you, Bridgette. It's good to be here."

"Well, let's chat. Rumor is, you've got some huge news for us today. Is it going to be another hit? I'm sure everybody is ready for your next concoction." She led, as the audience robotically clapped in agreement.

"Well, ladies, my next hit is about to happen right now, live on *Chatter Box*. Take a commercial break. Let everyone at home, or wherever you may be, spread the word for what is sure to be a shocking revelation. We'll be right back, folks." JB said into the camera, commandeering the show without even trying.

*ZZZ...*

"I tell ya', this burger has changed the course of my life! It's the melted cheese and the perfectly cooked onions on a toasted bun. Nothing's better than this. Nothing, I say! You just gotta' give me a minute while I take another bite of this life-changing burger!"

*ZZZ...*

"Remember, when you have to pay for something the rest of your life for something that may never happen, but is bound to happen someday, due to probability—give *Essential Crises Insurance* a call—and since we're such nice, trusting people, we'll be your family for the rest of your lives!"

*ZZZ...*

"If you're ready for something that eases every discomfort, brings unlimited happiness, and makes you a raging animal in the sack at eighty; then ask your doctor about Xenodrakseldophren, and see if it's right for you. Warning! May cause rectal bleeding, heart palpitations, and the inability to stand erect. Contact your doctor if any of these occur."

**zzz...**

Is your best friend's diet just not up to par? That cute little ball of fur just doesn't even have the energy to play anymore? Well, there's good news! Now your dog can eat like you! Do you eat from a large bag of dry food pebbles? No! So, why should your loving furry companion? Pre-packaged and packing a big dose of all the goodies of nutrition we humans enjoy, *Nature's Booty* is a dose of what we humans love the most: fish, veggies, desert, gluton-free, and yummy. Fresh and delivered to your door daily, *Nature's Booty* will put a natural smile on your best friend's furry face!

**zzz...**

"Welcome back to *Chatter Box*! We're here with Joshua Bannister of Wink Broadcasting fame!" Bridgette declared to the cheer of the audience, and the beat of jazzed-up elevator music. "So, I'm so excited to hear what you have to tell us."

"Ladies, this is a domino-effect today that's going to lead to a sizzling stick of dynamite by the end of it all. Let's get our eyes bugged out." He put forth confidently, steering his attention to the big screen mounted on the wall above them just below the neon pink Chatter Box insignia.

On the screen appeared a montage as JB began to narrate. "We all remember Loretta Crowley. Master conspiracy investigator Dane Shavers discovered that she was the long lost mother of Jeremy Boland-Bloom, or Gay J. I think we're familiar, ladies."

They nodded in unison, but Heather Douglas added, "Don't miss those days too much, but I do miss Jeremy. I thought we had a connection."

"Yeah, you just couldn't convert him." JB stealthily jabbed, as everyone let out an ooh. "No worries. None of you converted, but that's history. Right now, we're going to have Jeremy and Tamara Boland-Bloom joining us here on the show."

The applause was hearty as Gay J and Tamara appeared on the stage to everyone's surprise. Tamara looked ravishing in a soft pink dress flowing over her bulky stature, and Gay J looked healthy; the way he did back when he dropped albums. A re-uniting of the cast of *Conversion* was JB's first turn on the roller coaster none of them knew he had put them on. Two chairs were hustled out for them to sit in, and the clapping slowly died down.

"Welcome to the show, guys!" Bridgette said with enthusiasm. She immediately felt she may have slipped up and caused offense; so she quickly covered her tracks. "I don't mean *guys* in the male sense. I mean the *proverbial* guys. You know, like all of us. Anyways, good to see you both again!"

"Hi ladies, it's good to see all of you! And yes, Bridgette, I've finally healed from the fall from that crazy horse." Tamara teased, looking so much more female with her blonde hair pulled back tightly into an intricate bow.

Everyone laughed along for nothing as Gay J sat beside Tamara in his trademark ball cap and t-shirt, looking stoically hard. "How y'all doin'?"

Mistimed and mildly out of context, Barbie Red threw in her two cents on Tamara's appearance. "Ease up on the base, sweetie."

Gay J thought she was referring to the single off his new album, *Bass City*. Tamara was confused all the way around. Bridgette moved it along. "Well, Gay J, on top of a new album, you had some life-changing news here recently when it was revealed that you—an orphan—found out Miss Loretta Crowley was your biological mother."

"How was the reunion, J?" JB asked smoothly and unabashedly.

"Hell…kinda' weird. It was even weirder when she said my dad was some white dude with deep pockets. And, I guess, that she was a prostitute. But hell…I ain't no angel neitha'."

"Yes, you are." Tamara said, playfully slapping at his knee as the audience let out an aww.

"That's cute." JB said with a swipe of sarcasm. Tamara wanted to rip out his throat, but the show had to move along. It always had to move along. "A lot's been happening in the news lately. I think we can all agree on that, huh?"

"It seems like it's never going to stop happening. It's all so sad." Bridgette lamented, referring to the latest school shooting, which had taken the starring role from the nightclub shooting the week the before; the movie theatre shooting the week before that; and the bombing of a fair the week before that.

"Yeah, white boys be trippin'." Shonda Murano said, as the mostly white and female audience nodded their heads to agree that no other assessment could have been more correct.

Bridgette blushed at the socially acceptable slur with half a laugh. Barbie was less amused. "Shonda, does anything else come out of that balloon you call a head?"

Shonda waved her index finger back and forth through the air. "Listen here, mega ho!"

"At least I'm consistent, you phony bitch!" Barbie Red shot back, standing to her feet for a little face time if Shonda wanted it.

"Okay! Okay! We're getting off topic!" JB loudly interceded, as the quarreling co-hosts remained locked on each other. "Out next we have Johnston McCreeley; the hero of the Riverdale High School shooting!"

The audience applauded as prompted, but the confusion swirling through the Chatter Box cast on the stage only grew. Out came Johnston McCreeley in boots, blue jeans, and a brush popper. His thick salt and pepper moustache jutted over his upper lip, stained with dip. He went to shake each hand firmly as a chair was jetted onto the stage. He was old-fashioned. He looked each of them in the eyes. Some on the stage were rather offended. No matter for Johnston McCreeley. He just plopped down, seemingly un-phased by the recent spotlight.

"Welcome to the show, Johnston!" Bridgette said, as the hits just kept on coming.

"You're not armed, are you?" JB jokingly asked, as the audience laughed a bit.

Johnston released a chuckle of his own, and said, "No, I left it in the truck."

For some reason, the chuckling ceased. JB moved them forward. "Sad what happened at Riverdale. I'm sure it still weighs on you. Ralston Golden Jr. being so close to your family, and all."

"In the moment I just did what I thought had to be done." He dryly informed.

Heather Douglas just couldn't abandon her curiosity. "That's been a big question with this whole thing. Was it necessary for you, yourself, to end the life of Ralston Golden Jr.? I mean, the police were right there."

"Well, there's more reasons than just one. For one thing, he was on a rampage, and obviously out of his damn mind. I had told him to put the gun down. He wouldn't do it. I sure wasn't going to put mine down. Then the hit squad showed up."

"Hit squad?" Monica Brooks asked with a blank expression.

"Yeah, the SWAT team." Johnston answered, and then quickly moved on. "Anyways, I knew there was a chance when those boys rushed in it could've been both our asses. I'm sure they knew I was illegally carrying a firearm on school property, so in their minds, I was also fair game. Hell, in their minds, I was probably part of the whole damn deal. There wasn't a hostage situation, so negotiating was off the table. It was just a countdown to the use of lethal force. But still, the main reason…why I pulled the trigger…was that he wouldn't put the gun down and he was mentally unstable. I picked up a felony, and got away with my life.

Sure, I could've been the principle hiding away, or everybody else heading for the exit door, but I'm not them. What else can I say?"

"I know that felony has a high price tag on it." JB suggested.

"Yeah, the NRA is covering it." Johnston confessed, even drier than before.

Again, silence hit, but Barbie Red was going to break it. "You're a fucking bad ass, man."

"Okay! Wow, Barbie, thanks for that! Jeez!" Bridgette puttered out, shaking her hands and shrugging her shoulders. "Let's move on!"

"Okay, our next guest…" JB began.

"Our next guest?" Bridgette said, again taken aback.

"Yes, our next guest will not be joining us here on stage, but instead via the big screen. He is the Presidential candidate under the third-party Civic ticket in the final stretch of this general election cycle. Welcome to the show, Malcolm Grace!" JB introduced, as all of their heads swiveled upwards to the big screen. On it appeared Malcolm Grace with his trademark faint smile. He, like the other guests, had been told the important issues of the day were going to be mulled over. And, of course, a sizeable monetary gain. "Welcome to the show, Mr. Grace. Thanks for coming on."

"Thanks for having me." He politely replied.

"Yeah, thanks for coming on!" Bridgette wailed desperately, now fully conceding all the control she wielded was completely gone.

"You and the Civics are on the home stretch. I bet you're stretched yourself." JB implied with a smile.

"It's been a hectic schedule. It's really just a rehearsal for the real thing. The most important post in our nation: that of President of these United States." He replied without reserve.

"You think you got a chance?" JB bit, taking a sip from the coffee cup on the table.

"I think we all have a chance, Joshua. The trick is pulling all of the value from that chance. That's what we as a Party are doing, and are going to continue to do. But, to answer your question directly…sure…I think we got a chance." He replied, as the audience cheered him on. Following his admission on the campaign trail that he was going to lose; his stock had raised by ten points in the polls. He had dismissed the consideration to drop out at news of the uptick.

"I must say, you a fine ass white boy, Mr. Grace." Shonda Murano shot in, as the audience followed her with a laugh.

"Finally, something we agree on." Barbie Red said, gazing up at the monitor with hungry eyes.

Malcolm Grace blushed, responding with a courteous laugh. "Well, thank you for the compliment, ladies. You are all attractive to me, too."

The statement brought it back around to the *aww's* as JB pushed forward, having heard enough of their blustering. "Chairman Grace, I know you've been talking about the issues tirelessly on the campaign trail. Today, I was wondering if you could share your personal story with the viewers. I mean, we all pretty much know your political track record: hijacking Bill Doody's program, building a viably competitive alternative Party from the ground-up, and now getting really close to a residency at the White House. What about your humble beginnings? Let's hear that again."

Malcolm Grace was un-phased. His past was no secret from the public. "Well, I was born in Baltimore to…essentially…the state of Maryland. Some people use the phrase 'the government is not your daddy' in reference to social programs. In my case, the government actually was my mom and dad."

The audience gave a laugh at the light he made of the situation. He continued, "So, I bounced around a few foster homes, but I eventually landed with my adopted parents who inspired me to go on my own path that's led me this far. My adopted father was a liberal arts professor, and my adopted mother was an ophthalmologist. They both passed fifteen years ago from a car crash. Despite the tragedy, they are the reason I chose this path. And, ultimately, I have no regrets."

The sentimental audience erupted in applause. They all felt inspired by his reversal of fortune at being dealt a tough hand. JB even gave a phony clap-along, but cut the applause short with his next question. "Wow, what an American story! I wouldn't have any regrets, either. But, you know, it also makes you wonder…at least makes you ask yourself…*who are my real parents*?"

JB turned his attention back to the audience, and then over to Gay J sitting quietly and taking it all in. "Gay J, do you know the person who found your biological mother?"

Tamara lightly slapped him on the knee to signal he should sit up straight, which he did. He was off the coke for a while now, but he was blasted by the chronic. "That conspiracy guy. What's his name? Dane?"

"Dane Shavers, yes! I'm glad you brought that up. You've never met the man, have you?" JB asked.

"Naw, I never met him."

"When was the last time you saw your mom?"

"We've met one time. Ya know, when all this madness broke out."

"Would you like to see your mom now, Gay J?" He asked, as the suspense in the audience was bubbling over.

"Man, I really don't—

"Ladies and gentlemen, Loretta Crowley!" JB announced, standing to his feet before the word 'care' could escape Gay J's lips.

Out she came with her obese figure fully shrouded in a brightly colored flower-petal frock. She was already teary and emotional as the audience came to their feet with clapping hands. She moved towards the shocked Gay J as he oddly stood to unwillingly welcome her to the stage. In truth, he didn't know this woman; and deep down, he didn't even view her in a favorable light. His childhood grudge towards her was still set in place.

"My baby!" She cried out, forcing her embrace upon him as he reluctantly returned the gesture. Tamara was even more perplexed with feelings of jealousy.

Another chair was shuttled out as Loretta sat down next to her son. Bridgette was relegated for the remainder of her show to nod, smile wide, and say enthusiastically, "Welcome to the show!"

"Loretta, your life has changed so much, hasn't it?" JB posed, as they all settled down again.

"You wouldn't believe it, Mista' Bannister. It's all just such a blessing. Every day is just such a blessing." She proclaimed with cheers showering her. A tissue was shuttled out so she could wipe her eyes.

"What do you think about the man who really made this reunion happen? Dane Shavers?"

"Oh, I'm just so grateful. God bless Mista' Shavas."

"Would you like to thank him personally? Today?"

"Oh, yes I would, Mista' Bannister!"

"Ladies and gentlemen, Dane Shavers!" JB welcomed, as palms all around were beginning to sting and burn from the constant applause. JB was heading towards an eventual tingling numbness of his own.

The crew was running out of chairs backstage. Dane Shavers shook Johnston McCreeley's hand, hugged on Loretta Crowley, shook Gay J's hand, and then shook Tamara's hand; even though he questioned if that was the politically correct approach. It worked out all the same. Bridgette waved her hand at Dane as he sat down in the chair on the opposite side of the stage, clearly implying, *Yeah, I'm still over here!* Dane returned her wave with a smile.

Barbie Red looked confounded, following the look up with a rhetorical; "What the fuck is this?"

The applause had died down much faster, due to their fatigue. "Dane, who would've thought that your work uncovering conspiracies, real or imagined, would directly impact lives the way it has? It's just all so wonderful!"

"It's certainly not something I expected. It's been a chain of events that keeps surprising me. It all began with my coverage of Monty Lincoln's cult, The Fellowship of the Enlightened. Loretta, here, contacted me out of the blue. It reunited and introduced, in the same breath, a family who had no clue about the other. It's just such a special thing to be a part of." Dane explained, as the applause sign lit up once again. The audience hesitated, but JB subtly leered at them with eyes saying, '*Why aren't you clapping?*' They quickly followed suit.

JB smiled at their capitulation. "That's so great! Now, we all know what's happening in the California redwoods right now. The standoff continues at the cult compound. How do you feel about that, Gay J? I mean, we don't have genetic proof, but Monty Lincoln could very well be your father, right?"

Gay J was still stoned to the bone, uttering nonchalantly, "Nuthin', really. The only thing that threw me off was finding out I'm actually white. Not that there's anything wrong with that. But this is the whitest white guy. Nuthin's whiter than da' British."

"Whew, you right about dat now!" Shonda Murano agreed, slapping her hands together like the preacher had hit a chord, directly inspired by the Lord.

"Well, there's a reason you're on the show today, Dane?" JB said.

"Yeah, that's something we might all want to know." Bridgette said, holding steady to her begrudging smile.

"For Mister Johnston McCreeley sitting here and Chairman Malcolm Grace joining us on the wall there—your lives are about to change as well. Johnston, you have something in common with Gay J and Chairman Grace, just as they have something in common with you. You are also an orphan, aren't you?" Dane asked.

Johnston didn't want to be rude. It wasn't in him. But he really wanted to wring his little neck. JB's, too. He thought everybody else was pretty much alright. "Yeah, that's right."

"What if I told you that Gay J and Chairman Grace were actually your biological siblings?" Dane posited to the consternation of all, except Joshua Bannister.

"What the hell are you getting at?" Johnston stiffly queried.

"Please welcome to the show: Daisy Hunter and Diane Brewer!" Dane announced.

The audience's palms were finally itchy and numb. Bridgette's fake smile was now gone. She nearly yelled, "WHO?!"

Diane Brewer was in business professional attire; a fit woman in her fifties. She stood by the monitor on the wall where Malcolm Grace held a neutral expression in relation to the entire fiasco. Daisy Hunter stood next to Johnston wearing a sundress with a big hairdo crusted into place by the contents of a can of hairspray, wearing thick makeup, and worn thin cowboy boots. She was in her fifties, but looked to be in her sixties. The stage was set.

"I promise, folks. That's the end of the guest line!" JB said with a chuckle, looking back at Bridgette who returned a—'*Yeah, go fuck yourself*'—chuckle.

"Daisy, let's start with you. You're from Texas, right?" Dane asked.

"Born and raised in San Marcos." She answered with a pronounced drawl.

Johnston knew he had been born in San Marcos. That was about all. Dane continued, "Tell us your relation to Monty Lincoln."

"Well, it was a long time ago, but when I saw his picture on the news, I knew it was him. Growing up in San Marcos all we did each summer was float down the Guadalupe. I was a river rat. People always came from Austin to float the river, and a lot of those people were from out of town. Monty Lincoln was one of those people. I just loved his accent. We had a fling. Eight and a half months later I had a baby boy."

"I'm going to stop you right there, Daisy. I want to move onto Diane for a moment." Dane directed, shifting over to Diane standing nervously beneath the wall monitor. "Diane, you were born in New York City, correct?"

"That's correct. I was born and raised in Manhattan. I was attending St. John's University when Monty Lincoln came as a guest speaker specializing in global finance. I was a devoted student, and being such a young woman, I was naturally drawn to his presence. And like you, Daisy, that damned accent got me. It's very easy for me to believe he built this cult. He has that type of mesmerizing charisma. So, as it went, my tight-knit group of sorority sisters had dinner with him that night. He was full of amazing stories, full of confidence, and he decided to pick me to come back to his hotel for a night cap. Nine months later I bore a son."

"Okay, both of you opted for adoption just like Loretta. Daisy, why did you choose that option?" Dane shifted, as both women were becoming emotional.

"Well…I suppose I just couldn't take care of him." Daisy admitted with a crack in her voice, looking down at Johnston whose eyes increasingly bugged out. "I just couldn't do it at the time. I guess that's all I can say about that."

"And for you, Diane?" Dane pressed on in gentle tones.

She hesitated, bashfully looking up at the monitor to a face with eyes furrowed, lips pressed together tightly, and a jaw locked down tight. Malcolm Grace, the king of cool up until then, was getting anxious. He thought none of this could really be true: that he had walked into a trap. "At one time I saw my future not as a wife; not as a mother; but as a businesswoman. I was to establish myself. Set up my wealthy independence, find a man of my own class, and then build a family…the smart way." She explained, stopping just before her confession became any more detached and chilled. Before she said outright, *'You were just in the way, Malcolm,'* she looked up at the monitor. "I always knew where you were, Malcolm. I just left you alone. Obviously, you've become a wonderful mistake. Good for you."

"You know what that means?" JB broke in, incorporating the transfixed audience and those on stage with a simple swivel of his head.

"That Monty Lincoln is the dog of all dogs?" Shonda Murano unleashed, followed by an uneasy collective laugh.

"What it means is that you, Chairman Grace; and you, Johnston McCreeley; and you, Jeremy Boland, better known as Gay J…are all blood brothers! These are your mothers, and your father is none other than Monty Lincoln of the devil-worshipping sex death cult, Fellowship of the Enlightened! Let's all give them a standing ovation at this incredible family reunion story right here live on *Chatter Box*!" JB joyfully proclaimed, as the studio filled with deafening vocalizations, clapping, and stomping.

Most in the audience were crying deliriously, or were just on the verge. The only people not on their feet were Johnston, Loretta, and Gay J. Johnston thought, '*Why the hell did I come on this?*' Loretta was in a full bore bawl, and Gay J thought, '*So, this is the mutha fuckin twilight zone?*' Malcolm Grace had already removed his lapel mic, and stated leaving the monitor, "I'm done with this."

In the manufactured euphoria of the moment JB walked the stage to each guest and shook their hands. The new ratings were going to soar. The balloons began to drop from the ceiling as *We Are Family* by Sister Sledge began to play, drowning out any dissension at the moment's effectiveness. It was a celebration! A happy ending!

Frank Winkleshten was watching it all in one of his windowless dark rooms, sitting in his chair, wrapped in a blanket, and holding an oxygen mask to his face. He was a decrepit old man loving every moment of what he was watching. Coughing up some phlegm into a handkerchief, he gruffly said aloud to no one in particular, "Fucking brilliant!"

He didn't know if any of it was true, but that didn't matter too much as the credits rolled and the studio audience danced their little dances onto the stage—kicking and punching at balloons. Malcolm Grace just couldn't hack the fiasco. That was good enough; a skillfully crafted blindside. *Why wouldn't he want to know his mother? Why wouldn't he stick around for the celebration?* That would be a talking point on the 24 hour news channel in short order. Then, they would badger him with the same questions until it made him sick. Until he was rattled. That would put a dent in his points. All it had to be was silly, and that would be enough.

He flipped the channel to his news arm where the greatest coincidence was unfolding in breakneck drama. The aerial coverage showed the expanse of the Fellowship's redwood compound. "In the 21st day of the standoff here in the California redwoods there seems to be an advance in the negotiations with the cult leader, Monty Lincoln. It has been reported that he is going to release those held hostage in the compound. In fact, here they come filing out now!"

The scene switched to ground level at the gated entrance of the compound. Emerging with teary swollen eyes and hands held high were the Fellowship en masse. They were the beautiful wretched souls of the coffee shop back in San Francisco, the lurching hunchback Baltasar, Cindy carrying her baby daughter, and the woman carrying her baby who had given birth ceremoniously in the pool. Now the story given by the powers in charge would be validated, and believed absolutely.

"This is amazing! As you can see, there are two very small children that were held up in the compound. This was what the cult leader, Monty Lincoln, said did not exist. This has all been about the presumption by the authorities that people, and especially children, were being held against their will. This has been the source of debate about the entire situation. Now we can all see with our own eyes the authorities' assumptions are irrefutably true. Only one holdout is left, and that is the cult leader himself, Monty Lincoln!"

He was standing in the dark with only neon numbers streaming along the top edge of the wall. He knew the end was upon him. There was no more holding out. Supplies had been cut. Food had run out. He knew if he went hunting on the grounds he would be captured or killed. The presumption that any of his Fellowship were being held against their will was ludicrous. Monty had just begged them all to leave amid desperate tearful clinging. They loved the world they had built, but Monty knew it would not end on their terms. The outer world was about to lash its evil tail into theirs, and then the wrong people would be punished. It was those he had truly come to adore. He even played a trick on them. He said he would be the last to follow them out. He would follow just as they had followed him. He had to lie, even when doing the right thing.

As the numbers ceased their streaming against the wall, he knew he had to die. He knew now they had cut the electricity and water. It was the final phase of the siege. He was the devil incarnate meant to be destroyed, but he refused to be destroyed on their terms. He had done so much in his life—good and evil.

He heard the rumble of the vehicles coming down the driveway. It was time to act. He took the can of gasoline and splashed it over the walls of the room. He lit a match and threw it to the wall. It lit up in a beautifully mysterious, lively dancing glow of orange and blue. It began to envelop him in a warm embrace as he heard windows shatter from the advancing outside world. He grabbed the shotgun off the table. He wanted it as messy as possible. He was now ready to welcome them with a devilish grin, personifying the very monster they wished to paint him. He was not going to let them save him. This day he would dine with his Maker in the blinding heavenly light, suspended above the sparks and smoke of the living world. The inherent and ever-evolving silliness would now come to one blissful fiery end. He was delighted, after all the wealth he had accumulated, to finally be alive!

**Denouement**

**(This is the end)**

**Operation Sunrise**

She could feel the heat emanating from the diesel engine as it rumbled along. For her part, she was folded like a pretzel beneath the spare tire in the trunk of an armored vehicle. The time had come. Heading towards the demilitarized zone—the biggest misnomer on the planet—she was ready for action. She wasn't worried about the pieces coming together once the line was crossed, with a fierce forward trajectory being the only way out. The pieces had already been fixed in her by Master Chol. They themselves were an engine primed to be ran at a consuming speed.

All of it bundled together was a rolling tide in her being as the vehicle came to a stop at the entry point. The driver was simply a supply specialist tasked to keep the ammo coming during the live fire portion of the war exercises. Someone knew him, had offered him enough money to forget about the consequences, and then told him to keep his mouth shut. He was going to follow those directions to a tee as the front guard approached with the usual expression of stone.

"Identification."

The driver handed his badge over and the guard clicked on his flashlight. It illuminated the warm breath escaping their mouths into the cold, early morning hours. The guards' eyes darted up from the ID for no particular reason. He was that dead serious all the time. He handed the ID back and shifted his light to the covered trailer carrying the ammunition. He walked to the trailer and ordered the driver to unfasten the ties to the tarp covering the load. The driver did so speedily, pulling the tarp back to reveal the crates. Satisfied, the guard ordered it to be covered again. *That should do it*, thought the driver.

Fastening the tarp back down, he thought it wise to break the silence. "This is going to be a long couple of days, don't you think, comrade?"

The guard flooded him in the face with the light as the driver attempted to block it with the palm of his hand. The guard hesitated in his response, waiting for the discomfort to draw out. Robotically, he finally responded, "It is necessary, comrade."

He shifted the light from his face onto the trunk of the vehicle. Inside, Sun-rae had taken in breaths slowly and incrementally as her contorted frame was slowly becoming more and more compressed beneath the hulking tire. She had been listening intently. Her heart raced to a fevered pace, which she embraced wholeheartedly. Then she heard, "Open the trunk."

A few moments passed before she heard the lever unhinge. She felt the cold night air rush in to chill the beads of sweat wobbling on the surface of her face. She saw the light flood in and prepared for a deadly reaction. Being uncovered then was the least ideal, but regardless she was ready.

Nervous beyond any experience encountered, the driver affably noted, "This may be the strongest display of our great power yet, comrade."

The guard moved the light around inside the trunk. Its rays passed over Sun-rae's face through the lug nut holes. She kept her calm when the center beam of the light seemed to be shining right into her eye. She maintained it as she paused her breathing only to allow the sound of her heartbeat. The guard could have seen her breath now that the night air had entered the compartment. Seconds more passed in silence until finally the light left the compartment and she was shut back in darkness, not even allowing a sigh of relief to escape her. She knew there would be no relief until she reached the other side.

The guard quickly flung the light through the cabin of the vehicle. He holstered the flashlight and resumed his post. The only sliver of humanness he showed was when he said, "Let us have a great drill, comrade."

The vehicle rattled on as Sun-rae now knew she had a real chance. Penetrating the DMZ was the first domino to fall. It was all a chain reaction from there. The driver knew only as much as he pulled into the armory, parking in his assigned spot. He was nearly done with his role, which he would gratefully shed without incident. Cutting off the engine he exited the vehicle, opened the trunk, and walked away without as much as a whisper. Yet, Sun-rae knew he would have said, 'Good luck'—and she would have said, 'Thank you.'

Though folded and contorted underneath the heavy duty rubber tire, she had been trained it wasn't force that succeeded; rather the measured use of force patterned by a calculating mind. The bolt holding the tire down had merely been set on top of the threaded stud. It had also been the job of the driver. She snuck her slight fingers through the spokes of the wheel and snatched the bolt. Her head was oriented towards the rear of the trunk as she began to press the tire up from one end. Inch by careful inch she began to fold out of her contorted state, scraping her front and back side as the weight of the tire sandwiched her between the unrelenting rubber and railing of the trunk. The blood began to circulate back through her legs and arms as she squirmed and wiggled her way from the confines of the trunk compartment. She did it all in complete silence as she heard the chatter of soldiers taking in a smoke somewhere within the armory.

She was to crawl low; half like the slither of a snake, half like that of a quad-peddled lizard. From underneath the parked vehicles she spotted the huddled, olive-drabbed covered legs standing in polished combat boots. Stealthily she crawled towards them. She figured they would be close to an exit. If they did spot her, what they would see would be a small chiseled frame covered from head to toe in black; with a hard jaw line and blazing eyes of furious determination. It would be the last pair of eyes they would each behold.

They would be spared. Advancing her position was more important. The killing spree would have to wait. She slipped past the chattering soldiers who left the armory door open. Undetected, she slipped into the air of the cold night where the sun would break through shortly thereafter. Before it did, she had to cross the airfield in front of her with its watchtowers and resting antiquated warplanes. Broad spotlights weaved about the ground in timed rounds. She quickly pieced together the timing of each individual one, and how they related to the other. There were always gaps. She had to figure them. All the way across the airfield would be a hop, skip, and a jump. No do-overs would be had. None of it could be rehearsed. It was all about going to the next level.

A spurt of sprinting forward began it, and then an abrupt halt, standing stiff as a board. The goal was never to let the light hit her. She continued along through the mix, threading the needle. A mistake could not be fathomed. The fence was her destination; fitted ostentatiously with razor wire. She grew impatient at one point when she was nearly at the fence. It found her balancing on the tip of her toes with arms straight out to desperately avoid the light. It turned out her ballet training was more than about dance.

She crouched down close to the fence and pulled from her sleek utility belt—full of endless surprises—a pair of wire cutters. She quickly got to snipping at the foot of the fence, only removing enough of the links to safely slide underneath. The approaching light motivated her to move faster. She hastily shimmied through the opening, but it turned out to be too hasty. She then tumbled down a sloping plane of grass. It brought her down to the tree line of intermittent foliage. She did not expect company at the bottom, but it was exactly what she got.

The roving guard had slipped away from his patrol for a smoke of his own. Like her, he had not anticipated another body crashing into him unexpectedly. Jarred, yet remaining on his feet, he was unable to react in time for an effective defense. Sun-rae had already mounted his back, pulling a blade from her magic belt, slitting his throat cleanly—numb and thoughtless—just as she had been trained. She shut his mouth tight with the palm of her hand, and with legs wrapped tightly around his torso, he collapsed to the ground where she held firm to him until the futile squirming ceased signaling that life had left his body.

She dragged the unplanned kill into the fold of the wood line, and covered him with leaves. No harm had been done. She continued on through the heavy foliage until she saw a break in it all. She knelt down enveloped in the denseness. In her line of sight was the operation center headquarters for the DMZ. It was planned for her to be in that very spot. She would gather herself. The first glow of dawn would soon arrive. From then on there would be no rest, no mercy, and no shelter. It would all be decisive and definitive to the last.

Nostalgia she had been told to block out. It could lead to hesitation, which could lead to a fatal mistake, but as she lay in wait, she permitted herself a daydream. She thought of her mother. Would she ever see her again? Her mother was kept in the dark about Sun-rae's way to the other side. They had told her Sun-rae was simply going another way. Nothing could be helped. Everything had to remain secret. Everything had to be believed.

Then the nostalgia ran down the line of all she had encountered throughout her young life. It was the careful and thorough educators, her classmates, the doctors, the nurses, the rich, the poor, the disabled, and the mighty. She saw the entire breadth of the orchestrated grandeur. She saw the prisoner laboring in the penal camp. She saw those who enjoyed luxury and those who enjoyed their depravity. She saw the market district in its heyday. She felt the freedom of those dingy confines. She once again wound her way through tent city looking for the jolly, fat, graffiti-covered statue enjoying a beer and a turkey leg. She saw Jing's warm smile, and his bucked teeth. He had the ugliest face. She marveled at how beautiful it became when she knew him through and through. She missed her dear friend. She knew she would never meet another like him.

Then she was transported to the symphony where she was taking in the American rendition of *Arirang, Arirang.* Her soul had been stirred into a frenzy that day. Remnants of it still swirled as she knelt down in the foliage. That day ended perfectly as her father softly placed his hand atop hers, looking down upon her with a smile not needing a crease in his face. His eyes were like the sun on her skin, saying; "Isn't this wonderful! Aren't moments like these the best?"

She smiled in real time has dawn began to creep in around her. The round of nostalgia came to a halt. It had served its purpose, reinforcing her explicit will to kill all those bastards about to get in her way. It was time for battle.

She guessed it was in more ways than one as the alarms set off all around her. She could've been detected. It could've been the signal to begin the mock military maneuvers. Either way, she was moving towards the operational headquarters. The *inside* help began with the trunk left open in the armory. Now she expected some more help—another stash. This time she would encounter a single Pasque flower jutting up from the ground. It would be unmistakable. The petals were a full lavender. Cradled and huddled in the center were buds of bright yellow, and encircled within the yellow were pure white buds. It was Sun-rae's most beloved flower.

She spotted the flower halfway between the wood line and the headquarters. She remained flat to the ground as the morning light brought the flower to life. She unearthed it with her fingers at the base, expecting buried beneath a basic putty bomb fitted with a timer. It was there as promised! She soundly secured it, but halted from scuttling away so hastily, looking back at the unearthed flower lying on its stem with the petals contorted by the cold ground. She shuffled backwards, planting the flower to its original condition— erect and proud. She figured something had to be spared on her march through. Why not something beautiful?

She moved on, heading towards an emergency exit door at the rear of the command center. Without an emergency it was never trafficked, which made it the perfect entry point. She stuck the bomb to the door. She set the timer, and just as she was doing so, automatic gunfire began to whiz by her. She dropped down into the prone to face the threat; a single advancing soldier popping off his AK-47, yelling commands for her unconditional surrender.

None was close to forthcoming as she pulled a petite pistol from her back waistline. She aimed it true as bullets lifted the ground around her in tiny explosions. She put two consecutive shots into the frantic soldier's chest. Accurate as she was, they failed to fall him. He continued advancing, continued firing, and continued yelling for the impossible surrender. His wild shot grouping was zeroing in, but it only told her to now end it. She executed a single roll to the left to avoid the rounds that would have struck her, and fired a single shot. It bursts through the forehead of the soldier as he fell on his face. She imagined herself a secret agent amounting to a one-woman army. She had to say it. "The name is Rae—Sun-rae!"

She sprung to her feet, stripping the slain soldier of his weapon. She slung it around her body, released the diminished clip from the well, took a fresh clip from his flak, slapped it back in snugly, and loaded one in the chamber. As she did, the putty bomb took out the lonely exit door of the command center with a thrusting boom of billowing white smoke. The sneaky, rather quiet part of the mission was over. With sirens still spinning around her it was time to unload the absolute best of who she had become. She strutted through the door, emerging from the smoke, immediately drawing tight to the wall. She was never to be caught in the middle. She began along the wall at the ready, not having the slightest clue of where she was headed. It would all be fine. The fallen before her would lead the way.

She was approaching a corner on the opposite side of the wall. She zigged quickly over to the other side as she heard harsh, hurried voices pressing towards her. Just before reaching the apex of the corner a soldier rounded the corner into the open, but Sun-rae had the jump on him. Two quick pulls of the trigger brought him down.

Shots rang out from behind her, missing her entirely, but still striking the wall she scooted along. Hot and sharp pieces ricocheted off the wall into the back of her neck. It didn't stop her from spinning on a dime down to one knee; dead-sighting the two soldiers who were luckily lousy marksmen. Spinning back around to continue her advance she could feel the warm blood running from the back of her neck. It was okay. She knew she was going to bleed.

Rounding the corner she collided into an advancing soldier with two more behind him in tow. She tumbled to the ground at the point of impact, losing grip of the handle of her weapon as shots rattled off. She regained her grip quickly, simultaneously returning fire and throwing a heel kick into the soldier's knee. He had fired also, but the kick jeered him to miss as his knee dislocated, snapping the tendon. He had never felt sudden agony. The two in tow had been gunned down. So far, Sun-rae was the better marksman. She transitioned to the pistol without skipping a beat, putting two in the head of the soldier preoccupied with the pain in his knee. He wouldn't have to worry about the pain any longer. Three more who had gotten in her way bit the dust!

Another hot sensation began to radiate from her thigh. She glanced down to see she was shot, but nothing arterial had been hit. She tied it off, knowing the adrenaline would carry her all the way. In her mind, the wound wasn't there. It didn't happen. She expected to be drenched by the end of it all. It was the meter reading that things were getting done.

She pressed on around another corner concealing the unknown. At the other end of the hallway emerged more soldiers. They were embroiled in panic and were genuinely shook by the confusion Sun-rae stirred to life. She kept her finger on the trigger—remaining steady—until her clip was expended, and they were all lying in a heap.

As she dropped the dead weight of the automatic rifle to the floor she felt herself fortunate the clip had just enough to stave off their assault. One less, and it could have been her lying dead on the floor. She never believed in divine intervention, or even providence for that matter. She didn't believe in God. Neither did the regime. They believed they were the Gods who could use force indiscriminately without justice. She was going to bring justice back to the front of the line without courtrooms, without show trials, and without any phony political propaganda. That kind of justice was her God. This was her own divine intervention.

Her thoughts were running as such when she turned into an intersecting corridor continuing the sterile banality of the command center. She stopped dead in her tracks at the sight of the Bowibu officer who had led them to view her father's death. The same one who had entered their home with the intention to violate her mother. A single sliding door stood behind him at the end of the shaded corridor, only lit by the intermittent blinking of a red light. Their eyes locked, each possessing the same intensity. The match was set. The dual accepted. The sirens continued to roll, but they drowned out as she was now standing in the canyon on a clear sunny day. The circling hawk screeched above the heads of sworn enemies who were done with each other's very existence. The ominous whistling and the pluck of the acoustic strings she heard resonate all around her. All that was needed to stamp out the feud forever was a fast draw and a true aim. A commitment, for a short time, was all that lacked. How she wished she had a smoldering cigarillo clenched tight between her teeth.

The posture of the Bowibu officer reflected his lifelong accumulation of unrivaled, unwavering superiority. The expression was always the same. The difference between him, and those not holding his high rank was clear. None was going to match pure will and supremely sharpened expertise. Despite this lopsided confidence in his own abilities; the fact was that he hadn't fired the pistol holstered to his hip since his last promotion some ten years prior. This lapse, leaving his barrel cold and unused, failed to insert any doubt that none other than Sun-rae would be falling down dead that day. *After all*, he smugly thought, *she was only a girl.*

Sun-rae had entirely different motivations and skill sets. Rank was not a barrier to skill. She was fresh. The wickedness of his smiling face as her father swung from a rope sharpened her resolve to an icepick point. She witnessed his defiling hands gripping her mother into an unthinkable submission. The floating heads of the Bowibu officer and the Party official who had pulled the lever on the field were the most highly valued targets. And now, a dream come true. The floating head was now fastened down to the body in real time—a time that was now and hers alone.

She waited. He waited. The lawless Western frontier lay before them. The eyes probed for hesitation in the other. Throwing a playful wink of the eye was just to let him know he may have been thinking too highly of himself. It was also meant to enrage him. Never was he met with such disrespect. It was no matter. Her pistol pull was a blur—the shot unexpected.

His last sight of life was the muted, pounding, and dizzying view of Sun-rae approaching him with the perfectly mixed expression of pleasure and hate. He hadn't even pulled his pistol as the blood from his opened forehead filled his vision, switching to blackness as he crashed down to the floor.

She stood over him, imagined herself still puffing on the lit cigarillo with the desert sun bearing down on her reddened skin. She hawked up a hearty wad of spit, and said, "Vaya con dios!"

She relieved him of his pistol, loaded with a full clip. She popped a fresh clip in her own. She tore away the access badge from his waist belt, putting it up to the scanner situated on the wall next to the door. Volleys of gunfire were sure to be waiting for her on the other side. It was only a matter of being faster.

The door beeped and slid open. With precisely measured momentum she rolled her way forward into the heart of the command center. Her petite, tightly wound figure arrived at the center of the room with ease. She smoothly transitioned from the roll to a centered standing position. With arms extended, hands holding each pistol upright, she began to twirl in place. Four more officers who hadn't fired a weapon in ages fell to her blasts. She ceased the twirl of death to now face the Party official who was only there to view the exercises, and bring word of their progress back to the Dear Leader. He wasn't even armed.

Sun-rae was starting to believe in some kind of divine intervention, or providence; but she was definitely believing in dumb luck. Here was the lever-puller who had hung her father to death. She fixed both barrels on him as he stood before her, suspended in disbelief. It happened so fast the access door had just then slid closed behind her, shutting them in for a bit of privacy—a little bit of face time.

Behind the stunned and trapped Party official was a wall of glass. Beyond it was the battlefield littered with soldiers, armored vehicles, tanks, and a circling assault helicopter. Just beyond that, the South itself. She could taste it now, but there was still more work to be done. Still more of these bastards to kill through.

Facing each other she could see the character of Diego Montoya from *A Princess Bride*. He bled as she was bleeding. It was his father, and it was her father. The revenge was so strong that nothing could kill them. Death would be kept at bay by the love they harbored for the departed. Now it was only fitting to educate this Party clown before dispatching him. "Hello. My name is Sun-rae. You killed my father."

His eyes bugged. He knew exactly. He had taken great pleasure in the execution of her father. He was a man who had been a thorn in his side personally: never backing down, never giving an inch, always having the more sound idea. That's what had gotten him killed. He saw the same resolve in the eyes of Sun-rae.

She considered shooting him to be the easiest route, but decided to go a different way. She set down the pistols slowly at her feet, and stood back erect. He took it as a surrender, due to his stately power that could not be brought down by anything. Even the assassin before him could not deny the allure of his position. An assured smile swept across his face, but he had been deceived. Strapped around her thigh in a black sheath was her throwing blade. They were both about to find out how accurate she had become. She grabbed it and with an upward chopping motion she sent the blade on its way. The expression on his face remained like he was frozen in a block of ice. It was half smile, half terror as the blade stuck snuggly into his forehead. He attempted to take a few steps forward, but ended up crashing to the floor. She put her foot on his lifeless neck and used it for leverage to pull the knife from the seat of his forehead. She wiped the blade on his uniform and brought it back to the sheath. "I know you saw that one, Drip. Right between the eyes."

She picked up her pistols and stepped over him to look out on the expanse of the final plunge. On the other side of the 38th parallel were those in the South, mirroring what was going on in the North. The ROK (Republic of Korea) and US soldiers were conducting their own war games. It was a clear annual message from both sides—*Yes, we can do this, too!*

It was all about to go live. She fired at the glass in a tight shot grouping, grabbed a chair from the conference table set in the room, and threw it through the glass. She walked forward, stooping and stepping through the jagged opening. With her head held lofty she jumped down on the field of tire-shredded grass and cold mud. *One last push. One last stride through violent glory!*

She went forward with a sprint towards a passing armored vehicle fitted with a machine gun turret. Those taking part in the field exercise were clueless as to what just happened in the command center, but they were about to get clued in.

Leaping onto the rear bumper she began to crawl up to the nested gunner. He noticed her too late, attempting to turn towards her in defense. She reared up and buried two bullets in his chest, ending his field exercise. She jumped down into the turret with him, snapping his neck for good measure. As he crumbled down into the cabin she kicked him aside, dipping down to face the exasperated driver. She plugged him directly in the face, leaned over him to open the driver door, and kicked him out the vehicle.

She fixed herself in the driver's seat, looking out the windshield to see that the game may have been close to up. Soldiers were coming from all sides with guns blazing. She withdrew to the turret where she could exact an appropriate response. Fixing the metal stock to her shoulder and ready for the death-swivel, she began laying into them. The hot empty shell casings bounced at her feet. The machine gun drew from the belt as her finger held tight to the trigger. Soldiers were falling to the front and from side to side. Then she saw herself: the haunted vigilante upping the body count just to make a point, bellowing out a war cry from the deepest part of her bowels. Finishing the belt, she thought that's what it must have felt like to be Rambo.

She sunk back down in the driver's seat and put the pedal to the floor in a b-line towards the 38th parallel. Bullets were ricocheting everywhere. The bulletproof windshield was cracking and spider-webbing, but on she barreled forward. Then she heard the buzz of a helicopter situated above her. Those drilling in the South on the other side had gathered together to watch the show. All they could think was whether the longstanding cold war was about to get white-hot.

She was nearing the borderline. It wasn't close enough. She heard the deranged hiss and distinct whistle, which was the discharge from the helicopter. She was then flipped through the air where gravity left for the moment; she suspended in midair with floating fragments of glass and smoke. Just as quickly as gravity left, it returned with a stunning thud that instantly sent her into darkness. She had left the mission for the moment.

Submersed in the dark silence she heard the flutter of violins beginning the song. Then penetrated the gently plucked harp, whipping the air around in a dream. The lone flute penetrated the darkness with all of its simplistic beauty, cutting twirls of light into the dark fabric; sketching the misty mountain where she waited for her lover to return. The crescendo gushed forth in all its mystical accord. Hope became its direction where the refrain would have the waiting lover belt out the battle cry, "Arirang, Arirang!"

She saw a giant wave crash against the rock embankment, with the warm spray refreshing the cold mist of the trail leading back home. It all came to a stop as she found herself seated in East Pyongyang Grand Theatre, but this time it was empty. There was no New York Philharmonic Orchestra, not an instrument gleaning, and no other souls present besides her and her father. His hand once again rested gently over her own. She peered up at his kind face with that faint signature smile.

He lovingly leaned in, whispering in her ear, "You have to wake, Sun-rae. You have to get up. Rise, Sun-rae. Rise again, my love."

She felt herself being lifted out of a hole, rushed to the surface to meet the continued sounds of gunfire and chaos. Opening her eyes, captured in a seizing numbness, she took in a stifled breath of spent ammunition—metal and grit. She saw the turret opening as she dizzily came to her knees. The vehicle was on its side with flames dancing all over it. She saw daylight hitting the charred grass beyond the turret opening. She headed for it. She emerged from the wreckage and pulled for a fresher breath of air with an accompanying cough. There was only one option left. She was going to make a run for it on foot, ultimately living or dying through the rest of it.

Bullets whizzed and bunches of earth upheaved around her as she felt herself going in slow motion. Her eyes were fixed to the horizon of the South at the 38th parallel where something incredible was about to take place. It was clear. The South was taking live aim at those in the North heavy on her trail. She couldn't believe it. *They were covering her advance!*

The North quickly pulled up and redirected fire at the South. She continued forward thinking a war had just been sparked. *It was about time! Now they could have their war!* Covered in blood, charred black by the smoke, she was content to the bones. She had her vengeance, even if it was going to be the end. Smiling wide towards those getting in on the action from the South and laughing inside over the impossible odds—all she could think about was one day becoming one of those Silly Americans!